# THI /ITH
# HADDOCK

## Ever

ISBN-13: 9798483914419

ISBN-13: 9798483914419

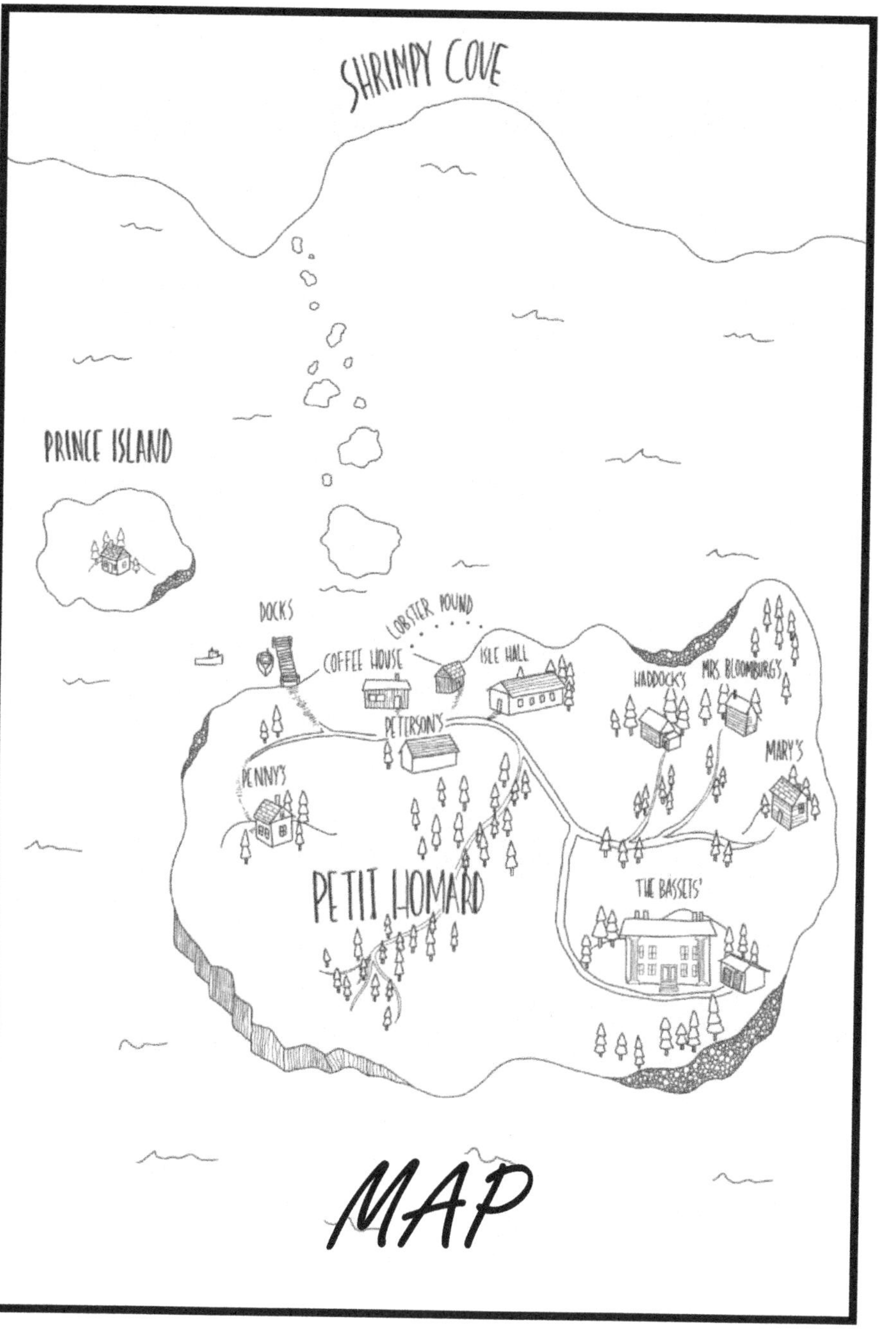
SHRIMPY COVE
PRINCE ISLAND
DOCKS
LOBSTER POUND
COFFEE HOUSE
ISLE HALL
HADDOCK'S
MRS. BLOOMBURG'S
PETERSON'S
PENNY'S
MARY'S
THE BASSETS'
PETIT HOMARD

# MAP

# Chapter 1

*Thursday, April 6th, 1961*

There once was a twenty-something-year-old girl named Jill Jopling. One evening, she was driving home in her car, minding her own business, *put-put-put*-ing down her street. It was a small, round kind of car, the kind where one gains an appreciation of their flexibility if they're able to get in and out of it. It was the time of year where no one was sure whether it was Winter or Spring. The seasons themselves are quite indecisive at this time of the year. The car she was driving was her late father's. "No, he's not unpunctual," she would say, "he's dead." As parting gifts, he left her his pessimistic witticisms to remember and an old car to drive, both being a bit backward sometimes. Her father had gotten the car for a tremendous discount, but only because it came with a tremendous fault—its pedals were switched around so that the gas pedal was the brake, and the brake the gas pedal. He got used to the peculiarity quickly, being a little peculiar himself, and since no one in the family drove it except him, things went along smoothly without incident. But when he died, and the wife declared that she didn't want it, the daughter took it gladly, quickly getting used to it as her father had.

But at the most inconvenient time, Jill got startled and reverted to the arrangement she'd learned how to drive with. The poor, young neighborhood mailman leaped for his life when she distractedly put on the brakes as he crossed the road. She was rather startled because he had unwittingly stepped out from behind a bush in her neighbor's yard. She put her foot down, not out of determination but surprise, only to become more surprised when she lunged even further ahead, seeming to threaten him with a rev forward. She only grazed him; only apologized with a regretful wave as she zoomed ahead; only just making it into her driveway without crashing into her house. She sat there motionless for a moment, catching her breath. The young mailman, bewildered as he was, dutifully marched up to her and wordlessly slipped a few envelopes through the driver's side window, like it was a mail slot in her door. He then tipped his cap and ran away, afraid of what she'd do next. She didn't recover in time to express her many apologies but was still grateful to him for delivering the letters. She came inside, sat down, and began reading one. Let's be very nosy and peek over her shoulder to see what the last paragraph said:

"I have to tell you something—I finally have just enough money to take the trip out there to come and see you. I am absolutely thrilled, my dear. My heart has been pounding ever since I got your last letter, thinking about finally being hand-in-hand with you, my sweet Janet-Lily. And when I come to Arizona and finally see your beautiful face, I shall ask you a question I've been longing to ask you for quite some time; longing like how flowers long for sunlight, how night longs for day, and I just know that your answer won't disappoint me. I hope you know by now just how much I love you, and how much I wish to be united with you forever in the blessing of an eternal bond."

Who wrote these unbearably poetic words, and to whom do they regard? You must be introduced. Miss Janet-Lily Marilyn Jopling, who allowed her friends to conserve their energy and simply call her "Jill", was the recipient of the letter that contained the words above.

"Oh, Steve! 'I wish to be united with you forever in the blessing of an eternal bond?'" she cried in mournful disbelief. "Flowers and night and day—why do you always do this to me, Steve?" she asked the letter, almost angrily. With eyes as wide as particularly broadly-rimmed teacups, she set down the letter flusteredly and looked out of a nearby window. The Arizona sun was now settling comfortably into oblivion, and its disappearing light reflected off of the plain stationary lying on her coffee table.

Enough has been said at the present time about the anxious recipient of the affection-dripped letter. It could only have been sweeter if it had been dipped into a vat of cotton candy and smeared over by a honeycomb. Now, whether you like it or not, you must be introduced to Mr. Steven Carey. He was the author of the poetic verse that was cleverly disguised as a letter. He was the age of 28, just when most men grow up. Just as the indirect proposal made in the letter was unconventional, the way the two met was just as, if not more, novel. It might have had something to do with the fact that Jill Jopling was a reserved young woman. Who she reserved herself for was never quite clear. Some might have even called her aloof. Many a time she would find herself walking around the grocery store, only to realize that she was in dangerously close range of a certain someone in her acquaintance who had a mediocre personality. Before the danger of an ensuing conversation occurred, she would dodge behind the celery. It really wasn't that she totally disliked her fellow human beings. It was simply the fact that human sociality tends to put pressure upon us all, pressure with which Jill Jopling did not enjoy contending with. She viewed socializing as an ingenuine ritual that we all happily condone. For example, the responsibility of appearing interested in subjects such as her acquaintance's eighteen-pound cat's diet, or that their gardening shed's resident lizard was nowhere to be found. Jill would just listen on, unsure of whether her acquaintance's gravity in tone about the subjects at hand was more irritating or amusing.

Now, if one was to *write* about such things in a letter, things would be quite different. She could take the letter in her hands, read it at her leisure, at her very choosing, and could react as feelings came, not feeling obligated to express them through an excruciated smile. Or she could find laughable the things that her friends thought serious without the worry of them detecting it. A perfect solution, indeed!

Has a negative picture been painted of Jill Jopling? Perhaps. But not to worry, you will see her better qualities in due time. She loved her family and friends with that intensity and depth that was reserved for them and only them. When speaking with them, there was no need to withhold from expressing the sillier of her thoughts as she pleased. This was especially the case with her sisters.

There was, actually, only one younger sister. She was the wild and free one. Between the sisters, it seemed that she had taken more than her fair share of the extraversion of the family. She moved to North Carolina to finish her degree. No one was quite sure what she was studying. She often didn't seem too sure, either. Clementine Jopling—her name and personality were so bright, that she could only live in states that matched their sunniness.

The other "sister" was not a sister by the usual definition. She was Jill and Clementine's older cousin, Peyton. Peyton Fargo. She was called "Peyton" by her acquaintances, "Penny" by her friends, and "Payton" by those who didn't know how to spell her name. Penny Fargo was the one to whom Jill tended to write most of her letters. That is to say, of course, mostly the most.

Clementine, obviously being the superior of Jill as far as socializing and mingling goes, sent numerous addresses of her quickly acquired college friends to her reclusive sister, to assist in the branching out she believed her sister must have desperately needed. The other sister, Penny, was too much like Jill to provide any such assistance, thus Clementine took on the assignment fully and very capably, being the responsible sister that she was. Clementine sent an address to Jill in 1960, one year before the beginning of this story, but this address was far different from any pen-pal that Jill had gotten ever before. The usual specimens were flighty, sociable girls who marveled at the thought of having their very own pen-pal. Jill noticed that their friendship fizzled after the novelty wore off, which was only after a few months, or even weeks. After a sufficiently boring time elapsed and a few ink splotches appeared on the other party's beloved dresses, communication began to cease. This isn't to say that Jill was lonely. She had a handful of successful pen-pals who generally cared more about friendship than a few unseemly ink splotches, and she was contentedly occupied with them. But despite all of the faithful pen-pals she had gained, there was still an emptiness in her life. The void she discovered she had is exactly what made the pen-pal of '60 and onwards special.

Jill Jopling and Steve Carey had been corresponding for one entire year. During these many months affection gradually grew, and even climaxed with Steve's words recorded at the beginning of the chapter. Jill, however, wasn't exactly thrilled with the climax. She desperately believed that she ought to have felt something—*anything*—remotely similar to what he seemed to be feeling for her. But, to her dismay, she instead felt fatigued, apprehensive, and even slightly nauseated. "Why? Why am I feeling this way now?" she asked herself while pacing around the little living room. "Ah," she said aloud, as the reason fully came to her. She was relieved to find that it was a very good, sensible reason: They had never met before in person.

How on earth could Mr. Carey babble on in that way? How could he even dare to suggest such a thing, if they hadn't even bothered to meet face-to-face? And, most importantly, why hadn't they ever met? These are all very good questions, and the last two have one simple answer.

It is the answer to a lot of problems faced by the general population: money. Jill Jopling was the secretary for the editor of a terribly tiny newspaper in a terribly large city—Flagwood, Arizona—and her wages were nearly as minuscule as the company's size was. And Steve worked in a relative's little grocery store in North Carolina. Suffice to say, the couple couldn't afford to visit each other, but they could afford stamps. But as Jill's father used to say: "Just remember, money's no object—it's all just imagined."

Clementine was the one who happened to meet Steve. She didn't meet him in any of the places where a romantic interest ought to be met. Not at a coffee house, not at a wedding. Not at a party, not on a street bench. They met in front of a bunch of lovely tomatoes. Upon meeting him, Clementine's complexion turned curiously similar to the fruit, looking like an infatuated chameleon. That coloration akin to tomatoes and that breathless feeling at the sight of him made her sure that meeting him was some sort of guarantee of the truest sort of love. Little did she know that she wouldn't be the eventual recipient of that love. Steve certainly didn't intend on provoking so serious a case, and only happened to be innocently taking inventory of the grocery's produce section. He noticed the young woman's dazed look, but not, of course, the cause of it. Little did he know that Clementine's behavior was nothing out of the usual. She always looked that way when encountered by a strongly featured face, brilliant eyes, and perfect hair a shade or two darker than the aforementioned eyes. The delightfully outgoing personality that complemented the features of his face couldn't help but enhance them. It was most likely for the best that Clementine was the first introduction to the Jopling family. For all that we know, if Jill had been the first one to meet him she might have dove into the tomatoes.

It soon became obvious to Clementine that there was no mutual awe caused by *her*. No reaction towards her, nor her strawberry-blonde hair, nor her adorably petite nose, not even her sparkling blue eyes. Taking all of this into consideration, it really was a wonder to her that she didn't awe him. Despite all of this, she decided not to be selfish. With the blessings of quick wit and outspokenness, she began talking about her lovely sister Janet-Lily, and how desperately *lonely* she was, all *alone* in a little house in Arizona, and how much she *longed* for a letter from *somebody*.

The end of the matter was that Steve Carey had a stranger's address written down on a note in his pocket. And a successfully dodged young woman expected him to, apparently, rescue her sister from dying of loneliness. Feeling adventurous, he decided to dash off a letter to her that very evening. "If nothing else," he said to himself with a chuckle, "it will make for a good story to tell." He sat down in front of an old typewriter that ought to have been retired long ago, wiped off its dusty keys, and began surveying the unusually arranged alphabet before him. Why such unusual words as "YUIOP", "QWERTY", and "ASDF" were written on certain rows of the keys beneath his fingertips was beyond his comprehension. Eventually, a roughly composed letter, complete with dings and scratches and angrily scribbled corrections was sent, and it arrived in the mailbox of a surprised recipient.

An enraged letter was fired off to Clementine, who hadn't considered the possible dangers of giving her sister's address to someone whom Jill had titled, "an impetuous creep." The titles for the mystery man fluctuated; Clementine defended him, giving him the innocent sobriquet "Sweet Steve," and told Jill to give him a chance. Jill cautiously renamed him "Sneaky Steve" and decided to reply. Steve Carey was surprised and pleased to receive a candid, stern letter from a strange girl across the country, and replied in an endearing, sincere way that Jill couldn't help but admire.

Now a year had passed, and Jill too started calling him "Sweet Steve." Clementine and Steve had mutual friends, and everyone loved him and there was nothing bad to say about him. And now "Sweet Steve" had saved up his nickels and dimes and was about to purchase a plane ticket to fly to Arizona and see what his future had in store for him.

# Chapter 2

Jill picked up the letter she had just received, took a glance at its words again, and then dropped it directly in the middle of the coffee table. After a long day of work, she knew that she had to eat, even if she didn't particularly want to. But the only dinner she could muster up the willpower to prepare was a dish of leftovers. She feared to guess how old they were, and so she decided to eat them before she could remember. She did remember what the cookbook called the recipe, "Italian Surprise". She certainly was surprised the evening she initially prepared it, when it gave her an enduring case of indigestion. She didn't remember what the surprise was in the present moment, though, and decided to find out as she ate it.

As she sat there in her little kitchen, stabbing meditatively at her Italian Surprise, she pondered over how she could possibly reply to Steve's letter. She stirred her cold food and munched reflectively.

"Of course I love Steve," she thought, "but enough to be a *wife*? Enough to be 'eternally bonded in the love that is lovingness', or whatever he said?"

She had seen too many girls run off with men they thought they knew well, but who realized they were terribly mistaken. How could she convince herself to marry, yes, *marry* someone whose face she'd never seen, whose voice she had only heard through a crackly telephone connection? But, despite all the obvious reasons not to, she did love him, and she did trust him.

After thoroughly enjoying her meal, which she confirmed was disgusting only after she began eating it, Jill slid her plate away and marched to her desk. She rented a little house from a family friend. It might not have been able to fit everything she wanted it to, but no matter what, it *would* fit a desk. She sat down and eventually found herself writing a letter, not to her yet-to-be-accepted fiance, but her would-be sister, Penny, the one to whom the Jopling sisters couldn't help but always look up to—and not just because she was tall.

Four years prior to this moment, Penny announced with tears that were composed of both happiness and sadness that she was going to move to Shrimpy Cove, an absurdly small town on the northern coast of Maine. Jill pleaded with Penny to stay, even when Penny was about to take off at the airport. Penny had always wanted to be where the trees were, and a friend of her mother's had a place for her to stay. Despite Jill and Clementine's entreaties, Penny was determined to try out a life that was the complete opposite of what she had ever known—sandstone, red dust, dry air, and automobiles whizzing past her window—and go as northeast as Flagwood was southwest. And when Penny had arrived, she found her new surroundings to be perfect.

Jill, however, found the situation disastrous. Her cousin, her sister, her friend, who had lived only three houses down since they were kids, was now suddenly abandoning her. It was the definition of terrible. Jill became thoroughly embittered, and she decided to show her resolute stand on the matter by refusing to write to her. Eventually, though, Jill's curiosity got the better of her, and she could no longer bear all of the irrepressible questions that crawled into her mind like persistent caterpillars. She began to constantly wonder if her dear Penny was safe and happy; if she had gotten the work she wanted to; if she had met any interesting people, (or any boring ones; Jill wasn't particular), and if she had even gotten a boyfriend, or at least someone who came close to the status.

Suffice to say, communication began flowing between them again, and Jill's curiosity was never disappointed. She heard wild tales of her cousin's experiences on the east coast, about a world that was so completely foreign to a girl brought up in the West. Penny satisfied her with many stories, such as the time when she embarked on a hike, only to run back after encountering a bear feasting on berries. Penny further told of clam-bakes, blueberry harvests, lobster dinners, the time she nearly fell off of a boat, the time her foot got stubbornly stuck while out snowshoeing. Even if all of this was not enough to convince her young cousin of her utter happiness and fulfillment, Penny constantly reassured her that there were far too many beloved things about the place than she could mention.

Perhaps the most exciting adventure of all was the news of Penny's second move. Shrimpy Cove was, apparently, not isolated enough, and so she accepted the offer to rent an affordable little house on an island off of the coast of Shrimpy Cove, a place called Petit Homard Isle. Moving to this place one year after her initial move, the event brought a further barrage of storytelling to excite and content Jill. Penny explained that the beauty of the island surpassed any she had ever seen before. All of her deliciously explained exploits were delivered to Jill in a signature little teal envelope. Jill devoured every letter, but despite Jill's delighted replies to her letters, she constantly refused the ceaseless invitations to fly out and see the unmatched beauty of New England for herself.

This evening, however, Jill wasn't seeking out any information from her cousin. Between the Italian Surprise, which she vowed to never be surprised by again, and Steve's distressing letter, filled with dangerous talk about flowers and moonlight and daybreak, Jill's hand jittered about as she scribbled on the stationery set out beneath her. The letter was asking for sensible advice, as

Jill couldn't trust herself to be sensible—it was a plea for help.

~~~

Two weeks later, Jill came home from work and opened her bright green mailbox, which she had proudly painted herself. The past few days had brought nothing more than irritating advertisements, worrying bills, and a young, sweaty mailman who delivered them all. He did so only after getting his daily exercise, getting chased by the neighborhood dogs, occasionally even the cats. He was easy prey, I suppose.

Jill always thought that he possessed the most hilarious ankles she had ever seen, which were unfortunately showcased by his uniform, composed of a collared shirt, Bermuda shorts, and socks that were only slightly whiter than his pasty skin. How they hadn't tanned out in the Arizona sun, she couldn't know. They really were too easy of a target for the canine residents of the neighborhood.

Today, David "Mangled Ankles"—as was the name given to him; Jill had a tendency to rename people for her pleasure—ran up to her in the usual, boyishly flustered way. Despite it being a day in April, when most places feel a nip of the coolness of Spring in the air, or at least a suggestion of it, here the blazing sun ignores the world's expectations of the seasons and burns the Arizona landscape with its warmth. Thus David dripped all the way up to her, heaving deep breaths, after being chased after by an assortment of creatures. Disregarding the mailbox in front of him, he plunged his hand into his mailbag and procured a small, teal envelope to hand directly to her.
~~~

"Hello, Miss Jopling. This is for you," he said, giving her a friendly smile despite the sensation of melting in the Arizona sun.

She thanked him, nodding with reserved congeniality, saddening him with being more interested in the letter than in him. She then walked towards her front door, much more occupied with the contents of the teal envelope than with David and his ankles. A dry breeze swept her bangs and flipped her hair back, and David couldn't help but watch on in admiration. He soon fled, though, at the sound of his barking canine foes.

After a long day of listening to Mr. Babcock's dull voice dictating uninteresting letters to her, she found grand relief in walking into the shade her home provided and falling into her bed. While laying there on her back, she smiled at the letter in her hand. With her weary typing fingers, she hastily ripped the envelope suspended above her open. To her surprise, three fifty-dollar bills rained down onto her face. At first, she sputtered as they made their unfortunate landing, but her eyes soon filled with shock and delighted tears as she sat up. She stared at the bills incredulously for a moment, then read the letter, which was composed of only two sentences:

"Come clear your mind on Petit Homard Isle, with me.
Love, Penny"

# Chapter 3

*Sunday, April 30th*

A week or so later, Jill stepped onto an airplane with a sigh of alleviation. What a relief, to be removed from the crowd of tired, irritated travelers in Flagwood's chaotic airport! She was grateful, not only to be out from the pushing and shoving tides of a disagreeable sea of people but also to have made it onto the plane at all. Despite the loudness of an incessant voice from above, the airport's speaker's volume did not always guarantee clarity. She could never be completely sure which one of its tyrannical commands to follow. Gate 1, gate 4, gate two billion, it all sounded the same to her. Finding herself exhausted and bewildered far too early in the journey, she would have gratefully obeyed the loudspeaker if it had told her to jump out of a window. The command would have been preferable to remaining in the overwhelming airport a moment longer than necessary.

But now she was on the plane, leaving behind all the anxieties and woes of the airport, finding a measure of peace as she settled into her seat. She folded her hands upon her lap and eagerly awaited take-off. In her countenance was found an unexpected excitement—why, it surprised herself—to be on a plane headed towards Maine. Yes, to Maine, the place she swore to never step foot into because it had dragged dearest Penny away from her.

Jill was happy to see that she was assigned the window seat. But as she settled into it, she realized that she would be a fellow traveler of a man whose corpulent figure threatened to encroach upon the personal space she felt entitled to. The threat was averted, however, when he sat down two seats down from her, in the aisle seat.

They took off, at last. After a time, Jill began trying desperately to tear herself away from the book the man in the aisle seat was reading. She had avoided detection of this unusual form of eavesdropping by suddenly turning her head whenever his head turned to look at her suspiciously. But soon Jill lost her crafty game. He caught one of her unabashed ganders, snapped his book shut, and stalked to the lavatory while giving what Jill thought was an excessively irritated look of disapproval. She raised her eyebrows and shook her head once he was out of sight. She recovered without a second thought, though, and now contented herself with attempting to recall what memories she had of New Hampshire. Jill was born in what she believed was an inaccurately named state, unless one considers 177 years of existence as "New." She lived there until she was three, and thus had no reason to remember it in any detail. Through the contents of a particular teal envelope, Penny had told her that New Hampshire was "somewhat similar to Maine," but "not as robust in beauty," and "without any ocean." Years ago, by the urging of Jill's aunt and uncle—Penny's parents—the Jopling family had the opportunity to move to the metropolis of Flagwood, Arizona, where Penny Fargo's family had been settled for a number of years. And so the Joplings moved to Arizona, where Mr. Jopling hoped to find better work after the Depression, and where Mrs. Jopling hoped the arid climate would rid her of her allergies. Mr. Jopling's hope was fulfilled, whereas Mrs. Jopling's nose was still never to be seen, as its dwelling was beneath a handkerchief.

The clearest memory Jill had of her three-year stay in New Hampshire was the overwhelming amount of trees. Inescapable trees. There was no hope of eluding them, no matter where one stood. Despite the disgruntlement she felt against their obnoxious omnipresence, she could not deny the beauty of the exploding colors that Autumn brought. She believed that the title given to fellow Autumn-leaves-enthusiasts was unfair; they were called "Leaf Peepers." She believed that the unfortunate bestowal of such a title was unnecessarily creepy.

There was a brief layover in Boston, during which Jill gratefully transferred to a smaller plane. She hoped that now she wouldn't encounter any more stingy bookworms who were disposed towards giving unfriendly looks at fellow passengers. As she boarded the plane and sat down, she realized that she again had the window seat and that she would be sharing a row with a thin, tall, proper-looking man with a neat suit and a cocked hat. There weren't any seats between them, however. After observing him for a moment or two, she decided that, despite their proximity, he would pose no threat to her enjoyment of the present flight, and so she again settled into her seat and closed her eyes.

A blissful period elapsed without any disturbances as she napped quietly, except for when she mumbled a little gibberish and squirmed around as much as her seat would allow her to. But her peaceful dreams about lobsters and Northeastern oceans took a frightful turn. She was suddenly stationed upon an old, broken boat, which was in a terribly stormy sea. She desperately tried to steer it, but with each turn she tried to make, the boat groaned and growled hideously.

Before she was thrown overboard, she awoke with a start. Her hand was pressed against her beating chest, and she was grateful to see that she was on a plane and not in the ocean. But her ears perplexed her. It seemed that although she was not remotely near any ocean, the boat her imagination created was still groaning. She turned to her right, then realized that the man she once thought of as so very proper was now feeding her mind with a series of horrid snores as he slumbered. She sighed agitatedly as she watched his unexpectedly large mouth gape open and produce several unpleasant noises. She decided that she'd rather be two seats away from a large, agitated man than right next to a deceivingly thin, loud, grating, one. She directed her attention away from the slumped-over gentleman, who had ruined the first impressions he had given her, and instead looked down at the land below her. It was easily distinguishable that she had entered New England.

"Mm-hm," she mumbled, noticing the density of the forests below, "exactly how I remembered it." These trees were nearly in bloom, and the others had not made up their minds as to if they wished to join their fellow woody friends. Snow had begun melting away only a little while prior, whereas Arizona began melting its citizens only a few weeks before. Jill leaned back and closed her eyes, wondering whether or not placing her shoe in the cavity in the gentleman's face would quiet him sufficiently. She decided that the risk would be greater than the pleasure, and so instead she rolled onto her shoulder and smiled, thinking about seeing Penny's dear face.

Although not intending on falling asleep, Jill again awoke with a start as the stewardess told her to fasten her seatbelt. She did so, and the plane soon safely descended upon the Portland airport. After begrudgingly removing herself from the surprisingly comfortable seat, and after nodding to the gentleman to her right with as much friendliness as she could scrounge up, she stumbled down the airplane ramp. The airport's bright lights nearly blinded her, which stood in contrast with the deep, dark sky that laid ahead. She sucked in a deep breath and got her first taste of New England air. And suddenly she felt amphibious. The air felt like she had accidentally walked into a raincloud. It was extremely humid in comparison with where she had just come from, as well as unusually natural-smelling. Even through the greeting of the smells of salty-sweet, humid air and oil fumes from the airport, it was refreshingly clear. With a shiver, Jill noted that the air was brisk, and she suddenly understood why Penny spoke so highly of wool sweaters.

Jill entered the building with her arms wrapped around herself. As she took her baggage, she looked around listlessly. There were barely any people in the "bustling city's" airport, (as Penny called it) and there was a lovely absence of the pushing and shoving she had experienced in Flagwood and Boston. Instead, there were many wool hats, wool sweaters, practical boots, and flannel shirts. With alarm, she quickly realized that she was unequipped. She didn't have any of the necessities that the people around her had. The only coverings she could brag about were a mid-weight sweater and a light coat, which was nearly lighter than the sweater. She regularly wore them during the wintertime in Flagwood, where they were effective. She frowned in disapproval as she looked at herself in a reflection of a window.

"Jilly? Jilly!" cried out a loud voice. Jill couldn't quite place where it was coming from. Very helpfully, the voice cried out again, "Over here!" Jill turned around, then smiled brilliantly in relief as she sighted Penny. She was jogging up to her in a winterized outfit. Penny's neatly-tied headscarf nearly slipped off of her head as Jill grabbed her. She crumbled into Penny's embrace, exhaustedly and happily melting into the warmth emanating from the sensibly dressed Penny.

"Oh, Penny!" was all that Jill could say. She was so relieved to have arrived in the same place and at the same time as Penny, safely and soundly. Penny released her, tickled pink, laughing loudly. Penny grabbed Jill by the shoulders to get a good look at her.

"Ah, Jilly! Look at you, you've grown up!"

Jill laughed. "I thought I finished growing up a while ago."

"Yes, but it's been a while since I've seen you last. You must have been seventeen the last time I saw you. Now here you are, as beautiful as ever." Penny now took Jill's hands. "You have no idea how much you coming here means to me." Jill grinned with a brilliance that was nearly brighter than the blinding lights that greeted her when she stepped off of the plane. Jill began giggling and shaking uncontrollably.

"I can't believe that we're here, together, right now, Penny!" Jill cried loudly, bouncing on her toes.

Penny put an arresting hand on her cousin's shoulder. "Easy, there! People around here aren't used to excitement." Jill looked around and noticed a few eye-of-the-chickens being directed at her. Although confused about why Penny was allowed to cry out earlier, Jill let it pass as innocent hypocriticalness. So Jill contented herself with a composed sigh and a large smile. Then the gentleman that sat to Jill's right on the plane entered the lobby. Upon sighting Jill, he smiled suavely. Penny looked at him, then slowly towards Jill with an eyebrow raised. Jill smacked Penny's arm.

"Don't you look at me that way, Penny, and don't be swayed—the unholy noises that come out of that man while he's sleeping aren't worth contending with for a nice suit. Listen to this little ditty I came up with on the plane—

'What an incredible noise
And what a disgrace
For a snore come out of a man of such poise
And out of that nice face.'"

Penny laughed, "Very good, Jilly," and then began looking at Jill up and down. She sensed that something was missing. No, the girl's luggage was present, she had her purse...

"Ah!" said Penny, at last, putting her hand to her head as the realization came to her. "Of course! You need some proper clothes." I forgot to mention that Penny was forgetful.

"You're telling me! Why did you think I huddled into you like a penguin in a blizzard? I don't own anything heavier than this poor excuse for a sweater," said Jill, as she picked up one of her cases.

"Don't worry about it, I've got a coat in the car. I think there's an old hat or something in there, as well," said Penny, picking up another case.

"Won't it flatten my hair? Hairspray isn't getting any cheaper, you know. I want to get my money's worth."

"Darling, it's ten o'clock at night," said Penny, wrapping her arm around Jill's shoulders. "Nobody is going to notice your hair, and even if they do, they'll barely care. Follow me," Penny said, taking long, assertive steps towards the exit. Jill obeyed, although struggling to keep up, as she happened to be carrying the bulk of the luggage.

The pair walked out to Penny's car. "It's such a nice, mild night out, isn't it?" Penny remarked with a pleased smile.

Jill nodded politely as she watched her breath become visible. "Ah, that's why my breath is turning into a solid." She couldn't help but wonder how horrible the winters were if this chilly night was considered "mild." She then began loading cases into Penny's car, putting them beside cases that were already there. Penny paused from searching for sufficient garb for Jill to look in disbelief at the growing pile of cases growing in the trunk.

"Jilly, what is all of this? Are you planning on clothing every family we come across on the way?"

"Those," Jill replied, seizing the case that was in Penny's hands, with laughably put-on anger, "are my hair curlers. I can't get this lovely flip in my hair without some assistance. And, besides, what if I *was* going to clothe all the families? Then you'd feel bad, wouldn't you?"

"I don't have a hairdryer."

Jill paused. "I'll figure out something."

Penny, without warning, began wrapping a yellow and white scarf from a bag in the trunk around Jill's neck. She then procured a child-sized, blue, knit hat, and fastened it upon Jill's head. Then came the final piece to the ensemble—a hideous, overstuffed, shaggy purple coat, at least four sizes too large for Jill. Penny held it up.

"Please," Jill begged, covering her eyes with one hand and rubbing her temples with the other, "put that thing back in the bag and never let it see the light again. It'll be for everyone's good, including the thing's." But then Penny held it up again, about to utter something, but then Jill cried out, "Please! Show mercy!"

"I know that it isn't..." began Penny, searching for an appropriate word, "...the most attractive coat..."

"It looks like someone fattened up an ostrich and then dyed it purple," Jill remarked tactfully.

"But it will have to do," Penny continued, undaunted even after the vivid simile, draping it over the shoulders of the ungrateful recipient. "You have the scarf and the hat, too... there, much better."

Jill stood by the passenger side of the car, staring helplessly at Penny. She plunged her cold hands into the recesses of the coat's pockets and regretfully discovered ground-up pieces of tissue in the pockets' corners. Flinging her arms out in a dramatic gesture, Jill asked her stylist, "What is the first thing you think of when you look at me?"

Penny, with great effort, refrained from stating her truest opinion, and instead said while adjusting the ugly coat's collar, "Warm. You look very warm and... and modest."

"Warm and modest, huh? Very good, Penny, now I've got the qualifications to be a housemother."

Jill and Penny smiled at each other, Jill endeavoring to be polite and Penny trying to look sympathetic to Jill's concern, but both struggled with their respective facades. Jill didn't like lying to be polite, and style was not among Penny's greatest priorities.

As they got into the car, Jill asked, "So, dear Penny, how far are we away from Petite Home-Lard, or whatever it is?"

"Oh, only four and a half, five hours. Oh, and then there's the fifteen, twenty-minute boat ride out there, to Petit *Homard.*"

Jill smiled at the correction, but soon the rest of the sentence caught up with her, and she abruptly gasped: "Oh, Penny! I just realized—you drove all the way down here! Four hours down and four hours back!"

Penny just laughed and patted Jill's arm. "Five hours, dear." She then said with a melodramatic sigh, "You know me, sacrificing self for the good of others. I'm just kidding—it really was no problem at all. I came down to Portland last night and stayed with friends."

"Ah, good!" Jill said with a sigh of relief. "What friends? Anyone you've written to me about before?"

"No, I don't think so. It's a lovely family. Their name's Hilton. They have this nice, big house with 300 rooms, each with a bed and a TV set. They've got a pool and everything..."

"Alright, alright," Jill said. "Now I feel even worse about making you drive all the way down here just for me. Four hours coming, four hours coming back..."

"Now I've got to say 'alright, alright' to you! Will you stop making yourself feel guilty? You're making me feel guilty somehow, too," Penny said while she merged onto the freeway. "You seem to have forgotten that *I* was the one who made you come out here."

"That's true, isn't it?"

There was a little pause, and then Penny started up again. "So you can only stay for a few weeks, hm? I already don't want you to leave."

"Mr. Babcock has graciously given me these three weeks off without a hint of apprehension. I think he thinks that it's the least he can do after The Toupee Incident." Only a few people in this world have ever been privileged with the details of The Toupee Incident, which happened one night during a staff party at the Flagwood newspaper office building. All that mattered was that Jill happened to be the one to save Mr. Babcock out of the predicament. Thus, there was a feeling of indebtedness which Jill would occasionally work to her advantage. Penny laughed every time she remembered the story, as she did now. Jill continued: "I could probably take half the year off if I wanted to, but I think that if I left for longer than three weeks it would do more bad than good."

"You're very sensible," Penny said after a pause, "but right now I wish you weren't. But still, I'm going to try to kidnap you for as long as you'll let me."

"You're very sweet, Penny, but," Jill said with a hesitant expression, "I don't know… I probably won't be able to stay terribly long... like I said, I don't know."

"Well, when is Steven arriving in Flagwood?"

Penny's words hung in the air for a few uncomfortable moments. Jill eventually replied, "He said in his last letter that he hasn't bought a ticket yet and that he was going to wait for me to tell him when's the best time for him to come."

"Oh, I see."

"Yeah," Jill replied baldly, with a poignant raise of her brow.

Penny shifted her weight in the driver's seat, deciding whether she should, or even could, bring up the problem that was Steve. "Em, Jilly, I've been meaning to ask you… have—did you decide to tell Steven that you've left the state?"

Jill stared out at the road ahead of them. "No, I decided not to, not yet, and I feel just terrible about it."

Penny nodded like she understood, even though she didn't. But she looked very much like she did, and this reassured Jill. "Hey, it's, it's alright… you know what's best." After another poignant pause, she continued more enthusiastically, "Don't worry about having warmer clothes, dear. It's only really cold during the nights, now, and I have plenty of things stockpiled in my closet that you can rummage through if you feel so inclined. Or we could go to the thrift store in Shrimpy Cove before we head out to the Island. It's no shopping mall, of course, but it's full of sensible items."

Jill nodded sweetly, even though the thought of a thrift store was nearly nauseating. She became concerned when she realized that pawing through people's old clothes—or, perhaps more accurately, old *people's* clothes—had become an indulgence for poor Penny. In any case, the thought of entering a building where there might be numerous coats like the one Jill was wearing was enough alone to make her heartily refuse the invitation.

Penny began smiling, and she began drumming on the steering wheel merrily. "Jilly, I think that you're really going to like the Island. You've never seen anything like it."

"Take me away from three weeks of melting in Arizona and I'm grateful already. What makes this 'Crow-Guard" Isle so special, anyway?" Jill asked, partly in a game to see how Penny would react to the mispronunciation.

Penny shook her head (Jill wasn't sure at which part of her sentence) and smiled. "It's just so… well, I'm not going to sit here and try to explain it. You'll see."

# Chapter 4

Although Jill made many considerate offers to assist Penny with navigation and driving duties, sleepiness won the battle fought between her and her drowsy eyelids. Her observations of the journey were brief and silent, as her eyes refused to remain open to look at the dark view lumbering past her window.

The next morning, she woke up to Penny shaking her bed. Jill rolled over, far too cozily arranged to immediately comply with Penny's request to "get up and going." She squinted as she looked out of a dimly sunlit window, then grabbed the top of her head. She realized that she was still wearing the unethically styled hat. She pulled it off, grumbled, and then asked, "Penny, where are we?"

Penny laughed, then replied, "We're in Shrimpy Cove, Jilly, and we've got to get moving. The mail boat is leaving soon."

A faint memory of what happened much earlier that morning finally came into Jill's mind. She remembered pulling up to an old house, then being awakened and greeted by an old woman who was very pleased to see Penny. Thereafter, Jill recalled stumbling drowsily into a room that the old woman directed them into. Although the memories were foggy, she remembered that in this warm, comforting room, she immediately took the opportunity to rid herself of the revolting coat, thereafter diving into bed while mumbling a goodnight to Penny. She fell asleep to Penny's voice telling her that it was, in all reality, a good morning. Jill was now sprawled out in a generously sized bed, which was beside Penny's already-made one.

"Even though I'm afraid to ask... what time is it, Penny?" Jill inquired, sitting up disgruntledly.

"It's twenty-of-six, and the boat leaves at six sharp. See, I gave you plenty of sleeping time."

Feeling a bit choked, Jill realized that she still had that awful scarf wrapped around her neck, just like the soft little noose that it was. She pulled it off flusteredly, then groaned reluctantly as she threw the warm covers off.

"You know, Jilly," said Penny as she milled around the room, somehow staying busy, "perhaps you and that nicely-dressed man who made eyes at you in the airport would make a good match. You both snore atrociously. I never knew that about you before, and I am quite disillusioned."

Incessantly squinting, Jill looked at Penny with sleepy indignation and said: "I can't understand how you're so cheery at such a miserable hour." Her frowning face then turned towards Penny's bed. Floppily gesturing towards it, she continued in a raspy voice, "And I thought that we were in a B&B, but here you've made your bed. Isn't that what the B&B people are supposed to do?" She fell onto her back into the messy bed and cried out, "And at six in the morning!"

Penny took Jill's flaccid arms and pulled her up to her feet. "Well, it's *going* to be six in the morning if we're not careful. C'mon, everything's by the door. All we have to do is walk outside."

Jill nodded while she stretched out and looked around the room. While she grabbed her cases, she caught sight of money on the nightstand. "Penny, only you would make your own bed at a hotel and still leave a tip." Penny shrugged with a self-pleased smile and nodded towards the door. They took a moment to laugh at each other and then headed outside. Once outside, they left the area hurriedly, Jill having only a few brief moments to admire the delightful simplicity of the B&B they had just slept in.

"That old lady was nice—what's her name?"

"That's Janice."

Jill seemed surprised. "You mean—*the* Janice? The Janice who gave you room and board when you first moved here?"

"The very one."

"Wait, Penny... the car. The—the—you don't own a car. Whose car was that?"

"Janice's friend's."

"You mean," Jill exclaimed, "that the coat, and—and the used tissues in these pockets aren't yours?"

"I don't put used tissues in my pockets!" Penny replied solemnly, offended that Jill would assume such a thing.

"Oh, Penny!" Jill cried. "Somehow I was more at ease thinking that these were *your* tissues," Jill continued, retracting her hands from the pockets, never to allow them to return to the darkness again.

As they got closer to the shore, Jill, for the first time, experienced the feeling of coastal fog surrounding her. It was an uncomfortably cold, humid, sticky sensation. The fog became heavier and more uncomfortable the closer they got to the dock. Jill was almost grateful that the fog blocked her view of the surroundings. Even with what little detail there was she was captivated, and the captivation made her slow down every few feet traveled. But with every few steps, she would remember that following Penny's lead was vital, and with a stumble she would regain her pace. They soon arrived at a little building, beyond which was a dock leading out into the misty sea.

"You told me that I'd be able to see Slow-Tarred—the Island, the Petite something or other—from here. Ha!" Jill exclaimed, looking out at the cool gray sheet covering the waters. Penny just smiled and nodded towards the little building, and so they entered it.

"Hiya, Mary," Penny greeted.

"Mah'nin, de'ah," replied an old, tanned woman with a wrinkly smile.

"What did she say?" Jill whispered.

"She said 'mah'nin'—it's Downeast-speak for 'Morning.'"

Mary nodded towards Jill with a smirk. "Who's the skinny thing?"

Penny laughed, as did Jill, but more in chagrin. "Mary Louis, this is my little cousin, Jilly. Jilly Jopling, that is. She's from Arizona. I'm hoping that I can convince her to stick around for a while."

"Oh, yes, yes, de'ah," said the woman, whose face became friendlier when she realized that she was a relative of Penny's. "Well, I'm guessin' that you want to catch the mail boat, right, Penny? You and this, this g'el from away?"

Jill decided to sit down on an old wooden bench while Penny took care of the proceedings. She figured that while being further out of sight, she might not get harassed as much. However, as she sat down, she began to worry that the rough bench would leave behind splinters in odd places.

"Yes, ma'am, that's right," Penny replied, "if we're not too late."

"Well, you'll be if you don't hurry. You know how particular ol' George gets about his schedule. He'ah, I'll getcha a couple of tickets."

Penny thanked Mary, and soon the girls, or "g'els", as Jill was confused to be called, were sent on their way. That is, they were pointed in the general direction of the ocean and were then expected to, half-blindly, make it to the mail boat without falling off the dock in the thick fog. As Penny intrepidly marched down the dock that she seemed to have made prior acquaintance with, Jill followed behind while questioning her own capability of avoiding a plummet into the unwelcoming sea beneath them. Jill's concern was heightened, of course, by the fact that she had not fully recovered from her drowsiness as Penny had. Jill's steps teetered from one edge of the foggy dock to the other, because of a terrifying combination of sleepiness and trying to avoid the especially rotted-out sections of the creaking structure.

"Morning, ol' George, are we too late for passage?" Jill heard Penny say. Apparently, they had reached the boat. From a distance, she couldn't tell by sight alone. She caught up with Penny, and she could see that a little distance beneath the docks was a smallish boat. Jill soon realized that it wasn't designed to provide comfort to any passengers it happened to carry.

"Yes you are, de'ah," groaned an old, leathery, captain-ish looking man as he emerged from the boat's cabin, "but I'll letcha board this time." At this he and Penny laughed. The snow-white-bearded man turned his sharp blue eyes to look at the shivering Jill. Glancing at Penny with a suspicious frown, he inquired, "She with you, Penny?"

Penny nodded confidently. Ol' George smirked at Jill, then took Penny's one or two cases as she passed them down from the dock. Jill approached sheepishly as she watched Penny board the boat with ease. Jill waited for a moment, testing to see if either Penny or ol' George would stop talking long enough to take her cases. Yet, somehow, these schedule-conscious people didn't seem to be in any hurry to demonstrate their finicky views on time management. Soon they were interrupted with the realization that Jill was not on board yet. Tilting their heads, they asked why. She raised her luggage-laden hands, and Penny laughed. "Come on now, Jilly. If you can pack all of that stuff, then I'm sure that you can manage to get it all aboard with you."

Accepting her cousin's challenge, she gingerly placed one loafer-shod foot into the boat. After her head bobbed for a few moments, looking between her imperiled foot and her luggage, she took a leap of courage and landed safely into Penny's arms. As she recovered herself, she was happily surprised to see that her luggage had made a successful landing as well. Although she initially thought that her luggage was a harmless extravagance, it was actually turning into a maddening encumbrance. As she stumbled forward to follow Penny towards where they would sit down, Jill realized that she hadn't arrived on the boat wholly.

"Ack, Penny!" Jill cried, hopping over to Penny to grab her arm for support. "Look, you made me lose my shoe."

"Your hair curlers made you lose your shoe, not I; there's a clear difference," Penny said as they watched the loafer sink into oblivion, producing bubbles in the water as a sort of farewell.

Penny helped Jill hobble to the boat's seating arrangements; a regal affair of a stiff bench that only held one comfortably. Although the beginning of the journey was not nearly as comfortable as Jill had expected, she couldn't help but feel a frisson of excitement when she heard the boat cough and sputter as it started up.

"She's been sputterin' like this for the past week," ol' George informed Penny, who thereafter gave him the sympathy due him, which was promptly rejected. It's a sort of ritual in these parts to share the happenings of one's life in this way. Eventually, the sputters developed into hopeful hacks, then at last the old boat started chugging, which prompted ol' George to loosen the knot that tied the boat to the docks and free the boat into its natural habitat. He steered the boat out of Shrimpy Cove, and at last, the girls were on the last leg of their journey.

As the sun rose further into the sky, the overwhelming fog cleared. As it did so, Jill felt a sensation that had become unfamiliar to her since her arrival in Maine—*warmth*! Glorious warmth! Jill wondered if the locals would ever become warmer as time went on, too. As Jill enjoyed the soothing, gentle movements the boat made, the swaying, the rocking, the occasional running over of slightly choppy waves, she began to see her surroundings with the clarity she desired all along. Looking behind, she saw the sun shining happily upon the fairly distant Shrimpy Cove, which was more delightful from the current vantage than the previously foggy view they enjoyed while within the cove. To her amazement, she discovered something else. With every few chugs from the boat, it seemed that they passed another little island. At first, the minuscule masses of land were nothing more than rocks with delusions of grandeur, but they began increasing in size. Very shortly after the overoptimistic rocks came landforms that could support a couple of people if they so desired to stand on them. The closer they got to their destination, the larger the landmasses became, some big enough to support a house or two. Jill had never seen such a thing, and she elbowed Penny and asked her every question that could come to mind through the drowsiness. The shape of the islands, in relation to the larger island they were approaching, was similar to a spilled cup of coffee. The puddle where the initial incident occurred could be comparable to the relatively large island, Petit Homard, and the smaller islands were like the little drips that followed the coffee spiller as he tried to get the coffee cup to the sink. Those series of landforms were to the mailboat route's left. After looking so intently at the series of little islands to her left, Jill was somewhat startled when she saw that there was a small, uninhabited, yet habitable-looking island to her right. And lastly, of course, she looked forwards, towards an approaching mass of land that was gigantic in comparison to its neighbors. She was sure that they were about to land on the island that Penny called home.

The sun did not limit its rays to Shrimpy Cove alone. It generously supplied Petit Homard Isle with brilliance, sparkling in a simultaneously beautiful and playful way upon the lapping waves that gently brushed against the shoreline. Jill had been occupied by listening to Penny and the conversations of prattling seagulls. When she realized that they were suddenly approaching the Island's dock, she became puzzled by the brevity of the voyage. Ol' George threw a rope out to another old fellow who was standing at the end of the dock. Jill noted with displeasure that this dock looked in even more rickety shape than the one they had just departed from. The old fellow who grabbed the line, and who was donned with a navy-blue knit cap, briskly tied up the line to the dock. He helped Penny and Jill out of the boat, with a kindly smile. Ol' George seemed to be a bit more obliging towards the transport of Jill's luggage, considering that she had just lost one out of the two articles which promoted her feet's well-being. He couldn't help himself from snickering at her thereon out, however.

"Jilly, this is Jerry, Jerry Miller. Jerry, this is Jilly, the cousin I've been telling you about. Jerry's been on this island practically his whole life."

"Nothin' practical about it, Miss Penny—I was born and raised here, and I plan on dyin' here."

"Well, don't do that until we at least shake hands, Mr. Miller," Jill said with a smile while outstretching her hand. Somehow, she forgot that that particular hand was occupied by her hair-curling case. Jerry's smiling expression quickly changed into a wincing, pained one as he "Ouch-ed" and "Oo-ed." He began hopping on one foot in a sort of excruciated dance to accompany the pained noises that were coming out of him, all because the case dropped on his other foot. Jill was immediately horrified to see the pain she had unwittingly inflicted upon him, but with ever more angst her eyes followed the case as it bounced off of Jerry's foot and landed directly into its demise: the watery deep beneath the dock.

All of the observers of the unfortunate event watched on in silence—even though all except Jill were ready to laugh—as water rushed over the case and sucked it into the bay's belly. Although Jill's hand was outstretched during the happenstance, she wasn't able to move a muscle.

"Well, Jilly," said Penny, grabbing Jill's shoulder, "I think we'd better get going. If we don't leave now, I worry that with your boating experience, you might lose *yourself* overboard."

The stiff, unnerved, nonplussed Jill nodded with a dry cough. They then picked up their luggage and left without a further word. Ol' George and Jerry, after seeing that they were a good distance away, began cackling. "Poor g'el... I didn't dare ask for any tip after that."

Jerry took off one of his battered boots, the left one, to be unnecessarily specific, and procured some change. "This oughta cover it."

"I'm not takin' your money!" replied Ol' George, offended by the good deed.

"Yes, you are! Costs fuel money, carrying all that extra weight—eh, from all those cases, that is."

Ol' George proudly resisted the offer twice over, but at last, his latent greed, or at least his sense of what was only fair, got the better of him and he pocketed the money. "You're an awful good man, Jerry Miller."

"Well," Jerry replied, squinting out at the ever-rising sun rather heroically, "I fig'ah that, to a woman, a sunken case is about as bad as one a' us sinkin' a boat. Oughta respect the arrangement."

"Yes sir," was Ol' George's reply, or, phonetically speaking, "Yessah," and that was about the end of the conversation. There was an admirable simplicity in the locals' conversation, a straightforwardness that would have pleased Jill if she had stuck around long enough to hear it. But she was far too bewildered by the past 24 hours to stay and enjoy the conversation. That time would surely come later.

Jill and Penny now bumbled away from the sea that devoured at least half of Jill's belongings. Jill then said, "Penny, that boat ride only took ten minutes. With all those little islands and rocks on the way out, couldn't they just build a bridge across or something?"

"Oh yes, they certainly could, and the mayor of Shrimpy Cove, who serves Petit Homard, has tried to repeatedly." She then paused as Jill stopped limping, leaned against Penny, took off her other shoe, and then continued walking, garbed with a puffy purple coat and now having bare feet.

"Hey, at least I'm walking evenly, now. Go on."

"The Mayor hasn't done it yet because every time he brings it up, the locals get all up in arms about tourists coming into their paradise. They think that they'll demolish the place, spoil their culture."

"Yes, their culture, or 'cul-cha', I suppose they would call it. Oh, Penny, why don't they say their R's?"

Penny shrugged. "I don't know, and I wouldn't suggest asking them."

"Why?"

"Because I've tried before, and they told me that they don't have an accent. It's much less frustrating to accept it than to try and convince them that they have one. Anyways, the simple answer to your question is that they don't want any tourism."

"It's hard to believe. They're all so friendly," said Jill sarcastically as she looked over her shoulder, towards the docks. "They'll probably be all politeness eventually. After all, they call you "dear," or "de'ah," all the time."

"They call everyone that, it doesn't mean anything, really, it's just a saying, like... well, I can't think of an example at the moment, but you know what I mean," Penny said as she unlocked her house door. Jill, unaware of her cousin's sudden stop, walked right into her. Penny smiled, put her hands on Jill's shoulders, and said with a sisterly smile, "And since you are a lot nicer than I am, they'll probably call you that eventually, too." She paused, then said with a droll twinkle in her eyes, "Provided that you don't drop all of their earthly possessions into the ocean." They laughed and giggled in that silly, sweet, sisterly way, and then they proceeded to go into the house.

# Chapter 5

*Monday, May 1st*

Jill awoke with a start. She had just had the most horrendous dream about pushing Mr. Babcock into the ocean. She couldn't remember if it was an intentional shove or not. As he swam up to the surface, he, in a very soggy voice, fired her. Now Jill was awake, and she looked around at her surroundings with a severity of drowsiness she had never known before. Her eyes eventually blinked away the majority of the lingering sleepy blurriness, and she could now recollect where she was. She was laying on a small, springy mattress, covered in an avalanche of blankets. It seemed to have completely buried her. As she looked at the foot of her bed, she noted with amusement that a rebellious toe decided that it did not wish to remain beneath the covers, and so it brazenly stuck out. Her gaze shifted from the shameless appendage and instead focused on the drawn curtains in the room, which happened to be directly above her head. Only one ribbon of light shined into the otherwise dark room. Not only was the room weighed down with murk, but also by what seemed to be an exploded clothing store. She got up with a groan and opened the curtains a bit wider. As she did so, she realized that her clothes had taken over the room. They hung from the curtain rod, sprawled across chairs and bureaus alike, and had even propelled themselves onto a retired ceiling fan. She smoothed her bangs back and kicked the central pile of clothes in the room. She then remembered that this particular pile of clothes was the one she had desperately searched through the groggy night before. She was very enthusiastically looking for her pajamas. She decided that the best course of action, according to her sleep-deprived brain, was to start flinging garments around the room until comfortable garb appeared. Upon smelling the lovely aroma of pancakes wafting through the air, she decided to remain indifferent to the messiness of the room. She was so moved by the compelling smell that she even decided to get dressed. She stooped down and dug a fairly complementary outfit out from the sea of fabric that was washed over her feet. She finished dressing and then opened the creaky door that led out of her room. She was hoping to come into close proximity with the pancakes that her nose informed her of. The distance between the bedroom's threshold and the beginning of the stairway, however, was alarmingly close. She was grateful that she was torpid while she emerged. If she had left the room at a speed equivalent to the excitement she felt at the smell of pancakes, she would have fallen right down the stairs and died without being able to enjoy the very pancakes that had tempted her. And to die without pancakes is one of the saddest ways to die.

Jill now carefully descended the staircase, with the prior profound thought in mind, and appeared in the kitchen. As she approached Penny, she closed her eyes tightly, making the apples of her cheeks protrude as her face turned into nothing but a grin. Penny laughed happily at seeing such a delighted reaction to her cooking, while she continued to stir cheerily yellow scrambled eggs with a huge wooden spoon.

"Good afternoon, Jilly!"

Jill squinted at the clock, and then her eyes widened when she determined where the clock's hands were placed. "It can't be two in the afternoon!"

Penny just chuckled in reply. She then said, "I figured that cooking something would get you out of bed more easily than if I tried to come in and wake you."

"You are a marvelous strategist, Penny."

"Oh, I try. Set the table, won't you? The plates are in the cupboard over there, and the silverware is in the drawer over there," said Penny, pointing in the respective locations with her foot. Jill traced the directions given by the toes and, upon finding the necessary items, began setting the table. As she did so, she began to admire the decoration of the house. Priorly, she didn't have the opportunity to take any studious ganders around. Early that morning, she was far too occupied with trying to find a bed, or any other decently comfortable surface to sleep on, to take note of how Penny decorated the exterior and interior of the little house. So now she looked around, noting the simple, homey flavor of the decor. The cupboards were painted a delicious, bright green, and the table and chairs were painted a rusty, rustic red, and the tablecloth had a tastefully checked pattern. As Jill set down the two plates, she admired the blue, hand-painted, flowery designs on them. It was all quite lovely, and all quite Penny.

Penny and Jill decided over breakfast that they would take a stroll around the Island, to see the especially scenic scenery and to meet some of the locals. The latter plan was not to Jill's preference, but she wanted to oblige Penny. She felt so indebted to her that she could offer no objection. So, after breakfast had been gratefully and ferociously disposed of, they put on their sunglasses and sensible shoes, both of which Jill borrowed from Penny, then marched out of the door, with vigor powered by the sugary, enlivening meal they had just shared. As they left, Jill glanced at the counter and saw that Penny had forgotten to drink her tea. There it sat, looking rather over-brewed and soggy. Penny was already too far ahead on their walk for Jill to remark upon the abandoned beverage, and so she decided to ignore it and close the door behind her. Jill then stumbled forward as she tried to catch up, although Penny's shoes encumbered her. They were very commodious. Jill then began staring at Penny's feet. She'd never noticed their extraordinary size.

"Jilly, I have a feeling that you'll like the folks around here. They're very forward, but good-humored," said Penny, taking Jill's arm, "but don't let any of their teasing scare you off. If they tease, it's their way of showing that they like you."

"Man, if they tease because they like me, what will they be like if they don't like me?"

Penny paused, then said, "Downright unfriendly."

"Lovely. They don't seem to be very welcoming towards anything out of the usual, hm?"

"Exactly. But, I suppose that it's better living around people that are too ordinary than too bizarre."

Jill nodded apprehensively, then stopped as she looked at little rows of buildings that were opposite of each other. The area was beside the docks. Penny smiled proudly, in her own quiet little way, and Jill smiled, too. "We call this part of the Island 'The Center,' since it's where most of the action on the Island is, with the docks over there, the Coffee House over there, the lobster pound over there, oh, and then the Peterson's store." Jill nodded, deciding that she already liked the quiet quaintness of the town that laid out before her, and she became assured that she made the right choice of coming to Petit Homard Isle to get away from the craziness.

Oh, but how disillusioned she would soon be! A large boom went off somewhere in the distance, and the idyllic calm that once claimed the atmosphere of the little town's center fell to pieces. Smoke plumed from where, assumably, the boom came from, and startled every living creature on the Island. Suddenly, an old, bald—yes, *bald*—woman came running out from the building furthest from where Jill and Penny stood, and she was shrieking while her pudgy arms were raised in terror. Only a moment later, a young man burst out of the same building. It soon became apparent that he was chasing her. But as if this were not strange enough, he was chasing her with a wriggling lobster in his hand! They soon disappeared around the building's corner.

Before the girls could believe what they saw, yes, a woman being assaulted with a crustacean, their heads turned at the sound of another door being flung open. Their attention was now turned to the opposite side of the street, where a white cloud of some sort emerged. It was actually a cloud of feathers, which precipitated to the ground while the feathers' origin honked in great distress. The swift goose ran, seeming to simultaneously gallop and waddle, as a middle-aged man chased after it with a stern expression and a broom. Perhaps the strangest aspect of the chase was that the goose and the man shared a peculiarly similar gait. After making a couple of circuits around the street, the chaser and the chased waddled speedily back into the building they had emerged from. A series of honks from both the goose and the angry man could be heard from within, along with a lot of crashing noises and multiple broom-thwackings.

Before the girls could even take a moment to blink in surprise and confusion, a shriek that was so womanly that it could only be a man's carried through the air. It seemed to originate from what appeared to be a coffee house. Jill and Penny, although afraid to look, slowly turned, and their breath was again stolen away as they looked through the window. There they saw a woman armed with a boot, beating a poor fellow over the head with vehemence.

The girls now stared at each other, pondering the absurdity they had just witnessed, both so alarmed that they could not say a thing. In wordless choreography, they turned on their heels and walked home with a frightened, decided briskness.

# Chapter 6

A few moments later, a stout, tanned, older than middle-aged woman with a determined stride walked into The Center of Petit Homard. She was there to get her daily fill of socialization and to take care of her errands. The first stop on her route was the lobster pound. Before continuing on, there ought to be an explanation of what a lobster pound is. It is neither a way of weighing objects according to how many lobsters the object would be equivalent to nor is it a place where people may go to retrieve their lost pet lobsters. It's an enclosure filled with circulating water, where lobsters may socialize until customers demand that they be ripped out of their natural environment and then be doomed to be put upon that evening's dinner platter. There is usually a building nearby where such deeds are done, and this is where the priorly mentioned woman was going.

As she swung the building's door open, her sharp eyes darted around. It was unusual to not see anyone. Even Tommy wasn't to be found anywhere. He was usually around, doing something or other in that chronically anxious way of his. When she heard distressed wheezes and sighs coming from around the corner, her eyes fell to the floor.

"Tommy!" she exclaimed, charging towards the young man.

"Oh, Mrs. Pine!" he cried, standing up from his kneeling position while twisting the soaked towel in his hands nervously.

"What on earth are you doin' on the floor like that?" this Mrs. Pine inquired. She was called Mary by practically everyone else on the Island, but the young man was particularly reverential in her presence. She'd babysat him more than once in her time, and he knew her methods. While she noticed that there was a puddle on the floor, he replied, "Oh, Mrs. Pine, it's awful, just plain awful, Mrs. Pine! Poor, poor Mrs. Bloomberg!"

An incredulous expression appeared on Mary Pine's coarse face. "What, did she melt or somethin'?" she asked, waving her arm towards the puddle.

"Oh, Mrs. Pine!..."

"If you say 'Oh, Mrs. Pine' one more time, I'm gonna have to put you in a worse state than that towel you're stranglin' is in. Now, what did you do to Mrs. Bloomberg?"

Tommy, a blond, blue-eyed jellyfish of a young man, swallowed his anxiety and said breathlessly, "Mrs. Bloomberg came in he'ah and asked if she could purchase a lobstah. She said that she wanted to cook it for dinnah, for old time's sake, since she and her husband used to eat lobstah every Tuesday night before he passed away. She said she had an aunt who..."

"Yes, de'ah, but I don't think I need to he'ah Mrs. Bloomberg's entire family his'try to know why there's a puddle on the floor."

"Well, anyhow, she told me that she's never cooked one before because her husband used to be the one to cook it. And so she asked me how I do it. So I told her how I season a good lobstah, you know, lotsa buttah and, and..."

"Sounds mah'velous, mah'velous, Tommy," said Mary in dry impatience.

Sensing her agitation, he hurried along, "Well, I came out from the back with a lobstah in a bag, but then she stah'ted insistin' that I put it in her's. So I took it out, and just as I was about to drop it in her bag, there was this big bangin' noise, and, well! I nearly jumped right outta my skin! And then, and then..."

"Go on, go on," Mary interrupted to show her impatience.

"...and then the lobstah slipped out of my hands, and it... it flew ov'ah her head, and its claw snagged her... well, I don't mean to be rude by mentionin' it, but, between you and me, Mrs. Bloomberg wears a wig..."

"Everybody knows that Mrs. Bloomberg doesn't have her own head of hair. I've seen more than a few seagulls take a gander at it, thinkin' 'bout usin' it for a nest," she said with a chuckle.

"Well, the point is that that lobstah took her nest—ahem, her wig with it as it went flyin' across the room. Then she went screechin' out like a cat up a tree. I tried runnin' aftah her with the wig and her lobstah, but I couldn't find her!"

"The'ah, the'ah, Tommy," said Mary.

"Thanks, Mrs. Pine," said Tommy, who was nearly in tears.

"That wasn't any comfort—you missed a couple of spots on the floor, *the'ah* and *the'ah.*"

"Oh," said Tommy, who knelt down again and began mopping up the splatters of saltwater. Mary was more upset that she hadn't come into the pound earlier to watch the happenstance than she was empathetic to Tommy's bewilderment. Tommy turned his head to briefly look at Mary as he asked, "Can I getcha anything, Mrs. Pine?"

"Well, I just came down from the camp to get some errands done. Just dropped in he'ah to see how your family's doin'."

"Moth'ah's doin' just fine settlin' into the house in the cove," ("In the cove" was one of those local ways of referring to Shrimpy Cove) "and Molly's doin' just fine takin' care of her." Molly was Tommy's sister. As you can probably surmise, Tommy was too snowflakey to yet have a wife.

"Good to he'ah, de'ah, very good. You stayin' outta trouble, takin' care of the pound all by yourself now, all in all?"

"Oh, yes, Mrs. Pine. Oth'ah than what happened today, I've been doin' just fine. My fath'ah taught me how to take care of the place real well."

"Yessah, he was a good man, your fath'ah was. You bringin' any lobstah to suppah tomorrow night?"

"Yes, Mrs. Pine, everythin' I can spare."

"Good, good," said Mary. As she walked out the door, she called out, "You'll do just fine runnin' this place, as long as you stop throwin' your merchandise at your customers, heh, heh!" Tommy smiled uneasily as he waved in farewell. He returned to his work, but then looked back up from the ground when the front door swung open again. Mary had reappeared, and she said from the door's threshold, "Or, at least, don't go throwin' them without me around to watch." With that, she again left while cackling.

She next went into a shop the locals called "Peterson's", a place where locals managed to find what they needed through the miscellaneousness of their merchandise. One day it could be a hardware store and the next a haberdashery. Candy, shoes, umbrellas, neckties, planks, fabric—Mr. Peterson was sure to have it, somewhere, somehow, bringing anything and everything he could find when he made his monthly trip to the mainland.

"Good aftah'noon, Mary!" greeted Mr. Peterson, the man whom Jill and Penny had encountered earlier, the man who possessed a goose-like gait while chasing one. He was now stooping down and standing back up, like a tireless see-saw, retrieving wares that had fallen and placing them gingerly back on the shelves.

Mary looked around the store with jocular disapproval. "What have we he'ah, Petey? Did a moose decide to come in and browse through your wares?"

"Oh no, somethin' small, feathery and spiteful did this to me."

"Mrs. Peterson with a feath'ah dust'ah?"

"Oh, no!" Mr. Peterson said as he laughed, "Mrs. Whitby came through and demolished the place.

"I don't know any Mrs. Whitby."

Suddenly, something angrily honked from the back room. "Shut up, will ya, you old goose?" cried Mr. Peterson.

"Must be a relative," Mary mumbled.

Mr. Peterson turned back to Mary. "Mary, I don't know what's got you thinkin' that all my relatives are out to get me. After all, Mrs. Peterson hasn't raised her voice in 10 ye'ahs. The last time I can remember was when she stubbed her toe."

"Who's this Mrs. Whitby, then?"

Mr. Peterson sighed. "Mrs. Whitby is old Mr. Basset's goose. The old man asked me to look aft'ah her for the week. Apparently, he was worried 'bout his butler's wellbein', thought he could use a break from caretakin' the plumy monstah. Now I understand why." Mrs. Whitby then began honking out again, seeming to take offense to the description. "Shut up!" cried Mr. Peterson, stomping his foot as he did so. He then turned back to Mary, putting on a placid smile. "You know how there's dog ye'ahs? Well, Mr. Basset says that Mrs. Whitby's 67 in goose-ye'ahs. Old Basset's so rich, I don't know why he doesn't send the goose to a home."

"If Basset takes the time to figure out goose-ye'ahs, I don't know why someone hasn't put *him* in a home," Mary remarked. She then pointed at the door that the honks came from. "You're keepin' her in the'ah, huh?"

"Well, it's the only place I could get 'er into."

"How'd she get out?"

"Didn't you he'ah that blastin' noise earli'ah? It sounded like it came from Mr. Basset's place itself. It jarred the door open, and the goose went honkin' and flutterin' out and through the shop."

Mary leaned towards Mr. Peterson conspiratorially and asked, "Why don't you eat the thing?"

Mr. Peterson shook his head and rubbed his fingertips together. "Money, Mary, money. You wouldn't believe how much money goose-sittin' rakes in these days."

"Too bad. I was hopin' you'd bring the thing to suppah tomorrow night."

Mr. Peterson laughed in appalled humor. "Old Basset would have me arrested for murdah! Besides, Mrs. Peterson's gonna bring somethin' special."

"Good to he'ah."

"Now, what can I get you, Mary? I've got plenty of feath'ahs, if you're in a pillow-stuffin' mood."

"Thank you kindly, but I just came in to get myself some fabric."

"Speakin' of which, Mrs. Peterson wanted to see if she could order a dancin' gown."

"Oh, I don't know, Petey. I've got a bunch of orders comin' in from all ov'ah. Besides, what use does Mrs. Peterson have for a dancin' gown? We haven't had a dance on this Island in twenty ye'ahs."

"Well, me and Mrs. Peterson... bah, nev'ah mind, she'll und'ahstand."

"What are you stumbin' all ov'ah your words for? What about you and Mrs. Peterson?" Mary inquired stubbornly.

"It's just that... we dance a little every Friday evenin', to some old records," he replied, swiveling on his heels and swinging his shoulders in evidence.

Mary frowned in distaste of the impromptu performance. "If you keep that up, I'll never tailor anythin' for you again."

Mr. Peterson laughed heartily and then shook his head. "Well, Mary, it'd mean a lot to us if you did take her ord'ah. We're comin' up on our 35th anniversary, and I thought it'd be nice to get her somethin' special."

Mary nodded thoughtfully, trying to determine whether or not she could possibly fit another project into her schedule. She also thought, for a fleetingly plaintive moment, about what it would be like to have the luxury of a 35th anniversary. "Yeah, well, I'll see what I can do, Petey."

"Thanks, Mary," said Mr. Peterson, who then turned away to continue to sweep up the remains of Mrs.

Whitby's escape. After Mary browsed through Mr. Peterson's stock and purchased a large amount of fabric, she put what she had bought into her basket and continued onward towards the Coffee House. She entered the little building and sat down at the usual barstool in front of the counter. She sniffed, then noticed that the air was distinctly smokey. After noticing this, she was surprised to find that the one person in the Coffee House didn't even give her a greeting.

"Jerry," she said to the very man, "what's that smell?" She then looked up with an awed expression, noticing that the smoke did not originate from any expected place, but from the top of his head. She was simply transfixed by the way the little stream of smoke rose from his hair and into the air. She had never seen anything quite like it. She was also perturbed by being able to see Jerry's head uncovered, as it tended to be concealed by his blue cap. A woman, who had the same height, shape, eyes, nose, and mouth as Mary, rushed out of the kitchen that was in the back of the Coffee House with Jerry's cap in hand.

"Bobbie!" Mary exclaimed at her sister, whose only real difference in appearance was her blonde hair, as opposed to Mary's dark brown hair. But now both were racing towards a complete gray. The sister also possessed a lighter, not to mention sweeter, disposition than her older sister. "What are you doin' with Jerry's cap? And why does his head look like a chimney?"

Bobbie just shook her head, too preoccupied with putting Jerry's cap in its proper place to reply. "The'ah," said Bobbie, putting the damp, slightly charred hat on Jerry's head. Jerry, however, remained expressionless, just staring ahead.

"Bobbie, what did you do to Jerry?" Mary asked while picking up a boot that was inexplicably on the counter, looking at it incredulously.

"Mary, let me pour us a couple a' cups a' coffee, and I'll tell you all about what I did to poor Jerry." Bobbie speedily filled the two promised cups. The coffee was brewed earlier on, and thus didn't have much warmth left in it. But neither of the sisters seemed to mind its mediocre temperature. Bobbie picked up her cup of coffee and put it to her lips. Then, both she and Mary rested their elbows on the counter while they stared at motionless Jerry, as Bobbie took her first slurp.

"Mary, did you he'ah that blastin' noise, went of 'bout a quarter of an hour ago?"

"Oh yes, de'ah," said Mary, unable to keep her eyes off of the curiously inert Jerry.

"Well, I had just lit a match to light the old lantern, and when that blast went off, that match went flyin' outta my hand like it was late for suppah. And I'll letcha guess where it landed."

Mary's eyes widened, then glanced at Jerry's hat. Bobbie nodded slowly. "How'd you get the flame out?" Mary asked in awe.

Bobbie raised her brow, then tilted her head towards the boot. "I beat it off of him."

Mary leaned forward to look at her sister in disbelief. "And why, de'ah, is the'ah a boot on the count'ah?"

"Joey shuffled in he'ah and wanted to see if you could mend it for him. He set it down and shuffled away—boy, is he a fast shuffl'ah—and the boot was the closest thing I could get my hands on when Jerry's hat caught on fire, so I clobbered poor Jerry ov'ah the head with it like he was a cockroach."

"Well," said Mary as she sat back, looking back at Jerry again, "I'm just glad that Joey didn't want me to mend his shovel." Mary held her coffee mug to her lips and squinted at Jerry contemplatively. With a suddenness that startled both Bobbie and Jerry, Mary threw the cup's contents into Jerry's face with an unapologetic thrust of the wrist. As Jerry sputtered and spat and shook all over, Mary laughed in her usual merciless cackle, while Bobbie was silent in shock. Soon after Jerry's recovery, he too began guffawing. "Well, now, Mary! G'els," he said, although the "girls" were well beyond the conventional definition of the term as far as years go, "I sure am glad that that pot of coffee cooled off good, oth'ahwise my cap wouldn't have been the only thing that'd been scorched!" At this they laughed together like they'd been laughing together for the past fifty or so years. They often were in the Coffee House throughout the years. Many fishermen enjoyed coming to the place, but Jerry the determined bachelor appreciated hot food and coffee more than them all.

"And not just any coffee would've brought you back from that daze of yours," said Bobbie with a quiet, knowing smirk.

"That's right, de'ah, only your coffee could cure me. You make it the best, state-wide, I do believe."

Bobbie nodded, not feeling any need for humility when it came to the matter, since it *was* true. She then proceeded to pour Mary another cup of coffee. Bobbie had been pouring coffee in the establishment ever since her father died. Her father built the place, serving simple meals for the fishermen on the Island. Nowadays, though, there wasn't anything in the place except coffee and Bobbie's baking, which was still enough to keep customers coming back.

"Jerry," said Mary, nodding towards the newspaper in front of him on the counter, "what's new on the mainland these days?"

"Oh, no *new* news, I'm afraid, just the mayor's usual blather 'bout buildin' his grandiose bridges. The sluggard won't do it anytime soon, though. We all know how all his threats have turned out ov'ah the ye'ahs."

"Not only *won't* he do it—as far as I know, he *can't* do it. He's gonna have to connect it to Prince Island, and that old crosspatch loner who owns it isn't goin' to let anyone touch it with a two-mile pole. He's got enough no trespassing signs on the shore that he could stack 'em up and use *them* as a bridge," said Mary.

"Well, I don't like it. The mayor knows that we none of us want that bridge built, but I've got a feelin' he'll go through with it at some time or anoth'ah," said Bobbie.

"Yes, de'ah, I'm sure he'll get his hands on that island as long as there's a promise of a buck or two. Well, Jerry, Bobbie," said Mary, putting her paw-like hands on their shoulders, "I'm not goin' to let anyone, not the mayor, not the economy, or any tourists ruin our island. You two with me?"

With that a hearty "Hear, hear!" was exclaimed, and they drank at least three more cups of coffee before the evening was through.

# Chapter 7

*Tuesday, May 2nd*

The next morning, Jill stumbled down the stairs, into Penny's kitchen. She reluctantly glanced at the clock. After examining it, her shoulders slumped in disappointment.

"3:00 P.M. today, Jill. A new record," said Penny, who appeared to be again preparing a large meal.

"I'm so sorry, Penny," said Jill, pulling out a chair from the kitchen table. She sat down defeatedly, sort of slumped over and sprawled.

"Oh well, Jill. You've got a lot on your mind," Penny replied, sliding a plate of waffles and eggs in front of her.

"Now *I'm* disappointed in *you*. You missed an opportunity—I have a lot on my *plate*, is what you should've said."

"The shame of it, Jill," said Penny satirically, sitting down across from her.

"Well, you may be losing your touch as far as witticizing goes… witticizing, is that even a word?"

"Probably not, but I'll allow it."

"Well, anyway, you may have lost your touch as far as witticizing goes," Jill continued, picking up her coffee mug and holding it under her nose, "but your cooking hasn't been affected. You know, you're being awfully good to me, cooking for me even though I've slept through most of the beginning of my vacation."

"Cooking woke you up last time, so I figured that I might as well use the method that works."

"Don't tempt me to sleep in every day."

"Oh, you don't have to worry about that. This is the last day I'm going to feed you like a queen. You've eaten through the last of my supplies. I'm going to have to go to the mainland to get some more. It's going to be oatmeal and tea until then."

"Tea?" Jill said, with a disgusted, twisted-up face.

"Tea. That's the last cup of coffee."

"Why didn't you warn me?" Jill cried, her voice breaking melodramatically. She looked at the last sip of coffee in her mug as if she were wishing it a mournful farewell. "First you dent my pancakes," she continued, looking at the waffles, "and then you tell me that I am going to be deprived of coffee. I could've savored this if I'd known it was my last cup."

"Just hush, Jilly," said Penny with a smirk, "you'll get used to tea. It has plenty of caffeine in it for me, and it'll do you just fine."

"Tea is coffee's unfortunate cousin, Penny, and I'd rather do without than substitute *my* coffee beans with *your* tea leaves."

"As you wish. We should go for a walk today, on one of the beaches."

"After yesterday? Booms from beyond? Lobsters? Geese?" Jill said while raising her eyebrows. She then shook her head determinedly. "Oh, no, Penny, not me. I'm staying inside until the end of the week."

"Why, do riflemen take weekends off?"

"Well, they'd better. Why don't we just stay inside and drink some tea or something, like a couple of old English women?"

"Sounds just fine to me. I practically *am* an old English woman."

"Penny! I've said it once and I'll say it again—29 isn't old."

"I'm 30."

"Well," Jill said, unsuccessfully hiding a grimace, "30 is... it isn't *that* old, anyway."

"Tell me that when *you* turn 30, dear."

"I'll try to remember to do that."

And so, with that, the old ladies adjourned to the small, cozy living room, where Penny sat and listened to Jill go on about her life. Particularly about how her boss, Mr. Babcock, was seeming to get more boring every day.

"What are you doing for work nowadays, Penny, now that Janice isn't letting you work for your room and board?"

"Oh, you know, just odds and ends for the Islanders. They always need their lawn trimmed, or their trims painted -"

"You paint their lawn trimmings?"

"No, no, the trims on their houses is what I paint. Sometimes I help Bobbie out with the Coffee House or help Mr. Peterson take care of his shop, or help Tommy with the lobster pound. Odds and ends, just odds and ends."

"Lovely. Sounds perfect for you." After being satisfied with this information, Jill went on to talk about her more serious troubles. "Well," Penny said, after having listened for a bit, "I think that it's admirable that Steven told you exactly how he feels about things."

"Admirable! Well, sure, he's got some pluck, but—I don't know, I keep getting confused. I've asked him over and over again to send a picture of himself, but he says that he wants to surprise me. And so I haven't sent any of myself—he doesn't deserve it."

"Mysterious men are the most obnoxious kind," said Penny.

"I think that millions of romance-novel-reading women would disagree with you. But I don't."

"At least you can talk to each other over the phone."

"But only once in a while, and even then his connection is so lousy, I can never hear him well."

"Oh! Jilly!" cried Penny, jumping out of her chair and running out of the room wide-eyed.

"What's wrong?" cried Jill, wrapping the blankets that were on her lap around her shoulders and running after Penny. Jill discovered that Penny was staring anxiously at the clock in the kitchen.

"Jilly! I absolutely forgot about dinner!"

"But, Penny! It's quarter of four, and we ate only a few minutes ago!"

"No, no, there's a community supper going on at the hall, at four, and I was invited! We have to get ready and go, Jill! I promised that I'd be there. I was going to surprise you—I told them I'd bring you along."

"Well, you certainly surprised me! You surprised yourself, to boot. But, Penny! I'm stuffed! And you must be too! And I'm afraid of your 'ordinary' locals. They're a little too 'ordinary' for me." Penny gave her an exasperated look. "Ok, alright, but I can't get ready in 10 minutes! Just look at me, I'm a mess!" Jill cried, pulling at her lopsided hair, then putting her arms out like a cormorant stretching out its wings to dry. Beneath her cape of blankets was a pajama outfit. Penny took Jill by the shoulders and looked at her up and down. "You'll be fine—just go upstairs and throw on a skirt or something and wear an overcoat, alright?" said Penny, ripping Jill's cocoon away from her and replacing it with a particularly shaggy, not to mention *purple*, coat.

"This doesn't seem to have a hood," said Jill after changing, patting her mussed hair with a frown. Penny's eyes darted around, and Jill sighed when she realized that her cousin began to eye the child-sized knit hat that was hanging off the coat rack. She walked over to it, plucked it off of its rung, and then stretched it over Jill's head.

"There," said Penny in satisfaction, taking a couple of paces back and crossing her arms, as if she were a critic admiring a work of art. "You look lovely." Jill just sighed in reply as she looked down at the unfortunately styled coat.

And so Penny opened the door, allowing Jill to step out of the house first. Penny, having gotten dressed at the early hour of 9 A.M., put on a light coat with particular haste and walked out the door even more hastily.

The daytime, Jill noticed with alarm as she buttoned up the strangely heavy coat, was much warmer than the nighttime. A wind picked up, and it slammed the door shut as Jill was closing it. "Be careful with the door, Jill. The handle is finicky. I've locked myself out at least five times." Jill nodded, although she secretly believed that Penny had probably lost or forgot her key, as opposed to the door handle being solely at fault.

They hiked towards the Island's Hall, Penny equipped with an old-fashioned, unlit hurricane lantern in hand for the trip back. As Jill traipsed alongside her cousin, she suddenly became grateful for her overcoat. A strong, salty wind picked up and chilled Jill's bones, as well as swept in every conceivable direction what hair her uncomfortably sized hat left uncovered. They soon approached a little white building. Windows ran along each side of it. Warm light shined out of these windows, contrasting the approaching darkness. Jill's stomach turned as Penny opened the door for her. The murmur of voices and smells of seafood, beans, and pie poured out of the humid building. Jill sheepishly entered the building, with Penny following close behind, the insistent shepherdess. Jill was in the mood for conversation as much as she was in the mood for any of the greasy, heavy food offered there. She hoped that Penny's enthusiasm would make up for the lack of her own.

To Jill's surprise, there were no outright greetings from any of the attendees, who all, in her opinion, looked, talked, and dressed exactly the same. But soon a few half-greetings came as Penny and she approached a table covered with food. Jill, at Penny's urging, regretfully picked up a large plate and began a long, arduous journey to the end of the food-laden table. Her hunger was already more than satisfied from Penny's breakfast. Although she sympathized with the stuffed potatoes, with a wince she graciously accepted each ladle-full of food offered by the women serving behind the table. Somehow, each of them looked like angrier versions of the lunch ladies from her school days.

"No lobster, please," said Jill, whose face was in the process of developing a green hue.

"Why not?" asked the server, rather perturbed by such a foreign request.

"I..." began Jill, who was then conveniently drawn into the next server, who asked in an attention-grabbing shout if she'd like blueberry pie. Jill accepted with grateful apprehension. She sighed in relief as she departed from the aggressively hospitable servers.

Jill now looked around the table-filled room, perusing it to determine the best place to sit, as well as where she could surreptitiously dispose of her plate's contents. She first looked to see where Penny had decided to seat herself. Alas, she was still standing up, talking to some old, toothless fisherman. Jill returned to her search, but soon realized that there was no possibility of sitting alone. But lo! She spotted a seat across from an old, slouched man who looked nearly as miserable as how she felt. Deciding that she and he were of a similarly unsociable spirit, she advanced.

She slowly pulled a chair out. "Excuse me, sir, is this taken?" There was no reply. The oldie simply continued to stare off into the distance, chewing with a morose frown. Jill took this as an indifferent invitation, and so she sat down. She poked and prodded at her plate of food, then attempted a few wary nibbles. She soon began imitating her companion's slouching posture.

Suddenly, Jill realized that she was hot. Unused to the warmth of a sticky, humid nature, she began to unbutton her overcoat. At the unfastening of the second button, however, she abruptly remembered that her upper half was clothed with garb intended for sleeping, not dining. She quickly rebuttoned her coat and glanced nervously with a crooked mouth at the old fellow in front of her. He was not affected by the quandary at all, though. In fact,

Jill was not certain if he had even noticed her presence yet. Growing uncomfortable with the silence, Jill actually said with a hopeful smile: "There's a lot of people here tonight." He still gave no reply, neither in word nor in expression. She couldn't blame him. She admitted that it was an extremely boring opener. She was rather jealous of his skill of ignoring people. She wished that she had the talent of disregarding conversations with such ease. She also considered, while staring at him unabashedly, what she had been told before about old people, that they like to do only one thing at a time. Apparently, chewing his baked beans was his one thing. Oh, but she did count one other—he managed to *look* like a baked bean, as well.

"Hey, the'ah, Joey!" loudly greeted a taller, sprier old fellow, slapping this Joey on the shoulder. Joey raised his head in surprise and gave a quick glance at the shoulder-slapper. When Joey looked up, he seemed to be startled at seeing Jill.

"When'd you sit the'ah?" Joey inquired, raising a bushy eyebrow.

The tall fellow leaned in towards Jill. "Joey's a bit hard a' hearin'."

Jill smiled. "Is he hard of hearing, or tired of listening?"

The tall fellow shook his head and laughed raucously as he walked away. Jill was surprised; she made a local laugh, and it wasn't even one of those derisive ones. A *real* laugh! But this triumph didn't help her situation any. She still was burdened with the responsibility of consuming the plate of food beneath her. But then came a stroke of brilliance. Yes, with a smirk, she got up, leaving her plate behind, and walked towards Penny. This way provided an anonymous escape, as she was sure Joey wouldn't remember to whom the plate belonged. Someone simply forgot to take their plate with them, and that was that. She was very gratified with her cunning. As soon as Jill came to Penny, she introduced Jill to a woman named Mary. After a few moments of Jill feeling unwelcomed by the woman, Penny looked at Jill's empty hands in sheer wonder.

"Jill, where's your plate?"

"Oh," said Jill with a smug smile, "I'm finished with it."

After this sly escape, Penny introduced her to at least five more Marys. Jill became acquainted with an endless barrage of fishermen, all of who were conflicted between being adverse to newcomers but also happy to be introduced to a younger, prettier attendee of the event. However alienated they made her feel, each of them encouraged her, if not put her under oath, to eat a lobster. She steadfastly declined every offer. It seemed that with every new person they met, they asked Penny about some upcoming project she was about to help them with—"You still comin' ov'ah tomorrow to paint my shed, Miss Penny?" or, "Remem'bah to come on ov'ah and dig my garden Thursday." And if these friendly reminders weren't the subject of the conversation, the recently ended winter was. "Haven't seen so much snow since the snowstorm of '38," or "Hope next year won't be as bad as '38."

"I can't tell, Penny," said Jill when they were by their lonesome, "are there a lot of people here, or does it just seem that way because this building's so small?"

"Oh, I'd say everyone's here."

Jill squinted. "What do you mean by *everyone*?"

"Everyone on the Island, of course."

Jill's eyes widened. "Everyone on the Island!" she exclaimed, looking around the room in astonishment. "I've been to parties that could populate three of these islands."

Penny laughed. "That's what I like about it here, Jilly. So, what do you think of them all?"

Jill smiled, then began: "They're stuck in their ways and like it. I've also learned the qualifications to be a Mainer: if you're a woman, you have to be named 'Mary.' If you're a man, there are a few more names available, but not many; You have to have at least one tooth missing, and if you were *not* born and raised here, and if you *don't* have a name that at least twenty other people have, and if you are *not* dentally challenged, then you will be promptly dubbed as being 'from away.'"

"Well done!" Penny replied. "You have nearly mastered the culture."

"They ought to give me a degree. Besides, I can't tell if they're giving me funny looks because of this ridiculous outfit or because I'm 'from away.'"

"Now, dear Jilly, go reward yourself with a lobster."

Jill's expression suddenly became severe. "If someone says the 'L' word one more time, I'm going to go screaming out of the building, or *waddling* out, anyway, I'm so stuffed."

"Why don't you want lobster?"

"You know why! I'm..."

"Ay," called out a woman, who was inevitably named Mary, "Whose full plate of food is this?"

Jill gave a stern look at Joey, a look threatening him not to open his bean-filled maw to reveal the plate abandoner. However, using his expertise to ignore Jill, he managed to hear the woman and he nodded towards Jill.

"Out of all the things to notice, you saw me leave my plate!" Jill thought as the woman took the plate of food and neared the cowering Jill, who took a step behind Penny.

"He'ah," said the woman, holding the plate out. "It'd be disgraceful to waste all that. You ought to put a lobster on the'ah."

Penny looked askance at Jill nervously. Jill pressed her lips together, stepped up to the woman with fiery eyes, then said in a trembly, faint voice, "I," she began, then her voice suddenly raised as she continued, "am very allergic..."—she took a sweeping look around, addressing the entire room of lobster-pushers—"...to shellfish!" After giving a brief glance at Penny, which seemed to say, "I'm a woman of my word," she inhaled a deep breath, then, in fluctuating tones, caterwauled right out of the building.

# Chapter 8

*Wednesday, May 3rd*

The next morning, Jill dressed in a bright outfit, then descended Penny's little house's stairs with a groan, rubbing her brow like she was kneading dough. There was a disheartening absence of the usual delicious aroma of breakfast in the house. With a depressed sigh, Jill realized that the house had entered a sad age, now that its more appetizing provisions were nearly out.

"Morning, Penny," Jill said blindly while stretching, shutting her sleepy eyes tightly. As she rubbed these compressed lids, she continued, "Yes, that's right, good *morning*, not afternoon. You should be proud of me, especially after yesterday's lobster incident—ha, isn't that funny; Mr. Babcock had a Toupee Incident, and now I've got an incident of my own." She expected to see Penny sitting at the kitchen table, slurping tea and reading some sort of useful book. But when her eyes opened, there was no such scene. No Penny, no slurping, no book, useful or not. Just empty chairs, and a forgotten cup of tea on the table.

"Penny?" Jill called out again with a quizzically furrowed brow. Jill slowly walked around the kitchen, as if Penny was there somewhere, perhaps hiding in the cupboards. After a moment, Jill charged into the living room. The bathroom was in no need of investigation, as its door was open. Jill's feet *thump-thump-thumped* from one side of the house to the other, like a rabbit friskily bouncing from one corner to the next. She went up the stairs, then down again, calling out Penny's name all the while. She came to an abrupt stop, attempting to calm the panic that was steadily setting in. Jill's eyes then darted towards the front door. Determinedly, she shod her feet with Penny's cosmically capacious shoes and scrambled out the door. As she stepped out onto the front step, the door closed behind her and clicked, in a foreshadowing kind of way. She was too preoccupied to take full notice, though, and so she called out "Penny!" again, although more calmly, deducting that if Penny was not indoors, it left only one option. The cries decreased in volume as the search around the house became increasingly hopeless. The breathless Jill's summons were shortened to the first syllable of her cousin's name. Finding that these calls were ineffective and that the "Peh, peh, peh" noises she was making only made her sound like a sputtering car, she decided that she would have to brave the outdoors to search for her missing Penny. It was not so much that Jill was concerned over Penny's well-being, (Jill trusted that Penny could take care of herself more than sufficiently) but she seemed to be feeling more anxious about her *own* welfare.

Jill ran—or *stumbled*—down the path from Penny's house towards a slightly larger path that could almost be called a road, if it tried very hard. After a short time running along it, she went by the docks, and then approached the little shops that were nearby. She set her hands on her hips and squinted as she searched. Unsatisfied, she walked directly to each of the shop's windows and peered inquisitively into them.

Business was taking place as usual in the Coffee House, where Jerry sat in his usual place on a bar stool by the counter, Bobbie poured herself a cup of coffee, and Joey sat at one of the booths. Whether or not he was reading the newspaper with droopy eyelids or just cleverly disguising his sleep was indiscernible. His state of consciousness soon became apparent, however, when he snorted as he was awakened by a sharp gasp from Bobbie.

"What's the matt'ah, Bobbie?" Jerry inquired worriedly. Bobbie just nodded towards the window facing the street, now with a more confused expression than a startled one. Jerry looked in that general direction, then, with squinting eyes, realized what caused the gasp. If he was disposed towards gasping, he would have done so, too. Now both Jerry and Bobbie squinted at the intruder that was looking in so suspiciously. When Jill squinted harder to see if Penny was among the Coffee-House-goers, Jerry and Bobbie squinted harder. They were a bit nervous. After all, they were present for the lobster incident. They had never seen such a strong, bizarre reaction in their lives, let alone towards their beloved resident shellfish. Jill backed away from the window while she shook her head, thinking that it was unlikely that Penny, the tea drinker—or, more often, the tea *forgetter*— would spend her time in a building devoted to the consumption of coffee. Jill was now an acknowledged terror among the locals since the supper, but at least now the feeling was mutual. She, upon her very first unfortunate introduction to the townspeople, was terrified of *them.*

Jill drifted from storefront to storefront, peeking in windows and yet not daring to enter the businesses, for the reasons aforementioned. She managed to startle at least one inhabitant per business by shiftily peeking into every window she could fix her peepers on. Finding that her search was ever unsuccessful, she stumbled further down the road, turning her head this way and that. At first, her pace was rushed and anxious, as was the expression on her face. But as the distance of the road dragged on, the speed of her run lethargically decreased to a graceless jog. She stuck her hands into her pockets and jog-trotted in a pretense of effort. Realizing that this pretense wasn't impressing anyone, especially herself, she resigned herself to simply walking hurriedly.

Upon realizing that she was entering a wooded area, she halted her confused march in the middle of the road. With growing agitation, she scratched her head and swept an awry piece of her bangs to the side. Jill now began to reevaluate her method of pursuit, acknowledging it was less than likely that Penny had been filled with an irresistible urge to go out in the middle of the woods and chop down a tree. "But I don't know," thought Jill as she put her hands deeper into her pockets while kicking a pinecone that a nearby tree had misplaced, "maybe she would!" Her foot bounced in deep thought, and finally she came to a conclusion as sensible as she could muster: she didn't know anything about the layout of the Island. This was the only road she had become acquainted with, and so she would follow it. She reasoned that it would simply be silly to go home and do nothing to retrieve her disappearing cousin. And so she half-ran, half-walked forward, like a confused lamb haphazardly searching for its spontaneously disappearing shepherdess. The illustration is rather backward, but you'll have to allow it.

The woods thickened into near darkness as what light there was shined through the awesomely tall pines that loomed quite imposingly above her. These faint splotches of light were splattered across the road as if a ditzy house-painter had walked along spilling his supplies. But Jill's capris, which seemed to have been colored by an ambitious dyer, could not be darkened by the loss of light. They were just as garishly green in the dimmed forest as they were in full daylight. Despite this, Jill had no qualms about wearing them. She saw no reason to discriminate against color. To her, they were no different from any of her other, calmer articles of clothing. Well, perhaps she would admit them to be a *tad* more assaulting to the senses than her other outfits. But Penny was not there that morning to warn Jill of how violently viridescent her trousers would be to the already bewildered locals.

Just as Jill was about to retreat from her self-imposed quest and head homewards, she instead leaned forward as her eyes turned into intrigued slits. Through a variety of meddlesome bushes and intrusive branches, her eyes caught sight of an extraordinary edifice, a scintillating structure, an awesome abode—yes, a magnificent mansion! All of this she could gather, even through the impertinent swaying of the twiggy foliage in the foreground.

Oh! But these moments of blissful abode-admiring were shattered as the splintering, soul-jolting sound of a shotgun blasted off in the distance! Jill had gained knowledge of what kinds of strange things such noises caused the locals to do. So with the fear of this in mind, as well as the uncertainty of where the shot came from and who its intended recipient was, she fled homewards in a hastier way than she initially planned, in a blur of green. Jill ran all the way home as fast as her oversized, borrowed shoes would allow her in an odd kind of shuffle. She looked rather like a frog with a limp. I have never seen an infirm amphibian, but I would imagine that the similarity between it and Jill Jopling would be striking.

The shuffler lunged towards the front door of Penny's house, alternating between looking hurriedly over her shoulder and eyeing the door handle. After a short, not to mention stressful, time elapsed, she began wondering why she was not yet indoors. She now concentrated more closely on the door handle, and she realized that her twisting wrist was making no progress. Suddenly, the sound of a distinct "click" echoed in her mind from when she had earlier rushed out of the house and slammed the door. Next Penny's words came to mind, "I've locked myself out at least five times."

Jill grabbed her head, spun around twice, then began walking quickly around the house in search of an alternate entrance. Still holding the top of her head, her elbows sticking up there in the air, she couldn't find any convenient method of ingress. She raised her eyes heavenward and saw an opening of tall order—the chimney. She shook her head, deciding that she'd rather not get sooty. After making this important decision, she looked in front of her at a more reasonable approach—one of the windows. Granted, all of these were shut, but Jill was prepared to pay the fee for a window replacement if she was forced to spontaneously open it with a rock. Being rather unadventurous, though, she heeded to her wisdom and instead attempted to try out her slier set of burglary skills.

She approached a window that was in the back of the house, then stroked her chin as she contemplated her method of crime. She didn't think to bring a glass-cutter. Soon, though, the plan came to her. She "tsk-tsked" at its simplicity as she approached the window and pushed up on the frame. To her shock, the window glided open with glorious ease! She sighed happily, but then took up the serious business of planning her trajectory. She looked behind, and she discovered that there was a sufficiently level runway. And so she jogged away from the window, preparing for takeoff. After going a fair distance away, she kicked off her encumbering footwear and charged towards the open window. As she flew upwards, her arms thrust in front of her, she began wondering if there would be any cushioning for her landing. But she did not soar far enough to find out. Instead, the barefooted eagle crashed into the window, but not exactly through it. She had either underestimated the height of her target or overestimated the strength of her legs. Whatever the case, she now hung by her underarms, her feet attempting to scramble up the side of the house. This proved to be difficult, as her bare feet were not particularly fond of the rough, splintery surface beneath them. She managed to struggle up enough for her torso to barely balance on the window sill, while her arms and legs flailed around. But it was all in vain. Her position was irreversible. She could not go any further forward without assistance, and she would have to plummet an undesirable distance if she decided to egress backward. The flailing ended eventually, when she realized that it wasn't helping her to progress to any kind of resolution. So there she hung in the balance, resigned to the fact that she would have to be left there until Penny came back from whatever she was doing.

"Oh, yes, Jill! This is exactly what you expected out of your vacation, isn't it?" she asked herself aloud, deciding to make conversation. "Stuck in the side of a house, running away from a rifle shot. And even if there was anyone around to help you, they'd run away themselves, after you made a delightful little spectacle of yourself with a lobster, or lack thereof, ha, ha, ha, ha!" Suddenly, she heard a disgruntled cough from behind. She was not in a position to make any further observations of the cougher, however, and so she coughed in reply.

"This your first burglary?" asked a gruff, womanly voice in a thick accent.

Jill bowed her already hanging head and sighed. "No," she replied, feeling rather sarcastic, "I've done twenty jobs like this, straight through the window. Best way to do it."

"Ah, so you're usually bad at it."

"Listen, ma'am, I belong here—or, at least in this house."

"I hate bein' called ma'am. If you've gotta talk to me, call me Mrs. Pine," said Mary (whom we've met earlier) while she watched Jill's green posterior wriggle about in the window.

"It's a pleasure, Mrs. Pine," said Jill in a muffled voice, who was now getting red in the face, both from chagrin and from her uncomfortable position. "Hey, I know that this might sound like a big favor, seeing how recently we've become friends, but can you help me get down from here?"

Mary laughed in that cackling sort of way, then rolled a large stone so it would lay beneath the window. "The'ah, try steppin' down on that."

"On what?"

"You'll find out soon enough."

Jill's toes cautiously stretched downward to feel around. It was soon realized that she was suspended too far in the air to make contact, so she attempted to lower herself slightly. The intended gradual descent happened all at once, however, and with a yelp she dropped to the ground, like a sack of disheveled potatoes. She had totally missed the stone provided for her leisure. Mary looked down at the collapsed girl before her. Although Jill's eyes were shut, she could somehow instinctively tell that this Mrs. Pine was smirking. When she opened her eyes, she looked up and saw the old woman reach out a surprisingly sympathetic hand.

"Thank you," said Jill, after being hoisted up by the short woman's strong arm.

Mary nodded, but was chiefly occupied with staring at the house before her. "So what are ya, Penny's sist'ah or somethin'?"

"Almost—we're cousins."

"Ah. Cousins are just siblin's that you don't have to live with."

Jill couldn't help but chuckle. But the humorous moment ended when Mary began squinting at Jill suspiciously. "Ay, you're that insane g'el who ran out a' suppah last night, aren't ya?"

Jill sighed. "Yes, the very same. I can't say that I'm surprised to hear that I've already made a reputation for myself here."

"Yes, missy, yes you have. You certainly have!" laughed Mary.

Jill, feeling her face grow flushed, then said in reply, "Well, I'm starting to form an opinion of this place myself, and I can't tell if it's a good one yet. I wake up this morning, and Penny's nowhere to be found. I then begin running around this island like a madwoman—which I'm starting to believe I *am*—and then I hear a gunshot from who knows where, and so I run back here to take cover, and then the dumb door is jammed. And as if this morning's and last night's events aren't embarrassing enough, some random woman comes out of nowhere and watches me fall on my behind."

Mary looked at her without any apparent expression of empathy. "Sounds like you've had a bit of a rough time."

Jill stared at her in disbelief. "A bit? A bit! Mrs. Pine," she sputtered, "may I please ask, what are you even doing here?"

"Well, Miss Fargo, I saw a flash of the ugliest green I've ev'ah seen in all my days go runnin' by like a frog with a bad hip, and so I decided to come ov'ah and make sure nothin' was wrong.

Jill's angry expression softened. "Oh, well, how considerate of you," she replied, trying not to sound surprised that this grumbly neighbor was concerned. "Mrs. Pine, do you have any idea of where Penny could possibly be?"

"She didn't tell you?"

"Oh, I'm sure she would have, if she remembered to."

Mary smiled as she looked off into the bay. "Poor Miss Penny. She's a smart g'el when she remembers to be. She always comes pedallin' on that bicycle of hers and throws a whoopin' on whatev'ah I need her to do around my camp—not that I *need* the help, I just like givin' her somethin' to do."

"That sounds like my Penny. But the question is, *where* is my Penny?" Jill asked desperately.

"Miss Penny usually gets her monthly supplies at the beginning of the month. She'll prob'ly be back by dusk."

"Oh," Jill replied, a little embarrassed that this stranger knew more about her cousin's habits than she did.

"Now that I've rescued you from this man-eatin' window he'ah, you can come up to my camp till Miss Penny comes back."

Jill was shocked by the downright neighborly offer. Little did she know that Mary liked her impertinence. "Well, that sounds better than hanging around a house I can't get into, waiting for the bears to get me."

"The'ah aren't any be'ahs on this island," said Mary, as if Jill should have known that the very thought was ridiculous. "I'd be more cautious 'round the raccoons, the creepy little creech'ahs." Mary then walked towards the road, prompting Jill to follow her. "Raccoons have every disease known to mankind—rabies, mostly, and who knows what else. They've prob'ly got the leprosy and the tetanus and the influenza, for all I know." Jill silently chuckled at the questionable medical accuracy of the ranting warning as she followed her. Before long, they were trekking up a steep hill. For all she knew, this Mrs. Pine could be kidnapping her, but she decided that she'd rather be kidnapped by the old grouch than fall victim to one of those villainous raccoons. Jill sighed hoarsely when they reached the top of the hill. With her hands on her waist, she admired the view, unable to help but be impressed by the cabin's vantage. "My! You can practically see the whole Island from up here, can't you?"

"Yessah, Miss Fargo. I keep an eye out ov'ah the Island, make sure no one gets into any trouble."

"You're like a friendly kind of stalker, then, huh?" Jill said belaboredly as she entered the cabin with a huff and a puff.

Mary laughed. "I do my best," she replied while opening a dust-laden curtain. As sunlight flooded into the room, revealing every single particle of dust the curtains had made sure to keep hidden, Jill realized that the room was filled with fabric and materials of all kinds, all textures, and all colors of the spectrum. All the more subdued ones, anyways. As the guest looked around the room, it seemed that the only company Mrs. Pine kept were stacks of cloth, which were casually sprawled across the single couch and a chair in what might have been called a living room. There was only one chair unoccupied by these textile guests, beside which half-finished articles of clothing sat with pins sticking out of them haphazardly. Other than the overwhelming majority of material in the room, there was little sign of any kind of a theme of decor. There were fishing trophies in one corner of the room, and in the opposite corner hung paintings colored in clashing hues. Then against the wall was a lovely, gold, ornate lamp, which was far too extravagant to belong in such an unpretentious home. To dampen its opulent character, fabric was nonchalantly thrown over the curve in its stem. Mary began cleaning the couch of clutter, removing fabric and pins and needles, and generally all of the things one doesn't like to sit on. "He'ah, sit down, sit down. I apologize for the clutt'ah, I don't have company too often up he'ah."

Jill nodded, having surmised that this was the case herself. She watched on as Mary moved the last of the seating impediments; two hand-embroidered pillows that featured Maine scenes, pine trees, mooses—meese? Did the plural form of "goose" apply to its rhyming counterpart? Jill didn't know—and a sparkling lake. How anyone could paint a picture with thread, Jill couldn't understand. What a skill! At last, Jill sat down, then noticed a picture frame on a little hand-hewn granite table between the couch and the unoccupied chair mentioned prior. Within the frame was a black and white picture of a young, handsome man in garb that made Jill feel like she stepped into the 1920s.

"Sit down, sit down, sit down," Mary went on as she tidied what she could, even though Jill had obeyed quite a while ago. Jill went on looking at the picture. Noticing that the man contained in the glass pane, frozen into a time of beauty and happiness, was close to Mary's chair, Jill decided that he must have been her husband. The man was obviously dear but departed. Jill, although being a grateful victim of Mary's hospitality, feared the woman too much to inquire of it or to offer what might have been unnecessary condolences. Jill gained much information from the contents of the room without having to inquire about them. But to Jill's surprise, Mary began a sudden tour of her artifacts, ranging from a vase her friend brought her from a cross-Atlantic tour to a quilt she helped her mother sew during the great snowstorm of '38. As Jill tried to follow Mrs. Pine's long, confusing explanation of how she acquired her lamp from an Italian shoe salesman, she realized that Mrs. Pine's choice of decor was chiefly guided by her sentimentality, as opposed to the traditional rules of coordination. Soon Jill was told to follow her hostess upstairs, despite the fact that many long minutes had been spent to prepare a place for her to sit down. As they climbed up, Jill acknowledged to herself that if Mrs. Pine was going to kidnap her, now would be her prime opportunity. Anything, to poor Jill, was possible, whether she could deem it crazy or not, as her past encounters with the locals had proven. But Jill didn't seem to mind the possibility.

Now Jill was shown Mary's workplace, which was fully devoted to her preoccupation with pins and clothing commissions. Jill soon learned that from this second-story, cramped perch Mary served as both the Island's tailor as well as its watchman, or as Jill would have affectionately titled the position, the Aloft Analyst, who knew everything that went on around the island, whether her objects of interest were aware of her inspections or not. Both Mary and Jill were surprised by Mary's sudden vivacity during the impromptu tour, yet both, however secretly, were delighted by it. As they walked back down the stairs and past what seemed to be a bedroom door, Jill pointed towards it and asked, "What's in here, your bedroom or something?"

Mary looked between the door and then Jill, then sighed, looking a little crossed, and said, "No, that was my—it's a spare. You can sleep the'ah tonight if Miss Penny decides to stay the night on the mainland."

"I certainly hope that she remembers that I came across the country to see her!"

"I'm sure Miss Penny will, Miss Fargo."

Jill half-frowned. "I'd rather you call me Jill, Mrs. Pine. My last name actually isn't Fargo, it's..."

"No, I'm not callin' you Jill," Mary interrupted. "I've got anoth'ah name. It'll suit you bett'ah." Jill smiled and cocked her head. Mary then looked down at Jill's bright green capris with a teasingly disapproving shake of the head. "Frog Legs."

Jill looked down, and although she couldn't deny the similarity, she flattened her lips as she took offense. "I happen to like these pants."

"Isn't that nice? It still doesn't make you look any less like a frog. And it ain't just the color," Mary said, then with a chuckle, continued, "You've got stick legs." Jill looked down again, sighed in hesitant acknowledgment, then walked ahead into the living room. Next came a rambling tour of the outdoors. "Yessah, my house is on the highest point of the Island, oth'ah than the Basset's place."

"Who are the Bassets? Is it a kennel, or something?"

"No, not at all. You could call it a looney bin if you wanted to. It's a fath'ah and his daught'ah. They're both a couple of cuckoos. They came he'ah about four ye'ahs ago from England, bought that old mansion. They don't come into the Center too often, thank goodness. They're downright strange people."

Jill nodded, wondering if they were actually mad or if being from a foreign country was enough to grant them the title of Cuckoo. "I see," she replied. "Is he the one who shoots off rifles?"

"No, surprisin'ly, though he likes to shoot off his cannon."

"His *cannon*?"

"Think it came with the house. He likes to blast it off once every great while and scare the daylights out of everybody. Mrs. Bloomberg's the one with the rifle—she's an old coot that comes he'ah from Florida in the summ'ah, an old snowbird. She's a widow just recently, and now that her husband's gone, she's taken up the rifle. She tends to shoot at anyone or anything she hears around her house. I don't think she intends on harming anybody. She's scared that everything's a wild animal comin' to attack her."

"The poor woman! There aren't any wild animals that would do that on this island, are there?"

"Nobody's ever gotten close enough to her to tell her that there aren't."

After Jill had gratefully been enlightened about her neighbors, they returned indoors to have an evening dose of coffee and to discuss all the adventurous times when Mary could've and should've died, but decided not to. Jill was impressed by these stories of stubborn survival and was so engrossed by them that dusk fell upon them quite abruptly. Jill stared out the window in amazement. Pointing towards the growing darkness, she asked, "How did that happen?"

Mary leaned forwards, then suddenly looked very disconcerted. She replied, "Not sure, Frog Legs. I'll go up and see if Miss Penny's house's lights are on."

"Thank you, Mrs. Pine," Jill replied with a smile that showed how surprised she was to be satisfied with the day's events. Mary left the room to go up the stairs. She stopped halfway up, then called down, "Just call me Mary, alright, de'ah?"

# Chapter 9

That evening, the circumstance of Penny's disappearance was fully and apologetically explained to Jill by the evaporated cousin herself. Penny anxiously told her nearly enraged cousin that she thought she left a note to inform her slumbering cousin about her journey to the mainland, where she went in a quest for supplies. She had left early that morning and didn't want to disturb Jill's sleep.

"I wish that my sleep was the only thing you disturbed!" Jill cried in reply when Penny had finished explaining herself. "All that you left was a cold cup of tea."

"I'm so sorry, Jilly. Was your stay at Mary's pleasant, at least?"

"Actually, it was. We had a cheery time. She kept surprising me, and I think she kept surprising herself, too."

"Well, *I'm* certainly surprised."

Jill expected that Penny would go on, but upon realizing that her elaboration would have to be provoked, she asked, "Oh really?"

"Yes," Penny said as she poured cold tea down the sink with a depressed expression, "Mary never has anyone up to her camp. Even her sister Bobbie only goes up there once in a while. Mary always just comes down to the Center, she never brings anybody up. It's taken me three years to convince her to let me do some yardwork for her. She must really like you or something." Penny looked like the joy of life had come into her again, by this point having poured freshly boiled water in her cup, into which a tea bag was thereafter plopped.

"I think she liked having a listener. She has the funniest ways of collecting things... Penny, is Mary a widow?"

Penny nodded while looking down at the tea she was stirring. "Yes, I believe so. She doesn't talk about her husband, though."

After a pause, Jill said with a prideful smile, "She called me 'de'ah,' and told me to just call her Mary, and not Mrs. Pine."

"Well, well! In your first week! Not bad at all. It's sort of nice to be called 'dear' all the time, even if they don't mean it, don't you think?"

"Are they in the habit of calling people 'Frog Legs', too, or is my nickname just a fortunate fluke?"

Penny was justly confused by the question. She paused, then replied, "I hope they don't call people that."

"I must be special, then. Unless they nickname everyone after the color of their pants."

Penny then took a moment to look at the article in question, then laughed. With a cringe, she agreed, "They are pretty loud."

"I know that, but nobody's ever said a word about them in Arizona."

"Well, Jill, that's because you live in the Wild West. Now you're in the... in the Unexcitable East, if you will."

"I will, I certainly will! But I can't help but like it here. I haven't figured out why, but I want to try and figure it out before I leave."

~~~

The next day, Jill, feeling confident and adventurous after having an actually pleasant experience with a local, decided to explore her surroundings with a renewed sense of curiosity. Penny, in reply to Jill's invitation to join her ramblings, declined in favor of staying in the house to
~~~

recover from her shopping expedition. You may wonder how the noble endeavor of stocking up supplies could take an entire day. Penny not only received many foodstuffs, but also a pretty portion of socialization. It was a custom of hers to visit with old friends on the mainland, who although but a mile or two away seemed to be reachless. She had left the Island by the morning's mailboat and had returned on a lobster boat, escorted by the couple who had entertained her.

Although the absence of Penny's companionship brought Jill due apprehension, she braved onwards, courageously packing herself a sandwich to take with her, fearlessly loading it with peanut butter and jam. Penny insisted that Jill slather the delectable bread with blueberry preserves. Jill, similar in character to the peanut butter that stuck so closely to its bread, did not always like to try out unfamiliar things. She wavered in this characteristic, however. Some things were perfectly admissible, despite being new, and others were beyond bearing. But she could only know how much she didn't want to change when the change came up to her face to face. And the blueberry jam was one of those things that she nearly slapped in the aforementioned face of change. But politeness ruled, and Jill acquiesced to Penny's suggestion, without any slapping.

Jill took the little canvas bag that Penny suggested she use to carry the precious meal in hand, and carefully shut the door behind her. The air was warm, and she could hear the distant sounds of seagulls crying out like spoiled children, and the sound of waves approaching the beach then quickly retreat to their origin. Jill walked into the wind with her back straight and her face raised towards the sun. She wasn't exactly sure where she was going or what she would do when she arrived at nowhere in particular. She knew of a few places that she didn't want to go; not near the Center where perfect moments to be had would surely be interrupted. Neither did she want to go towards the south-eastern side of the Island, where she heard people often accidentally discovered cliffs. She was determined to end up where the sea would meet her toes, and so she allowed her nose and ears to pull her closer to her goal. She followed the salty breeze and the sound of water crashing and fizzing when it met the rocky sand. She was filled with excitement when she, at last, arrived at the destination that was once unknown to her, the ocean's noises greeting her before the sight of it could. She ran up the hill that separated her from her destination, and upon coming up to its summit, she looked down and smiled widely, sighing in a musical sort of way. There is not a word between a sigh and a hum, but if there was one, this would be the place to use it. She took off her shoes once she reached the bottom of the hill, and was surprised to feel her feet squish into cold, sandy soil. Strands of grass tickled her toes as she descended upon the rocky beach. She did not expect a beach of the sort that was before her, however. She found it strange that she had been more surrounded by sand in a landlocked state than she was now, standing on a beach. But after a few moments of appreciative adjustment, she began to like the idea of a rock-covered beach very much. Another gust of wind blew, and with it entered a sweet, flowery aroma. She turned her head, then discovered that the flowery smell sprung from a leafy hedge, which was peppered with white and pink flowers. She walked towards it, tripping at least six times while journeying across the unpredictably sliding rocks beneath her. Upon arriving at the bush, she paused to admire it. She reached out to caress the flowers that had given her such pleasure. Jill retracted the loving hand with a yelp, however, when the bush suddenly made her aware of its thorny nature, to which she replied by flinging the afflicted hand around in pain. After recovering, in flesh but not in spirit, she began examining the prettier, more delicate portion of the attacker; yes, its wide, glimmering flowers. She cautiously approached it nose-first. But her nose too fell victim to the bush's protection when a shriek from behind startled her, sending her head forward. She turned around, plucking a minuscule yet sinister thorn from her nose. She realized that the shriek just came from a seagull that was soaring above, looking with intent greediness at the canvas bag that contained her sandwich. Realizing what intentions it had, she clutched the bag closer and made a face at the bird.

She then sat down on an especially large rock, which was a wary distance away from the bush that had victimized her twice now, to eat her lunch. She carefully unwrapped the blueberry-stained paper from the sandwich and closed her eyes as she was about to take a large, altogether perfect bite out of it. But her eyes fluttered open when she heard a feathery, swooping rush of noise. To her anger, a plucky seagull had attempted to dive-bomb the sandwich she had eagerly anticipated enjoying. Jill was as stubborn as the seagull was determined, and with an incandescent, galled—dare I say "*gulled*"—glare at the annoying avian, she held the exposed, tantalizing bread closer to her mouth, like a possessive squirrel, in hopes of protecting it. For an average, lackadaisical gull, her posture would have been a sufficient deterrent. But this gull was a resident of Petit Homard Isle, and thus was not timid as a mainland gull might be. The island life had hardened the gulls and the people alike. Self-sufficiency was key for survival, whether you were an experienced fisherman or a hungry gull. Thus, the gull's predisposition towards obstinacy was heightened by its fewer opportunities for scavenging. And so with this dangerous nerve, it swooped again, but with more accuracy. Although it did not capture what it aimed for, it managed to thoroughly terrify Jill. It crashed into her with another fell swoop—or another "*fowl*" swoop, if you'll allow yet another bad pun—and left behind an array of gray and white feathers. Jill, on the other hand, jumped up and fled, leaving behind her sandwich, the attacking bush, and the bombarding gull. She did manage to grab her shoes, although her feet were still wet from a brief stroll in the waves. After she had gotten a sufficient distance away, she bent forward and leaned on her knees as she caught her breath. She frowned, realizing that the gull had come off the victor in this battle of wills. "Ah!" she exclaimed in offense as she saw further evidence of this. The gull squawked happily as it danced over its conquest, hopping over it and gulping down the bite Jill should've had. But soon an angry mob of whom Jill guessed were the gull's cousins began quarreling over the gull's violently acquired bread. Jill, although out of a sandwich, was very entertained by the war that played out before her. Crumbs exploded as each gull would accidentally release the sandwich, while another would push its way through the cloud of squawks and screeches and white feathers to intercept the bread. It would then land, rejoice over its brilliance, and then go to swallow the sandwich's remains whole. But the mob found him out before he could enjoy it, and so it was stolen and the cycle would begin again. Jill found not only amusement but also a sort of satisfied revenge in seeing that the original gull would not enjoy its plunder with such ease.

She meandered away from the battle scene she had unintentionally instigated and went towards the Center. Arriving there, she sighted many of the folks whom she had met at the now infamous community supper. Beginning with a few fishermen hanging around by the docks, each of them would without fail grin mischievously and offer a greeting that went along the lines of, "Af'tahnoon, Frog Legs." The first two or three greetings of this nature perplexed her, but soon she remembered that Mrs. Mary Pine had influence over the Islanders. Without a doubt, Mary's sobriquet for the newcomer had been gladly shared with the general public that morning. So with each mention of the name, Jill would smile flatly and nod at them, feeling both amused yet playfully irked. Frog Legs eventually made it past the zone of name-callers and began walking down the same road she had embarked upon when she heard Mrs. Bloomberg's gunshots.

Although she felt wary of this path, she couldn't help but be drawn to it after being mesmerized by what she now knew was the infamous Basset's mansion. She just had to get another peek at it.

Jill soon came to the point where just yesterday she stood and admired the splendor of the enormous residence. She was at the bottom of a steep, gravelly, winding drive that seemed to be heading in the general direction of the place. She smiled—or, perhaps more accurately, smirked—at Mrs. Mary Pine's contemptuous thoughts of the Bassets, which was one of the few subjects she expressed her opinion of with fervor.

Suddenly, the sight of an airy, delicate object tumbling down the precipitous drive interrupted Jill's amused musings. She wasn't totally certain of how to define its movements—she couldn't be sure of whether it carried out its descent by means of a series of tumbles, or if it was just floating down while taking a few rests. The manner of descent of the object directly *behind* it was much more easily discernible. It wasn't floating, to say the least. This other object flung its arms about in a most un-demure fashion. With the help of closer proximity, the thing behind the forthcoming thing was found to be a young woman. Atop this person was a mass of thick, blonde hair thrashing around as the legs beneath stumbled down the near-ravine in an apparent attempt to retrieve the thing that Jill had first seen. Jill couldn't help but be bewilderedly transfixed on the girl's lengthy fall, which was cleverly disguised as a heavy run. Jill was so distracted by the chaser that she did not even notice that the chased (a parasol; much daintier than its owner) landed directly yet delicately upon Jill's feet as if it were mocking its chaser's strenuous attempts to retrieve it. Much alarm arose within Jill when she realized that, although the parasol had come upon her in a very genteel manner, the solid, tall blonde who followed would not. She had gained much more momentum than her parasol, despite having taken regular pauses to stumble and trip as if a herd of affectionate cats was winding around her legs.

"Oh, no!" Jill cried as the barrelling blonde was about to careen directly into her solar plexus. Jill now had an unexpected understanding of what it must feel like to be in a football game. She closed her eyes tightly, deciding that she'd rather listen to than see what was about to happen. She heard a yelp, then a sound equal to screeching tires. She braced herself for immediate impact as she heard the noise of sliding gravel. Jill opened her eyes with hesitation, knowing full well that she would have to look at the crash scene to see who required medical attention. To Jill's great surprise and joy, neither one of them seemed to be injured. The blonde, of course, was half on her feet and half on the gravel. The girl then began laughing in a guffawing sort of way, slapping the ground. She quickly abated from the gesture, however, when she remembered how sharp the gravel was. Jill too began laughing, but more in perplexed surprise than anything else. The blonde, although having taken more of a beating than Jill, was much more entertained by the affair than shocked by it. Jill wondered if this was because the blonde was used to such fiascos. The blonde then spoke, in a delightful British accent: "Well, there I was, minding my own business on top of the old hill, when a nasty wind pinched my parasol and flung it down the drive. And now here I am, laying at the feet of some poor, rattled girl. You look as white as a sheet, yes indeed, as white as a sheet bleached by a fanatical laundress, ha, ha!"

Jill managed to smile, but couldn't begin to comprehend what had just happened. She barely noticed that the blonde had stood up, dusted her bright, pretty dress off, and then started going on about how windy that part of the Isle got on a day like this.

"Are you a Basset, by any chance?" Jill finally asked, interrupting the blonde's cheerful prattling, which was very chirpy for someone who had just taken a substantial tumble down a gravelly ravine.

"I *am* a Basset!" replied the girl happily. She then corrected, with a little laugh at the end, "But I'm not a hound, of course, am I?" She said everything with such heartiness that made Jill either want to shrink away from her or become the best of friends. Jill decided that further acquaintance would make her more determined.

"Well, you can call me Jill, Miss Basset," Jill said while bravely putting out her hand for a shake.

"And you can call me Dahlia," replied the blonde, while grabbing Jill's hand and shaking the life out of it. "Where are you from? That is, where do you live? Have you lived on the Isle for long? Do you live in a tree or something of the sort? You must, seeing how you came out of absolutely nowhere, ha, ha!"

"I live in Arizona, but I'm staying on the Isle with my cousin, Penny. Are you alright, Miss Basset? You took a terrible fall..."

"I'm from London!" Dahlia said, managing to exclaim and interrupt at the same time. The ignorance of Jill's question seemed to indicate that the tumbler was fit as a fiddle.

"Unless, of course, 'from London' is some British expression for being hurt," thought Jill. She came to the conclusion that Dahlia was simply, in a delightfully compact adjective, a spaz. And Jill liked it. Jill replied, "From London? Do you like it there?"

"Oh, no," Dahlia said, as flippantly as she announced her origin emphatically, "I like being wherever my dad is. Say, won't you pop into the house for some tea? It would be absolutely marvelous."

Jill, although wondering if it would be, accepted and was promptly dragged up to the house. Quick-thinking Jill grabbed the parasol that had so cordially introduced them to each other. Dahlia seemed to have forgotten all about it.

Jill laughed at her prior astonishment at the mansion as they neared its grounds. She thought that the mere view from the drive was magnificent. Now she fully appreciated its mind-boggling beauty. It was a grand, white mansion equipped with pillars, railings, statues, and all that sort of thing. It was befriended by climbing ivy, which had begun to take the house into its embrace many years prior. It was the kind of house that had two sitting rooms, a coffee room, a tea room, maybe even a lemonade room, six bedrooms, servant's quarters, servant's dimes and nickels; suffice to say, a room for every activity you could possibly imagine. All of the house's windows were perfectly aligned in their respective rows and were obviously specifically designed to give the house's occupants a view of the gorgeous sea before it. And there in the offing was a cannon which Jill was already familiar with, having heard it before, which pointed out towards the sea.

Suddenly, without warning (as the word 'suddenly' would indicate) an alarming honking noise began blasting in the air. The dreadful sound reminded Jill of a noise she had heard somewhat recently. The noise's origin soon made itself known. With a dramatic flapping of its wings, a large goose came charging towards the property's intruder. Jill's eyes widened, and she quickly ducked behind her abruptly acquired hostess.

"Oh, don't get your feathers in a knot, Mrs. Whitby!" Dahlia said calmly, with a disapproving shake of her head, as one might look at a mischievous little puppy. She was more disappointed in the goose's impolite behavior than alarmed at its aggressiveness. "Come along!" Dahlia called to Jill, continuing ahead as if nothing traumatic had happened. But Jill was traumatized. She stuck close to Dahlia's side as she kept a wary eye on Mrs. Whitby. Mrs. Whitby hissed, obviously still displeased, and then went waddling back to wherever she had come from.

Now they entered the grand house. Dahlia opened the towering doors as casually as one would enter a gardening shed. If Jill was left with the responsibility, she would have thrown open the doors with more of a regal flair. They stepped into the entrance, and everything was perfectly spotless—the vases, the paintings on the walls, the floors, the fresh-cut flowers—everything was perfect. Jill supposed that if one could afford such a house, then they couldn't help but afford to keep ten servants scuttling around the house, keeping everything a tad immaculate. "I certainly *hope* that they have at least ten servants," thought Jill as she looked around the room with awe. "Any less taking care of the place would be cruel..."

"Dahlia!" cried an old, British voice from above. Jill's head swung upwards, and she discovered that the grand staircase directly in front of them led up to a catwalk-hallway, which ran along every wall, except for the one the door was in. From his suspended position, the old man calling down was nearly hanging over the edge of the railing, an action which aroused considerable anxiety within Jill.

"Dad! Look who I stumbled across while on my daily walk."

"Your daughter's a literal girl," put in Jill.

Whatever the girls' way of meeting each other was, the old fellow was caught up in pure delight at seeing a guest in his home. His whiskered face smiled down brightly upon them, and he ran down the stairs in a comically bumbling way.

"And who is this, who is this, my pet?" inquired the old fellow as he ran towards his daughter. Now that he wasn't ten feet above them, Jill realized that his daughter was about a foot taller than him. Reaching their sides, his eyes sparkled in joy as he shook Jill's hand more vigorously than his daughter had.

"This is Miss Jill, Dad. She lives in Texas, or Dallas, or one of those southern states," Dahlia informed him.

"If she lives in the state of Dallas, what is she doing here?"

Jill just laughed, then said, "I'm from Flagwood, Arizona, Mr. Basset, and my name is Jill Jopling."

"My! I say, my, my! What an exquisite name, for such an exquisite young lady!" cried Mr. Basset. "Do I make you blush with all these compliments?"

"No, not at all. I'll take any compliments I can get."

"Oh," said Mr. Basset, seeming to be disappointed. Nonetheless, he began smiling again, his smile getting so large that there was getting to be no more room for it on his face. As he rambled on in excited, fatherly, friendly tones, Jill realized that except for his being short, mustached, and old, he looked and behaved exactly like his daughter. She guessed that he was at least sixty, but his joviality and utter vivacity hadn't faded over the years as his silver hair had. Soon the hands that were gently patting Jill's were now tugging her towards the tea room. "Tea, tea, we shall have tea!" sang Mr. Basset as they rushed into the tea room. She stumbled into the room as Mr. Basset's pace accelerated suddenly. She felt rather like a hesitant dog being forced ahead by a leash wielded by an overexcited walker.

"Sit down, please, please!" cried Mr. Basset and Dahlia in turns. Dahlia rang a little bell, which Jill guessed was used to call servants. Jill, although unsettled by the peculiar entrance, was happy and contended to be amused by the affair. They were eccentrics, but not cuckoos. Not yet, anyhow. Although initially she was slightly nervous about having to make conversation with them, she was put at ease when she realized that they were more than happy to do the talking for her.

"Addie!" cried Mr. Basset abruptly, in the middle of a story being told by his daughter. Jill assumed that the creature he was calling was a pet of some sort, by the playful tone of the command. She became anxious, wondering if he was calling the goose.

"Have a mint while we wait for Adkins, Miss Jill," said Dahlia, holding up a golden bowl from the table that was between the couch she and Jill were sitting on and her father's chair. Jill politely declined the offer multiple times, but soon acknowledged to herself that neither of them would let themselves sit back until they had the satisfaction of persuading her to partake of the ready refreshments. She thus succumbed, drawing one of the oddly-shaped little mints from the bowl and popping it into her mouth. The entire process was going very well until the taste struck her tongue. An overwhelming array of sensations overtook her when it did so. With a series of coughs and winces and tears from its strength, she did her best to endure the pain of swallowing the horrible little thing. But she couldn't bear it covertly. She could not identify exactly what it tasted like, but whatever it was, it was deathly strong and horribly vulgar to her taste buds. Her hosts did not bother to notice the scrunched-up expressions on her distressed, twisted-up face. The Bassets were too preoccupied with telling her about how they had happened to come to America. It was quite a story, to them. Jill could not tell if it was truly uninteresting, or if she was simply distracted by the refreshing taste in her mouth to fully enjoy it.

"Dear Mrs. Basset died much too early, in the prime of her life," said Mr. Basset in a strong voice, as he grabbed the lapels of his tweed suit and turned his head towards an oversized painting on the south-facing wall. Jill looked up as well and, involuntarily, her eyebrows jumped and she was thrust back into her seat. She earnestly endeavored not to let the woman's undeniable ugliness deter her from showing the subject deep respect. Nonetheless, it was a struggle. "It was probably for the best that she wasn't around during our move here when I retired. It wouldn't have suited her. No, the house would've been much too small for her liking. Ah!" he suddenly exclaimed in delight, "There's ol' Addie, now! What took you so long to come?"

Jill turned to look at this Addie calmly, but then again had reason to jump back in her seat at realizing that he certainly wasn't a puppy or a kitten. He was a stout, somewhere between 35 and 40, serious-looking, balding butler dressed exactly as a butler should be, like in the movies. Jill's surprise was equally divided between realizing that this Addie was a man and not a cockatoo, and at how unusually stereotypical he was.

"It's Adkins," Jill heard the miffed butler mutter as he walked into the room, in reply to the "Addie" that had been called for. He then stood up straight in that butler-ish way, and he replied to his employer in the driest, politest way Jill had ever heard a human being speak: "I apologize for the delay. I was preoccupied with preparing dinner, sir."

"Oh, bumbershoot, Addie, what use do we have for dinner? It's only two-thirty. What we really need is some *tea*."

"Perhaps you misheard me," replied the unflappable butler, while eyeing Jill suspiciously, "when I informed you that I was *preparing* dinner, *not* serving it."

"I am not concerned with how you do or do not prepare my meals—my, what were we talking about, anyway?—all I want is some tea!" cried Mr. Basset, getting quite riled by the discussion.

"Shall I prepare the tea according to your custom, sir?" the butler inquired stiffly.

"Yes, Addie," replied Mr. Basset in a rather peeved voice, "do it how I like it. It wouldn't be much of a custom if I went about switching it up, now would it?"

"No, sir. Contemptible of me to have suggested anything otherwise," he replied dryly, without an ounce of remorse in his tone.

"Yes, quite right. On with it, then."

The butler bowed, and as he left the room, he directed an almost apologetic look at Jill. She could tell that he certainly wasn't apologizing for anything *he* had done. She assumed that he was merely empathetic to her entrapped position as a guest. She seemed to be getting into a lot of hospitable hostage situations lately.

"What a cheeky little man," Jill thought as he left the room, the British vocabulary brushing off on her.

"Adkins has been serving our family since I was only twelve," said Dahlia. "Such a good, honest, polite fellow, wouldn't you agree!"

Jill found that she thought the opposite of him, but Dahlia's question was not phrased in such a way to be answered, so it all ended well. Nonetheless, Jill couldn't help but like that dry wit embodied by him and which constantly carried in his voice, a sort of tone that wanted to make her laugh even if he wasn't saying anything particularly funny. Ah, that conscious, sarcastic intelligence that carried in the simplest reply! He had only been able to get away with it, of course, because of the unaware character of his employers.

"Now, Miss Jill, what do you like to do with yourself, hm?" Mr. Basset asked. "Sailing? Yachting? Bicycling? Painting? Writing? Poetry-ing?"

"Poetry is one thing that—" Jill began.

"Perhaps Miss Jill is a professional woman! Perhaps—" Dahlia interrupted.

"Yes, yes! How lovely it is to see a young woman go out and—" Mr. Basset interjected.

"Perhaps she is a seamstress! Or—" suggested Dahlia.

"Or a waitress! A model, she could be!—" the father exclaimed.

"No, no, not a model!" Jill was able to exclaim, now feeling free to interrupt, as they didn't seem to have any aversions to it, "I am a secretary for a newspaperman in Flagwood."

"Oh! Oh, yes! The most intriguing profession for a young lady!" cried Mr. Basset, not seeming to mind the transition of Jill's occupation from a model to a secretary.

"Yes, yes! Look at her fingers, Dad—the best suited for typing I've ever seen," said Dahlia, grabbing Jill's hand for better inspection.

"Oh, indeed! The perfect fingers for such an occupation!" agreed Mr. Basset, leaning far forward in his chair to admire them. Their observations of Jill's fingers (which Jill had, until this moment, taken for granted) were cut short by Adkins' reentrance into the room. He entered the room with his arms totally occupied by a tray of tea things, stiff as anything. "Never have tea-things been arranged so masterfully," Mr. Basset said proudly as he watched his butler. Everyone in the room agreed, including Adkins. As he set down the tea in the center of the table, he directed another apologetic glance at Jill, which was soon followed by a stern look at the tray before them. Jill couldn't help but feel that she had been tacitly warned, and was now in further dread of the refreshments to come. Never before did she realize that she could fear such warm hospitality. Such a fear she had acquired only after arriving in Maine.

Mr. Basset's wish was to talk endlessly with excited gestures and quickly sputtered words, some so rapidly expressed that Jill could not hardly tell if he was talking about "lovely scenery" or "ugly machinery," or "horrid weather" or "torpid feathers," even "prevailing crumpets" or "sales of trumpets." Whichever of these meanings were what he intended them to be, if either of them, they were always said with emphatic passion. No matter how unbelievable the sentences sounded, Jill could believe that anything was possible for Mr. Basset to say. He fired off cannons for the fun of it, for goodness' sake! Jill had never seen so short a man be so excitable. She didn't know how it could all fit into that compact little frame.

The tea was soon delivered to her, which she accepted with a smile and nod that was so polite that it was obvious that she was uncomfortable. The butler again gave her a subtle apologetic look, then meaningfully glanced at the platter, after which he turned to go stand in the corner to be both motionless and emotionless. Jill was confused, although she ought to have been anxious about what was to come. Innocent as a dove, she politely sipped her cup of tea, even though she didn't like tea enough to voluntarily partake of it when at home. In the situation, her pinky raised involuntarily. But everything proper left her when she realized that the only thing she could taste was hot water. Abominable! Serving such weak tea! It was in vain that the Bassets even had a room dedicated to tea if they were going to betray the beverage! All of this indignation was raised in Jill, even after she once called the drink "coffee's unfortunate cousin." Well, *now* it was unfortunate, being abused by people who pretended to be experts of the stuff. Perhaps the fact that indignation was stirred up even in Jill adequately explains the injustice done to the tea. She could tell that her reaction to it was being watched by Adkins, even though he was staring ahead in a very straight line. She suspected that he had very good peripheral vision, being so cheeky as he apparently was.

Oblivious to the cruelty her father had unintentionally shown Jill and his favorite beverage, Dahlia abruptly asked, "Do you have any family on the Isle?" When they were thereafter told of a cousin, they were absolutely delighted! Perfectly enthralled! This cousin *had* to be invited for tea, as soon as possible, even the next day, if she was available, and if she was not, then she must make herself so. Jill declared that the cousin loved tea. Adkins was then asked what he thought of the idea.

"I fear that Miss Jopling might have an aversion towards inconveniencing her relations with invitations of this nature, sir," Adkins interjected, provoking a mortified smirk from Jill, but absolutely no offense from the Bassets. Mr. Basset was hard of hearing, easy of forgetting, and Dahlia was too enraptured by the thought of receiving another guest to take notice. Even if she had heard, she wouldn't have comprehended it enough to feel anything about it.

"Well," said Mr. Basset after a large sip of tea, "I believe that I must offer you the position of being my personal typist..."

"Oh, yes!" cut in Dahlia. It amazed Jill to see with what ease they interrupted each other, and with what absence of annoyance they could do it! "I tried and tried to be his typist, but either I or my fingers would be too stubborn and get in the way of the process. But it's really alright," Dahlia continued, gazing at her spread-out fingers and wiggling them appreciatively. "They serve me well."

"As do mine," agreed Mr. Basset. "Don't you think they could be used for some talent or other, Addie? Maybe I could become a pianist, or some sort of botanist, or something of the sort. "

Adkins glanced down at them, then said, "I am sure that your talents are left to be discovered, sir."

Jill decided that Adkins found his own audienceship to be sufficient. She shook her head and said, "Thanks for the offer, Mr. Basset, but, I thought you said that you're retired."

"Oh, but he almost is!" exclaimed Dahlia.

"Yes, indeed I am almost retired, but the old fellows at my company keep me in the loop of business affairs out of respect, or pity, or something of the sort, isn't that right, Addie?"

"One can be sure of their motive, sir," said Adkins. Jill tried not to encourage him with looks of either shock or amusement, even though she felt both.

"I appreciate the offer, really, Mr. Basset, but I'm not going to be staying on the Isle long enough to need a job—"

But this sensible argument was no match for their excitement. They soon rushed her out of the house with irresistible insistence. They were wholly diverted by the thought of Jill coming up to the mansion regularly. It was all settled on, and somehow, there was nothing she could do about it. She cautiously avoided their attack-goose as they led her out of the house and escorted her down to the bottom of the drive. She was grasped by the hands, her hosts refusing to let her go until she promised to return. She anxiously obliged them, and then happily regained possession of her hands as they merrily waved goodbye.

Although she didn't like that Adkins character implying that his master deserved pity, she couldn't help but feel just that for the Bassets. They treated her like she was their queen, like an old friend, as a guest of honor, when really she was just an impediment to Dahlia's parasol. Jill now knew that the "infamous" Bassets were nothing but completely sincere. Eccentric? Of course! But they weren't deserving of the ill-will the locals treated them with. She argued with the locals mentally; simply being strange did not mean that the Bassets were unfriendly or unworthy. On the contrary, it only made them better acquaintances to have. Jill wondered if Penny had been affected by the prejudice that was against them. She was sure that Penny hadn't any prejudice, but was nonetheless ready to defend them, even though she had been personally unnerved by their unusual behavior. And through it all, she could've sworn that Mr. Basset kept saying something about trumpets.

# Chapter 10

*Friday, May 5th*

The next day, Penny happily rang her bike bell to passerby as she zoomed past them. It was a warm, lovely day and the salty, cool breeze energized her with each eager pedal forward.

Although Penny and Jill's vehicles differed greatly—one being a bicycle, the other a car—they shared one exciting flaw. The handlebars on Penny's bicycle were similar to Jill's car's pedals—they were set up backward. Penny needed a way to get around, and the only transportation she could find was an old, chipped bicycle out from behind Mr. Peterson's shop. She was offered it for free, and she thought it was an awfully kind gesture until she realized that it was a contrary machine. If she turned left, the bike would go right, and if she turned right—well, you get the picture. She had looked it all over but was never able to comprehend how to put it back the right way around. Fishermen and womenfolk alike couldn't figure it out.

As she rode along the road that fine day, Penny couldn't deny that she was apprehensive about meeting the Bassets. The previous night, Penny could hardly believe Jill's story about how she had met them, and even more incredulously did she accept the invitation from the Bassets for tea. As much as Penny was apprehensive about going to the "Big House," as the locals called it, her curiosity, however cautiously maintained, won out. The

Bassets moved onto the Isle only a few months after she had, so she had heard the Islanders' opinions of them at their most prime. Such misgivings couldn't help but rub off on her.

Penny didn't come with Jill to the Bassets. Jill arrived half an hour earlier. Penny had promised Mr. Peterson her assistance taking care of the shop that morning and thus could not come to tea immediately. The ride to the Basset's was a welcome one, though. It was better than staying cooped up indoors. Penny frowned when she approached the steep drive that led up to the big house. Her mere bicycle, although cherished and trusted, was not built for the uneven, gravelly mess of a drive that was before her. Nine out of every ten pieces of gravel looked capable of popping the bike's tires, and so she dismounted and walked up the hill. Although her arrival at the top of the hill was utterly graceless and exhausted, she was grateful to see the view that awaited her. It was undeniably breathtaking—though not as breathtaking as the journey *up* the drive—even though her view was partially blocked by a row of evergreens near the shoreline.

Ah! But the brief moment of happiness was ruined when she heard a honk that breathed threat and murder! Penny's eyes darted towards the sound, and there before her stood a goose. If it had arms, she was sure that its hands would be indignantly placed on its hips. Whatever the case, it definitely *was* scowling. It was now a standoff. Penny, although a little frightened by its affronted gaze, resolved not to be intimidated by something that could just as easily be on her dinner table. Penny straightened her back and squinted at it. The goose replied to this assertion by waddling furiously towards her.

"Hey!" Penny cried angrily, too taking a couple of steps forward. She waved her arms at it, but the goose was undeterred. The goose had made up its mind; Penny was an unwelcome alien, and it wasn't going to let her take a step nearer. Seeing this resolve in the fowl's beady, deliberate eyes, Penny could no longer hold her ground.

As the goose's aim seemed to be one of harm, Penny took her bicycle and made a run for it.

Penny was shocked by the speediness of the chase! She had no idea that geese were such expedient creatures! Instead of simply removing herself from the property the goose was endeavoring to protect, Penny stubbornly decided to run around the back of the monstrous house and hope to somehow get to the front door. She only hoped that the goose wasn't smart enough to think to double-back. Penny ran into the shadows of the opposite side of the building, looking over her shoulder to see if the honking, hissing thing was still chasing her. She was quite surprised when she looked ahead again.

"Oh!" she exclaimed. If she had tires, she would have screeched as she came to a stop. She had almost tackled a well-dressed man, who was innocently hanging laundry up to dry on a sun-light portion of the back of the house. He was not terribly alarmed or flustered by the interruption. Maybe 'agitatedly confused' is the best way to describe what he looked like. He soon perceived what was chasing this unexpected guest, and in a commanding voice, he said, "At ease, Mrs. Whitby!" The goose stopped all at once. Recognizing that the command was from one of the house's occupants, it squawked in awkward defeat, turned around, and waddled back to wherever it had come from. It occasionally would turn its head and hiss while giving Penny a look that said, "Watch it, lady."

Now that Mrs. Whitby had been taken care of, although not in the sense Penny would have liked, (she would've preferred to "take care of it" by braising it in a lemon sauce) the chased guest and her rescuer were at their leisure to look at each other. Both were rather speechless, but perhaps for different reasons. The fellow, who, as you have probably guessed by his characteristic perturbation, was Adkins, the Basset's butler. Penny's reason for being speechless was perfectly expected, having been, for the first time in her life, threatened by a goose. But Adkins' reason was, to say the least, unusual. There, in that very moment, for the first time in his life, while holding a wet pair of stockings, he fell in love. Yes, love! He was absolutely taken with her. But even at this moment, his usual disgruntlement was present. "Why," he thought angrily, "did this moment finally come whilst I was performing the most inglorious of my duties?" He silently and repeatedly lamented this thought over and over as he looked (with a scowl, nonetheless) upon her lovely, simple features. But his expression was unchanged. He looked like an angry butler, not like a lovesick admirer. All of that changed, of course, when he attempted to speak.

"Could I, would you—would you, em... " he said, becoming increasingly sheepish. "Fool, fool!" he cried out mentally.

"No," his ungracious lover replied with amusement, glancing at Miss Basset's pair of stockings, "I have plenty of stockings of my own, thank you." His rapture was so great, that he'd now forgotten that he was holding them. "But," continued Penny, "if you'd be so kind as to tell me where the nearest door is, I'd appreciate it."

With a swish of the stockings, he gestured towards the general direction of the front door. She nodded gratefully, then walked away with her bicycle in hand. Adkins watched her walk away in that determined way of hers, then angrily looked down at the stockings. If they weren't Miss Basset's, he would have most gladly thrown them to the ground to begin stomping on them.

Penny approached the front door cautiously, unsure if the command given to that goose by the stocking-armed man would be enough to deter it from trying to attack her again. She slammed the fashionable metal door-knocker hurriedly. Although she would never have thought of letting herself in, she quickly decided to toss her politeness aside when she saw the goose slowly poke its head around the house's corner. Now Penny was inside the house, and she was very unsure of what to do next. She heard bubbling conversation from on yonder, and so she decided to follow the excited noises to their source.

She walked ahead while wondering why there wasn't a servant to let her in. If there was a specific servant hired to wash stockings and patrol geese, it certainly seemed like there should be a doorkeeper. With this thought in mind, she walked towards an open door. Blue light poured out of it and into the hall. She cautiously approached its threshold and then heard a woman's voice say, "Why, Dad's the leading trumpet man in the whole world!" Penny was now far too intrigued to not enter the room. As she came in, she saw Jill give her a slightly exasperated look. Penny only simpered in reply, while Mr. Basset, upon seeing the young woman enter the room, stood up with an expediency that made both Penny and Jill fear that he would immediately topple over.

"Hallo, hallo! Welcome, welcome!" cried the old gentleman, approaching Penny speedily. Penny, although startled, shook his hand graciously and smiled.

"Mr. Basset, this is my cousin, Penny, Penny Fargo," Jill put in. "And Penny, this is Mr. Basset, and this is Dahlia."

"It's very nice to meet you both," Penny replied. She was pleased to see that the Bassets weren't the crazy ninnies everyone presented them to be. Dahlia too got up and shook Penny's hand with a vehemence nearly matching her father's. "I'm sorry that I'm late. I had an encounter with a rogue goose and a surprised laundryman—"

"You mean Mrs. Whitby and Addie!" Mr. Basset exclaimed.

"Well, I guess I do."

"Mrs. Whitby is our pet, Miss Fargo, and Addie is our butler."

"I can certainly understand the need for a butler in this huge house, but why do you have a goose? I admit that it's an excellent watchdog, but—"

"Mrs. Whitby came with the house, actually. The realtor didn't know exactly how she got here, but she seems to have lived on the property for a while, and she treats it like it's her own. I've taken it upon myself to give her the best of care."

"And to give her a name?"

"Yes, yes, I thought the name was fitting. She reminded me of my wife's sister," Mr. Basset mumbled.

When they all sat down and settled from the excitement, Dahlia said with a start, "When you came in, Miss Fargo, I was just remembering that I forgot to tell your cousin Jill about what Dad does for a living." Penny then turned to look at Jill, with a confused expression that said, "You took a secretarial job from this guy, not knowing what he does for work?" Jill translated the look with ease, and just shrugged in reply.

"Did I hear you saying something about trumpets, Dahlia?" Penny asked.

"Anyone Who *Hounds* You Can Lump It," said Mr. Basset spasmodically, "As Long As You Purchase a *Basset* Trumpet!" He then laughed heartily. "It's a brilliant little slogan, isn't it, girls?"

Jill and Penny began laughing once they understood that it was a slogan, and not just a spontaneously concocted poem. Penny leaned towards the table as if to take a cup of tea. But she was taken by surprise when she realized that there wasn't any tea to be found. She politely coughed, then said, "This tea party started very well, and I think it'll just keep on getting better as long as we get some tea to go along with it."

Mr. Basset nearly jumped out of his seat. "Oh!" he cried in a sort of hooting sound, as if an owl had sat on a pin. "We've been having such pleasant conversation with your cousin Miss Jill that I forgot to get ol' Addie to get us tea! Oh, how beastly of me!" he continued while tinkling a bell by his fingertips.

After the cousins giggled forgivingly for a while, Penny asked Mr. Basset, "So, Mr. Basset, what got you into the..."—she got unsteady, not sure what to call the trade—"...the, em, trumpet business?"

"Well," began Mr. Basset, slapping his hands on his knees as he leaned forward, "It began way back in 1898 when my grandfather heard of a wondrous opportunity. His good friend offered him a partnership in a brilliant business. While they were in one of the nicer tea shops in London, his ol' chappie suggested the idea to him. Well, my grandfather didn't have very good hearing, and he thought that his chappie was talking about the crumpet business. My grandfather thought that the business of manufacturing crumpets was a good, English sort of thing to do, and—"

Just as the story was getting to its climax, Adkins entered the room in a bluster, which was strange, since he usually entered in a whisper. He was quite out of sorts, just having fallen in love and all. Even Mr. Basset noticed his butler's unusual state. "Why, Addie! What is all this bluster of fluster about?"

"I apologize for not coming sooner, sir," Adkins replied, anxiously plucking clothespins from his lapel.

"Oh well, don't think of it, old man. I forgot to tell you to make us some tea."

"Yes, sir."

"Right. I again apologize, ladies, for forgetting the most essential part of a tea party," continued Mr. Basset ashamedly, then pointed to his head as he said, "the old bean failed me."

Adkins, who was about to leave the room, turned sharply and said with a confused, almost alarmed tone, "Sir?" He was mortified, thinking that he had been called an old bean. Not only that, but he and his pride would have hated to have the onlookers think that he had failed in his duties. Especially *one* particular onlooker.

"No, no, not you, Addie, *this* old bean," replied Mr. Basset, knocking on his own forgetful head. Adkins was both relieved and ashamed about having misunderstood. He was thankful for the necessity of leaving the room to bring the tea things in. "Now, where was I?" continued Mr. Basset. "Ah, yes, the crumpets! Yes, my grandfather was quite interested in widening his profits, and so he shook hands on the deal. He then asked his chappie if he could take a gander at the merchandise sometime. Imagine my grandfather's surprise when he went over to his chappie's place, and he pulled out a brass trumpet!" Mr. Basset paused to let out a loud, wheezing laugh. After recovering, he turned to Dahlia and said, "Oh, what was it your great-grandfather said when he saw it?" He didn't wait for her recollection, remembering it himself: "Oh, that's right, he said: 'I was rather expecting something smaller.'" At this everyone laughed, except for Adkins, of course. "That little slogan I mentioned earlier popped out of ol' Addie's mouth one day," said Mr. Basset proudly. This statement alarmed Adkins, too.

"Pardon me, sir, but I will not be so haughty as to accept the compliment of thinking up the slogan. It was your business associate, Mr. Johnson."

"I don't remember any Mr. Johnson! Who is Mr. Johnson?"

"The one who bets on duck races," Adkins clarified.

"Duck races? Well, if I made a bad bet, I'd hate to get the *bill*," Jill said with a smile.

"You don't have any shame, do you?" Penny said as she shook her head. Then Adkins, after acquitting himself of the crime of coming up with a silly slogan, quit the room.

Despite the strange and droll situation that brought them all together, the girls enjoyed the conversation that accompanied their tea immensely. But Penny couldn't help but think it strange that every time she simply went to pour herself a cup of tea, Jill's brows bounced up like they were jumping on a trampoline. Penny kept persisting, but every time was warned off by the hairy acrobats. Soon Penny gave up and contented herself with simply taking a mint. Jill nearly jumped out of her seat, but she wasn't quick enough to stop it. To Jill's amazement, Penny placed the thing in her mouth, as calm as could be, and didn't react to the unbearable refreshments at all! Jill stared at her, dumbfounded, wondering if she simply got an unloaded mint, or if she was just incredibly self-possessed.

The group soon began discussing the fine area surrounding them, explaining the notable features of these surroundings to an enraptured Jill. The Bassets, of course, were silent when it came to having to explain anything beyond their own property. Although they had lived on the Isle for the same length of time as Penny, they were as clueless about it as their Arizonan visitor was. Penny was thus forced into being the authority of the Isle.

"So, what is the little island next to us called?" Jill asked. "I've been wondering for a while, but I keep forgetting to ask."

As Penny breathed in to give an authoritative answer, Dahlia broke in, having unusual excitement about announcing the island's name, "Prince Island, is what it's called. Oh, for as long as Dad and I have been here, I have been dying to go out to it! I have heard that no one's stepped foot on it for at least 10 years. I just must know what it's like! I must go on it before I die. As far as anyone's concerned, I think that I've stared at it so much that I *have* stepped foot on it. I've stared at it for hours upon hours, just to imagine what could be on it, and what secrets lie within it!"

Although Jill had brought the subject up, she couldn't comprehend the appeal of staring at a large, scarred chunk of rock for hours on end. Five minutes was enough to feed her curiosity. Penny, in the meantime, was raising her eyebrows. "I thought that the reason why nobody's been out to Prince Island for so long is that there's an old recluse who's scattered no trespassing signs around its shore."

"Oh!" said Dahlia in an indignant, drawn-out way, "who goes around purchasing islands and keeping them to themselves? It's an absolutely horrid hobby. The old man doesn't matter, anyway—Dad gets worried about me, even if I just stare out at it. I've nearly bribed fishermen to take me out there, but somehow Dad gets to know what I'm all about, and he makes me come back."

"A million things could go wrong, at least that's what Addie tells me. Think of the dangers of the sea! A storm might throw you over, or a shark might jump out of the water and nab you, or at least a rogue seal. And who knows what sort of fellow lives out on that island." Penny and Jill nodded seriously but were actually in very good humor. They both were amazed, wondering why anyone with beautiful grounds, a house, and a beach like the Bassets' would want to go trespassing on some old coot's barren piece of rock.

Only too soon did the visit come to its end, but only on the terms that Jill would come back the next day to do secretarial work for Mr. Basset, and that Penny would return for tea. As Adkins showed them the front door, Penny and Jill nodded at him very politely, while Penny said, "Happy stocking-washing, Mr. Adkins." As Penny walked away, anxiously waiting for an opportunity to answer the inquiring, confused looks Jill was giving her, little did she know that her sass did far more damage to Adkins than the mere tease intended. Somehow, that teasing curve of her mouth just made him fall for her even more.

# Chapter 11

*Saturday, May 6th*

The next day's weather was, surprisingly, next to perfect. Usually, if the weather was perfect one day, it couldn't help but be miserable the next. Jill was extremely happy that this wasn't the case, so she insisted on walking to the Bassets' instead of riding Penny's dear but very backward bicycle. The weather just had to be enjoyed with a walk. And besides; Jill didn't feel like riding a bicycle off a cliff. It was too nice of a day for it.

Jill decided to celebrate the day's beauty by wrapping a punchy scarf around her neck. It was light and free, coincidently very similar to how Jill was feeling. Penny, fearing that because of the wind, the scarf might be *too* free, heartily suggested that Jill tie it tighter around her neck. Jill tactfully agreed, but by the time she got out of the door, she had either forgotten about her agreement, or she simply didn't care enough to choose to remember it. She proceeded towards the Bassets' drive, solitarily. Penny would come later. As Jill walked on, she smiled, feeling very majestic as her scarf flowed in the tastefully strong breeze, a breeze that made the wildflowers wiggle happily and the trees sway as if they were slow-dancing.

Jill's walk and heart stopped simultaneously, however, when something roared, sounding like a pack of lions operating chainsaws. The noise got nearer and nearer, and as it did, Jill came to the studious observation that it was the sound of an old motorcycle nearing retirement. Along with its roaring came more unpleasant noises, sputtering and popping and—well, all sorts of indescribable sounds, but you know what I'm talking about. Anyhow, she got over the initial jolt, resolutely decided to not let it bother her, then continued walking. It filled her with wonder to think that there was a motorcycle on the Isle. She hadn't seen anything nearer to modern technology on the Isle than her cousin's backward bicycle.

As she pondered over this, she got to see the very thing that caused such confusing thoughts. She stumbled further towards the edge of the road, endeavoring to not get squashed by the blur that appeared to be what she had assumed it was—an old motorcycle, who, like retired people, had the will to race like its days of glory, but a body that wished to sputter and cough instead. She tried very hard to scowl at the driver, since he was barreling at an idiotic speed, but the very reason for her disdain for him prevented her from doing so. She couldn't direct her looks at anything except a decrepit blur. Now, what happened next was dreadful. Violent, even, I'm afraid. Whether it was an unfortunate gust of wind off of the ocean or the wind rushing by from the speeding motorcycle, Jill could not say. But she *did* know that it ruined the beginnings of a lovely day. The scarf which she had neglected to tie with sensible firmness around her neck, instead being cavalierly flipped over her shoulder, now took flight. It flew away from its owner with glorious freedom. But just as it was at its height of liberation, it somehow got sucked into the path of the passing abomination of a vehicle. It flew directly into the driver's face, and with flailing arms, he swerved from one side of the road to the other until his hands managed to find the handlebars again. Jill stumbled off the road, wide-eyed as she watched. After seeing that the driver was not headed towards a crash and thus in no danger, Jill put her hand to her neck and felt perfectly justified in feeling deep mortification and outrage. Her face twisted into a graver scowl, and while sputtering angry mumblings, she shook her fist at the thing while standing on her toes, as if the added two inches made her more intimidating. The unintentional scarf thief, though, was not around to enjoy it by the time she had her wits about her enough to make a fistful of a reply. It was all over, all past, all gone. She stalked ahead, mumbling to herself about how not only did this scarf thief steal her beloved accessory, but also her valuable time. She hurried along, hoping that she wouldn't be terribly late. Of course, the time of her arrival was of no consequence to the Bassets, who barely could remember that she would be returning at all.

~~~

But who is this scarf-offender? Who mortified Jill Jopling, and who was this mad driver of chainsaw-bearing lions?

Haddock.

No, not a fish—although some might have called him a silly fish, no doubt with good reason—it was a man. A young man, with a fishy sobriquet and a wreck of a motorcycle.

Bobbie dropped her coffee cup when she saw him walk through the Coffee House's front door. "Haddock!" she cried, first with her arms outstretched, then with her hands over her mouth in delighted surprise, then her arms out again as she ran towards him.

"Why do you two sist'ahs always *do* this to me?" Jerry cried, standing up, saturated with coffee. He was within the range of Bobbie's dropped coffee, and after being victimized by it he frowned, recoiling from the dripping counter and haphazardly wiping himself off with a nearby cloth.

"Bobbie!" said this Haddock as she ran into his arms and squeezed him so hard that he wondered if he'd live long enough to see the rest of the Isle.
~~~

"Why, it's little Haddock!" exclaimed Jerry when he had a moment to look up from his mopping work. "Well, you're not so little anymore, are ya? You were a lot short'ah the last time I saw you."

"And you were a lot taller, Jerry," replied Haddock as he reached out to shake his hand. He wasn't in Bobbie's embrace anymore, but certainly was still being clung to. "And a lot drier, too."

"I don't know about these Pine g'els, Haddock. I nev'ah gave 'em the impression that I liked coffee enough to bathe in it, heh, heh!" said Jerry, heartily shaking the extended hand.

"Oh, Haddock!" said Bobbie in a happy, breathless sigh, "It's been what, now, about fifteen ye'ahs? Just a baby, you were."

"Well, why don't we go and have a chat, see what ya' been up to between then and now, eh?" invited Jerry. Haddock obliged them gladly. As he sat down on a creaky bar stool, he took a deep breath in and smelled what he smelled those fifteen or so years before—old wood, old coffee, old fishermen, and old bait, the latter two being synonymous. But he was deeply endeared, and happy that nothing had changed in the room, except for a few more wrinkles on Bobbie and Jerry's faces, and a few more dents and chips in the counter. It was perfectly unchanged, just to his liking.

Haddock, being a handful as a child, if you could imagine, was sent to Maine for three summers in a row, with his uncle. His uncle liked the boy well enough but was not exactly the fatherly type. Back in '39 or '40, he was more of the go-ahead-play-with-the-shotgun-while-I-have-a-drink-and-take-a-nap type. Bobbie, having a son just a few years older than Haddock at the time, immediately saw the danger of a well-meaning but rambunctious boy left to his own wits, and so she took him under her wing. He and her own son got along well, played together, laughed together, got into plenty of trouble together, all while being governed by her watchful, loving eye. But, because children have the insufferable habit of growing up, Haddock stopped coming back to the Isle. He was now older and, coincidently, easier to handle, after being under Bobbie's guidance for those few years. But more brought him back home than simply growing up. The War had begun, and he was sent to live with an aunt or someone of the sort, not to return until this very moment. For Bobbie to see that boy all grown up into a young-ish man was so exciting that—well, I'm sure that Jerry could tell you as he wiped his shirt off, being the victim of this excitement.

"What ah you doin' he'ah, de'ah? Why didn't you write and let us know you were comin'?" Bobbie asked. Haddock smiled down at her cheerily, but then half-frowned and sighed. "Oh, right," Bobbie said, now also frowning. "Your poor uncle. I'm sorry, Haddock, of course that's why ya he'ah. It just slipped my mind—"

"No, no, Bobbie, don't worry about it at all."

"He died down South, right? Where he moved aft'ah movin' off the Isle?"

"That's right. He had a stroke."

"So you're he'ah to take care of what he left behind, right?"

"Yeah... well, actually," Haddock continued, wanting to smile even though the subject didn't call for it, "he... he left his place and everything in it to me. Not that there's much in there, but I'm honored, anyway. I got the news about my uncle leaving me everything up here, and so I decided that I'd spend a week or two with you all, maybe longer. I've been wanting to come up and visit you, Bobbie, but you know how tight money has been."

"I know, de'ah. Seems like everyone is strugglin' these days. So, I see that you got ol' Jimmy's bike runnin'?"

"Oh, yes. Tim Johnson gave me a ride out here on his fishing boat last night, and I've been working on the bike all morning. It still sounds like it's about ready to keel over and die, but I'm telling you," he said, his eyes lighting up, "you should've seen how that old thing went down that open stretch between here and Uncle's camp!" He said this while clapping his hands, one speeding away from the other in illustration.

"Oh, we didn't need to see it, Haddock. I'm pretty sure that folks could he'ah it all the way from Shrimpy Cove," said a disgruntled voice from behind him. Haddock then turned around and saw Mary entering the Coffee House.

"Oh, hi, Mary," said Haddock with as much of a smile as he could muster up. But all that seemed to come out of it was a wince, the corners of his mouth turning up only half-convincingly.

"Well, well, what brings you up he'ah, Haddock?" Mary asked as she sat on a barstool, not looking at him all the while.

Haddock uncomfortably eyed Bobbie, who was looking at her shoes. Haddock wished that he could, too. They brought him far more comfort than Bobbie's sister did. "I came to fix up my uncle's camp, Mary."

Jerry, getting a bit uncomfortable himself, said with a start, "Oh, Mary, ya' shoulda seen it when little Haddock walked in he'ah. Bobbie spilled coffee all ov'ah me. Seems to be becomin' a habit of you g'els. I haven't seen Bobbie so lit up in quite a while."

After well-meaning Jerry said this, the begrudged feeling in the air got a little heavier. Mary's resentful silence soon made everybody take a sudden interest in their shoes. "Oh, yes, I bet she did," was all that Mary said in reply.

You may have surmised by now that Mary Pine had the ability and tendency to dampen any commotion. However, the discomfort that she caused the room to feel now went beyond any characteristic flaws she may have had.

Mary and Bobbie, about fifteen years ago, were both wives and mothers, having had children a little later than usual in life. They had both married the Pine brothers. No trials ever arose between their families. They were happy mothers and happy aunts. But one summer, a boy from away came to the Isle, and, naturally, befriended the sisters' boys. Bobbie couldn't help but be the more kind-hearted one out of the two sisters, unable to refuse to take in the boy with open arms. Mary's arms, on the other hand, were crossed when she met the boy. He was from away; her son wouldn't get along with him. Or maybe he would have if he'd been without her help.

As if being from a different part of the country wasn't enough to fall into her disfavor, Mary also began to detect that Bobbie was beginning to neglect her own nephew in favor of taking care of this boy. Bobbie even gave the boy a cute nickname, "Haddock", while Mary's own son never got even a nick out of his name. These offenses always abated when summer ended and took Haddock back where he belonged. But as summers have the tendency to go away, they also like to come back.

Year after year, more and more resentment built up in Mary's heart, to the point that even now, when Haddock was grown up and the sisters' children were gone, Mary couldn't treat him with any of the motherly affection she ought to have had. But the reasons for such resentment didn't end there.

Jimmy, Haddock's uncle, reserved a special place in Mary's heart, years after being widowed and Haddock having moved on. But Mary's irritation with her sister again sprung up. Whenever Mary mentioned Jimmy or expressed her admiration for him, her sister, her dearest friend, would just say, "I never liked Jimmy very much. He neglected Haddock somethin' awful." Yes, even after Haddock's childhood irritations had finished plaguing her, a bitter reminder of her sister's preference for Haddock lived on. Seeing Haddock again struck another bitter remembrance of her life's troubles. Just as Mary began to believe that Jimmy might man up and propose to her, just as she began to have hope, Jimmy moved down South to be closer to family, without a word of farewell or anything like it. You can now imagine her chagrin, presently hearing that Jimmy had left everything he had on the Isle to Haddock, a camp that *she* loved, a camp which reminded her of the only man that she had ever loved since her husband's death. She told Jimmy how much she loved it in times past, but now here was Haddock, returning to tell her that again he was here to take away something she wanted, to tell her that his uncle would, in essence, rather leave his camp to a foreigner than to a woman that he cared about, a woman who expressly told him how much that camp meant to her. Yes, Jimmy left it to a nephew he didn't care much for, and not to a woman he was near proposing to. This entire history played through her mind as she scowled at the counter.

"Well, Bobbie, you can't guess what happened to me on my way over here," said Haddock in a good-humored tone, turning away from Mary. He hoped to bring at least *some* cheer back into the room. "I nearly died."

"What are you talkin' about?" Bobbie exclaimed.

"Bet that old bike's the cause of it—or your *drivin'*, at least," commented Mary sullenly.

Haddock glared at Mary for a millisecond, then continued with an unrepressed smile, "No, not my driving, Mary—*this* thing nearly killed me." He pulled out a bright scarf from his sport coat.

"Ack!" exclaimed Jerry, covering his eyes, "That thing could blind a man."

Bobbie squinted as she tried to safely look at the excessively bright thing. "*That* almost killed you, Haddock?"

"Nearly kills me," said Mary, while blinking in recovery. "It's like lookin' too long at the sun."

"That's right, Bobbie. I have to admit, if I had to die because of a scarf, I wouldn't want it to be *this* one, but, anyway—I was zooming just fine down that stretch, thinking that it would be alright because I didn't think anyone would be walking down it, and as I took that corner 'round the drive up to the big house, there was this—this *girl*, walking right down the middle of the road! I couldn't believe my eyes! And then something flew right into my face. I tried to steer away from her, almost landing in the ditch, but after a few seconds I got the thing off my face and got back on the road."

"And it nev'ah occurred to you to brake, mister?" Mary inquired.

"No, I couldn't do that! The bike could've stalled out and ruined my run." Mary only rolled her eyes in reply.

"I'm glad you didn't get hurt, de'ah. What a shame that'd be," said Bobbie, thwacking his arm affectionately.

"Well, I'd hate to have this hideous thing be the last thing to flash before my eyes. Do any of you know who this could belong to?" Haddock asked, dangling it from his fingertips disdainfully.

"Hey, you know what—that looks like somethin' that Frog Legs would wear, doesn't it?" said Jerry.

"For sure," Mary said, gesturing towards Jerry with her coffee cup in agreement.

Haddock, looking thoroughly lost, needed an explanation. "Frog Legs is Miss Penny's cousin," Bobbie supplied.

"Oh, right," Haddock said, in a way that pretended to understand what they were talking about.

"On my way ov'ah, I think I saw 'er walkin' towards the big house. She's been visitin' the Bassets a lot lately," said Mary, who then mumbled, "Shows you what kind of g'el she is." A raise of her eyebrows added, "She's a cuckoo."

"Did I hear you all right when you said that her name is, is *Frog Legs*...?" Haddock asked.

"No, silly, 'er name isn't Frog Legs. She's some g'el from away. Jill Fargo's her name, I believe," Bobbie replied warmly. "She seems like a nice enough g'el—a little strange, but I'm sure she's got a good heart."

"Good-hearted or not, she likes to wear stuff like *that*," put in Mary, nodding towards the limp scarf in Haddock's hand. "She wears these bright green pants. Looks like she got half-dipped in bright green paint," Mary continued, shaking her head with a chuckle. "She stayed up at my place the oth'ah night. Locked herself outta her cousin's place. She doesn't have any manners to write home about, but she's nice enough."

"Look who's talking," Haddock was tempted to say, but refrained. He didn't usually like to refrain, but he didn't want to upset Bobbie. He decided that if this girl could get along with *Mary*, then he wouldn't be particularly disposed towards getting along with her himself. Thus, he decided to change the subject. "So, what other newcomers are here these days? Has anyone left?"

"Oh, no, nobody's left since your uncle moved. Oh, but Mrs. West, you know, Tommy's moth'ah, did move to the mainland with 'er daught'ah Molly."

"And we've been gettin' plenty of newcom'ahs, I'll tell ya," said Mary with another shake of her head.

"Yessah, we've got the Bassets now—crazy old fellah and his daught'ah, a couple a' Brits who moved into the big house, and Mrs. Whitby," Jerry added.

"Is she an aunt of theirs or something?" Haddock asked.

"They're looney enough, they might think she is—nah, she's a goose. Wicked loud thing. It'd be shot, plucked, and on the suppah table long ago, if I had anything to do with it, heh, heh!" said Jerry enthusiastically.

"Then the'ah's Mrs. Bloomberg," said Bobbie.

"What's she, a pheasant?" Haddock asked with a chuckle.

Bobbie slapped his arm. "Don't go callin' 'er unpleasant. I taught you bett'ah than to go around disrespectin' your eld'ahs. Mrs. Bloomberg stays he'ah for the summ'ahs, and she's a respectable old woman."

"No, Bobbie, I called her a *pheasant.*"

"Don't think that's much bett'ah, sonny, heh, heh!" laughed Jerry.

"Besides, Bobbie, Mrs. Bloomberg *is* unpleasant," Mary put in, "unless you find rifle blasts outta nowhere pleasant."

"Rifle blasts?" Haddock echoed dubiously.

"Mrs. Bloomberg thinks that anything rustlin' in the bushes is somethin' out to get 'er. I don't know what her late husband was thinkin', leavin' a rifle behind to a paranoid wife. She's nearly killed me at least three times," said Jerry.

"Between her rifle, Basset's cannon, and that goose, I don't know how this island is still in one piece," said Bobbie quietly.

"Alright, how about Miss Fargo, the Frog Woman's cousin?" Haddock asked.

"Oh, yes, Miss Penny is a good g'el," said everyone in their own way. Bobbie added, "She's helped all us old folks out a lot. She gardens, cleans sheds, fixes anything—"

"Does she fix drinks? I could use one right about now," Haddock said, rubbing his temples as his throbbing brain tried to catch up with all the changes to the Isle since he'd been there.

"Goodness, Haddock!" laughed Bobbie, "Everyone's looney enough as it is, we don't need the help of liquor. Anyhow, yes, Miss Penny's a good g'el. She's a tough, sassy sorta thing, but you'd prob'ly like her." Bobbie then began looking at him with a mischievous smile.

"Don't you start looking at me like that, Bobbie!" laughed Haddock, "I don't need you hunting girls for me. Besides, what makes you think that I don't have a girl of my own by now, anyway?"

Bobbie's eyes lit up. "You don't mean that you're—you're *married*?"

"No! Oh no, not that!" cried Haddock. "But we're closing in on it. She's a great girl, Bobbie, you'd love her."

"So you and Miss Penny will just have to be good friends now, eh?"

"Well, as long as she doesn't own large birds or shoot at unsuspecting visitors, I imagine that we'll get along just fine. But this Frog Girl, you said that she's up at the big house?"

"Yessah. You gonna give 'er that—that *thing* back?" Mary asked in disgust.

"Well, *I* certainly don't want it," Haddock replied, thereafter hopping off of the barstool and towards the door.

"Promise me you'll be more careful drivin' that bike, Haddock," Bobbie pleaded.

"Alright, Bobbie, but I don't think I'm going to take it up to the big house. That drive is pretty steep, as far as I can remember. I'll just walk over and give the thing to her, get it over with."

"Alright, de'ah. Be careful. Wicked windy out the'ah," Bobbie warned. Haddock merely waved goodbye in reply to the warning. Bobbie then sighed proudly as she watched him walk away.

"Hasn't changed one bit," remarked Mary with a side-eye at the door.

"He's grown up so handsome, hasn't he?" said Bobbie with a smile.

"Good lookin' boy, yessah," agreed Jerry.

"He's still got that mark on his face," said Mary.

"It isn't exactly the kinda thing someone grows out of, Mary," said Bobbie, turning to put on another pot of coffee, "He wouldn't be Haddock without it. I'm half-disappointed that he's found some g'el—he and Miss Penny would make such a good match."

"Give the fellah a minute before you go off marryin' him to Miss Penny, Bobbie," said Jerry.

Mary, who happened to like Penny very much, interjected, "Besides, they wouldn't get along well at all."

"Why not?" asked Bobbie, sounding disappointed.

"She's a toughie, and he's a milksop."

"Mary!" Bobbie exclaimed in offense.

"Hold on, what I mean is that, well, sure, he's a strong fellah himself, but he's a loose cannon. You know that, Bobbie," Mary continued, then half-mumbled, "you practically raised the boy." Bobbie then proceeded to wipe down the counter feverishly in upset silence.

Haddock, in the meantime, was taking a happy little stroll towards the Bassets, feeling very curious about what Frog Girl and company were all about.

# Chapter 12

"Why, *we* know a Michael Angles!" cried Dahlia. The exclamation was in reply to a story Jill was telling her about her mailman, who, as you know, was less gifted in the ankle department than most. "Mangled Ankles" is what Jill called him, but Dahlia misheard. Dahlia Basset wasn't deaf but certainly wasn't present in mind enough to hear things correctly. Up to this point, Jill was giggling while telling her new friend about how the ambitious canines in her neighborhood found his ankles to be perfectly bite-sized. But now Jill had difficulty explaining to the girl that the name she bestowed upon him wasn't his actual name.

"No, Dahlia! It's just a *joke*, just a little joke—"

"Dad!" Dahlia called out, summoning her father into the coffee room that she and her guest were in. Mr. Basset toddled in before long. "Dad, Jill here has told me that she is acquainted with a Michael Angles, and I am convinced that we've met him at some time or other."

"Why, that name *does* sound excessively familiar!" agreed Mr. Basset warmly. "Where were we introduced to him?"

"Oh, no, Mr. Basset!" cried Jill, deeply mortified by the miscommunication. She was severely discomfited when Mr. Basset entered the conversation, intending to share a girlish laugh with Dahlia alone. Now things were getting much too complicated. "I was just telling Dahlia about my mailman whose ankles… ahem, anyhow," she continued, uncomfortable with elaborating to a sixty-year-old, "it's just a joke. It's just a nickname that I gave the guy, for fun, for *fun*!" But now the Bassets were far too engrossed in trying to remember who they *were* reminded of to give up the subject. Jill crumbled into the couch and quietly ran her hands through her hair. Finally, someone came in to end it all.

"I believe that the gentleman you are thinking of, sir," said Adkins, even though nobody noticed that he had entered the room, "is a Mr. Angles of Gloustershire, a boot manufacturer." The Bassets let out a relieved "Ah!" in unison, and to Jill and Adkins' relief, (the former not knowing that the latter shared her torment, having eavesdropped on the conversation for longer than Jill would have liked him to) the Bassets turned to a different subject at last.

"Well!" said Mr. Basset, "that is to say, well, well, then! I am glad to see that you have had a bit of fortification in some afternoon coffee. A young woman like yourself needs the nourishment, I am sure! Especially after working so hard learning about what your duties are as my secretary."

"Oh, I'm very strong, Mr. Basset, you don't have to worry about that! But please remember that I'm only going to be staying on the Isle for another week or so, and—"

"Oh, yes! It's no trouble, no trouble at all, is it, Adkins?"

"Miss Jill's vacation is of no inconvenience, indeed, sir," Adkins replied from the corner of the room.

"Well, I won't give you any more reason to tire yourself out, Miss Jill," continued the oblivious Mr. Basset, "so I insist that you take my automobile back to your home."

"No, Mr. Basset! Believe me, I love walking back and forth. I'm not as weak as you seem to think I am," independent Jill replied. "Wait—you have *cars* here?"

"Yes, my dear, I brought them over with me from London! It cost a little to ship them by boat, and we had a dreadfully hard time getting them onto the Isle, but I'm terribly attached to them. And really, I couldn't let you go without taking one of my automobiles from the garage!"

"For goodness' sake, Jill! Listen to the old man. Dad never drives the old things anywhere, anyways. It'd be good for the automobiles to get out and about. They need fresh air, just like we do." And so with this reassurance, which was nearly a command, they went out of the coffee room in a clump and walked towards the garage. Jill was appalled at its size and thus was anxious to see what sort of vehicles lay behind its monstrous doors. She rubbed her hands together at the thought of being behind the wheel of some neglected, imported Italian car. She grinned as she did so, watching Adkins press the automatic button to open the doors. They rolled up, squeaking hideously from years of disuse, seeming to complain about their unemployment. Her excitement accelerated as tires appeared beneath the slowly upward-moving door. But her grin collapsed into a frown.

"Ah!" exclaimed Mr. Basset breathily, looking upon the two cars—yes, only two!—with a proud smile as he clapped his hands. "There they are! Beauties, aren't they?"

"Oh, yes," said Jill gloomily as her shoulders slumped. Instead of a once-driven Italian sports car, there in front of her was a rusted-out, pink boat of an automobile. It seemed to be a convertible. The pink wasn't a fashionable rouge. It was a sickening, rancid sort of color, like rotting bubble gum. You can imagine how affronted Jill was at seeing the thing. But then her spirits were lifted high when she caught sight of the second car, the little Italian she was dreaming of—a jet-black convertible. It was sporty, fashionable, the kind of car that any girl claiming to be chic wouldn't be ashamed to be seen in. She couldn't help but envision herself in a spy flick, fitted up with a black hat, some shades, and black satin gloves. The exciting reverie was rudely interrupted when Mr. Basset slapped the hood of the sickly pink car. Jill winced when she realized what bonus her employer was about to give her

"Well, Miss Jill," said Mr. Basset, "here it is—my late wife's automobile. It might have been prettier in its day—well, come to think of it, the same could be said of my wife, but anyhow—it is now at your disposal." He slapped the hood again with a cheery grin.

Jill smiled. She thought that the matter had been clarified, and she was relieved. "Oh! You see, I didn't realize—I'd be happy to dispose of it for you. I just didn't know that there was a junkyard on the Isle."

Mr. Basset looked at her with a confused smile. "What, my dear?"

"Well, it's just that you said that it is at my *disposal*, so I just assumed that you wanted me to *dispose* of it." As she said this, her eye caught a smirk on Adkin's face.

"Oh, no! No, no, no, no, no, my dear!" Mr. Basset replied, shaking his head with each "No", "I only meant that you may make use of the vehicle whenever you wish." Jill's slouch reappeared. "Now, old Pinky's brakes aren't in the tickity-tockiest shape, but the rest of her runs as well as an automobile of her age ought to—"

"'Pinky?'" Jill repeated, like an incredulous parrot.

"That's the name my wife gave it. You may call it that if you'd like." Jill nodded respectfully. "Addie! Get Miss Jill the keys."

"Yes, sir."

The keys were soon in her hands, the car door was opened for her and then shut behind her. She smiled nervously in reply to the Bassets' eager grins. "Hey," she said with a smile, looking at the dashboard, "somebody put the steering wheel on the wrong side."

"Oh, did they?" said Mr. Basset, quite surprised at the "mistake." "Too bad! I don't suppose that there's anything we can do about it now. I believe the warranty has run out by now, hasn't it, Addie?"

"Undoubtedly, sir."

Jill chuckled, put her hand on the starter, took a longing glance at the superior car beside her, then finally turned the key. She nodded to her audience as she idled pathetically out of the garage. The sounds coming out of the car expressed her feelings aptly. It coughed tentatively, sputtered hesitatingly, and rumbled disgruntledly as it got to a speed sufficient to be called slow. The Bassets cheerily waved farewell, as did she, while veering towards the side of the drive. Adkins sighed—she missed the goose by two yards. He walked back into the house behind the Bassets, consoling himself with the hope that she'd have better aim next time.

"Can you believe that the steering wheel has been on the wrong side of the automobile all these years, my dear?" Mr. Basset asked his daughter. "No wonder traffic is always so congested in London."

While these profound realizations were being made, Jill was slowly approaching the top of the hill. She frowned at its pitch. She was sure that the car wouldn't have any issues going *down* the hill—she had seen gravity at its work marvelously with smaller objects on this very hill. She only worried that gravity would be less friendly the next day, when she attempted to return Pinky to where it belonged—well, where it *belonged* was another matter, but anyhow—she considered simply parking it at the bottom of the hill, beneath a friendly-looking, fluffy tree, and then she would just walk the rest of the journey. This satisfied her enough, and so she proceeded downwards.

With a hesitant press of her foot, she jolted ahead clumsily. Although the throttle forwards was intended to be practice, she found that momentum and gravity, things that didn't mean much to her before, were now rolling her full speed ahead down the steepest hill she'd ever seen. Her hair swept forward and back again as the descent began, blown about by the chaotic breeze. Having now lost a substantial amount of eyesight, behind blindfolded by her hair, she was more determined than ever to put the stubborn jalopy to a stop. She stomped on the brakes desperately, even harder than the time she stomped on a scorpion that decided to make itself a guest in her home. But the stress was more acutely felt, remembering that she was responsible for Mr. Basset's beloved vehicle, which she felt certain was going to land itself directly into an evergreen tree and leave her up in its branches. As she pounded on the brakes with increasing vehemence, it only resulted in a squeaking noise. Jill, as you could imagine, was not in the mood for squeaks. She would have preferred to come to a stop. But by the time she realized that the car was completely out of control, she compromised and merely hoped for a painless death.

As if the circumstance of her certain demise wasn't bad enough, she now saw something in front of her that caused further alarm. About twenty feet from the front of the car walked up an innocent young man, whistling merrily as he was about to turn up the drive. Jill now decided to stand on the brakes and lay on the horn simultaneously, while the only effort Pinky made was to squeak. But at the critical moment, the brakes finally decided to start working. Jill shut her eyes, gritted her teeth as she heard a little "thump", then felt herself come to a gradual stop. She opened one eye, her hands clenched onto the steering wheel. Seeing that the young man wasn't in front of the car anymore, she nearly somersaulted as she tried to get out of the car. Her steps towards the front of the car, though hesitant, were quick. Her hands automatically clasped over her mouth when she saw the young man lying there beside the car, with a leaf stuck in his hair, unconscious. Somehow, although her hands had covered her mouth, the shriek that followed didn't seem to be muffled very well. After a few moments more of observation, she realized that he looked very alive and was breathing superbly. Other than a bruise forming on his head, he looked peaceful, as though he was there of his own volition, like he had decided to lay down right there and take a restful nap. Jill was amazed—he was even *smiling.* She wasn't exactly sure what to do next. She hadn't had much practice in running into people. She was familiar with *almost* hitting people, but she was left without a clue of what to do now. She decided to attempt to lug him into the car, and then get him to a doctor. "Who knows," thought Jill mournfully, "Maybe I'll give the doctor a few more customers on my way over."

But this charitable idea was cut short by the floppy arrival of Dahlia, who was running down the hill like a madwoman. Adkins followed behind, in very dignified form. "Jill! Jill!" Dahlia screamed out, as she slid to stop, grabbing Jill's arm, "What happened? We heard a horrible scream, and—" then Dahlia also shrieked when she saw the young, smiling man by their feet.

"Dahlia!" Jill cried, "You almost stepped on him!"

"Oh, says the woman who bumped into him with two-thousand pounds of steel!" Dahlia looked down then shrieked again.

"Oh, no!" Jill cried, "What's wrong with him?"

"Sorry, not to worry—I just didn't realize how *handsome* he is! It rather startled me, is all."

"Well, I'm not about to stand here, gawking at his chiseled face—if it wasn't chiseled before, it certainly is now," said Jill with a frown as she knelt down and brushed a piece of gravel off his face.

"You don't suppose he needs CPR or anything, do you? I'm quite good at it," Dahlia said.

"I'm sure you are," Jill replied with a sideways glance. "Mr. Adkins, could you please help me get this poor man in the car?"

"Yes, miss," Adkins replied, walking over and lifting him single-handedly.

"Oh, well, that works, too," said Jill with raised brows and a surprised voice, comparing Adkins' short height with his unusual strength, picking up a man much taller than him with no complaint. "Em, Mr. Adkins, why don't you put him in the back? It'll be more comfortable for him, I think," Jill directed, gesturing towards the back shakily.

"In the trunk, miss?" Adkins asked in horror.

"No, no, the back seat!" Jill clarified hurriedly. Adkins stepped forward to do so.

"No, Adkins!" protested Dahlia, "Put him up front, next to me."

"Yes, Miss Basset," replied Adkins, turning towards the front of the car again, his violent swings left and right looking like the motions of a bucket brigade. Meanwhile, the victim's flopping limbs increasingly resembled a teddy bear's being handled by a careless child. At long last, he set the victim down heavily into the passenger seat. The victim's eyes opened for a moment, but his first sight was Adkins' panting face. As if he decided that the view was not worth opening his eyes for, the victim closed his eyes and passed out again. Jill jumped into the back seat, while Adkins attempted to do so himself, but instead of finding himself seated in the vehicle, he was thrown back as Dahlia stomped on the gas pedal and careened away.

"Dahlia!" Jill shrieked, bracing herself as they zoomed away. "Where are we going? Dahlia! The passenger door is open!" Dahlia then made a very sudden u-turn, while Jill lunged forward and grabbed the victim's lapels to keep him in the car.

"I'm taking him back up to the house!" was Dahlia's belated reply.

"Shouldn't we take him to a doctor?"

"Probably—but Adkins is the closest thing we've got to one out here," Dahlia rejoined calmly as the car's wheels revved up.

"You mean, there's no doctor out here?"

"Unless you happen to be one, no."

At this point, Adkins had picked himself from off the ground and had dusted off his suit. Now the car was violently returning towards the drive, the back door opposite of Jill also having been carelessly left open. He straightened his tie and his posture, then began calculating the exact moment he could jump into the automobile's open back door. He was certainly too tired to walk back up the drive. The car screamed up, and he barrelled towards it in a sort of sideways run. He squinted, he jumped—he missed. Unless, of course, his actual target was a group of welcoming bushes in the ditch. But as it was, he had taken flight, but being just an inexperienced fledgling, he failed.

A few moments later, while grumbling and regretting his unfortunate trajectory into the bushes, he heard something approaching, like a bicycle's wheels on the road. All he could see from his vantage were madly pedaling legs. Eventually, he could see the whole figure, and—dear goodness, it was Miss Fargo! He nestled into the bushes, hoping that she wouldn't see *him*. He rustled with extraordinarily bad timing, however, and Miss Fargo's head swung around and caught sight of him. Her eyes were glued to him and her mouth hung agape. She then toppled over, her descent happening so quickly that she didn't even have enough time to yelp. She got herself back up quickly, picked up her bike, and stalked over to Adkins with an uninterrupted, inquisitive stare.

"Mr. Adkins! What on earth happened?" she cried. "I heard a scream, and so I came over here as fast as I could. What are you doing in the bushes?"

"Oh, you know," he replied with a dry smile, "I often spend my spare time in the bushes. It's quite relaxing."

"Well, I see that you're no help. But I'll help *you*," Penny said agitatedly, reaching down and helping him up.

"We ought to meet in less unusual circumstances, I know," he said with a lovelorn sigh. As she helped him up the hill, he explained the entire circumstance to her.

Meanwhile, Dahlia and Jill managed to get to the top of the hill, despite Pinky's best efforts. Dahlia then took enough time to stop staring at the victim to help Jill carry him into the house. They quickly realized, however, that young ladies' arms aren't burly enough to lift a man of his height. After debating about the best way to carry him, as well as dropping him a couple of times, Dahlia suddenly left Jill and the victim, running towards the back of the house. She ran back to them, armed with a rickety, old wheelbarrow.

"Can't you afford nicer transportation?" Jill cried, looking at the rust-bucket disdainfully.

"My mother loved this wheelbarrow. She gardened with it all the time."

"Tell me, Dahlia, did your mother only like old, decrepit things?"

"Well, she did marry Father, after all," Dahlia replied. They then deposited the victim into the wheelbarrow and wheeled him over to the front door. "Terribly, terribly!" Dahlia muttered.

"Are you starting to see how serious this could be?"

"No, I was just thinking about how terribly good-looking he is!"

"Oh!" cried Jill in disgust as she opened the door.

Mr. Basset, upon hearing a great amount of commotion, decided to emerge from his upstairs office. He came out, then looked down on the entryway from the catwalk above. His eyes then bugged out of his head when he saw a wheelbarrow—and its contents—in the middle of his grand entryway. "Golden grasshoppers! What, what?" cried Mr. Basset.

"Do you have a guest bedroom downstairs we can put him in or something?" Jill asked Dahlia, her anxious voice echoing in the room.

"Would someone please tell me what is going on?" cried Mr. Basset again.

"No, we only have one upstairs," Dahlia replied.

"Would someone—" Mr. Basset began again.

At that moment, Adkins and Penny hobbled into the entryway unannounced.

"Penny!" Jill cried.

"Jill!" Penny cried.

"Adkins!" Dahlia cried.

"My back!" Adkins cried.

"Will someone *please* tell me what is going on?" said Mr. Basset, his English accent getting thicker with each desperate question.

"Jill ran into this man with Mum's car, Dad," Dahlia replied calmly.

"And Miss Basset pushed me into the bushes with the aforementioned car, sir," said Adkins.

"And I fell off my bicycle because Mr. Adkins rustled in the aforementioned bushes, Mr. Basset," Penny informed.

"Now, was that so difficult? Come now, let us get this poor chap into the guest bedroom!" said Mr. Basset with a swing of his arm towards the upstairs.

Adkins and Penny soon surmised from Dahlia and Jill's helpless looks that they could not carry him. With perfect synchronization, Adkins and Penny effortlessly lifted him up out of the wheelbarrow and took him up into the bedroom. They dropped him onto the bed, and then Adkins dropped himself into a chair.

"Adkins," said Dahlia, "go get the smelling salts, hurry!"

"Mr. Adkins isn't in any condition to be getting smelling salts!" cried Penny.

"Miss Fargo," said Adkins breathlessly, limply beckoning her to come closer, "the smelling salts are on the top shelf of the closet at the end of the hall." Penny nodded and went off on her smelling salt mission.

"Shouldn't we be getting a doctor or—" Jill cried, but halfway through, she remembered, "—oh, right, no doctor, unless I'm one, and I'm not. Do you have ice or anything? It'll probably help with the swelling."

"Ice, ice!" Mr. Basset agreed, leaving the room to retrieve it so hastily that he looked like he was slipping *on* ice. A moment after he left, Penny rushed back into the room and practically threw the salts at Dahlia. With shaking hands, Dahlia then conveyed them further by throwing the salts at the victim. Adkins, perplexed by the arrangement, managed to get up and look at the box Penny had brought into the room. He picked up the box to investigate. "These aren't *smelling* salts—they're fragranced *bath* salts!" he exclaimed indignantly.

"Really?" Penny cried, "I'm so sorry—they were the only salty thing I could find in the closet."

"Since when have smelling salts been kept in cardboard boxes?" Adkins asked incredulously.

"They could be kept in goldfish bowls, for all I know. I didn't know that people still use the stuff, let alone know what kind of container they come in!"

"Well, all this does is make him smell and look like he was mugged in a lavender field," Jill remarked with a frown.

"Wait!" Dahlia cried in a whisper, "I think he's waking up!" Everyone went quiet, then stared at him like they were watching an egg hatch. The victim moaned quietly, then began slowly opening his eyes.

"The best thing we can do now," said Adkins in a very soft whisper, "is to try to be as quiet as possible." Everyone nodded in silent agreement.

There was then a *thump-thump-thump* up the staircase, which then burst into the room. "Ice, ice!" exclaimed Mr. Basset, rushing in and placing a cold pack directly onto the victim's forehead. The victim yelped, but the alarm ceased when he reflexively shoved the old fellow away.

"Well, if the accident doesn't kill him, our doctoring will," Penny remarked quietly.

"Alright," the unexpected visitor said in a moan while stretching, "where am I, and why do I feel like I was run over by a train?"

"You were," sputtered Dahlia, "that is, you were run over. Not by a train, of course. Train tracks don't even run through here, come to think of it. No, it wasn't a train. It was *her—she* ran you over." Jill was mortified as Dahlia's accusatory finger pointed at her, watching the victim's head slowly turn to look at her.

"*You*?" the victim said, pointing at her, too. Jill hung her head as she nodded. "You—you don't like you could knock over a *bicycle*, let alone do all this to me." Now Jill was mortified *and* offended. The victim then rubbed his head with a pained expression.

"Oh, my! Poor soul," Dahlia cried, "What a terrible bruise there is around your eye," she continued, picking up the cold press that was knocked to the floor, then pressing it to his eye.

"No," he groaned, pushing her hand away, just half-conscious enough to not have to be polite.

"But it will help with the swelling! I know that it feels dreadful, but—"

"It's not a bruise," he said.

"Oh—well, it must be dirt, then. Here, let me wipe it off, we can't let dirt get into your eye—"

"It's not dirt, it's my face," he said shortly. "Yes, yes, I know. Kids in school used to call me the only kid that was ever born with a black eye—it's a birthmark."

"Oh!" said Dahlia, retreating from her efforts with the cold press. "Well, then, perhaps you'll allow me to introduce you to everyone here—it's sort of like a party, isn't it?—my name is Dahlia—*Miss* Dahlia Basset—and the kind man who brought you the ice is my father, Dad—or, Mr. Basset, I suppose you'd call him."

"Well, Mr. Basset, that was a very *cool* thing to do for someone you've never met," the victim said as he smirked, soon desisting when he realized that smiling was painful.

"Oh, oh yes! I wouldn't do anything less, young man," replied the old man proudly.

Penny shook her head at the stranger's poor pun and said, "I suppose we'll have to forgive him—he *did* just get run over, after all."

"Well, I'll smile at his joke for him, since he can't," Jill said.

"And this is Miss Penny Fargo. She carried you upstairs," Dahlia continued.

"Well, I appreciate that," the victim replied with a nod at her. Jill now became even more offended by his not being surprised at Penny being able to carry him, but saying that he'd be surprised if Jill could knock over a bicycle.

"No trouble," Penny said, "this gentleman helped." She gestured towards Adkins, who was looking more ill than the victim.

"Oh yes," said Dahlia, seeming to have forgotten about poor Adkins, "this is our butler, Mr. Adkins."

"What happened to you?" the victim asked in astonishment.

"I've thrown myself into the bushes more often than I would have liked to today," Adkins replied defeatedly.

Before the victim could express his concern over the man's choice of exercise, Dahlia turned towards Jill and said, "And this is my friend and Miss Fargo's cousin, Jill. She's the one who ran you over with my mother's car."

"Well, if you had to do it, it was smart of you to do it with her mother's car. No one would've traced it back to you, that way," the victim said with a smile. Jill wished that she was wearing a turtleneck so that she had something to bury her face into. "By the way, I want to thank you all for the part you each played— Miss Jill ran me over, Miss Fargo and Mr. Adkins carried me up here, Mr. Basset threw ice at my face, and Dahlia introduced everyone to me. But I think that your butler is in worse shape than I am."

With that, everyone turned around to look at Adkins and realized that it was so. Everyone rushed out of the room, Penny and Dahlia supporting the butler to his own quarters. All of this excitement was too much for a man whose days were usually filled with making tea and ironing socks. Jill followed the rest out of the room, but then stopped at the threshold of the doorway. When she turned around, she realized that the stranger was staring at her with an amused smile. When he realized that she saw that he was looking at her, he gave her a sweet smile, the sweetest smile she'd ever been given.

"Wait a minute," she said, "Dahlia introduced us all to you, but you never introduced yourself to us. Who are you?"

"Just call me Haddock."

"An odd request, but I'll do it. It's the least I can do after..." she said, then broke off. She sighed, twiddled her thumbs, then began again, "Mr. Haddock—"

"Just call me 'Haddock'. Adding the 'Mister' just makes it sound like you're mocking me."

"Oh! Well, I won't call you that, then—alright, Haddock, I really just can't even begin to tell you how *sorry* I am—"

"No harm done, Miss Fargo. I already had one black eye. Might as well have a matching set."

She smiled bashfully in reply. "My last name's actually not—" She paused. She didn't have the heart to correct him. Besides, she wanted to be on as friendly terms with him as possible. "Just call me Jill, please."

"Alright, Jill, could you pass me that cold press? My face doesn't need it, but my neck sure does. You got me pretty good."

"Well!" she said as she passed him the cold press, "I'm just glad I didn't get you any better."

"Me too!" he said with a laugh.

"I—I wanted to get you to a doctor, but I just found out that there isn't one on the Isle—"

"Yeah, I know, there's never been. But I think that I got the best care that I could've. After all," Haddock said, picking up the box of bath salts that were spilled across him, "I got a spa treatment, to boot."

"Oh, yes... my cousin accidentally brought you bath salts instead of smelling salts."

"People still use smelling salts?"

Jill gestured towards the spilled box. "Apparently not very well!"

Haddock looked down, then looked back up at her and laughed. Jill then explained the droll story about how she accidentally began working as a secretary for Mr. Basset, then how he insisted that she drive his late wife's car, and how it happened to have very bad brakes...

"...as you probably already know," Jill finished with a nervous laugh. "What were you doing, walking up the road, anyway?"

Haddock reached into his jacket pocket with a wince. Jill gasped when she saw what was in his hand—her beloved scarf!

"Of all the—you're that awful man who stole my scarf and nearly ran me over!" Jill exclaimed angrily.

"Awful man?" Haddock replied with a disbelieving squint and rise in his voice. "Awful man! Well, of course! I couldn't be anything else! How rude of me to almost hit someone who was, was *waltzing* in the middle of the road! I mean, *you'd* never do something like that, would you?—Oh! That's right, you *did*! At least *I* had the decency to *miss* you."

"Oh, I see! And careening eighty miles an hour on a reckless joyride *is* decent? At least I wasn't speeding downhill by choice! Mark my words, if I hadn't just run you over, I think I could thwack you." She then snatched her scarf out of his hand indignantly and tied it around her neck.

"I didn't know it was possible to tie a scarf so angrily," Haddock said, watching with a fascinated expression. Jill inhaled sharply, about to retort, when Penny suddenly walked into the room. Noting that the air in the room had turned unfriendly, she coughed uneasily and said, "Jilly, I'm going to stay and help Dahlia take care of Mr. Adkins and Mr. Basset."

"What happened to Mr. Basset?"

"He went to get Adkins another cold press, and he slipped on some ice."

"Oh, great," said Jill with a sigh, putting her hands to her face and pulling her cheeks down in exasperation, "I've nearly killed three people in one go."

"Four, if you include yourself," Haddock added cheerfully. Jill threw her head up in the air, sighed angrily, and then stalked out of the room.

After looking between her cousin and the victim, Penny called, "Jilly, wait up." She ran after her. "You can take my bike back to the house if you want."

"No, no, I'll probably injure fewer people if I just walk."

"Jilly, what happened while we were gone? It's like you became enemies in two minutes."

"Well, we sort of did. He's that awful man who stole my scarf!"

"*What*?"

"Oh, forget it—I just can't stand reckless guys like that."

"Jilly, you almost killed the man! The least you can do is be nice to him."

"I know, I know," Jill replied quickly. "Listen, Penny, thanks for everything. I'm pretty shaken up, I... I've just gotta go walk it off, then hopefully I can sleep it off."

"You're just going to *leave*?"

"Well, if you need help, I can stay, of course..."

"No, you don't look so good, actually. Go ahead and go home. I'll see you tonight."

# Chapter 13

*Tuesday, May 9th*

It only took Haddock a few days to fully recover. It might be said that it took Jill longer. One afternoon, Jill was alone in the house writing away at Penny's desk. She was often alone, as it became apparent that she was turning more into a housemate than a guest, which suited the home's two occupants very well. The sun was shining, and all the windows were opened in the house, the resident allowing the very salty breeze to go on as it liked as a very welcome houseguest, gently blowing the light curtains in a romantic way that Jill very much liked. The breeze took the sunshine along as a fellow guest into the friendly house, and they were quite a fine, pleasant couple, entertaining and soothing Jill better than any human guests she could think to invite. Everything was quiet, still, and happy. Such are the perfect conditions for the breeding of creative juices in a writer's mind—in Jill's mind, anyways.

Poetry had always fascinated Jill, and she had always admired how its rhythmic ways allowed the conveyance of either happiness or sorrow, humor or seriousness, lightness or darkness, buoyancy or flatness—whatever the writer felt, *splat*! There it went on the written page, either to be admired deeply or laughed at, but either way enjoyed. Jill always had a knack for coming up with sound-alike words, her mother often proudly recalling to her friends the odd names little Jill would give household objects—the "hot pots;" the "slouched couches;" and the "graceless vases." But Jill eventually outdid even these brilliant thoughts, and her abilities as a poet increased so much that her written words ended up being very pretty little pieces, enjoyed by no one but herself, occasionally shared with her mother, sometimes Penny—when she pressed her to—and Steve, who received the sweetest bits of her scribblings. She was so very inspired by the view out of that window to the right of the desk that she just *had* to sit down and write. She sighed, closed her eyes, and first listened for her inspiration. She jotted down a few clever thoughts—

"Beyond me, I hear the chugging of boats,
And the sound of gulls' demanding cries;
The engines create nearly musical, but grumbly, notes,
While the gulls the captains continue to utterly despise."

Jill then turned her pretty little face upwards to fully admire and observe the view. Seagulls wavered in the air, patches of tall grass blew, trees swayed, lobster boats motored around, a couple of locals walked down the path in the distance—but all of a sudden, things got very unromantic. A new figure appeared, quite suddenly, on the path that led up to Penny's house. The hill that supported the path had a tendency to hide the sight of any approaching visitors from anyone in the house until they came over the rise and threw the house's inhabitants for a loop. Jill was in the worst state of mind to be thrown anywhere, especially a loop. Interrupting creative genius is always a bad idea. But the very person approaching hadn't yet been forgiven from a past offense, so to add this one on top of it convinced Jill that she wouldn't be able to face him without exploding. She was sure that Penny didn't want any spontaneous combustion going on in the house, and so she ducked under the window to avoid being seen by him. But being curious about why he dared to approach in the first place made her more curious than she'd like to be, so her eyes peeped over the edge of the sill, not being a Leaf Peeper now, but a Haddock Peeper.

Now he was heading towards the front door. But to her surprise and confusion, she didn't hear a knock. Jill couldn't see the front door from where she was, so with cat-like sneakiness, she crawled across the living room and into the kitchen, hoping to somehow get a peek at what he was doing. She waited by the door to listen and try to get a clue about what he was doing, but she heard nothing. She smirked—maybe the Fish had come to apologize for nearly squashing her, but he lost his nerve and turned around. This thought amused her, so much that she wanted to see his expression as he walked away. She stealthily stood up and peered out of the kitchen window. Imagine poor Jill's surprise when she saw him standing next to Penny's bicycle, its handlebars in his hands, him looking at it admiringly as if he were at a bike shop, then hop onto it and begin riding away! She couldn't believe her eyes—was he actually *stealing* it?? No! He couldn't be! But she couldn't help but laugh when he tumbled over, not yet the master of the backward mechanics of the thing. But he was a dexterous young man, and soon got the hang of it, and was able to continue his thievery without any problems. Jill rushed out of the front door and ran after him.

"Hey! Hey, what do you think you're doing?" she called out. To her great chagrin, the conscience-less young man looked over his shoulder, got a look of fear in his eyes, and began pedaling faster! In Jill's eyes, this criminalized him completely, so she ran after him in Penny's slippers, calling out his name and waving her arms. At last, she caught up with him as they sped down the hill. Feeling so indignant at his stubbornness to not give it up, she shoved him to make him stop, but she shoved harder than expected and actually pushed him right off balance and onto the ground! Jill the policewoman stood over him quite contentedly, waiting for him to recover so that he could confess. He was quite out of sorts, not injured beyond a few scrapes, but very bewildered.

"So? What do you have to say for yourself?" Jill asked, mercifully lending a hand to help him up.

"I'm disappointed that I can't out-pedal a girl in big slippers," he mumbled, dusting himself off. Their heads turned when they saw Penny running up to them, wide-eyed and flabbergasted.

"What happened?" Penny cried.

"The Fish tried to take off with your bike. I can't blame him—yours is in better shape than his."

"And Miss Jill decided to play the hero and knock me over before I could make away with the goods," Haddock said mockingly.

Jill expected a proud word of thanks from her cousin but instead received a reprimanding "Jilly!" as Penny picked up her bike and checked to make sure it was intact. "Jilly, I *asked* Haddock to take my bicycle!"

Jill got quiet and lost that heroic shine in her eyes, then peeped, "What?"

"I heard that Haddock likes to work on motorcycles, so when I met up with him on my walk, I asked him if he'd take a look at my bicycle."

Jill's heart felt like an overworked elevator at that moment—it went up a few floors into her throat, then sank down to ground level. "Oh," she squeaked.

"Well, ladies, if you don't have any objections, I'll be off," said Haddock, nodding to Penny in farewell, then taking a quizzical look at Jill as he shuffled off with Penny's bike in hand. And all that day, Jill had to refrain from satisfying her desire to go jump off the cliffs on the north-eastern side of the Isle.

# Chapter 14

*Wednesday, May 10th*

The next day, Penny saw Jill sitting at the desk in her living room. "What are you writing?" she asked.

"A letter to Mr. Babcock."

"What, are you quitting? Did Mr. Basset offer you a bonus you couldn't refuse?"

"Oh, no..." Jill replied absentmindedly, "...I'm writing to ask for another couple of weeks off."

Penny, who had begun drying dishes, frowned while squeaking away at a glass. "You have the nerve to ask him for another two whole weeks off?"

"No, no, just a *couple*. It's much less. Besides, you know I can ask him for whatever I want. He's indebted to me, after all, after the Toupee Incident. Ever since, he's had..."

"...*toupee* for it, I know," Penny finished with a smirk, hearing the pun many a time before. She then cocked her head. "So, that means you want to stay. How come? Haven't you been traumatized four times over?"

Jill dropped her pen and half-frowned as she thought. She then smiled as she looked up at Penny. "I, I don't know exactly why, but I actually like it here. I love the ocean, the scenery—yes, even the people—and I love staying with you."

"I can tell by the way you mentioned me first," Penny replied sarcastically, putting a plate into the cupboard with a smile. "But really, it's good to have you here, kiddo."

"I didn't realize how much I've really missed you since I've spent this time with you."

"Well, no matter how much you love my company, I must admit that if I were you, I'd be anxious to leave after what happened yesterday."

"Believe me, I haven't stopped thinking about that. Before I realized that the Fish—Cod? Haddock, that's right—was my scarf thief, I thought that I'd like him. But afterwards, I realized that he's just the type that I hate—a cocky, reckless smart-alec. I know that we'll meet up again at some point or another, but I still hope that I don't run into him again."

"I'm sure he doesn't want you to run into him again, either. Sometimes you take things a little too literally."

Jill smiled a little, then continued on with her letter, and Penny continued drying spoons. "Well," Jill started up again, "at least he's not staying at the Bassets' anymore. I hated having to work there knowing that the jerk was just upstairs."

"I wouldn't call him a *jerk*, Jilly..."

"He nearly squashed me!"

"You *hit* him! *And* knocked him off a bike, *and* accused him of being a thief..."

"I know... but at least when *I* ran him over, I didn't *mean* to be going that fast. That Fish was just, just *flying*, and he *wanted* to be. I just can't like anybody who could kill himself just for a thrill. I keep trying to be mad at him, but then I remember that I ran him over. Then I feel like sinking into nothing when I think about the bike incident." There were then a few moments of peaceful silence, but Jill started up again, "What kind of name is Haddock, anyway?"

"Oh, Jilly, people name their children all sorts of strange things. Well, that's what Mrs. Peterson told me after she went to the mainland for a visit. Of course, she said that while thinking that Joanne without an 'e' was nothing short of insanity."

So Jill sent the letter off on the mailboat, and all that she could do was hope for the best.

~~~

The following Saturday was chillier than the increasingly warmer days that preceded it, and so Jill bundled herself up in a sweater and tied her scarf—*securely*—around her neck. Despite the chilliness, she preferred the cool air to the stuffy indoors she had just emerged from. There was no reason to prolong her stay there, as Penny had put on her dungarees, tied a stained scarf 'round her head, and set off to go chop down a tree or plant a garden or something like that. Jill could never predict her cousin's agenda. So Jill was again left unsupervised.

Jill squelched down the muddy path from Penny's house to the main road, her hands in her pockets, her hair turned damp and stringy. Nonetheless, she was happy. The slight fog over the sea and the damp air contributed towards a romantic mood and state of mind. She walked through The Center first, finding that she was at last able to wave and say hello to the locals without being given the side-eye, or, at least, a less severe one. She waved with special friendliness at Bobbie, who waved back from within her warmly lit coffee house, with a shy but earnest smile. Jill and Penny had visited the Coffee House a few days prior to enjoy coffee and tea—the latter being Penny's order, which inevitably went cold—while Jill got to know Bobbie splendidly. Jill was concerned, of course, when she learned that Bobbie was practically Haddock's mother. She was put at ease, though, because the subject of her nearly fileting Haddock was never brought up.

Jill walked out towards the Bassets'. Conveniently, there were plenty of tall trees to block the cold wind that began to come up off the sea. At first, she contemplated
~~~

journeying towards the Bassets' beach. It was an absolutely perfect day to walk on their stone faced beach, yet she knew that walking anywhere near Dahlia would ruin her hopes of remaining solitary. So Jill pressed on, ignoring the steep gravel drive that had allured her. Jill shuddered—she was now in the very spot where she had nearly fried the awful Fish. She relived those moments as she walked on. Laughter and tears both seemed to be suitable at the recollection.

Next came the drive heading up to Mary Pine's house. It was another residence that afforded a marvelous view, but alas! Jill's wish for her own company exclusively deterred her again from walking up yet another drive. Now Jill had walked past all the houses she was acquainted with, and now there was no guilt in passing by friends' homes. She could now walk past stranger's homes, where knocking on *their* doors uninvited would be more rude than simply passing them by. Jill was delighted to be polite in this way.

The road grew lovelier as she went further down it, although it was densely populated by trees. This didn't concern Jill, although she had unfriendly thoughts towards them in the past. They had grown on her, or, perhaps as a better way to phrase it, she got used to them and actually enjoyed their company. She was content with having these residents wave in the breeze, since she didn't feel any obligation to wave back. However, as she went even further, the swaying trees became less friendly-looking and more invasive in demeanor. They blocked what little sunlight the cloudy sky allowed to shine through, and the road seemed to be coming to its end. Jill frowned, remembering why she had misgivings towards trees. She took these misgivings up again as she gave an indignant look at the intruding evergreens and the impudent dead end, then turned around.

She had passed two paths to the left on her way to the dead end. Turning back homewards, she nervously and quickly passed one of the paths that was now on her right.

She had anxiously half-ran by it when it was on her left, because she knew that Mrs. Bloomberg lived down that path. That woman was a deadly combination; miserably old and trigger-happy. The next path, as far as she knew, didn't pose any threat to her. She couldn't tell if it was a drive up to a house, or simply a path headed to the shore. But she intended to find out.

Jill was very pleased with herself. She discovered yet another part of the Isle, and she was extremely curious about what laid ahead of her. But as she continued down the path, it seemed unpromising. There were trees, trees and trees thickly lining it. Jill's pace quickened, however, when she saw light in the distance. At last she came near the clearing, and through the thinning trees, she spotted a little cabin peering out of the forest. She smiled at it as she came directly into the clearing. It was a delightful arrangement. There, a simple, humble cabin nestled itself into a few huddling trees. She only hoped that these trees wouldn't fall in the wind and destroy the delightful scene that they helped create. She then looked around the cabin —her mouth hung open when she saw what was parked beside the cabin she had grown so attached to—it was that awful, junky motorcycle that had nearly squashed her! She now shut her mouth to frown angrily, then glanced up at the trees she was previously so worried about. She now wished that the trees leaned more precariously over that bike. Her chagrin rose steadily when she heard merry whistling from behind the motorcycle. The bike was parked horizontally towards her and, from a distance, it momentarily blocked her view of the whistler. But even though she couldn't see the whistler's face, she knew that he was distinctly fishy.

Jill was now frozen. She looked up at the clearing sky with a lengthy sigh, deciding that now was as good a time as any to offer a true apology. She had come to admit that her grudge was a ridiculous one to hold. Besides, her apology might provoke one from him. And so with this incentive, she bravely walked ahead. Her steps slowed with increasing hesitation as she approached. Thankfully, the whistler didn't seem to be very interested in who was walking towards him. She came towards the bike and stood on the opposite side of it for a moment, getting more and more confused by the continuing silence. There was no greeting, no exclamation of surprise. Even a shocked inhalation would have satisfied her. But he remained aloof, elbow-deep in machinery. Jill was sure that he would have heard her approaching footsteps by now. She felt that if she coughed, it would just be obnoxious. After all, if he didn't hear her footsteps, he certainly wouldn't hear her cough. And likewise, if he was simply ignoring her, he would ignore her cough just as easily.

"Hey," he suddenly said, holding out his hand from the opposite side of the bike, "whoever you are, could you hand me that wrench that I left over there?" Jill recoiled in surprise, then, after recovering, reached down and, without saying a word, obeyed the request. "Thanks," he said, without looking at her all the while, taking the wrench she placed in his hand and continuing his work. Jill couldn't take the silence anymore.

"For all you know, halfway in the engine, I could be a burglar. I could've decided to hit you over the head with that wrench. It would have been a very convenient opportunity. After all, you *did* ask for it."

"Miss Jill," Haddock replied, looking up, "burglars are much quieter than you. Your footsteps were so loud, I thought a draft horse was stomping up the driveway."

Jill, offended by this equestrian comparison, reached down and picked up another wrench. "You know, I don't want to steal anything, but I'm tempted to knock you over the head anyways."

"Besides," continued Haddock, ignoring her threat while taking the wrench away from her, "you'd be a *robber*, not a burglar."

"I'd like to know how you got that bike on the Isle," she said, ignoring the correction. "The way people scorn technology out here, I'm surprised that they didn't sink the boat it came on."

Haddock smiled as he wiped his hands off of a distressed-looking rag. "The bike was my uncle's. He lived here for a long time, and everyone liked him, and he loved this bike. So when he brought it over, there wasn't much argument."

"Now, how did you get this adorable little house?"

"Wait here, and I'll tell you," he said, throwing the rag at her and heading towards the house.

"And I'm left holding the rag," Jill said with a sigh. She impatiently carried out her assignment, holding the nasty rag by her fingertips. Haddock returned minutes later, with his shirt now buttoned up all the way, his hair slightly combed, and with a cup of coffee in each hand. Jill was surprised with each improvement, but was especially delighted with the coffee.

"I could nearly cry," she said, taking the little, white, chipped mug from him very gratefully. "Penny has been neglecting my need for coffee. She forgot to get a tin of coffee the last time she went to Shrimpy Cove."

"Too bad!" he exclaimed in sympathy. He put a hand on the bike and leaned on it, and then they appreciatively sipped their coffee in unison.

"Well, thanks for the coffee, Haddock… say, is your name really Haddock?"

He laughed, then replied, "Oh, no, it's just a cute little name Bobbie gave me when I was a kid. She saw the birthmark around my eye and said that it reminded her of the dark spot that's near the eye of haddock, and it stuck—the name, that is. The birthmark stuck around by itself."

"People around here are quick to notice things out of the usual, aren't they?"

"They sure are! I promised to tell you about how I got the camp, didn't I?"

"I've been dying of anticipation."

"My uncle kindly went out of his way to make sure I could have it."

"Oh, really? What did he do?"

"He was nice enough to die and leave it to me." Jill gasped. "Yeah, the poor guy died too young. I do miss him. He used to show me how to fool around fixing this old beast. He even gave me a job in the store he opened after he moved out of Maine. It feels strange, trying to fix the bike while just making things worse, without his help."

"I suppose that explains why it's in such rough shape," said Jill as she kicked one of its tires. He looked at her curiously. "I dunno, it seemed like the right thing to do," she explained.

"My uncle took pride in taking care of himself the same way he took care of this bike—come to think of it, *he* always looked in rough shape, too. Can you believe that my father, who took better care of his health than anyone I've ever met, died ten years before my uncle?"

"I think I could. People around here seem to think that death is more of an inconvenience than a threat."

Haddock laughed. "No kidding. I first started coming to the Isle when I was a kid, spent the summers with my uncle."

Jill suddenly remembered that she hadn't offered any condolences yet, and so she put in abruptly, "I'm so sorry to hear about that."

"Well, the summers weren't *that* bad..."

"No, I mean I'm sorry to hear about your uncle's death."

"Oh, well, thanks anyways."

Jill drove her hands deeper into her pockets and bounced on her toes. She looked up at the clearing sky for a moment, then said, "Well, I was about to comment on the weather, but I think that discussing whether or not I should be wearing a sweater would be a waste of our time."

"I have to admit that I didn't think that you walked all the way down here just to get my opinion on your sweater—which *is* nice, by the way."

"Oh, thanks. It's Penny's, anyways. People like to comment on my clothes around here."

"Oh, that's right—you're Frog Girl."

"Just because these are green doesn't mean that—well, what's the point of getting upset? *I* like my clothes, and that's what matters in the end. 'You are what you wear,' they say."

"Isn't the saying, '...what you eat?'"

"You eat clothes?"

He decided to say "Yes" to confuse her, then said, "I think we got a little off-topic. We were going to talk about why you didn't come down here—did that sentence make sense?"

"No, but I'm fluent in nonsense. I actually didn't mean to walk down here at all. I thought that this was just another one of those paths that start out promising but then just end up leading you to an uprooted tree. I certainly wasn't expecting to help you fix your bike."

"Would you rather see a rotting tree than me?"

"Well—yes, to be truthful."

"So, are you going to get to your point, or are we just drinking coffee and talking about the weather? Because, to be honest, I only gave you a cup of coffee because I thought you were going to apologize to me. But," Haddock said, reaching to take back the mug he had offered her, "if there aren't going to be any apologies..."

"Wait!" Jill cried, desperately clutching onto the precious beverage. "Alright, alright, you threaten to take my coffee away, and I'll do anything. Haddock, I overreacted the other day, and I'm sorry. Can I keep my coffee now?"

"Which other day? The day you ran me over, or the day you pushed me off a moving bicycle?"

"All the other days."

"Despite all of your best efforts, I'll forgive you." He gave her a side-eye, then continued, "There's something about you that makes a guy can't help but be in a forgiving mood. Do me a favor: next time you see a guy trying to peacefully ride a bicycle, don't push him off, alright? And next time you go up to the big house, could you tell the Bassets how much I appreciate how well they took care of me?"

"Hm!" Jill said in a laugh.

"And what does that sassy little 'Hm!' mean?"

"Oh," Jill faltered, "I'm not used to people noticing my little 'Hm's'. I was just thinking about how much Miss Dahlia cared for you. She was quite taken with you."

"Ah, Miss Dahlia... Nice girl, but as goggly-eyed as a scuba diver. Just think what my girl would do if she saw her."

"You have a girlfriend?"

"Don't sound so surprised."

"You should've told Dahlia, the goggling might've eased up."

"How was I supposed to blow her off, while she and her father were taking care of me?"

"I wouldn't call that 'blowing her off'—if anything, it would've been a kindness."

"Well," he replied, taking the coffee cup from Jill, who was willing to release it only because it was empty, "it sounds like you're a lot more scrupulous than I am, Miss Fargo." After saying this, he walked back towards the house.

The faux "Miss Fargo" couldn't take it anymore. She followed him, saying, "Scruples or no scruples, my last name isn't 'Fargo', it's—"

Her correction was interrupted by the blast of a shotgun. She saw a bullet knock over one of the logs stacked near the cabin. The noise thoroughly startled Jill, causing her to yelp, trip, and bonk her head against the corner of the cabin. Her vision dimmed, and she stumbled over to lean on the porch's railing. "You're such a sissy," she mumbled in a scold to herself as she felt a faint coming on. Haddock, looking back and seeing what was about to happen, tossed the coffee mugs aside, ignoring the smashing sounds they made as they landed, and ran over to catch Jill. He was just in time. As he came near, she stumbled around floppily, then finally fainted, after stepping on his foot. "I almost think that you meant to do that," he said, looking down at the unconscious girl suspended peacefully in his arms. "Oh, no need to thank me. I couldn't have let you dent the bike," he said, continuing the conversation while the other party was absent. Having never rescued someone in this way before, the rescuer felt quite unequipped. He sighed, looking for a place to put her that wouldn't weigh as heavily on him. He then lifted her onto the nearest platform available—the porch off of his cabin.

At first, he felt very inconvenienced. There she was, just laying there, all sprawled out. As the seconds that ticked by turned into minutes, however, he got more concerned about the fact that she hadn't woken up yet. He tried squeezing her hand, then tried shaking her. "Out cold, like a broken light in the fridge," he mumbled. He considered slapping her, but then reasoned that the tactic only seemed to be appropriate in the movies. He instead patted her on the cheek, saying in a low, polite voice, "Miss Fargo! Wake up, please!" Little did he know that she wouldn't have responded to the name, even if she was conscious. "Miss Fargo!" He then sighed anxiously. "Now you're scaring me."

"And you're scaring *me*!" said a familiar voice from behind. Haddock spun around, and there he saw the real Miss Fargo bicycling towards him. She came to an ungraceful stop, stumbled over herself as she set the bike on its kickstand, then ran over to him. When she saw the motorcycle nearby, then Jill, she gasped. "Oh, no!" she cried, her hands over her mouth, "You didn't run her over too, did you?"

"No, of course not!" Haddock replied, offended.

"Then what is she doing laying on the porch like that? I heard a shotgun go off and a shriek, so I came over as fast as I could. It seems like I'm always running to and fro to see what Jill's screaming about."

"That old woman Bloomberg lives twenty yards away, and she's always blasting that thing off. I think Miss Jill got startled and tripped and hit her head. I caught her just before she fell over, and I, I didn't know where else to put her. I thought she'd come to by now."

"And putting her on something that's *not* as hard as a rock didn't occur to you?"

"If I had a down mattress nearby, I would've been happy to escort her to it, but I happen to be a mechanic, not a nurse. She's heavier than she looks!"

"You have a couch or something in the camp, don't you?"

Humbled, Haddock replied, "Sure I do, but—"

"Oh!" Penny exclaimed in an exasperated sigh. Without a further word, she took Jill into her arms and carried her off without any difficulty.

"What are you doing?" Haddock cried, half humiliated, half confused.

"I figured that you're unqualified to help me get her back home, judging by the nursing skills you've demonstrated so far."

Haddock just stood there, his mouth agape in amazement as he watched her carry Jill away like she was as light as a kitten. But he soon regained his senses. "Wait! I'm qualified! You wouldn't *believe* how qualified I am," he said, now having something to prove.

"You're right," Penny called back over her shoulder, "I don't believe it." Haddock frowned, then ran up to Penny. "What," she asked with a quick look askance, "do you want me to put her on the ground or something?"

"Just let me help!" Penny did so, and they walked back to her house, taking turns carrying her. Both Penny and Haddock were shivering nervously like wet puppies, but Penny hid it better. In a flurry of fear, they rushed Jill up to the front door. "It's locked!" Haddock cried while jiggling the door handle.

"Of course it is!" Penny growled in exasperation. "Alright, let's go through the window in the back."

"The window!"

"What other choice do we have? Well, I shouldn't ask *you*—you'd want me to put her on the PORCH," Penny said in disdain as she led the way to the back.

"Oh, would you get off it?" he said while trying to pry the window open.

"Here, hold this," Penny said, thrusting Jill into his arms, "*I'll* do it." She then threw the window open without any effort.

"Alright, smart guy, now what do we do? Toss her through the window?"

"Well, the window *is* right there in front of the couch..." Penny said, stroking her chin thoughtfully. Soon it was agreed that they would lift Jill up and aim her lifeless body through the window.

"I hope you're as good at bean-bag tosses as I am," Haddock remarked. They counted to three, then shoved her in. They heard a springy noise and guessed that she had landed on the couch.

"Something just occurred to me," Penny said, stroking her chin again, "Jill probably can't unlock the front door for us."

Haddock, who was bent over and panting, shook his head. "You have to admit," he said breathlessly, "that this tops the porch thing."

"Yes, yes, now go wait by the front door and I'll let you in," Penny snapped. Haddock jogged off wearily while Penny planned her approach. She remembered that the couch was her usual landing spot of choice whenever she came into the house through the back way. But now the couch was occupied. Penny, being skilled at breaking into her own home, having locked herself many more times than she admitted to, scooted methodically up the side of the house and began her inevitably awkward landing. She usually employed a half-somersault, but with this new obstacle, she had to adapt. She didn't adapt very well, however, so she ended up elbowing and kneeing Jill simultaneously as she rolled over her as lightly as possible. Penny continued rolling right onto the floor, and she lay there for a few moments. She then heard intense knocking on the front door. "Coming, coming! I didn't forget about you, already!" she called out, as if her forgetting things wasn't commonplace. She swung the door open while Haddock kept on knocking, and, in fact, knocked her right on the head.

"Oh!" he cried.

"It's alright, I'm learning about how you deal with crisis very well, now," Penny replied, looking at the floor and holding her forehead. In this same stooped position, she led him directly into the living room. "Would you mind carrying her upstairs to her room? I have a little headache," Penny said. Haddock readily obeyed, scooping her up like a clumsy knight in dull armor. He tripped up the staircase and kicked the door open. "That's *my* room—" Penny cried, but she stopped, deciding that it didn't matter. All of his clumsiness wasn't noticed by the blissfully unaware Jill, though. She woke at the suavest moment of the rescue, as he gently set her down in Penny's bed. "What happened?" she mumbled in a pitiful, sleepy voice, like a child woken up by its mother.

"You fainted and I carried you up here," Haddock replied with a reassuring smile and a soft voice.

"Right," said Penny sarcastically as she entered the room, "he's quite the hero."

"You—you carried me all the way from your cabin?" Jill asked, coming to a bit more.

"He carried you all the way to his PORCH," Penny clarified, while Haddock half-frowned at her.

"Well, whatever you did, thank you very much. And I think that you should thank him too, Penny."

"Alright, alright, I admit that I've been pretty hard on him. Sorry, Haddock. I get cranky when I'm scared."

"And I do dumb things when I am, so we're about even. Is there anything else I can do? Anything at all?"

"No, you've done enough. She looks alright now, anyways, just a bruise on her head," Penny replied, sitting next to Jill on the bed, examining her face, "but thanks for asking."

"Yeah, sure, it's the least I can do. I'd better leave you alone, I've bothered you two enough."

"You call helping a bother?" Jill asked, surprised.

"If you were around to see what happened, you wouldn't ask," Penny replied. She then turned to Haddock. "Still, thanks for getting her up here. You're right—she *is* heavier than she looks."

"Hey!" Jill cried. "Well, how do you like that? Talking behind my back like that."

"We'd never do that, Jilly."

"That's right. We said those things right in front of your face," Haddock reassured her.

"Here, let me show you out. This seems like a good time for you to leave," Penny said to Haddock.

"No, no, it's alright. I'll let myself out."

"Don't break anything," the girls said simultaneously.

"Goodbye, goodbye!" he called out breathlessly in heroic farewell, tripping as he shut the door behind him. Jill's dazed eyes followed him all the way out of the room, and Penny followed Jill's gaze. The way Jill looked at him made Penny wonder if Jill's post-faint stupor simply made her gaze at him longer than was necessary, or if the gaze was actually as fond as it looked.

# Chapter 15

*Monday, May 15th*

"You getting the mail?" Jill eagerly asked Penny as she watched her tie her scarf around her head.

"No, I've got to get over to the lobster pound and help Tommy out."

"Tommy, *hmm*?" Jill said with a simper.

"'Timid Tommy', as you call him, means as much to me as your 'Mangled Ankles' means to you. Why are you excited about the mail, anyway?"

"I'm expecting a letter from Mom. I miss the lady. Well, I guess I could just walk down to the docks to get the mail myself..."

"No, no, I'm not letting you go down there with that woozy head of yours. I'd go down and get it in a heartbeat, but it looks like I'm a little late already... you know what I'll do? On my way over, I'll ask someone to grab the mail and bring it up to you."

"Don't do that, Penny! They'll think I'm even more of a sissy than I am."

"Eh, who cares what they think of you?"

"I do! But oh well. Like dad always said, 'Cheer up, they've never been right about anything before.' You're a peach, Penny, thanks."

And so Penny went off to find a deliveryman for the sissy's mail. And she happened across Haddock.

"Morning, Haddock," she greeted dryly.

"Morning, Miss Pen—"

"On your way to the Coffee House?"

"Yeah, actually—"

"Then would you be a dear and get any mail for Jilly from the mailboat and bring it up to the house for her? She's still a bit woozy and is expecting a letter. Thanks a lot!" With that, she kept walking, without considering that Haddock might have been walking down the street with a purpose. He watched her walk away with a confused frown, then shook his head with a sigh and continued on to the Coffee House. Anyone who didn't come to get their letters fresh off the boat knew to go to the Coffee House, where they were dropped off. So he went in and apathetically asked Bobbie if there were any letters for Miss Jill. Bobbie handed him a letter, and without a second look at it he stuffed it in his pocket and walked back out.

"Morning, Jerry!" he called out to the fisherman, who he saw from afar. Jerry was on his bobbing boat, working on something. Jerry's "Mah'nin!" was so inviting that Haddock decided to take a break from his task and stop to talk to the far more interesting Jerry Miller. "What are you up to on this fine morning?"

"Just fixin' ol' Miss Geraldine for the tourist season comin' up," Jerry replied, leaning to one side and resting his elbow on a stack of lobster traps. "Thought I'd straighten 'er up, tune 'er up, clean 'er up." He then directed a foul look at a little bench by the wheel, where seagull droppings of an assortment of sizes were left. "Now what do you suppose those gulls were doin' ov'ah the'ah, of all places?" Jerry asked with an annoyed wag of his head.

"Isn't it obvious?" Haddock rejoined. "Say, Jerry—I didn't ever think of you as being the vain type, but here your old boat is named Miss Geraldine..."

"Now, don't you start with that!" Jerry laughed. "My name is *Jeremiah*, mister, not Gerald. Geraldine was my moth'ah's name. It's not right to name a boat after somethin' as ugly as me, is it?"

"I wouldn't say that, Jerry. After all, Joey named his boat after his sister."

Jerry attempted to scold and laugh at Haddock simultaneously, but the effect was anything but reprimanding. The conversation continued with Jerry explaining what he planned to have done on this Miss Geraldine, and it carried on for quite a while without either noticing how much time was going by.

In the meantime, Jill was getting rather impatient. She had allowed enough time for Penny to find someone to get her mail for her, then for the impromptu mailman to actually go and get the mail, and then get up to the house, but something was amiss. She quickly reasoned that Penny probably forgot to ask. And so with this thought in mind, she groggily got up, stumbled from one side of the house to the other to get to the door, and went down to the docks to see what she could find.

Haddock and Jerry had, by this point, wrapped up their conversation. Jerry returned to his work and Haddock completely forgot about the letter that was crinkling in his pocket. And so they went their separate ways, while Jill was on her way to find out what had gone wrong. Jill approached the docks, not knowing anything about the proper procedure of how to receive a letter on an island. She soon remembered that the mailboat was very efficient. It dropped her and Penny off, then practically threw the letters at the people that gathered around to receive them, then went sputtering back to the mainland as fast as it could go. Jill wondered if this was simple efficiency, or a wish to get her, the strange girl from away, off the boat. Whatever the case, she got to the docks, but there was no mailboat in sight. She did see a fisherman on his boat, though. He was back-to, however, and she didn't want to startle him. But somehow, whenever we try our best *not* to startle someone, the effect is only that we startle them more than if we yelled out their name at the top of our lungs. And this was the very case with Jill and Jerry. She crept up slowly, her dainty steps creaking the dock slightly as she approached. "*Dee da doh, dee dah day,*" was the merry song he sang as he bent over the engine, which was concealed by a board in the boat's floor that was now uncovered.

"Mr. Miller?" Jill whispered. Finding that the whisper was not heard over the emphatic humming going on, she stepped into the boat and cried, "Mr. Miller!"

Mr. Jerry Miller's song took a sudden turn, with a dissonantly startled "Ah!" and a clang from the heavy wrench he dropped into the engine. His cap even abandoned ship, jumping off his head and into the water. Not that this was any great novelty—he'd lost it overboard 63 times, somehow always fishing it out of the sea, no matter the condition—but it was startling, nonetheless. He was so perplexed that he lost his balance, tripped over the side of the low-backed boat, and fell face-first into the salty water beneath, with a resounding splash.

"Mr. Miller!" Jill shrieked, not expecting so much excitement from going to collect her mail. His sudden departure made the boat sway, nearly throwing her off, but she somehow held her ground. She then balanced herself over the edge of the boat, hoping to fish him out from a precarious angle.

Haddock, the unwitting instigator of all this, ran back towards the docks at the sound of a shriek. He was nearly too confused by the suddenly-created scene to do anything but watch. But after getting his fill as a spectator, he too ran down the dock and jumped into the boat, helping Jill pull poor Jerry back in.

Everyone coughed and sputtered for a while after recovering Jerry. "Well, that's number 64!" Jerry said to his rescued cap fondly. "Now what were you doin' jumpin' in my boat and makin' me jump outta my skin and into the wat'ah?" Jerry asked through teasing chuckles.

"If it wasn't for the nincompoop who didn't deliver my letter, I wouldn't have even been here!"

"And I'm the nincompoop," Haddock said sheepishly.

"You—" Jill said, pointing at him with wide, confounded eyes. "*You're* the nincompoop? What took you so long to simply take the letter from *here* to up *there*?"

"I admit, I forgot. Jerry distracted me with his talk about birds and boats."

"Ay, now, don't take me down with ya, mister! *You're* the nincompoop he'ah!" Jerry said, thoroughly enjoying himself, although wetly.

"If you weren't so careless, none of this would have happened!!" Jill exclaimed, the large, circular gestures accompanying the "this" seeming to indicate that it was far more all-encompassing than the singular event.

"I'm not the one wandering around on stranger's boats!"

"You left me no choice!" Jill rejoined, then sighed, feeling rather defeated by life. "Will you at least give me the letter now?" Haddock slowly drew the letter out of his pocket, and upon noticing its state, passed it to her nervously. She took it, then looked back up at him with a nearly tearful frown. "You dented it! And it's from my mother, too! And it's wet! Just look at all these wrinkles—look, Jerry, have you ever seen so many wrinkles?"

"Nevah! Exceptin' on the womenfolk's faces around he'ah, heh, heh!"

"You can't even let a girl have a minute to recover from one bewilderment before you bewilder her again!" Jill fired at Haddock.

"I'm not solely to blame here, am I?" Haddock asked, turning to Jerry, who suddenly became a judge, jury, and witness all at once.

"Even if not, I don't suggest that you try and prove it!" Jerry replied to the largely rhetorical question.

"Well, that did it!" Jill said conclusively.

"Did what?"

"*It*—the big, ugly it. I've at last decided that you're the most careless person I've ever met, Mr. Haddock!"

"—just Haddock—"

"—*Mr.* Haddock—I'm mocking you, can't you tell? Now if you'll excuse me, I have a letter to iron."

And so all of them again went their separate ways, all a little wet, all a little riled. Haddock went home to sulk, Jerry went home to change, and Jill went home to flatten out her letter.

~~~

Despite the effort it took to receive the letter, it really all was worth it. Jill and her mother were closer than... than... well, I can't think of anything to compare them to, but it's definitely something close. The point is that the two often sent letters back and forth, despite the fact that they only lived across town from each other. Now was the first time in Jill's life that letters to and from her mother were practical. Her mother's letter read this way:

"Dearest Janet,

I have barely survived without our Sunday afternoon coffee together, Janet, dear. You seem to be going farther and farther away—first, you move out at twenty after your father died, then you travel to Maine, leaving me to drink coffee with awful Mrs. Riley. You'll be glad to know that her cat lost another five pounds, and she's celebrating the return of her gardening shed's resident lizard. But I've been struggling through life just fine without you. Don't worry about me a bit. I have plenty of things to keep me busy and excited. For example, a few days ago I tuned into the live broadcast of the first American in space. Were you able to catch it? I'm not sure what kind of television reception you can get up there. It was incredible. Can you imagine being rocketed into space like that? If I were strapped in there, I'd be afraid of burning up. Speaking of getting burned up, the temperature hit 95 today. I'm terrified that my daffodils are going to get fried, and you know I never was one to like dried flowers.
~~~

Well, my daughter, you've written me one letter so far, and it was a very interesting one. It even made me miss the East coast a little bit. That shows you how good of a letter it was—you know how much I don't miss the East, excepting the bumblebees. You don't suppose that you could catch one in a jar and bring it back here, could you? I could use a pet to keep me company.

Janet, if it wasn't for your feminine handwriting, I'd swear that your father wrote your letter. You take after him in just about everything, don't you? You two are the drollest people I've ever met. Even on the day you were born, you looked droll. I've never understood how a baby could be droll, but I saw it with my own eyes. Anyhow, I adored your poem—it was bee-utiful, as all of them are. And your descriptions of the people there are delightful, with your "Timid Tommy" and "Miffed Mary." But I have to warn you, dear, that your drollness is dipping its toes in the water of pessimism. I suppose that's like your father, too. Perfectly funny and kind, but pessimistic. I think you'll get along with all of those people just fine eventually. Ever since you were a little girl, you didn't trust any of the other little girls. You were always running after them during your tea parties, convinced that one of them was set on taking one of your teacups. Your father and I balanced each other out—he always thought the worst, and I always thought the best. Maybe that's why you and your sister turned out so differently. Well, dear, try not to assume the worst of people anymore. You don't have anybody to balance you out. And when something's not balanced, it's sure to topple over and fall on its behind. Don't do that. Maybe if you just think the better of people, people will think the better of you.

Enough of my motherly advice. I know that you'll tell me everything that I need to know, so I won't ask any questions in this letter. I hope the rest of your little vacation goes well. Send my love to Peyton, and find me a nice bumblebee.

All my love,

Your Mother."

# Chapter 16

*Tuesday, May 16th*

"Your stitching looks like it was done by a one-eyed amputee." This commendation was given to Jill's handiwork by her encouraging sewing instructor.

"Thanks, Mary," Jill replied. Mary nodded, and they continued sewing. After the business of critiquing her work was settled, Jill said, "I got a letter from my mother yesterday, and you know what she said? She said that she watched a man get shot up into space on television—and I *missed* it! Do you know what I was doing while a man was leaving the atmosphere? I was drinking tea. *Tea*, of all things!"

"Eh, nothin' to get too upset about, de'ah," Mary said without batting an eyelash.

Jill was in total disbelief. "I miss the chance to watch a man go into space, and you say that it's nothing to get upset about?"

"I don't see how some man flying into space affects us any. Pass me the pincushion, will ya?"

Although Jill could not comprehend how someone could reply to the subject of the second man to ever go into space with "pass the pincushion," she stopped herself from elaborating on her incredulity at Mary's flippancy and merely stared at her sewing instructor with wide, confounded, indignant eyes as she passed the pincushion.

Since she knew that only an event that took place within Mary's sphere could be discussed at greater length, Jill felt that it was now appropriate to begin to tell her chronically disgruntled companion an exciting story that took place on the Isle. And so she told her about Haddock's heroism. Mary's arm, which was nearly fully extended, stopped sewing midair at the mention of the name. "Haddock?"

"Right. I didn't think much of him when we first met—"

"You mean when you bulldozed into him with your cah?"

"Well, yes—but that was only after *he* nearly squashed *me*."

Mary, inclined towards believing the worst, inquired further into the event. She nodded as Jill vented her frustrations, Mary being only too happy to agree with any negative opinions that conveniently coincided with her own. "Keep stitchin', de'ah, and I'll tell you all 'bout Haddock," Mary said with a smile. Jill's attention was now divided between pleasing her instructor's exacting sewing expectations and her intrigue about hearing another opinion about the Fish who threw her own opinions into controversy. "I think you're a good kid, Miss Jill, and I've always liked you and your cousin—well, I don't like anybody at first, but I like most everybody eventually." Although confused by this sentiment, Jill appreciated it. What happened next was quite unexpected. Mary stuck her needle into her pincushion, set aside her cloth, and patted Jill on the knee. Jill, though initially so surprised by the maternal motion that her first instinct was to recoil, instead put down her sewing and smiled uneasily. Mary now sighed, looking down. "Miss Jill, I've gotta warn ya—Haddock is a bad egg."

Jill, who was expecting a more serious revelation, was disappointed by this mediocre comparison to a spoiled poultry product. "I appreciate the warning, Mary." Mary nodded solemnly, then returned to her sewing. "Is—is that all?" Jill asked in confusion.

"Haddock is a selfish, obnoxious fellah who doesn't think about anybody except himself." Jill thought that the first and last accusations were redundant, but she allowed Mary to go on. "And everybody thinks so much of him when really, he's just an egotistical, self-centered—"

"Well," Jill interrupted, never one to bear redundancies well, "he must cover it up pretty well, for you to be the only one who's noticed."

"Well, I haven't let myself be blinded by that easygoin' nature of his. What's good about bein' easygoin', anyhow? I'm proud to say that I've nev'ah been called easygoin' in my life. Easygoin'," she mumbled disdainfully, "just another way of sayin' 'lazy', and I certainly am not lazy!"

"No, that you aren't!" Jill cried. Mary was beginning to sound argumentative, as if Jill had called her the hated word. Jill then returned to her sewing after the outburst. "Weave up, weave down, weave up, weave down," echoed Mary's voice in her mind. But Mary's voice wasn't the only thing in her head. In fact, the last thing on her mind was her sewing. Of course, having a sharp object in proximity to one's fingers should never be the last thing thought of. Nonetheless, Jill's mind was more importantly engaged. There were endless conflicts, endless paradoxes wrapped up in Haddock! He was sarcastic but nice, thoughtless, yet thoughtful, careless, yet caring. One report varied from the next, even her own thoughts about him weren't consistent. Up to that day when he carried her back to the house, she disliked him, but ever *since* that day, she wanted to just talk to him, get to know him. He added to his good favor by stopping by the day after she fainted, bringing her a few wildflowers and a thermos of coffee—well, the wildflowers were picked by Penny, but they were synonymous with his visit because Penny had brought them up at the same time as Haddock came to bring her a coffee, a brief visit, and a smile. He left another thermos on the doorstep the day after he failed his role as the mailman. "He's no Mangled Ankles, that's for sure," Jill said to Penny after she'd cooled down from the incident. But that smile of his! Just when she could hate him, she remembered that smile. It wasn't like any other she'd ever seen.

These thoughts took her by surprise. But, in reality, they didn't. Positive opinions from the Islanders, as well as her own better opinions, had been wearing at her. But until this moment, she never classified them as anything more than a mild interest in a neighbor. Mary's warning snapped things into clarity. Why did she warn her in the first place? It was a motherly interest, and maybe it was even to protect her from falling for him.

"Falling for Haddock!" she exclaimed in her mind, "Ha! What a thought!" But as soon as the internal exclamation was made, she realized that she was playing tricks on herself. He certainly couldn't be called unattractive, despite the splotch around his eye that became his namesake. "Silly, all silly," Jill thought with a smile. Silly moments they may have been, but she had to admit that they were moments of clarity. Her thoughts had been foggy for the past few days, being both positive and negative, happy and chagrined, all haphazard and random—but they were all about *him*! This she couldn't deny.

"Weave up, weave down, weave up, weave down…" Jill mumbled as she became a little more focused on her sewing. She noticed that the stitches were wandering even worse than before. Jill put herself at ease, deciding that she wasn't falling for him—maybe *tripping*, a little bit—but *falling*! She could never do that! This would be the end of the silliness, for her own sake and her Sweet Steve's sake. And all of these discoveries were made during a good, old-fashioned sewing lesson. Besides, it was easier to disregard the silly thoughts, now that a burning anger was lit in her heart. She was mad at him, for being a brat to Mary and causing her misery throughout all her days, and mad that he made her think differently about how she felt about Sweet Steve. Thus, somehow, the discovery that she could fall for him made her not like him at all.

Mary, though not in tune with her companion's matters of the heart, could immediately notice the lingering silence. So she decided to start talking about the snowstorm of '38, and how she, her husband, her son, her mother, and the Petersons had to stay under the same roof for 37 hours and 16 minutes because they were snowed in together. They drove each other crazy the entire time, and both couples never let the legend die. Jill smirked—she had heard the Petersons too state the exact hours and minutes of the countdown as if it was the worst experience of their lives. But Jill was too preoccupied in the brain to reply to Mary's cheery storytelling. So silence began again. Mary was more bored by this silence than worried by it, so surmising that she had done her best with this student (that is to say, her student's skills had plateaued) she led the way to the end of the visit. "Well, de'ah, it's about time we'd be finishin' up, eh?" Mary said, putting her work aside in a more permanent manner than before. She then stood up. Jill smiled and nodded, although still feeling distracted. She attempted to simultaneously put aside her project and get up, but the task, for some reason, was strenuous. She looked at Mary, hoping that she didn't see her unusual struggle. Thankfully, Mary's back was turned towards her. Taking advantage of this audience-less moment, Jill looked down to investigate what happened, and why the project did not slip off her lap when she rose... the realization then came to her—she sewed the cloth right into her pants! Just as her deepest mortification was setting in, Mary turned around and added to it. "Oh, Miss Jill!" she cried while laughing. Jill wished that her first time seeing Mary laugh hard wasn't at her own expense. All Jill could do is squeak out a little upset "Oh!", tug at the cloth, and head towards the door. There weren't just a few stitches; she had somehow sewn the entire length from her hip to her knee. "I told you that you had to watch your stitchin'!" Mary said while scrunching up her face and laughing. Never had Jill seen the prevalence of her wrinkles until this unfortunate moment. Jill then half-smiled, you know, that awkward smile all of us have had to make at one time or another, when we want to seem like we're laughing it off when really we feel like crying.

"Thanks for the sewing lesson, Mary," Jill said as a genuine smile emerged. She had to admit that it was terribly funny. Of course, she was still determined to leave the room as quickly as possible. And she did, with a needle dangling from a single thread and excess fabric flapping in the breeze as she exited the house.

Walking back to Penny's house on the road, she happened across Haddock. He took one look at her pants, then grinned, only saying, "Well, like they say, 'you are what you wear.'" Jill gave him a strange face, then stalked homewards.

# Chapter 17

*Wednesday, May 17th*

"You know what I'm going to do?" thought Jill as she looked around Penny's kitchen with her hands dangerously industrious-looking on her hips, "I'm going to cook a lobster for Penny." As she put on some shoes and walked down to the lobster pound, the thought continued: "She's done so much for me, the least I can do is go out and try and cook something nice for her while she's out working away. How hard can cooking a lobster be, after all? It's like boiling potatoes, I'd imagine—you boil some water, throw 'em in, and there's your lobster. As long as I don't eat any, I'm sure I won't have an allergic reaction to them." She tried not to think about the more alarming appendages that lobsters possess, deciding that if they really were dangerous, they wouldn't be sold to the public. But a fear of the crustaceans lingered in her mind as she came into the lobster pound. She walked in while a bunch of *incrustations*, taking the form of various locals, were hanging around, a few talking about how their day of fishing went. They noticed that Jill was in the building.

"Lookee the'ah, the'ah's the little miss From Away—Toad Feet, isn't it?"

"Frog Legs," Jill corrected indignantly. It suddenly dawned on her that the correction didn't help her dignity any.

"What's little Miss Frog Legs doin' in he'ah?" questioned Jerry with a smile.

"I—I came to buy a lobster," she faltered.

"For Penny, I'm guessin'? Considerin' that you screamed out of the room that last time you were in the same room as a lobstah."

"That's right—it's for Penny," Jill squeaked humbly.

"Well, Miss Jopling, come on ov'ah and pick one out," said Tommy bashfully, leading her over to a tank of the water-breathing creepy crawlies.

"What are those things in their claws?" Jill asked Tommy.

"Those are wooden pegs the lobstermen whittle out. They put 'em in the base of the claw to wedge 'em closed."

"Poor little creatures!" Jill exclaimed.

"You'd be sayin' the same about us if we didn't put those pegs in their claws," called out one lobsterman. As they all cackled at her naivety while she continued to survey the candidates, Mary Pine came in.

"Nobody told me 'bout the party," Mary said, looking around at the small crowd gathered there.

"Next to Bobbie's place, this is the only place to hang around," said one lobsterman.

"Then why don't you go ov'ah the'ah and buy yourselves a cup of coffee or two to make yourselves useful? Bobbie sure could use the money."

"We could use it, too. It's cheap'ah to hang around he'ah— Tommy's too timid to kick us out."

"Hey, what's Frog Legs doin' in he'ah?" Mary questioned upon sighting her.

"Frog Legs is trying to pick out a lobster to feed Penny tonight," Jill replied, her eyes set on the lobsters, mortified as she watched the biggest one in the tank pulling on an underdog's leg. The big one only had one claw with one of those wooden pegs in it. The other claw's peg was missing, and the lobster was putting its unrestrained claw to use.

"You sure you want to try cookin' a lobstah? You haven't had much success with 'em so far, have you? Well, de'ah, better choose the feistiest, they've got the best meat on 'em," Mary recommended.

Jill gasped as she watched the underdog lobster's leg get pulled off. After recovering, she turned to Mary with a suspicious look. "The feistiest, eh? How do I know that you're not pulling my leg?" Her eyes then widened, and she looked mournfully at the poor lobster in sympathy.

"I'm not pullin' your leg! But if you do choose a feisty one, I'll give you a warnin'—they'll fight'cha back."

"Kick and scream, they will, once ya put 'em in the pot," said another lobsterman, very helpfully.

Jill threw another suspicious look around at them. She felt certain that they all were just trying to scare her for the sake of a laugh. Her pride ran high, and so she bravely pointed towards the violent lobster she had just been watching, feeling sure that it was the feistiest out of the bunch. She didn't choose him because she was taking their advice—things were getting personal, now. She would prove to them all that she could handle a little lobster with no problems. She also felt pity for the legless lobster and felt that this could be her way of showing him support, by removing the ruthless bully. Tommy, without a word, took the lobster out of the tank and into a paper bag. Jill then gave him the money, carrying out the transaction out quite haughtily.

"I could come ov'ah and cook him for ya if you want," said Mary. She said it rather derisively, although she didn't mean to. Her voice just was used to sounding like she knew best about everything.

"No, Mary, I'll manage just fine, thank you," said Jill as she walked towards the door.

"You'd bett'ah leave the pegs in his claws, missy—or he'll *getcha*!" said one fisherman, the sudden snapping gesture that accompanied his warning startling Jill. She straightened her shoulders and sailed out, feeling ever more confident in her own abilities, because they were challenged.

Jill returned home, threw the paper bag in the icebox, set the largest pot she could find in the kitchen on Penny's old stovetop, then fired up the burner. She smiled proudly at her work as she watched the pot of water come to a nice, rolling boil. But she knew that the most trying part of the process was to follow. She pulled the paper bag out of the icebox and set it on the counter. She peeked into it apprehensively, as if the lobster would jump out at her like a pouncing lion. She began to regret her choice, remembering what this particular lobster did to its fellow's arm. She was comforted by the fact that at least one of its claws was restrained, and so with a brave spirit she stuck her hand into the bag and pulled him out. She had never felt anything like it before—it was like picking up a smooth, cold, wet, living rock with legs. The lobster seemed to not be feeling itself, having been out of the water for a while. It wriggled its legs, claws, and tail, but not as spiritedly as it had in the tank. She began looking at the splintery peg in its claw and decided that she'd rather not have the possibility of Penny eating splinters with her lobster. Jill already was beginning to worry that she'd somehow kill her cousin in the process, and so the precaution was taken to somehow remove the peg from the claw. She didn't consider it any danger. The suffocating creature was downright docile at the moment. So she went to work trying to remove the peg, which was firmly wedged in. But with the help of a little effort and willpower, the claw was released. Not completely assured of the safety of her fingers, though, she carefully took it by its tail and plopped it into the vat. She put the lid over the pot and sighed, feeling very accomplished. The worst part was over. She looked out of the window, seeing that the sun was beginning to go down, then began setting the table. It was a happy little domestic picture—until, of course, she began hearing *thump-thump*ing from the general direction of the stovetop. Then she began hearing the oddest sort of squealing. "Goodness, the thing *is* screaming! What a horrible noise!" she thought as she cocked her head and stared at the pot, then jumped back when the lid of the pot began opening and closing as if something within was trying to push it off... "Oh, no you don't!" she cried, running over to the stove to clamp her hands over the lid to keep the lobster from kicking it off. But she didn't make it in time—the lobster, a regular boxer, thrashed its claws and tail around, not going down without a fight, actually kicking the pot so forcefully that it tipped over the edge of the stovetop and clattered as it hit the ground and spilled boiling water all over the floor. Jill managed to jump back from being completely scalded. She angrily stared at the mess, then waited a few moments for everything to cool off before running over to try and begin the process again.

As she was about to put up her biggest fight with her cousin's dinner, Haddock was walking Penny's bike back up the hill, feeling quite ashamed at the fact that he had been defeated by the thing. There was no fixing it without irreversibly disassembling it. With a sigh, he set the bike on its kickstand by the front door, then hopped up the stairs to knock on the door. But just as he was about to, he heard angry screaming from within, and a voice yelling—"Oh, I hate you, I hate you, you little fiend!"

Haddock's brows jumped, feeling a bit surprised to hear such language being spoken between cousins. Inferring that this wasn't a good time, he confusedly turned away and started to leave.

"You awful lobster—you try that again, and I'll—" The threat ended with a pain-stricken shriek. Utterly bewildered and frightened, his first instinct was to run away, but his more heroic side decided to go in and try to break up the apparent catfight going on within. He flung the door open, and instead of seeing a female brawl, as the noises coming from within would indicate, he instead saw Jill flinging her hands around, one of her fingers occupied by a lobster's stubbornly clamped claw. She turned around in shock at seeing Haddock, flinging her arm around and smacking Haddock with it. Surprised by the smack as well, the lobster seemed so confused that it, at last, let go of Jill's finger and flew through the air and again smacked, except this time against the window. Jill then began hopping and writhing simultaneously around the room, while Haddock could only laugh until tears rolled down his face.

"You're not bleeding or anything, are you?" he asked.

"No," she grunted in reply.

"Oh, good, I don't feel as bad for la-*ha*-aughing!"

"This must be how it feels to be inside a nutcracker," Jill cried, stumbling around the room, then finally sitting down with a melodramatic sigh at the table. Haddock giggled all the way over to the table and inspected her red-ringed, throbbing finger. "Ooh, hoo, hoo—that looks ba-*ha*-ad," he said, trying to be sympathetic and recover from his laughter at the same time. The effect was insulting to Jill.

"If all you're going to do is laugh at me like an owl or a sheep, then get out of here!"

"Oh, c'mon, Jill, if you-*hoo-hoo* walked into a room and saw what I-*hee-hee* saw, you'd be laughing, too!" Haddock said, ha-ha-ing right out of the house. But as soon as he left, Jill too began laughing, pausing intermittently to inhale sharply when an especially painful throb came up. And so as Penny walked up to the house, she saw something wet splattered against the window, and her bike by the front door. She ultimately came home to a wet floor, a smashed lobster against the window, and a laughing Jill at the table.

"This isn't exactly how I planned the evening for you, Penny— ha, ha, hoo, hoo!" Jill said, her forehead on the table, exhausted from the hysterical laughter. "Oh, Penny, Mom was right!—I thought the worst about people, and I fell on my behind! I thought everyone was joking when they warned me about the dangers of lobster cooking, but look where that got me! Ha!" And soon everyone on Petit Homard was laughing.

# Chapter 18

It can be easily guessed that Jill only deepened her impression on the locals by the Lobster Incident II. But we mustn't forget that Frog Leg's pants only added to their infamy by means of the previously mentioned incident when Jill's distracted, silly thoughts led to a silly addition to her trousers. Not to worry, though—the extra material was removed with careful effort, and the pants suffered no harm beyond the usual ridicule and abuse. But we will not go on forever talking about Frog Leg's pants or her various run-ins with lobsters. In fact, we will barely even consider her in this chapter. The focus will now be shifted to another interesting character—Dahlia Basset.

As you have probably discerned by now, Dahlia Basset was a lonely young woman. Her only companions were her father and their butler. The Islanders never had any intentions to welcome them, and with the passing of four years, it became increasingly unlikely that they ever would. Her father could be said to be less lonely than she, he who was occupied with his imaginary importance in his business, and who had such an entertaining daughter, as well as a "good-natured" butler. He hadn't any need for any happiness that couldn't be found beyond his perfect little sphere. Thus, the utter isolation didn't weigh quite as heavily on the father as it did on the daughter.

One might have to give an argument about Dahlia Basset before allowing themselves to completely pity her. She was, after all, in the best sense of the word, a simple girl—simply happy, simply amused, simply going through life with the ease that obliviousness brings. She was liked by everyone in her home country, England, and was very popular. But she was forced to move with her aging father where he would retire—*New* England. At first, the newness and the hustle and bustle that a move necessitates satisfied her quite enough. The locals' negative response to the Brits' arrival was unnoticed at first. The newcomers were too wrapped up in themselves to pay any attention. But after a few months more, the inattention was no longer unnoticed, but instead cheerfully ignored.

But really, if it weren't for the move, Dahlia Basset might not have known what to do with herself. The Bassets had a delightful bubble in England, too. But bubbles do not last forever. The mother's death popped the bubble resoundingly, and the poor daughter didn't know how to behave. She had never experienced any kind of loss in her life, and to begin experiencing it in this way! But the move helped distract what was left of the family. But, Dahlia's world was shattered, and with each passing year on the Isle, her world shrank littler and littler. She soldiered through it all bravely, though, not knowing how to be sad. Now she had a duty, her very first, and a very serious one: she had promised her mother that she would take care of her father for as long as he lasted. And so closed up every opportunity to travel, to associate, to do anything to satisfy her innate curiosity. She became settled with the idea of living around two old men for the majority of her youth. At least she liked the geezers. She loved them, really. But she loved everyone, which perhaps explained how she could manage to like Adkins. She was oblivious, and being oblivious helps one to like everybody. There's a lovely blindness that comes with the quality. And as far as living with her father went, she was too much like him to not enjoy his company, both being generally too unaware to not like each other. Thus, they were a contented trio, stuck on an unheard-of island together.

But ever since Jill Jopling had come to live amongst them, Dahlia experienced a sensation she had never known before—dissatisfaction. Jill didn't do anything out of the ordinary to make Dahlia feel this way. No, Jill was cataclysmic enough just by being a single, independent girl, living an average, independent life. Dahlia had forgotten that such creatures exist. Ever since she became Jill Jopling's friend, these unusual feelings gradually seeped into her mind and heart. Before Jill's arrival, these feelings were mere tricklings. But now the thoughts, at last, gushed open, like floodwaters, after the two friends had a particular conversation.

"Jill, dear," Dahlia said one sunny, humid day as they lolled across lounging chairs, "brace up—I am going to ask you a silly question."

Jill was rather afraid. "Oh? What is it?"

Dahlia smiled broadly, even cheekily, then looked out over the ocean that laid beyond the trees in front of them. "Have you ever been in love?" Jill couldn't be sure if she was relieved about the question's contents. Considering the questioner's initial description of the impending inquiry, Jill was happy that the question wasn't any more awkward. Nonetheless, the question, for her, was awkward enough. "Oh!" said Dahlia in drawn-out intrigue, "Your blush says it all!"

"Oh, yes," Jill replied, putting her hand to her cheek while smiling hesitatingly, "usually my cheeks give the answer before my mouth does." Dahlia was not yet satisfied. So her cheeky grin grew. "Yes Dahlia, I will tell you that I have been in love. And, in fact, I am in lo..."—Jill conveniently choked on an hor d'oeuvre here—"...well, I don't have any intentions of loving anyone ever again."

Dahlia was expecting to have more fun with the answer. She found herself instead receiving a depressing one. "Why don't you try falling in love again? It's great fun, I've heard."

Jill smiled knowingly. "It is fun, at first, but it—it gets complicated, too often for my liking. But," she continued with a despondent sigh, "I *do* have a boyfriend." She added a mumbly "I think," to the end of the sentence, but Dahlia was far too enraptured to notice.

"A boyfriend? Well! Is it a serious case?"

"I—well, yes, it is."

Dahlia was ecstatic. After a little pause, Dahlia broke out and exclaimed, "Are you *engaged*, Jill? Is that what you mean?"

Jill's face scrunched up as she looked at the blinding reflections off of the sea. She shook her head. "I'm not sure."

Dahlia, who had been thrust upright in her chair by the discovery, was now halfway out of it. "Well, if *I* was engaged, I'd make sure that I really was!"

Jill laughed but didn't have the motivation to explain the situation fully. "Well, Dahlia, I—I don't know if he loves me anymore, and I'm not sure if..." She stopped herself. She liked Dahlia very much, but she decided that she'd feel guilty if she shared something about her feelings that she hadn't shared even with her closest family. She couldn't tell this new friend that she was having doubts about if she loved Steve before telling Penny, Clementine, and her mother. So she changed course and finished with, "...I'm not sure if he thinks that I love him."

"If *I* had ever been in love, I'd make sure that he knew it!" Dahlia cried, finding that this method of reasoning was worth using twice.

Jill smiled again. If only she knew! "Come on, Dahlia! You can't tell me that you've never been in love, not even once?" Dahlia colored a little, but other than that, the hint didn't go far. "What about that one nice fellah who spent three days recovering in the same house as you? The one you wanted to take a drive with, even though he was unconscious?"

Dahlia now laughed heartily. "Ah, of course! Mackerel—"

"—Haddock—"

"Yes, he *was* very nice, wasn't he? I haven't seen a young man in so long, you'd think that I would've fallen in love very well! But, I have never been in love. I've liked a great deal of 'em, but I think that love is only love if it is returned."

The statement, though simply put and quickly blown off by Dahlia as she rambled on, touched Jill. Actually, her conscience rapped her on the knuckles—maybe she and Steve weren't in love at all, according to this definition. Day by day, she was growing more uncertain if she even loved him at all—bah, silly, silly thoughts! But the phrase "I love him" didn't perfectly fit what she was actually feeling. This disturbed her.

Anyway, enough about Jill. You were told that this chapter was devoted to Dahlia, and the issue isn't going to be confused any longer.

At last, Dahlia finished her ramblings with, "...yes, he *was* handsome. Is this boyfriend of yours handsome?"

Jill almost laughed. "I don't know," was an answer that would provoke questions that she didn't feel like answering, so she only said, "People have told me he's handsome, but I think he's cute."

"Is there a difference?"

"Certainly!" Jill replied resolutely. "'Handsome' is a serious, movie-star kind of good-looking, but 'cute' doesn't even have to necessarily be good-looking, just sweet. Just listen to me—I've worked it into a stupid kind of science, haven't I? Anyways, Steve's *cute*, trust me."

"Well, now that I know that there's a difference, I've had an opinion that I didn't know about 'til now—I'll take seriously handsome over your ugly but sweet cute any day."

"Well, you can take your pick, but I'm sorry to disappoint you, Dahlia—handsome as he is, Haddock told me that he has a girlfriend."

"Oh, I see!—you think Haddock is handsome!"

"No, no, that's not what I meant—" Jill protested, even though it was.

"This science of yours is getting sticky, isn't it? Well, scientifically sound or not, his having a girlfriend is no bother to me. He's too sharp for me, too quick. I don't want to call him 'mean'—that's too strong of a word. He's really just a wonderful person, but on the brink of being waspish. But I still think that he's first-rate. He got along with my father very well, and he got along just fine with me."

Now Jill was confused—confused about whether Dahlia's paradoxical opinions about Haddock could confirm her own opinions, or if Dahlia's thoughts were just a result of her usual optimistic wishy-washiness. If they could confirm Jill's confusing feelings, then they would hold great meaning. If even Dahlia—the most positive person Jill had ever met—could acknowledge that there was both meanness and kindness in Haddock...

Ah, there I go about Jill again. Anyhow, all of this talk about love and such made Dahlia think about her own life with some depression. Here her friend Jill had some delicious drama going on in her life, but the only drama Dahlia could scrounge up was lately seeing a bright green crab on the beach, or seeing more beached jellyfish than usual. She almost stepped on one, recently. That entertained her and her father for some days. But now, the poor jellyfish was nothing in comparison to the excitement of love. This all put her in a romantic, daring frame of mind.

~~~

On an afternoon when distant clouds looked like they were on the verge of tears, Dahlia announced to her father that she was going to go on a walk. And it was true — partly.

Dahlia deciding to go on a walk was nothing out of the usual. Neither was her destination. What was unusual was where she planned to go *after* she reached her destination. Singing and whistling accompanied her
~~~

journey towards the docks. She had a merry tweed hat on, with a delightful pouf at its crown, and a nice little brim on the front. Her blonde, teased hair fell out beneath it, bouncing as she went skipping closer to the docks. She looked up at the heavens with an adventurous smile and saw a group of seagulls squawking at something or other. Seeing how free and mobile they were only encouraged her to do as she planned.

Although she was often envious of the free and easy birds, there was one in particular whom she always noticed with pity. By some unknown traumatic circumstance, there was a poor little seagull whose tongue permanently stuck out to its left. She named it Frederick, but after knowing him for a while, she felt comfortable enough to call him Fred. The docks were now about fifty feet away. She was so distracted by the seagulls that she walked right across the fifty feet, onto the dock, and nearly off the edge. A few fanciful fishermen watched as she "Ooh!"-ed and swung her arms back and forth, trying to regain her balance. She convulsed like an imperiled caterpillar, trying not to plummet into the unwelcoming water beneath while beating her arms like a gull too heavy to take off. The fishermen didn't feel any motivation to help, and instead only chuckled and simpered, while others had faces of granite. The locals' coldness towards newcomers—yes, Dahlia Basset was a *newcomer*, although having lived there for four years—cannot be explained in a single way. Was it their disgruntlement towards change? Or a sort of fear of the unknown? Or a feeling of defense, wanting to protect what they viewed as their own?

Jerry Miller wasn't afraid of the artless, oblivious girl. In fact, he called out to her: "Say, missy, whatcha lookin' at?"

Dahlia, not embarrassed in the least by almost unintentionally diving into the ocean, smiled at him, delighted to be addressed by a local. "Oh, goodness! I was looking up at those poor dears in the sky."

Joey, happening to be nearby as well, looked up to the heavens with a severe squint and a deeply confused scowl. "Ya mean the *gulls*?" It should be noted that lobster fishermen despise seagulls, who tend to bombard bags of bait, leave droppings, and laugh disrespectfully as they do so.

"Why, of course I'm talking about the little dears!" Dahlia replied earnestly, with a plaintive frown. "Do you see Fred up there? Yes, that one—or is it that one—oh, *there* he is!—yes, he's just landed on that post over there, now," Dahlia continued, now pointing at her object of sympathy. Her appearance on the docks had now drawn a small crowd of fishermen. "See how ill the poor dear is? It must be awfully hard for him to eat his dinner with such an impediment."

"Eh?" said a few fishermen in unison, the reason being that most of them were hard-of-hearing, but all of them were in disbelief. If they didn't like the foreigner before, her friendship with the gulls was sure to cement their misgivings.

"How would you feel, sir," she continued, addressing a random fisherman amongst the crowd, "if you had to eat your dinner whilst your tongue was constantly like this—" She then demonstrated the disability, jutting her head forward and sticking her tongue out, all in admirable similarity to Fred. All the fishermen laughed derisively in reply, as they turned away to return to their work, except for one. Jerry stayed and laughed.

"Well, de'ah," he said, his sun-worn face wrinkling further as he smiled, "anyone who can feel for a rotten gull must have a heart a' gold." With that he turned away, his shoulders bouncing in laughter as he walked back towards his boat. Dahlia then walked away from the docks and towards a slope that ran down to the water.

Being a perfect optimist, she appreciated the attention that had just been given to her, not bothering to notice that most of it was derisive. But now she had walked a little way up the path that one takes to go to Penny's house. After reaching a certain point, she looked around, making sure that nobody was watching her. She grinned—not a soul around. So she steadily crept down the slope. It led down to what an optimist might call a "beach," what a pessimist might call a "mud pile," but what a realist would call a "rocky shoreline." Dahlia didn't have much interest in debating about what to call it. Her main interest was in what was in the water. Her first introduction to the spot was similar to the one that made her meet Jill. She had tripped and fallen down the steep slope, but stopped tumbling about halfway down, thanks to a small indentation in the side of the hill that seemed to be put there for the very purpose of catching trippers. While regaining what she had of her senses, she looked beyond that which might have given her a broken leg, and there she discovered, with a proper amount of romance, a little rowboat. Its front was dragged onto the shore. It looked like someone had tried to tie it to the shore, but it was a meager, half-hearted attempt. The rope hung slack between the boat and a midweight boulder, while it seemed that the boat was secured mostly by a large rock beneath it. The rest of it bounced gently in the lapping waves. She adored it and thought about its quaintness and sweetness all the way back to the big house. Every time she walked past that spot, she intentionally stumbled down the slope a little ways to check on its well-being, and, in fact, made it into a little friend of hers. This, of course, demonstrates her utter loneliness. To my knowledge, one generally does not befriend rowboats unless they are exceedingly lonely. The rowboat never seemed to move an inch out of its usual place. It just loyally sat there, calmly bobbing around. She had no idea who it belonged to, but she decided to become friends with the owner, as well, by imagining him, or her, rowing away in Rowboat, (as Dahlia cleverly named it) splashing off into a darling adventure. The owner always came to her mind as an old, widower fisherman, with a long, silver beard and dark brown eyes. She imagined him back in his younger days (with a shorter beard and lighter eyes, of course) rowing around the bay with a secret lover, a rich girl from Spain who jumped overboard a yacht, running away from her tyrannical father. She and the lowly fisherman rowed and rowed together in the summertime as they courted, then got married on a sunny day in Fall. But soon thereafter she died of malaria. (How she got malaria, Dahlia couldn't tell, but she thought it was an interesting way to die.) And so the old fisherman abandoned the little rowboat, never stepping foot in it again, in fear of it bringing back painful memories of dear Agatha, (not a particularly Spanish name, but Dahlia didn't know any Spaniards, so she had to make do) and instead he devoted his days to staring out despondently over the sea, saying softly, "Oh, Agatha, why, why?" So this afternoon she decided to borrow her hypothetical friend's boat, to row away into the bay. It wouldn't be any inconvenience to Rowboat's owner. After all, it wasn't Rowboat's fault that its owner was a depressed, negligent widower. Dahlia would show it a good time, and it would be grand.

Dahlia half-walked, half-stumbled, half-tripped—oh dear, that's too many halves. Well, change the proportions into thirds, and we'll continue on—down the slope, then, at last, she set her feet on the muddy shore. Her heart pumped an excited feeling through her whole body, and everything throbbed happily. It was an adventure! An actual adventure into the unknown! She then frowned, but only for a moment—entering the boat required a brief stroll through salty mud. The ankles would have to be submerged. But she began smiling again. She reassured herself with the words, "*Adventure*, Dahlia, dear! *Adventure*!" She secured her hat with a couple of tugs, then advanced through the slimy element before her. But soon another inconvenience cropped up—the proper way to get into the boat with mud-enveloped feet. "Quite," she mumbled. She then began before she knew exactly how she was going to end. She threw her arms out and grabbed the opposite side of the rowboat. She then pulled, and the right foot was released easily. But her left wasn't about to be emancipated. "Quite!" she said again, now somewhat angrily. The anger empowered her, and she used all the force she could muster to remove herself from the predicament. The mud suddenly became compliant to her wishes. So suddenly, in fact, that she went flying forward, headfirst, into the boat. "*Adventure*, Dahlia! *Adventure*," she repeated to herself happily, as she stiffly readjusted herself into an upright position. Her feet were wet and muddy and her face was hurting, but somehow, she was extremely happy. As if to test the resilience of this happiness, a few clouds that seemed distant just a few minutes ago were now looming towards and nearly over the Isle, growing darker as they got closer. But these clouds didn't do anything except fuel her adventurousness. She grinned, rubbed her hands together quickly in excitement, then placed them on the oars beside her. They were coarser than she expected them to be, but it didn't matter too much to her. As long as they were in her hands, she was content.

She stretched her arms and back, then began her voyage. While trying out the oars, she tried her best to imitate the movements she had seen in movies. They were usually circular. She soon came to the realization that in order for the oars to go *up*, she must press the handles *down*. But to her surprise, they required more effort than she'd assumed they would. But being a beefy, determined girl helped her to push past her worries and to push the oars downwards. She soon realized that to properly set out into the sea, one must be unattached to any land. The boat's front—or *bow*, I suppose I should call it like a proper mariner—still clung to the shore. The boat was small, though, and could be easily maneuvered. Pushing off was no great pain, with the help of an extended, wooden arm.

Things began to feel ever more exciting when she felt the sensation of buoyancy. Yes, she was floating! She was absolutely free! It was an utterly sensational feeling to float away from shore, being free to change directions, free to glide away from it all—powers she didn't have in her own life. Soon, however, Dahlia realized that it would be necessary to learn how to steer the vessel. So she broke away from her reverie to teach herself how to be a captain. She was already proud of her ingenuity, using her oar to push herself off of the shore. The oar could not be said to be unaffected by its newly acquired skill. It was now more chipped and dented than it once was. But as long as the newly appointed captain hadn't any clue about the damage, everything was rosy. The oncoming weather, though, was anything but rosy. Dahlia was not a reckless person, as you might be thinking. She was anything but. It simply did not occur to her that anything dangerous could happen. She only thought of adventure, and adventures could only end up happily. If she were to ask certain transcontinental explorers if they'd agree with her opinion, I believe that she'd be shocked by their replies.

She quickly—well, somewhat quickly—learned how to maneuver Rowboat, just enough to get her out a little ways, and just far enough away to put herself into danger. As she settled into her new role, the approaching clouds began cooling the bay. It was a humid sort of cold, a distinctly wet feeling in the air, the kind that is indicative only of rain. It didn't bother Dahlia, though. She was confident that she wouldn't be gone for terribly long, and if she was, a little rain wouldn't hurt her.

I will not allow you to go on thinking that Dahlia was planning to wander off into the middle of the ocean, flounder around a bit —goodness, maybe even *see* a flounder—and then somehow return to shore. She was not purposeless. She was going to row out towards a mass of land that had filled her days with curiosity—Prince Island, where she hoped to crawl around on the large rocks on its magnificent beaches and go up to the house and become marvelous friends with the shy little man who lived in it.

What could possibly go wrong? Or, to those who prefer to be less naive, what could possibly go right?

The smiling flower Dahlia shined amidst the dark, watery field surrounding her. Her sturdy arms caught on to their assigned motions, and the waves kindly assisted her on the voyage out. The waves' hue at the beginning was as inviting as the waters were calm. Gradually, however, both the ocean's hue and temperament began to sullen. The cheery blues that once greeted her now faded into a stormy gray, and the playful laps against the boat's sides grew into bullying shoves. As Dahlia began to notice the symptoms of impending disaster, she also noticed that, no matter what she tried to do, she could not make Petit Homard come closer. Her arms complained with shivers and trembles, and the power gained by excitement began to wear off.

Something curious then occurred—she heard a low rumble. She looked inquisitively down at her stomach. "Why, I just ate an hour and a half ago!" she thought, wondering why her stomach was grumbling so gratuitously. As if to clarify its origin, the rumble repeated itself. Indeed, its source deeply surprised her—it came, not from within, but from a dark mass looming above her. You could call it an extremely hungry cloud. It began accumulating other famished clouds, and then they began to shed communal tears. Dahlia began shaking all over now, because of a feeling virtually unknown to her—fear. Optimism and obliviousness had carried her through life without any excessive anxiety, but now danger stared at her in the face and even poked her in the eyes.

The "waves" that had assisted her journey out turned out to be more sinister than obliging. Their power increased and could now be properly identified as "currents." The "waves" that were once too happy to help now emerged as "currents" that were sure to drag her to who knows where. And Rowboat, which was once so easily controlled, now obstinately refused to be guided by anything except the path it was already on. Dahlia struggled valiantly, but even her stocky arms proved to be no match for the infinitely more powerful foe, the sea.

Now the English flower shriveled as waves began throwing Rowboat around. The wind picked up and threatened to toss her out of her vessel. She now discerned that the currents led her away from her intended destination, and instead chose a different one for her—the open ocean. The further out she went, the rougher her surroundings treated her. Dahlia was now in no position to think. So, finding that she could not stay awake during the plight, she involuntarily fell asleep. It saves one a great deal of trouble to go unconscious when they're in a situation they don't particularly like. I'd recommend fainting to anyone who likes the easy way out of problems.

# Chapter 19

You may be surprised to learn—as she was surprised, herself— that Dahlia Basset survived. Yes, when Dahlia opened her eyes, she happily discovered that she was not dead. A setting sun, spreading out its golden arms, embraced the scene with glowing, warm hues. It had broken through the assembly of clouds and created a peaceful end to an eventful day. This warmth was one of the only sensations Dahlia could consciously feel. She was breathing, she was salty, she was cold, and she was sun-struck. So far, her senses hadn't recovered enough to be put to any further use than to ascertain this.

The sun's beams curved over every protruding surface on the beach—numerous stones and boulders, calmed waves, and this young woman's restful body. She rallied enough strength to open an eyelid. Initially, the effort seemed to be fruitless. The only view her eye afforded her was a bleary, hazy-looking sky, which was in the process of turning from day's brilliant blue to night's darkness by means of an orange interlude. Her sense of hearing gradually came back into working order. She could now hear the gentle sounds of water stretching out across numerous rocks, then dragging them into its embrace, the rocks clattering as they took a few steps closer to a submerged state. This soothing sequence of noises strongly contrasted the noises she had heard exactly prior to her unconsciousness. They were fearful, loud sounds—crashing waves, sonorous thunder, and her own hearty cries. Now she was laying on a bed formed by the ocean. Waves would cover her, although the sea would rip away the blanket intermittently. It would then seem to be sorry and replace the blanket with another wave. Her pillow, she realized, was composed of an uncomfortable rock and some sporadically placed seaweed. She closed her eyes again and, with labor, moaned. She wished to be either totally revived or completely unconscious—this in-between business was miserable.

An hour elapsed before she opened her eyes again. And when she did open them, it was involuntarily. She awakened at the sensation of something breathing warm breaths upon her face. She opened her eyes to a wide, curious snout with a woolen frame staring into her face. She gasped out of surprise. She then began hearing its colleague's opinion of her: "*Baa! Baa!*" were its exact words. She heard their four-legged footsteps shuffle around, and then the sheep that initially greeted her turned away, and immediately afterward another one took its place. It was as if the herd was taking turns to examine her. The startling effect of the sheep's presence on her weak body caused her to feel woozy again. But before her consciousness slipped away entirely, she heard footsteps that didn't seem to be trodden by four hooves—they were two feet.

"*Qu'est-ce que ç'est?*" cried a masculine voice from above. She might have thought that his words were translated into gibberish through her waterlogged brain. However, her ears were not to blame for the strange language. He was speaking perfect French. The tone of his question combined feelings of concern with inconvenience and irritation. Whatever misgivings the owner of the voice had to unexpected company on his island, he nonetheless performed the bare minimum of his duties as a fellow human being, deciding to take her up to his house. He scooped her soaked body up into his arms and grumbled another French phrase as he carried her towards his cabin. The annoyed tone of his voice and his disapproving looks at where her wetness contacted his torso seemed to indicate that his complaints were about his now wet sweater.

The misfit couple now approached a humble, cabin type of dwelling, which was nestled within a few protective trees. In fact, those trees were amongst the few that were on the otherwise bare, grassy piece of rock. The grass was exceptionally green this evening. Everything was—the trees, the grass, the water, even poor Dahlia's face. But despite the greenness, she couldn't help but look beautiful in that evening's romantic lighting. Thankfully, the French-speaking hero wasn't too distracted by her beauty to not take care of her properly. If the roles were reversed, Dahlia would have been too taken with him to be of any use.

He faced a conundrum upon approaching the door of his dwelling. The handle was commonly stubborn, tricking and troubling him even when his arms weren't occupied by a pathetic castaway. He gritted his teeth in anger and perplexity. He grunted as he tilted forward, awkwardly trying to perform two tasks at once. But yes, he managed to somehow wiggle the handle, shaking Dahlia in the process, then kick the door open in a heroic stride. Now in the cabin, he looked around the two-roomed home. It was shoddily wallpapered some time ago, as its peeling edges and brown tinge revealed. He had left the decorating to its previous tenant, who died at least 40 years ago. The only alterations given it since then were the incidental ones created by a young, careless, artistic bachelor. In a word or so, it was a cluttered mess.

His quick eyes darted around the room, which was filled with books and canvases, searching for a resting place for the fair maiden in his arms—or, to him, for a way to remove the troubling wet thing from his soaked sweater. He first spotted a conventional place to put recumbent people—a bed. Half-concerned about the untidy state of it, and half-disgusted by the thought of having to dry wet blankets, he impetuously set for the one table in the entire house. One in a less distracted state might question the elderly table's structural integrity, being large and wooden. Dahlia was too similar in structure and was at great risk of collapsing it, being thickset in that healthy way, and, at this moment in unconsciousness, nearly wooden. Her rescuer didn't bother to notice these precarious similarities, and so with impressive flexibility, he kicked a mug off of the table and heavily set her down on it. After heaving a deep sigh, he breathily said in a soft exclamation, "*Elle est,*"—something, something—"*lourd*" or something or other. He seemed to be languishing over the fact that she was heavier than she looked.

Between the smashing of the kicked mug—an unsightly thing that he was grateful to be rid of—and being set down abruptly on a hard surface, Dahlia began to awaken. At first, she was all moans and groans, but when she awoke to a sight much more pleasant than that of curious sheep, she was instantly delighted. Standing over her was a much better-looking greeter. He was frowning, but she didn't mind. She smiled merrily.

"*Que fais-tu ici?*" he questioned coldly, without pity, asking what she was doing there.

"Dear, me! Did I float that far away?" Dahlia asked with a mortified expression, imagining that she had landed in France.

He smiled a little, but very wryly. "No, mademoiselle, you are not in France."

"Would it trouble you too much to tell me where I am, exactly?" she asked with a groggy, but dreamy, voice.

"I can, but only if you tell me what you are doing here."

"I was—I was—" she began, but turned green and began to faint again.

"Never mind, never mind!" he cried, deciding that he'd rather have a conscious trespasser in his home than an unconscious one. His resigned words weren't enough to stir her, so he gently slapped her salty face. She then began coughing violently. "Sit up, mademoiselle," he quickly said, trying to help her up. He soon realized, however, that even sitting up was a definite challenge for her. Begrudgingly, he realized that he would have to carry her again. Before her consciousness again fizzled away, he desperately asked, "Where do you come from?"

"England," she replied in a muffled, sleepy grumble. He looked at her in serious examination, ascertaining that if she indeed *did* float all the way from England, she'd be dead. He recalled seeing a rowboat washed ashore, a little distance away from the cloud of sheep that had formed around the girl. Another realization struck him—she couldn't have been from a place terribly far away, if her means of voyage was the flimsy vessel he had seen on the beach. This realization brought him great relief.

"You mean you were born in England, don't you, hm? But I do not care about where you were born. All I am worried about is getting you off my island."

"Awfully considerate," was the drowsy reply.

"Ah, ha!" he exclaimed, "You are awake enough to be funny, so you must be able to tell me where you live currently."

"Oh!" she said in a cry as forceful as her state would allow it to be, "Don't say 'current', those nasty things are what got me here."

If the Frenchman's patience hadn't been tested before, it certainly was dried up now. "Tell me where you are from, or I swear that I will throw you back where I found you!"

"Anywhere would be preferable to this dreadfully stiff bed."

"Agh!" he cried, his anger swelling, "Listen to me, or—"

"Well," Dahlia exclaimed, her sleepy eyes clearing up enough for her to survey the room. "Why, you only have one chair in the whole house!" If she were more with it, Dahlia would have done well to be more cautious around her indisposed host. Her befuddled condition, however, intensified her usual candidness and flippancy. One could not be sure, though, if she really would have behaved less aggravatingly with all of her faculties. Perhaps if she *had* all her wits, she would have gotten herself thrown into the ocean much sooner.

The Frenchman now seemed to be resigned to her ridiculousness. "*Oui*," he replied to her surprised exclamation, not feeling impelled to defend the sum of his furniture.

"In *my* house, we have at least sixteen chairs in every room."

The Frenchman now saw an opportunity to find out where she lived. "And where is ze place that has sixteen chairs in every room?" he inquired dryly.

"Petit Homard," she replied groggily, at last.

"*Enfin*!" he cried victoriously. His jubilation was cut short, though, when his guest involuntarily closed her eyes and slumped over into his arms. But if she was in a state where she could fully appreciate his good looks, I'm sure she wouldn't have minded the state of things.

With the necessary information finally received, he could now deliver her back where she belonged. He, however, had no idea where exactly the girl lived on the Isle. This would mean that he would have to go around and make inquiries. But this was something extreme to him. Avoiding such interaction was the very reason why he lived as far away from civilization as his circumstances allowed. The only way he could think of getting her off his island would be by shipping her off with the boat that brought him his bi-weekly supply of food. And that interaction brought him enough agitation in itself. But he decided that he would rather undergo the inconvenience of conversations with strangers than have to provide room and board for the girl until the next week. He hoped that the little boat that had so graciously deposited her onto his island would be good enough to take her back where she belonged.

So with this hesitant heroism as his drive, he slung her over his shoulder like she was a lifeless sack of potatoes and walked down to the very place he found her. The sheep had dissipated, with the exception of one, who affectionately butted its wooly head into the Frenchman's knees, almost making him throw the sack of potatoes into the sea like he once threatened. He skidded, but recovered, thankfully. After doing so he took a thorough look around. With another relieved sigh, he sighted the boat that bestowed Dahlia. His gratefulness increased when he realized that the boat didn't look as decrepit as the girl did. He threw the potato-y girl as cargo in the back and then pulled the rowboat into the water. With great ease, he rowed towards Petit Homard. When they got closer, he realized that she was looking slightly more awake. He might not have to ask around to find out who the girl was and where she lived after all! He paused from rowing and shook her shoulder. "Mademoiselle," he asked casually, "where do you live?" Only a murmur could be heard in reply. "What!" he returned, in more of an angry exclamation than a question. Her reply was agitated as well, but it couldn't be heard very well, because she was curled into a ball, her arms covering her head as if rocks were falling from the sky. He flattened his lips in irritation. He paused, then leaned back and shook her again. "Eh? Where do you live, eh?"

"None of your business," was the reply, which would have been a very wise one in any other situation involving a stranger.

The Frenchman sighed while looking up at the evening sky that was closing in. The sun was setting gently in the west, the sky dishonestly looking like it had been calm all day long. While looking around at all of this, he remembered their discussion about the proper amount of chairs a home ought to have. "How many chairs did you say are in your 'ouse?"

"Oh, hundreds, undoubtedly," was the carefree reply.

"And where is zis 'ouse zat contains zese uncountable amounts of chairs?"

"By the sea."

He laughed a laugh of utter frustration. "A big 'ouse, ay? Big enough to hold anywhere from sixteen to hundreds of chairs?"

"Some might even call it a mansion."

"Ah, ah! *Un manoir*!" he cried in excitement, feeling the closest thing to happiness that he had felt in a number of years. He recalled once hearing the man who delivered foodstuffs to him talk about a mansion on the eastern shore of Petit Homard. Now the Frenchman could deliver her to her house with as much ease as a milkman delivering his product with nothing more than a knock on the door. Now knowing the general direction to go in, he rowed up to the east side of the Isle, avoiding the docks, a place where questions would be raised and answers would be required.

Beneath a deep blue sky that slowly enveloped the Isle, the little boat inched up to the little beach that was in front of the Basset's mansion. Rowboat gently ran aground against the sloping mass of rock that formed the majority of the lovely beach. The Frenchman who once was so concerned about his shirt getting wet was now wading hip-deep in the water as he dragged the little rowboat onto land. Looking back at the boat's contents, the potato deliveryman now began to notice the beauty of his delivery. Her prettiness was augmented by the cool highlights of the approaching twilight. The realization that the young creature was actually ailing made him pick her up more carefully. In his eyes, she transformed from a sack of potatoes to a crate of fragile eggs. Not a very romantic comparison, but it will do. With the belated acknowledgment that here in front of him was a young woman who was actually imperiled came more conscientiousness and urgency. With Dahlia in his arms, he walked as quickly as he could towards the huge house that loomed ahead of him. Other young men might be intimidated by such a house, but the Frenchman was beyond intimidation. He didn't fear anything. He was just vexed by everything.

With the sudden gallantry that overtook him came the decision to not just knock on the house's door and abandon her, as the indifferent milkman of a few moments ago would have. There was no time for a knock, and he became too concerned to leave her on the doorstep like some sort of baby orphan. Instead, he would enter this grand dwelling like how he usually entered his own humble home, with a kick.

Wiggling the handle and kicking the door open was no challenge for him. The door acquiesced to the harsh treatment given it, and he busted into the entryway like some sort of bank robber. Thankfully, Adkins wasn't attending the door at that moment. He was engaged with preparing dinner. This included the task of tenderizing the meat. As Adkins had plenty of aggression to release that afternoon, he couldn't hear anything beyond the meat mallet in his hand, not even the rash entrance of the Frenchman. Mr. Basset, though, wasn't tenderizing anything at the moment, so he happened to hear the violent opening of the front door. He appeared just as the Frenchman was considering what to do next.

"Oh!" said this Mr. Basset upon seeing a young man in his entryway. The Frenchman seemed to be more rattled by Mr. Basset's sudden arrival than Mr. Basset was at seeing an utter stranger in his entryway. "Allo, there, good fellow! Awfully nice to see a new face around here," Mr. Basset greeted as he jauntily walked down the stairs. "I suppose that you're one of our neighbors, and you dropped by to introduce yourself." The Frenchman looked at the old fellow in utter disbelief. Now on the same floor as his visitor, Mr. Basset realized that Dahlia was limply hanging there in the visitor's arms. "Oh, there you are, Dahlia, you sneaky thing!" he said to her, the thought that something bad had happened being so far away from his mind that he treated her as if she were standing upright. "You've been gone for hours, my dear! Old Addie came up and said to me, 'Sir, Miss Basset has been gone for half the day.' He said it in that boring, serious voice of his, you know. But I said to Addie, "No, no, there is no doubt in my mind that dear Dahlia is just fine, just fine, indeed. She's practically a grown girl, and she's probably just gallivanting in the forest.' Of course, I wasn't expecting you to come back here with a young man, but see, you prove me right to Adkins, yes, here you are, perfectly safe and sound..." But just as Mr. Basset looked more closely at his daughter, surprised that she hadn't interrupted him yet, he realized that things weren't as peachy as they seemed to be. The Frenchman shifted his posture, and her arms then flopped down from their folded position and dangled there in the air. Now Mr. Basset was horrified. "Addie!" he cried out, his butler's name being his usual reply to distress.

"Where is her bedroom?" the Frenchman asked curtly. "She looks a little tired." The father replied by running out of the room to get Adkins. The Frenchman gave up on the old man and decided to look for a place to put her down on his own. He repeated what he had said before, about her being heavier than she looked, then began ascending the staircase.

Mr. Basset, on the other hand, was headed in the opposite direction, to get the man who could do everything Mr. Basset couldn't. The perplexed and terrified father skidded into the kitchen, like a cat on ice skates. For the first few moments, Mr. Basset could do nothing more than play a game of charades. Adkins watched on, setting down the tenderizer that was suspended in the air when Mr. Basset came in. Adkins' brow furrowed in absolute confusion. He was never one for party games, and he wasn't in the mood to amuse his employer. Finally, though, he got a clue from the flailing Mr. Basset.

"Is something the matter, sir?" the butler calmly inquired. This moved the charader to reply in a gasp—"DAH-lia!" The butler now began to feel the concern he ought to have been feeling all along. Mr. Basset wheezed a few more times, then ran out of the room, breathless both from excitement and from the fact that he hadn't run in at least ten years.

Adkins chased Mr. Basset up the stairs, while the Frenchman had quietly taken care of matters without anyone else's help. The men of the house ran around, searching each room in a frantic game of cat and mouse. Eventually, they found the one they sought. It wasn't with any skill that they did so. The Frenchman found *them*. He exited Mr. Basset's bedroom and softly shut the door behind him. He stopped, looked at the fellows that stared consternatedly at him, squared his shoulders as if he was about to say something, then walked directly past them. The fellows were, at the moment, more concerned about Dahlia than him, so his sudden departure suited them all equally. Adkins swung the bedroom door open, then Mr. Basset peeked over his butler's shoulder. Beyond lay Dahlia in the bed, the covers neatly over her, looking exceedingly peaceful. Adkins then turned to Mr. Basset in alarm. "Sir, we must find out who that man was!"

"Why, yes, yes, of course!" Mr. Basset replied emphatically. So the great chase continued back down the stairs that they had just scurried up.

"Stop where you are, young man!" cried Mr. Basset, like a fatherly policeman. The Frenchman stopped walking and nodded at them. Having thus adequately obeyed, he walked through the front door that had been left open without a word. The fellows stumbling after him persisted, though, following him outside. But it was almost too dark to hope to catch the details of any particular object.

"What is the matter with Miss Basset?" Adkins asked authoritatively.

"She doesn't 'sink that I 'ave enough chairs," he replied as he kept walking away.

"But, but," Mr. Basset sputtered, "won't you at least tell us your name, good fellow?"

"As ze girl once said to me, 'It is none of your business.'" With this strange farewell, he jogged down to the beach at a pace much faster than the older fellows could keep up with.

# Chapter 20

*Friday, May 19th*

To everyone's relief, Dahlia eventually woke up. The day that Dahlia went missing, Jill had been working for Mr. Basset. Both Jill and Adkins worried about Dahlia's unknown whereabouts, but they couldn't convince her father to be, so they satisfied themselves with worrying about her in the privacy of their thoughts. Jill came to work for him the next day, and upon arriving there she received a full account (or, at least, an account as full as it could be for someone who was unconscious through most of the adventure) from Dahlia. So instead of being Mr. Basset's secretary for the day, Jill was assigned to be Dahlia's nurse. If nothing else, Dahlia was provided with an enraptured listener.

After listening for a while, Jill said thoughtfully, "It seems like ever since I've come here, people keep getting hurt."

"It is a gift of ours!"

"Accidently hurting people?"

"Precisely!"

Jill sighed. "Why couldn't we be prodigies or virtuosos, like other gifted people?"

"Well, the harm we cause always seems to lead to us meeting good-looking blokes."

"Well, maybe it's a gift after all. We all have our methods, don't we?"

As Jill finished saying this, the girls suddenly began hearing agitated, confused noises from downstairs. They then could hear hurried, heavy footsteps coming up the stairs, and before they could guess what was going on, the bedroom door swung open, and there before them was yesterday's rescuer. Dahlia could hardly recognize him. Whether this was because she was half-awake when they first met or because his appearance had been altered since then, she couldn't tell. Here at the door's threshold was, not yesterday's rugged, messily groomed and disheveled-in-dress hero, but a *less* messy, *less* disheveled gentleman. Dahlia and the hero took a few moments to stare at each other in confusion. Jill looked between them with an amused smile, then got up, smiled at Dahlia (who didn't notice), and left the room. The hero only acknowledged Jill by stepping aside slightly to let her pass through the doorway.

"Hello!" Dahlia said.

"Bonjour, mademoiselle."

"Please, call me Dahlia, sir. I am so pleased to meet you," she replied while thrusting out her hand for a handshake like a harpoon.

A smile appeared on his face. It was an unusual smile, a kind that he'd never had before. A sort of bashfulness was discernible. While he stood over there bashfully, Dahlia was smiling brilliantly at him in delight. He was even better looking than how she remembered him. While she based this abrupt improvement of looks on her complete consciousness, the truth of the matter was that he had actually gone out of his way to improve his looks himself. Although the "improvement" would still be deemed "disarranged" to the average eye, the changes, to him, were drastic. He combed his hair, (he ran his fingers through his hair in a deliberate way) put on his best sweater, (the one with the least amount of holes in it) and his best boots (the ones with the least caked-on mud on them.) The boots were even shined, though unintentionally, by being rinsed off in the briny water he again had to wade through to land on the Basset's beach. There was even the suggestion of a necktie wrapped loosely around his neck, tied in a half-hearted cravat style.

"As you wish—*bonjour,* Dahlia," said the greatly improved man, stepping forward and firmly shaking her hand.

His accent made her smile. It was unique—she had heard French accents before, and this wasn't the kind that she remembered. She then frowned worriedly. "But what should I call you? I hate calling you 'sir, sir' all the time. Even your polite little name for me—'made-moist-elle' (she said in a very proper voice)—makes me feel like a queen, but what does 'sir' do for anyone?"

"It might make zem feel like a knight."

Dahlia's heart melted like butter on toast. "I'd—truly, I'd like to thank you for saving my life, sir—oh, there I go again. Knight or not, I do not like 'sir'."

"Remi," he said quietly.

"What?"

"I have not introduced myself in many years, and I don't like to do it."

"But, what was it? What was the name?" Dahlia asked eagerly.

He cleared his throat. "Remi," he said more clearly.

"Remi!" she cried in immediate adoration. "How perfectly lovely! What is your last?"

"Ay?"

"Your last name, what is it?"

"Oh—Roy. Remi Roy."

"I adore it! Two R's in a row, like that! Oh, what is it called when that sort of thing happens?"

"Ay?" he asked again.

"Oh," she said in an antsy way, "you know, when the letters are all the same—goodness, what on earth is that called?"

"*Alliteration,* Miss Basset," came an unsolicited reply from Adkins as he happened to be passing by the open door in the hallway. Although the helpful comment was startling, the interlocutors quickly returned giving their undivided attention to each other.

"Ehm, Dahlia," Remi said, pulling out something from behind his back, "I brought you zese—em, *fleurs.*" The gift now came into full view, a delightful assortment of wildflowers.

"Oh!" Dahlia cried, "they are just beautiful!" As he brought them closer, Dahlia's smile diminished, but only slightly. "Oh, look—these poor dears are more of invalids than I am!"

Remi, noting her dismay, quickly explained, "Ze sheeps did it."

"Ze sheeps?—I mean, what sheep?"

"Don't you remember zem?"

"Well!—I remember having some strange dream about sheep staring down at me."

"It was not a dream. Ze sheeps are what made me find you. I was walking by the ocean, and I saw zer fluffy bodies down zer in a circle. Zey never go down to the beach. So I went down to see what zey were maa-ing about."

"My, I don't even know where you live!"

"Mouton Île."

Dahlia frowned—she knew that she didn't float away to France, but his island couldn't have been anywhere near Petit Homard. He quelled her confusion and continued, "But ze people around call it something like, like 'Prince Island', I 'sink. But I prefer to use ze French name—"

"Thank goodness!" she said in a sigh of relief, interrupting him. "I didn't go too far from home after all. But wait!" she then exclaimed, pointing at him with wide eyes, "You—you're that terrible man!"

"Ay?"

"You—you're the recluse, the, the man who keeps that lovely island to himself! But you're supposed to be old, aren't you?"

"Am I?"

"Yes, you are! You're supposed to be old and, and ugly and mean and—"

"Am I!" Remi said with a laugh, "But I am not old—ugly and mean, maybe, but—"

"Surely you're not! But—who is that terrible old man, then?"

"Perhaps you 'sink of my uncle? He lived on Mouton Île many years ago. But he is very dead, now."

"So—you aren't a recluse?"

"No, I *am*."

"Oh… well, alright, be a recluse. It doesn't seem like a very nice way to live, but if that's that, what can I do about it? Anyhow, I quite like your name for Prince Island, it sounds so regal—tell me, what does it mean?"

The man who once seemed unafraid of anything now bowed his head hesitantly. He soon decided to take whatever he was about to say in stride, and so with a smirk he said, "It means 'Sheep Island.'"

"Oh!" Dahlia exclaimed with a delighted laugh. "But how on earth did sheep get on your island? Did someone drop 'em out of an aeroplane?"

"My uncle brought zem on a boat from Quebec to begin a little farm. But he died, and ze sheeps began running ze island. Zey are terrible pests, now," he explained, thereafter mumbling something in French angrily.

"So they ate the flowers, hm? Oh well—the greenery's quite good, at least."

"*Oui*, I'm glad you noticed." After replying so, he looked around the room, looking uncomfortable. But he quickly regained composure and, while turning towards the door, said, "I must go now. I leave you to rest."

"But," Dahlia protested anxiously, sitting up straighter in her bed, nearly jumping out of it, "I'm very rested! I feel very well!"

"*Je ne*," he said, but not intending for it to be heard.

"What was that?"

He said, "I'm not" in French, Dahlia, but you didn't hear. "No, I cannot stay," he said firmly, "I apologize for using your rowboat to return to my island, but I had no other way to get back—"

"It's no matter to me, it's not even my boat, after all."

Remi was shocked. "You—you *stole* it?"

"No! Well, I—I borrowed it. We're old friends."

"You and ze owner?"

"No, I and the boat." This confused Remi's indignant mind even further. Not able to comprehend the perplexity, he turned to leave. "Wait—perhaps you and Adkins could row out together, and then Adkins could row the boat back!"

"Who?"

"Adkins, our butler!"

"No, no, no," Remi replied decidedly, not liking the idea of being confined to a small boat with a stuffy butler, "I'll swim."

"Don't be ridiculous!"

"Did I hear you call, Miss Basset?" asked Adkins, who suddenly appeared again, stiffly standing in the doorway.

"Is your name 'Ridiculous?'" Remi inquired smugly. "It fits you." Adkins didn't attempt to repress an angry expression.

"Well, Adkins, I was just suggesting to Mr. Remi Roy," said Dahlia, taking an opportunity to enunciate the entirety of his delicious name, "that you and he take Rowboat back to Prince Island, and then you can row it back! What fun you'll have!"

"I am afraid that it is out of the question, Miss Basset," was the immediate, curt reply to the suggestion.

"It is, it is!" Remi enthusiastically agreed, then grabbed Adkins' arm and began examining it. "I am not sure if ze twiggies could row all the way back, anyhow."

Adkins, who had been too shocked to recoil, now shook Remi off. Adkins glared at the arm connoisseur and was about to retort when cheery Mr. Basset walked up and stood between them. "What is this, what is this? An odd place for a party, but I must admit that I quite like it. Now, what were you chappies talking about, anyhow?" he asked while clasping his hands together.

"His arms," said Remi with a wry glance. Adkins came near fuming. Even Mr. Basset, as fanciful as he was, could not reply to the reply, so he stood there and just blinked at them. Then Dahlia explained her brilliant idea of Remi Roy and Adkins rowing out together.

"But why row out at all? Why don't you skip it altogether, while we have you as a houseguest, Mr. Roy!" Both of the Bassets lit up. The other two, however, glanced at each other with mutual abhorrence of the idea. They began quickly presenting the challenges that would prove the invitation impossible.

"Mr. Roy does not have any clothing with him, sir—not that I imagine he has many changes of clothing," said Adkins with a snobbish look up and down at the guest.

"But I changed just last week," said Remi in droll reply.

"Well, Mr. Roy can borrow my clothes, Addie," said Mr. Basset, "so there's no need to worry yourself, though it was awfully considerate of you."

"Ah—'considerate'—*zat's* ze word I was trying to 'sink of to describe ze Adkins," said Remi.

"Although, I am afraid that my clothes might be a tad large on your toothpick figure," Mr. Basset continued, "but I hope that you won't mind."

"It seems, sir, that Mr. Roy would not mind, seeing that it is his custom to wear his clothes a few sizes too large, anyways," said Adkins, looking down at Remi like some fashion pundit.

"Then you'll be right at home!" Mr. Basset said excitedly.

"You must 'ave good vision, Mr. Adkins, being able to look all the way down your nose at me," Remi said, while Adkins covered his nose with his hand in horror. Now Remi's worst fear had been realized. He was a victim of hospitality that he could not refuse. Mr. Basset was in such a grand state of jollity that he couldn't do anything for the rest of the day except rejoice in having another house guest. Jill was invited to stay for the evening, Adkins assigned himself the task of returning the rowboat to its owner, and Remi was forced to accept an invitation to the dinner table that evening. There were only two advantages to his coming to dinner; the first, being able to look upon Dahlia's pretty face, which glowed upon the certainty of his extended stay, and the second was that his arrival moved Adkins to make the meat especially tender.

# Chapter 21

*Sunday, May 21st*

Never had the Islanders ever been so intrigued by the Basset's affairs until Jill spread the fantastic account of their adventurous introduction to Remi Roy. Whether Jill was responsible for this spread could be a matter of controversy. She *did* tell Mary Pine about it, after all. Mary then told Bobbie, who then told Haddock.

Two days after Remi had been convinced to stay as a houseguest at the Bassets', Jill and Penny decided to pay the happy little group a visit. On their way over, they began discussing the many invalids the Bassets had hosted since Jill arrived, which inevitably led them to start talking about Haddock.

"I find it very funny, Penny, that the self-proclaimed bike mechanic couldn't figure out your little bicycle," Jill continued, laughing a little in evidence.

"Oh, I wouldn't judge his mechanical skills by that. That old bike has baffled mechanic and layman alike. Besides, after he brought it back, I realized that I'd be sad if it went back to being a normal bicycle, just like how I'd be sad if you ever decided to be normal—oh dear, look, he's coming up behind us!"

Yes, Haddock happened to meet up with them on the road, since they all had decided to visit the invalid and her hero. While the Fish and Jill's cousin talked about the weather, Jill kept glancing at his birthmarked face. Somehow, that dark splotch on his face gave it a nice effect. Admiration grew, an admiration that was getting less silly and more significant by the day. This happened with the acknowledgment that his good qualities shone out at the most opportune times. These distressingly positive feelings about him were routinely checked with recollections of Mary's opinion of him. But even this thought was tempered with the knowledge of Mary's dislike for things in general. So Jill decided that she would have to judge him for herself. So far, she couldn't help but like him, but she was determined to find out exactly why.

The unlikely trio walked up to the front door and were permitted entry. Adkins gave them the expected dry, generic greeting due to each of them. Penny was given the unexpected, confusing pleasure of receiving a greeting that might have been called personal. There was a certain apprehension in his air, and he nearly looked her in the eyes. He managed to address her in a way as dry and subtle as was possible, considering the strange intensity of his admiration for her. But it would take more than a dull "good afternoon, Miss Fargo" to catch her. Adkins, thoroughly unversed in these kinds of things, did not yet understand this fact, and was thus disappointed when the only reply given was an empty echo of what he had just said to her.

They all went up the stairway, being led by Adkins to a sitting room. The door to it was open, and within could be seen Remi sitting in a little wooden chair beside Dahlia, who was languishing on a couch. When the four arrived, Remi stood up in a peeved kind of way. They had interrupted their conversation.

"You have visitors, Miss Basset," said Adkins with that insufferable formality of his. Having fulfilled his duty, he took leave, deciding that he'd rather not run the risk of having his arms, or lack thereof, insulted by Mr. Roy.

"Oh, my, what a delight to see you all!" cried Dahlia, clasping her hands together in the same exact way her father did when he was excited, "Look, all my dearest friends. Is there anything I can get any of you? Tea, perhaps? No? Well, have a mint." Haddock, unaware of the trap set before him, smiled and nodded, took a mint from the bowl raised to him by Dahlia, and popped it into his mouth without a second thought. Well, the second thought *did* come eventually, as did buggy eyes and a stifled cough. "Now how is that, Haddock?" Dahlia inquired. If she wasn't oblivious, one would think she was utterly evil.

"Now, Haddock," Jill said, patting him on the shoulder, "don't *mints* words."

Dahlia continued onwards with the conversation: "And now I get to introduce you to a very good friend of mine—my, it feels like we've known each other for ages, doesn't it?—this is Remi Roy, from Prince Island—oh, sorry, Remi—from *Mouton Île*." At this, all three of the friends stepped forward at once, in eager choreography, making Remi recoil.

"Pleasure to meetcha, Remi," Haddock said with a cough, reaching Remi's hand first.

"But, Haddock!" Dahlia cried, "you are not saying his name right."

"It is no matter, madmois—" Remi interjected.

"But it *does* matter! Mr. Roy has told me that he is full French-Canadian—"

"—*Quebecois*—" he put in firmly, a man proud to be born in Quebec.

"And so we ought to say our R's as he does. Come now, say your name so that we can learn how to say it right."

Remi, feeling a mixture of amusement and embarrassment by the girl's insistence, then said "Remi" in full French fashion. Dahlia then invited his audience to participate. They then gave a weak attempt.

"No, no!" Dahlia cried disapprovingly, "you have to sound like a cat hacking a hairball to make the R's sound right. Now, let's practice the noise together!"

"I really do not think zat zey must—" Remi began.

"Now, repeat after me," Dahlia continued unswervingly, "*Hhgh, hhgh, hhgh, hhgh.*" Her students repeated the hideous noise in chorus. "Much better!" Dahlia cried, feeling very proud of them. She then turned to Remi. "Wasn't it much better?"

"Yes, yes, much!" he replied, in delighted awe of her oddities. In fact, he was actually *smiling.* The sensation of the creation of a smile on his face made the muscles required sore, as he was so terribly out of practice. If muscles could creak because of disuse, then his certainly would have at that moment. Dahlia's command went out again, "Alright, again!" Soon the room filled with a guttural rhythm. Adkins happened to reenter the room at the height of it. Realizing that he had come back in, the room gradually went silent. He looked around at all in the room, as if to make sure that he hadn't accidentally walked into a psychiatric ward, or, if nothing else, a room filled with asthmatic pugs. After he had recovered as much as he could, he nodded at Mr. Basset as he jounced into the room. Apparently, Adkins had informed him of the sudden party.

"How perfectly spiffing to have a party of this size so unexpectedly!" Mr. Basset exclaimed with sparkling blue eyes. He considered any gathering of four or more as a party, whether the guests agreed with the definition or not. "Say, Dahlia, are you well enough to get back to your constitutional?"

Dahlia gasped, responding with great exhilaration: "Why, we all should go walk on the beach together! The day was made for it! Won't you come walk with me, Remi?" she asked, turning to him with puppy-dog eyes. Remi, though not one to usually be so affected by puppies, acquiesced to the invitation. Seeing that he did, the rest were only too happy to comply as well.

So Dahlia and her troop set out of the house as quickly as possible, the herd traipsing behind their host and the Frenchman—or, as Remi would put in, "the Quebecois." The pace of the herd increased as they got closer to the sunny destination. On the expedient hike, Dahlia disclosed Remi Roy's entire family history to the group. Her self-assumed role as Remi's historian served everybody well. The audience was curious about it, and Remi didn't have to say a word. Remi Roy, as it turned out, was *not* a Frenchman, but a Canadian. "A *Canadian*, could you believe?" Dahlia exclaimed, her bright eyes flashing back at her audience. "Yes, he was born and raised in Que-neck—"

"*Québec*, mademoiselle—" Remi cut in.

"Oh, yes, yes, Que-deck, how could I forget?" she said in quick acknowledgment of the abrupt clarification, not bothered by it, and continued without losing any momentum, "And his father is very successful—he owns a huge shipping company."

"He makes a lot of money—he's no success in any other way," Remi put in with a grumbly voice.

"Oh, yes! And because Remi got so fed up with his dad's nasty business, he pushed off from the whole thing and bought Prince Island."

"Huh!" said Haddock, "You just decided to go and *buy* an island, eh?"

"Yep," said Penny sarcastically from the back of the group, "it was between an apartment and a personal island for me once, but I took the apartment. I figured that the island would be too much upkeep."

"I didn't buy ze island at all!" Remi cried. "Ze island's been in my family for a very long time. My great uncle bought it a long time ago, for ze same reason I came here, to get away from all ze crazies in ze world. But my family despises ze island because it's so far away from zer business."

"So what do you do for work? Or are you one of those privileged sons who've never worked a day in their lives?" Haddock asked.

"No, no, no! I detest idleness and hate monotony. I am a painter."

"Oh? What do you paint?" Penny asked.

"With all the beauty around here, the question is what *don't* you paint?" Jill added.

"I like to paint boulders."

"*Boulders*?" everyone said.

"Mm, well, *a* boulder, on Mouton Île's beach."

"Why?" Haddock asked.

"Its shape! Its shadows! Its, its meaning! I will show you my work one day, and you will see what I mean."

"When I was laying on your table in your little house and I saw all those paintings of rocks, I thought that I was seeing double, but perhaps that's not the case after all," Dahlia said thoughtfully.

"Out of all the things to paint, he paints rocks," Haddock muttered.

"You speak excellent English, Mr. Roy," Penny remarked amiably, although she was thinking what Haddock was mumbling.

"I like to read, mademoiselle, both English and French books. Besides, my father made me learn English. It is the language of business, he says," said Remi, as if English was a burden.

"And here we are," said Dahlia with an adoring smile at her Quebecois guest. The group now stopped walking, their feet having reached their destination. "I am going to take my shoes off," Dahlia announced, kicking off her sandals. Everyone thought it a cheery sentiment, except for Adkins, who raised his brows. She explained, "Really, the rocks are too warm to not enjoy. Won't you take your shoes off, too, Remi?"

He hesitated. "No, no, I don't 'sink so."

"I'm disappointed!" Haddock said, dropping to a rock adequately qualified to be a bench and loosening his bootlaces, "Looks like I'm going to have to man up and be the only guy brave enough to let my feet see the sunlight."

After watching Haddock labor over his shoelaces, Jill said, "Well, I can't let the men outnumber us, Dahlia."

Mr. Basset then proclaimed that if were about thirty or forty years younger, he would have joined in himself. But after expounding, to an unwilling audience, on the nauseating maladies that afflicted his feet, he decided to sit on an even section of the beach where he could set down a lawn chair without any great inconvenience. The only inconvenience would be having to tell Adkins to go and fetch it for him.

After this point, the group broke off into three distinct couples. Mr. Basset is not included among these, as he had settled himself on a portion of the beach which the younger generation deemed uninteresting. Having sufficiently set the scene, we shall now eavesdrop on each of the couples.

~~~

There Miss Penny Fargo was, standing there, quietly amusing herself with watching the others. Although she knew that she wouldn't like to throw her own shoes off so flagrantly as the others did, she enjoyed watching them enjoy themselves. She was not mortally offended by their conduct like her secret admirer was. Adkins felt so emboldened, at just the sight of her, that he daringly considered starting a conversation with Miss Fargo. "No, no," he thought in a scold at himself, "Preposterous! Far too forward a notion—"

His pious thoughts were then interrupted—and his notion suddenly gratified—when a man, who was gradually supplanting Mrs. Whitby the goose as Adkins' foremost antagonist, called out to him: "Ay, why does not ze Englishman take off ze shoes?" This was, of course, Remi, who himself had submitted to Dahlia's whims and removed his feet's encumbrances.

Mortified, Adkins replied instantly, "Surely not! I'll never take off ze shoes—my shoes."

"Mm," the taunt continued, "zat will make things interesting in ze bathtub."

"I'm not particularly inclined towards taking off my shoes," Penny commented while looking at Adkins' fuming
~~~

expression with a smile, “but I think that if they want to, let ‘em knock themselves out.”

“I’ve never been happier to hear a woman say I should be knocked out,” Remi replied.

“What do you have against it, Mr. Adkins, hm? Stuck in the 19th century, as usual? You ought to give the century up, it’s been over for a good sixty years,” Penny said.

Adkins, who had been involved in this conversation from the distance of Mr. Basset’s lawn chair, now reasoned that continuing the conversation from this distance would be impolite. And so he walked over to her, contentedly stumbling upon a way to talk to her without having to initiate the conversation.

“I don’t believe in uncovering any portion of my feet for the observation of the public eye. It is a silly and ungentlemanly practice,” Adkins said, giving a stinging look at Remi. The look went unnoticed, however, as Remi had begun walking along the beach with Dahlia.

Noticing the look, Penny said, “Seems like your look was wasted. Too bad, it was a good one, too.”

Adkins turned his head away and stared out at the ocean, hiding his discomposure with a frown. Penny didn’t seem to mind, or to even notice. She was distracted by looking at his shoes, imagining what lurked within. She was thoroughly diverted, as the wry smile on her face revealed. “I bet you have funny little toes.”

His head now swung around, completely shocked. “I do not!” he exclaimed.

“No, no, I’m positive that you do. They’re probably like little white sausages.”

“They are not!”

“I’d imagine that they’d have to be pasty, considering your policies about proper shoe removal. Your poor toes probably haven’t seen the light of day in decades.”

“I will not stand here and let you abuse the character of my toes!” Adkins cried, never feeling so flustered in all his life.

"Alright, I'll stop making fun of your toes if you'll walk with me down to that ledge over there. Do we have a deal?"

Adkins's emotions had never fluctuated as much as they did when he was in her company. Adkins smirked in disbelief as he looked into her expectant, no-nonsense eyes, then recollected himself and shook hands with her. "It is a deal, miss." He then confidently offered her his arm. If he wasn't an admirer of her previously, he would've refused the contract she offered. But, as it was, he was only too happy to consent. "Say, you aren't going to push me off the ledge, are you?"

"No, sir! That would be *most* unladylike."

~~~

"Do you ever get lonely, Remi?" Dahlia asked as they carefully climbed over precarious rocks of differing heights, getting closer to the water. She was careful to pronounce his name in proper French fashion.

"Please, mademoiselle," he said, cringing politely, "I prefer you to say my name in your English way."

"Why?" Dahlia cried, pausing in the middle of his assisting her in climbing from one rock to another, "After all, I don't want to be a hypocrite after teaching the party to say it correctly."

"But you don't say it correctly."

"I don't, don't I?"

"*Oui*—I don't like coming into a room and being greeted by something zat sounds like a—a—oh, what is it in English—a *carlin*, you know, one of those dogs with a, a face that looks like it's been hit with an iron but is still wrinkly—"

"A—a pug?"

"Yes—I don't like being greeted by people who sound like pugs with ze sniffles."

"I suppose that's reasonable—but Remi, you didn't answer my question."

"What was ze question, mademoiselle?"
~~~

Dahlia pursed her lips angrily. "If you can make me say 'Remi' the English way, then I can make you call me Dahlia—*just* 'Dahlia', no 'Miss' or 'Mad-muss-elle,' or whatever it is."

"But I thought you *liked* 'Mademoiselle.'"

"Well, I did, but it's much too formal for two whole day's acquaintance! Now answer the question."

"Ay?"

"How is such a pleasant, friendly young man like you able to sit alone in a house all day long?"

Remi laughed. "You call me 'friendly? Pleasant?' No one calls me zese 'sings."

"But you've been so friendly to me!"

Remi thoughtfully looked down at his bare feet. "Well," he said after this pause, "this is just because I 'sink you are—" He caught himself, then slyly encrypted his compliment in French: "You are *très gentil, et très jolie*."

Dahlia, unfortunately, was too occupied with losing her balance to fully appreciate the compliment. As the man helped her down from a large rock, suavely speaking in his fluid mother tongue, the smaller, slate-like rock beneath him decided to humiliate him. It flipped over, making him lose his own balance, thus ruining any chances of Dahlia maintaining her own. Dahlia yelped as she awkwardly stumbled down, while Remi regained his composure just in time to clumsily catch her. He groaned as he did so, again being victim to Dahlia's unexpected weight. With effort, he propped her back up on her feet. Dahlia opened her tightly shut eyes, then looked down at her sides, where Remi's rescuing arms were placed. She looked up at him and said, "Awfully like when we first met, isn't it?"

~~~

By this point, Haddock and Jill were walking in the opposite direction that Adkins and Penny were, and were a little distance from Remi and Dahlia. Finding that the
~~~

others had broken off, Haddock and Jill were forced to take a pleasant walk together. But the conversation left much to be desired.

"Nice weather," said Haddock, even though he didn't really want to say anything to the snob.

Annoyed by his laziness in choosing a subject, she replied, "Don't try that conversation out on me—I already heard your material when you were talking to Penny on the way over here. I don't think I can listen to it all over again."

"Fair enough," he said, even though he didn't think it was very fair at all.

Jill now frowned as they walked on—she realized that she had just extinguished the one subject either of them could think of things to say about. "How about we talk about, em—well, what can we talk about?"

"How about those new pants you had on as you came out of Mary's?"

Jill smiled, then frowned. "That experience was actually a little traumatic."

"Ah, yes, I could understand. Clothes seem to be the only love of your life."

Jill's frown changed into a scowl. "Well, speaking of which, how's that old rustbucket you call a motorcycle?"

"It's a *nice* rustbucket, and it's doing just fine." After a pause, he decided to proceed cockily, "I did sixty on the stretch. But you don't want to hear me talk about myself—how's your stay here on the Isle going?"

Jill couldn't keep pace with the transition to a polite question, so she replied, "It's going well. The locals are nice enough. Funny thing is, the only real complaint I have is about the people that are from away."

Haddock abruptly stopped walking. "Ok, that's it," he said, swaying as he made cutting motions with his arms. He looked straight at her, then leaned forward and asked: "What's your problem with me?"

"I—I don't really know," she cried angrily, her expression confused.

"I wish you did! Maybe then I could fix it, and you'd stop treating me like I'm a jerk! I—I brought you a thermos of coffee, for goodness' sake, doesn't that get a man anywhere anymore?"

"Well—I just can't *tell* if you are a jerk or not, that's all!"

He walked onwards, shaking his head. "Well, missy, I'm having some difficulty deciding what I think of you, too."

"Oh?" she said, running after him. "Well, I guess I can't blame you for that."

Haddock then smiled. "Mary got to you, didn't she?"

"I resent that you think my opinion is totally based on what someone else thinks of you!"

"So she did, huh?"

"I've been coming to conclusions on my own, and—and she merely reaffirmed things I know about you already."

"And what, pray tell," he said like a pious professor, "do you know about me?"

Jill, taken aback by the question, took a few steps closer with every few words she spoke: "I know that you do a lot of things accidentally. You accidentally steal young womens' scarves, and you happen to catch fainting girls. You've brought me coffee, but you've also made fun of and even insulted me, and laughed when I was mortally pinched by that awful lobster. And I've never heard you apologize to anyone, including myself. So what do I know about you, you ask?" A placating cloud moved, allowing a beam of sunlight to glint across his upset, hazel eyes. Jill sighed both in admiration and exasperation. "I don't know anything about you do I?"

"If you do, you aren't using what you know very well."

Jill "Hm!"-ed in agreement. "Want to know how Mary described you? She used the word 'selfish', or well-chosen synonyms, at least ten times."

"Are you sure she wasn't describing herself?"

Jill looked at him in shock. "Haddock! She's an ancient crank of a woman—treat her with some respect!"

"But can you blame me? It's... it's been a rough year, and I guess I've been letting it get the best of me."

"More like the *worst* of you."

"Alright, Miss Jill, I'm going to give you a full education about me. You desperately need it."

"Oh, my, I didn't realize that I was enrolling in a full course."

"Well, now you have. You like to judge by first impressions, don't you?"

"First impressions are like concrete to me. They're set, and it takes a jackhammer to get 'em out."

"Miss Jill, prepare to be jackhammered. You are going to hear *my* side of whatever stories you've heard about me." And jackhammer her he did.

Afterward, Jill concluded, "So Mary hates you because Bobbie liked you better than Mary's kid?"

"I think she wants my uncle's cabin, too."

"Mary's very resourceful—you'd better watch your back. She just might find a way to get it."

"I can't really blame her for holding a grudge. The poor old woman's been through a lot."

"Oh? What happened to her?"

Haddock sighed, then stopped walking. "In the summer of '42, just before the draft went out, Mary and Bobbie's husbands took their boys to go way out on the fishing boat. A storm came in unexpectedly and..." he explained, looking pained, "...well, to just say it... they never came back."

Jill listened intently. Her head drooped as they started walking again. "That's terrible, I'm very sorry to hear that."

"Thanks... it was a long time ago now, but I do miss those boys. We all do. And as far as Mary goes, I think that losing just about everyone that I loved would make me a bitter person, too."

"You've been through a lot, too, haven't you, Haddock?" Haddock's head jerked towards her. "What? Why are you surprised that I'm trying to be sympathetic?"

"Well, Jill! I wasn't expecting you to say something—something—"

"Something *nice*?"

"That's the word."

"Watch your back on account of Mary—watch your mouth on account of *me*."

"There's the Jill I've come to know and lo—" Haddock began, but the sentence stumbled awkwardly to an end. "Alright, I'll admit, I've had my share of heartache. First, my mother died, then the Pine sisters' boys, then my dad, then came the War, then my uncle died, and now my girlfriend is mad at me... it's all a mess."

"I'm so sorry, Haddock. No one should have to lose so many people." He simply nodded in reply. "And I've had my fair share of complicated relationships, so I think I can sympathize with you about your girlfriend."

"Well, maybe she'll come around. I don't understand her sometimes—she's usually the sweetest creature on earth, but now she's just left me in the lurch!" he said, with anger lingering in his exasperated voice. "Anyways, I don't think you'd like her."

Jill, though internally riled, managed to smile and reply, "We don't have much in common, huh? She sounds too sweet to get along with me."

"Now, how am I supposed to answer that?"

"Don't. Let's talk about someone else."

"Who?"

Jill's eyes turned towards Dahlia and Remi, who were arm-in-arm, walking ankle-deep in the water. "Like Miss Basset. She's a real cutie." Haddock turned around to look at the couple, then smiled. "Well, Haddock, it looks like you're not in danger of Dahlia anymore."

"Things sure look that way, don't they?" he said with a chuckle. "I ought to thank Remi. Well, Miss Jill," he said, taking her hand and giving it a quickly executed, but firm, shake, "thanks for the walk... say," he took her hand and held it close, examining her fingers, "how's the lobster bite healing up?"

"Oh, just fine—now, don't you start laughing again!"

"I-hee-hee can't help it! Just remembering you flying around the room with that lobster—"

Before Jill could defend her dignity, she too started losing it, and soon everyone else on the beach turned their heads quizzically at the heartily laughing couple.

"Hoo, hoo," finished Haddock, wiping away a tear, "thanks for the laugh, I needed it."

"I have to admit—heh, heh—that that afternoon was awfully funny. I take myself too seriously sometimes, but you taught me not to."

"If you need any more lessons on the subject, I'm available to tutor you anytime. I'd better be getting back to the camp. I'll see you around, Miss Jill." With that, he walked away, while looking askance at the blooming lovers, Remi and Dahlia. He chuckled again. "Not in danger anymore, ha!" He then waved farewell to everyone, somehow escaping the entreaties made by the party's adhesive hosts. Jill now began walking back towards the rest of the group. She wondered if what Haddock said about Mary applied to him, about how losing those she loved made her bitter. *He* certainly seemed bitter. His girl, she decided, was obviously a loser, a twit who didn't give two hoots about him. No wonder he had been acting so strange. Their conversation taught Jill the lesson that took twenty-two years to learn. It all fit into place, like putting a key in the keyhole, then learning which way to turn it—people are more than their exterior. After that day, whether she realized it or not, Jill thought differently about the people she met, all thanks to the Fish.

As she came back to the reconvened group, she looked over her shoulder as she watched Haddock walk away, muttering to herself, "Yes, sir, Haddock, you're in no danger at all." She continued walking, then suddenly stopped as if she'd run into an invisible wall. She fully turned around, then whispered to herself in confusion, "I'm not sure if *I'm* not, though." And, for the briefest moment, she thought she saw a flash of light come from the general direction of Adkins' feet.

# Chapter 22

*Monday, May 22nd*

The next afternoon, Jill was sitting in Penny's living room, sewing *very* carefully. She made special efforts to keep the cloth as far away from her pants as possible. She stopped when she heard the front door open. "I'm back, Jilly," Penny called. Jill heard the rustle of Penny taking off her raincoat.

"Hiya, Penny. It's really coming down out there, isn't it?" Jill replied, looking outside with a shutter—pardon me, that was the *windows—she* looked out with a *shudder.*

Penny then came into the room. She paused, then began laughing at the scene before her. There Jill was, in the corner furthest away from any windows. Next to the fireplace was a spilled box of matches, and within the fireplace was a thick log, which had failed in fulfilling its role. To complete the pathetic scene, Jill was covered with at least three quilts. "Jilly, you're acting like it's the middle of January, and we're almost into June!"

"I've never seen so much rain in my life! Don't you ever worry that it'll never stop and you'll get flooded out, then get washed out to sea?"

"I've never worried that. I suppose that my imagination isn't as pessimistic as yours."

"I'm used to flash floods, you have to remember, where two drops out of the sky mean that you've got to stay away from any crevice." Jill sighed, then continued meditatively sewing. Penny walked over to Jill, then cocked her head, watching her cousin's strange methods. "Whatcha' doin' there, Jilly?"

Jill's held her sewing project directly beneath her nose, her hands resembling the paws of a dining chipmunk. "I'm trying not to include my pants in this quilt I'm making," was the muffled reply, as Jill had just placed a pin between her lips.

"You learn how to sew one day and then make a whole quilt the next?"

"Your Maine weather inspired me. Mary gave me a bunch of her old scraps, so I figured that I'd try to piece 'em together. Anyways, did you get any good mail?"

"No, not really, but you got a letter."

Jill looked up from her sewing with wide eyes. Well, they were wide to begin with, thanks to her reading glasses. They seemed to be composed of two magnifying glasses. The effect made her look like a surprised goldfish looking through a telescope. "For me? It's not from—from *Steve*, is it?"

"No, no, it's from Mr. Babcock," said Penny, giving the envelope a glance then tossing it into Jill's lap. Jill tore into it, hastily unfolded its contents, then began reading it. Her lips parted as she frowned, and she slowly put the letter down. Jill's magnified goldfish-eyes stared blankly at Penny. Penny had to suppress a smile while looking at the depressed fish's eyes. Penny was now sitting across from her, having to put her elbow on the armrest and surreptitiously disguise her smile by putting her hand over her mouth. "What's wrong, bad news?"

Jill nodded, then removed her glasses, to Penny's relief. Now her sympathy could take full effect. Jill set her project aside, removed blankets from her lap, then walked towards the fireplace. She stared into the cold cavern and said, "Mr. Babcock says that I have to return to work within the next week if I want to keep my job. He sounds pretty upset, but it's a little hard to take him seriously—

he's a terrible speller without me there to type for him: 'Get bak here as soon as possibowl, or yool be fyred by Monday. Sincelery, Mr. Babcock," Jill read, pronouncing each word phonetically. "*There's* an improvement—he spelled his own name right this time."

"How'd he ever become an editor?"

"I don't know, and I don't know what's so sinful about celery, either."

Penny frowned. For the next few moments, the only noise in the room came from the rain beating mercilessly against the windows. "Sounds like you've got a choice to make, Jilly."

"Yeah..." Jill said distractedly, "...well, uh, I guess I should go start packing or something, shouldn't I?" Jill replied, hugging herself as she took a few steps towards the staircase.

"Up to you, Jilly."

At these words, Jill stopped, then sharply turned around. "I don't want to leave, Penny! I—I just can't. Not yet, anyway. I love being with you, I love this little house, I love the people here, I love the ocean—I *hate* the rain and mosquitoes, but I can get over that—"

"You've never been here for Winter."

"Oh, what's a little bit of Winter between friends? I'll get used to that, too, but heaven forbid that it be like the storm of '38," said Jill drolly, rolling her eyes. "But wait," Jill said, now pacing around the room slowly, "but I also love Arizona. I love living near Mom, I love my own little house... Oh, Penny! I've never had to make a choice like this before."

"It isn't the only choice you have to make."

Jill turned and looked at Penny quizzically. "What do you mean by that?"

"Oh, c'mon, Jilly," Penny said, sitting back in her chair and crossing her legs. "You don't know what I'm talking about? Well, alright, if you want it, I'll give it to you with both barrels—the way you looked when you thought that Steve sent you a letter... I've never seen you look so, so *fearful* before! And that's not all. I... well, maybe I shouldn't say anything."

"You can't leave me hanging like that!" said Jill, even though the better half of her didn't want to hear the other barrel.

"Alright, alright, well, here it goes... I was watching when you and—and Haddock were walking on the beach yesterday, and let's just say that I've never seen *that* look in your eyes before, either. You certainly haven't ever looked that way when you talk about poor Steven."

Jill, feeling very overwhelmed by now, heavily sat down in a nearby chair. "'Poor Steven' is right. Oh, Penny! How could I actually fall for someone I've only known for—and why have I been so... ack! Steve and Haddock... they're so completely different, Penny. Steve is sweet and caring—sometimes *too* much; reading his letters is like getting smacked across the face by a book of poetry—and then there's Haddock, over there being blunt and teasing and sometimes a little cranky—Penny," Jill said, breaking off from her disjointed monologue, teary-eyed, "Why do I like him more than sweet Steve?"

"Oh, Jilly," Penny said, getting up and walking over to Jill's chair, then consolingly wrapping her arms around her tearful cousin. "All that I know is that you've got to be honest—with yourself, with Steve, and with Haddock."

"But Haddock's—he wouldn't *ever*—" Jill said through the sobs.

"Well... all that matters is that you make a choice and stick by it. I know you'll make the right choice. I've got faith in you, kid."

That very evening, numerous choices were made, right at the desk in Penny's living room. Jill sat solitary at this desk, while Penny had gone to bed at a reasonable hour. Jill was beyond any reasonableness and thus didn't feel the need to be confined by reasonable hours. But she made herself stop and try to think reasonably, and the product of it was this: two letters were written, and she didn't pack her suitcases. The first letter was to Mr.

Babcock, politely informing him that she would not be returning to Arizona until at least the end of the month. But the second letter wasn't as easy to write. Jill nearly used up all of Penny's stationery—she was in the habit of turning failed drafts into paper airplanes, which, with remarkable consistency, flew into the fireplace. They also were often crumpled up into wrinkly spheres and tossed into the fireplace to keep the airplanes company.

Eventually, every emotion, every detail spilled out onto two pages. Without giving herself time to overthink things to the point of having the pages join their predecessors in the fireplace, she sealed them in an envelope, licked a stamp, fastened it on, then placed the letter on the designated out-going mail shelf by the front door.

# Chapter 23

For a week, at least one of the Pine sisters and their closest friends were abuzz with excitement. Haddock had come up with the brilliant idea of getting his elderly friends to hold an old-fashioned dance in the Coffee House. Bobbie was convinced, Mary was skeptical, and the rest were invited. The night of the little dance finally arrived.

Gradually, the invited trickled in, their personalities governing their punctuality respectively. Mary was, of course, the first to arrive, to help Bobbie set things up properly, or, if nothing else, to redo whatever Bobbie thought was proper. Next arrived Penny, but without her cousin. Jill was not the punctual type. She was having difficulties deciding how to look and what to wear.

"Penny," she said while looking at herself in the mirror with a critical frown, "does my face look wider than usual?"

"I don't know, is your face in the habit of changing dimensions while you're not looking?"

"I don't know, I just feel like my face looks wider than usual sometimes."

"As Adkins likes to say: 'It's just another delusion—ahem, *illusion* of yours.'"

"Adkins is one of those people that I can't tell if I like or not."

"Put what your mother told you into practice and try liking him. She's a smart lady."

"Yes, I don't want to fall on my behind again. I've done that more than enough lately. You know, Penny, I didn't think that I'd be going to a dance when I packed my clothes. Now there's nothing to wear. You'd think I'd be cured of my vanity, after sewing my pants in the wrong places and accidentally wearing a lobster for a ring, but nonetheless, here I am." Soon, Jill found that Penny didn't have anything she would deem suitable, besides the dress that Penny was wearing herself. Even then, it would have affronted Jill to be prevailed upon to wear it. So after making many fruitless suggestions to her frantic cousin, Penny left Jill behind to worry herself sick. After Penny's arrival, in came Jerry and Joey. The two old gents showed up in their best sweaters and with thoroughly spit-shined shoes. Shortly thereafter came Mr. and Mrs. Peterson, the latter wearing a smashing dress. Smashing in an old-fashioned kind of way, that is. The Petersons looked very jolly, as if the event transported them back thirty years or so. Back then, they might have been a little younger, a little thinner, a little less gray, but their insides hadn't changed a bit. Mary kept glancing over at Mrs. Peterson and smiling, admiring her own tailoring work. And then came Jill, at last. After all the turmoil she had put herself through, this is what she came up with: A knee-length skirt paired with the best blouse she had packed. The only thing she lit up the room with were the jewels she had frantically put on; her *mood* certainly didn't add any luster to the party. She was feeling restless and apprehensive about the arrival of her favorite Fish, Haddock. She kept scanning the room, and every time her search came up empty, she wasn't sure if she felt disappointed or relieved. She was caught by surprise, though, when *another* gentleman walked into the room—yes, there was *Adkins*! It was perplexing to see him without his proper butlering attire. Jill was shocked to see him, looking so underdressed without all the starched collars and waistcoats he always wore. A tweed sport coat and plain slacks—what a sight! She watched on as Penny sighted him, then walked over and greeted him, taking his arm and leading him to a booth. Jill was too muddled in the brain to think of the occurrence as anything more than a kind gesture on Penny's part to invite the lonely old man. (But bear in mind that Jill thought that anything on the other side of thirty was old. He looked like he was somewhere before forty, so according to her views on the subject, she should've been running to get the elderly man a wheelchair.) Now all Jill could do is succinctly converse with the locals as she waited for Haddock's arrival. The minutes ticked by, and he kept not showing up.

The Coffee House was perfectly cozy. It always was, but the gathering of friends made its quaintness complete. When there is almost absolute darkness outside, and nothing but a few well-placed oil lanterns to light up the indoors, there's a quiet warmth, a lovely intimacy that soaks the atmosphere of the room and makes anyone within feel entirely at home. Despite the utter chaos charging around in Jill's insides, and the convulsions within her brain, her contentment with the hominess of the room was inescapable. Penny sat down at the piano and tickled a few keys in preparation for the evening, while Jerry pulled out the fiddle he'd brought. He blew on it mightily, sending a long-undisturbed layer of dust into chaotic flight. Soon those tough, scaly hands that spent a lifetime wrestling with ropes and catching lobsters suddenly transformed into a pair of nimble, gentle hands that drew out the sweetest notes you could hear. The sprightly old man tapped out the beat of a measure with a bouncy leg, and soon the bow in his hand hit the strings and created a lively beginning to the evening. Bobbie and Joey promptly replied and got up to dance. Yes, Joey, the old mossback that Jill didn't think could walk or talk, the man whom she'd never seen take any more action than the occasional blink, or the lifting of a mug of coffee, was now cackling and spinning around the room like he was sixty again. The Petersons joined in, stepping out onto the floor while the rest clapped along. The way that Jerry played that fiddle could make anyone want to get up and do a jig, even if they didn't know how. There was only room for three couples, but thankfully, at the moment, only two couples wished to dance. The song played through, accelerating everybody's hearts, whether they were dancing or not. Penny finished the song off with a playful, ascending arpeggio, while Jerry ended with a drawn-out, resonant note. Everyone applauded, then turned to look at who entered the Coffee House. It was Haddock, who was applauding as well.

"Hey, everybody! I didn't hear the whole thing, but I'll applaud you anyways," he said as he walked in. Everyone heartily welcomed the newcomer, except Mary, who found his tardiness more nettling than endearing. Jill, too, didn't respond to his arrival as the rest did, but for altogether different reasons. All that she was, at the moment that he entered the room, was a tremble. She wanted to tell him everything at once, but say nothing. She wanted to speak to him alone but stay as far away as she could. She was a messy paradox bundled into a confused container. Blissfully unaware of the turmoil he was causing, he walked around the room, unknowingly being followed by Jill's eyes. Everyone was equally pleased to see him—except Mary, of course, as is a given—but some showed their pleasure more than the others, Bobbie being the most expressive. Jill's eyes eventually, that is to say, *finally*, got tired of watching all of the good times he was having. If she were in a better frame of mind, she probably would've noticed how amazing it was that he hadn't made one motion towards her, no greeting, not even a look. Jill sat down at a lonely table. That isn't to say that she was alone at the table. Joey was sitting across from her, having what seemed to be a smile on his face. She sat down with a duly dramatic, emotional huff, and, as she expected, Joey didn't seem to notice.

"Bobbie, I'm sorry that I came late. I tried to get here early, but Mrs. Bloomberg shot my bike's tire, so I had to walk over," Jill overheard Haddock say.

"No problem, no problem, de'ah," was the forgiving reply.

"Well, is there going to be any more dancing?" he asked as he looked around the room. "I'd hate to think that I missed out on it."

"Ah, look at the young fellah, thinkin' we're spring chickens or somethin'," Jerry said while bending over and wheezing demonstratively.

"I'll tell ya, young man, I get outta breath just tyin' my shoes, let alone dancin' like this!" remarked Mr. Peterson, who was in a similar state as Jerry.

"Don't worry, Haddock, we'll get the folks dancin' again aft'ah a bit. Don't you worry, de'ah," Bobbie said with a reassuring pat on the back.

Haddock smiled, then took a rather long glance at Jill. Jill, having given up at looking at him, was too disengaged from her surroundings to notice the look he gave her. I think she would've been pleased if she had seen it. The look got so soft that it was nearly jelly in substance. Seeing that lonely, depressed slump made him feel a little ill. Well, I suppose it doesn't matter whether she saw it or not, considering that she *definitely* noticed the action that his look led to. All her emotions rose to a climax when she realized that he was walking over to her. Looking over Joey's illuminated, bald head, she straightened her posture and tried to look demure and contented.

"Evenin', Joey, hi, Jill," Haddock said, nodding to each one respectively.

"Hello, Haddock," came only one reply. That it was a singular reply didn't discontent Haddock. He wasn't expecting anything from the other person at the table, and his main purpose in coming over anyway was just to talk to the slump that was Jill. She looked like she needed cheering up. Joey didn't require any cheering up. He had a chronic case of the slumps.

"How's it going, Miss Jill?" Haddock asked.

"Oh, I'm—I'm fine," came the politely deceitful reply. "And you?"

"Oh, fine," was the aptly invented answer. "Do you like dancing?"

"Yes, yes I do!"

"Really?"

"Why are you surprised?"

"Well," Haddock said, now having to attempt to pave over what he had ripped up, "I didn't see you dancing when I came in, that's all."

"Nobody asked me to," Jill said, then added with a smile, "that's all."

"I think it's in my power to remedy that. Would you like to dance with me, once everyone else has taken a good hour to catch their breath?"

"I'd love—" began Jill. She realized that she was sounding too enthusiastic, and so she finished with a subdued: "Sure, why not?"

Joey suddenly began coughing in a way that required them to question him about what was on his mind, as opposed to an inquiry after his trachea.

"What's the matter, Joey?" Haddock asked.

"Well, ah," came out his gruff voice as he crossed his arms, "I just asked Miss Jill he'ah if she'd dance with me, and she said yes."

"Did she?" Haddock and Jill said at the same time.

"Yessah," was the infallible reply.

"I'm so sorry, Joey, I," said Jill, looking between the two suitors apologetically, "I must be out of it tonight."

Joey laughed in full agreement, like "out of it" was an understatement. "I'll say, missy, yes ma'am!"

Haddock glanced at Jill's nonplussed face, then said, "No problem, no problem. I'm pretty sure Bobbie wanted to be the first one to dance with me, anyways. You two cats have fun."

"Cats?" Joey said with a scowl.

"Alright, we'd better get up, sounds like Jerry's at the fiddle again," said Jill with a laugh. Soon Jill and Joey, Sandy and Haddock, and the Petersons stood up on the dance floor. Jill was so distracted by thinking about her would-be dancing partner that she couldn't fully appreciate her current one. If she had, she would have been surprised by Joey's fatherliness, his talkativeness, his everythingness. She gave him polite, preoccupied smiles, but devoted the remainder of her looks and thoughts towards Bobbie's partner. As often as Jill was carried away by her thoughts, this occasion was especially notable. She didn't even feel like she was in the room. It was as if she was watching the whole thing through a TV set. But when the music ended, she changed the channel and everything came back into focus. The moment she had waited for all night had finally arrived. After a moment of casual applause from the dancers, moving Jerry to take a little bow, Haddock walked up to Jill.

"Boy, Penny's terrific!" was the first thing he said.

After a millisecond of confusion, Jill asked, "Generally, or at the piano?"

"Well, if I choose one, you'll think I don't think the other. So I'll just be a gentleman and say both."

"But I don't think of you as a gentleman, Haddock," Jill said thoughtfully.

Although taken aback, Haddock raised his brows and managed to reply, "Well, then. At least you're honest about it."

"Oh," Jill cried, "you know that's not what I actually meant to say!"

"I can't tell anymore with you."

"Well, what I *meant* was that... well, look at Adkins, for example," Jill said, motioning towards the off-duty butler in the corner of the room, who was sitting in a chair that was in convenient proximity to Penny, who was still at the piano. "Adkins is a 'gentleman', but who wants to hang out with a stuffy old guy like that all the time?"

"Who invited him?" Haddock asked in a distracted exclamation, slow on the uptake. Jill sensed that he was missing her point. She shrugged, then said, "I think Penny might have." Haddock looked surprised, then began grinning mischievously. “What are you grinning about, all, all roguishly?” Jill asked.

“Just look at Adkins over there, next to Penny—I’ve never seen the guy smile, and now look at him! He’s smiled twice in a minute. I can’t help but grin roguishly, seeing him breaking records over there.” Haddock looked back over at Jill, who looked confused. Not only confused but also impatient. So, although in disbelief that she hadn’t caught on about what was going on over there by the piano, he asked her what she was saying. This satisfied her.

“What I was trying to say is that... that you’re too mellow to be a gentleman, in the stuffy sense of the word. I mean, well—you’re a nice guy and all, so maybe you just have all the best parts of a gentleman without all the seriousness... you’re, you’re *comfortable*, sometimes, is all that I was trying to say.” Jill, throughout the whole of the confused compliment, worried that her face might catch on fire, as it progressively got redder and redder with each word that came out.

It could hardly be told if Haddock was more unsettled or pleased by her words. She was one of the most satirical girls he’d ever met, so seeing this moment of sheer sincerity took him even further back than the affronting beginning of the cryptic compliment. If got taken any further aback, he’d be out the back door and into the ocean. The silence that followed made Jill feel sick. Sick, but a little impressed with herself. “I’ve made the man who never runs out of things to say speechless,” she thought with pride. It took a few seconds of wordless, perplexed staring before he could turn his head away to recuperate. But soon, that arch smile of his reappeared right back where it belonged. “Well, Miss Jill, you’ve got quite a way of complimenting a guy,” was all that the Fish could say. But the way he said it was enough to let her know that her stutters were duly appreciated. Presently after Haddock finished his sentence, the conversation was gladly interrupted by the sound of a squeaking fiddle.

They turned around to look, and they saw that the Petersons were no longer dancers, but were now performers. Mr. Peterson stood up there with bow in hand, and beside him sat his well-dressed wife, who replaced Penny at the piano. Jill's head swung around the room, searching to see where her cousin had gone. Ah, there she was; she laid her eyes on Penny, who had already joined hands with her dancing partner. Jill turned back towards Haddock, satisfied in knowing where Penny was. But a double-take was in order when her brain finally caught up with her eyes—yes, there Penny really was, about to actually *dance* with Adkins! Jill knew that Penny must have felt enough pity for him to *invite* him, but for her to *dance* with him was an absolute riddle! Jill turned to look at Haddock, but they ended up simply running into each other like a couple of bumbling rams. After a brief recovery, Haddock gestured towards the other dancers. Jill nodded, he took her hand, and they joined the others.

As the song began, everyone could immediately tell that a slower dance would be required. That is to say, Mr. and Mrs. Peterson's fingers were not as limber as their predecessors'. Thus, a slower melody was chosen. Haddock and Jill swayed together, enjoying the tune, and, whether they would admit it or not, each other's company. Jill kept spasmodically swinging her head around, curiously looking around at the other dancers. She smiled as she watched Jerry and Bobbie. Their eyes were closed and they both had sweet little smiles on their faces. They were so delighted to be together. Jill's smile grew; she had always sensed that there was a subtle fondness between the old-timers, and this moment proved it. They seemed to have abandoned subtlety and decided to simply relish the moment. Jill half-frowned, wishing she could do the same. But her nerves were far too wound up to allow her to.

She was less delighted and more disoriented when she looked at the *other* couple on the floor. Adkins and Penny... she couldn't comprehend it. The thought of any sort of, dare I say *romance*, hadn't even crossed her mind. The thought was so far away that she'd have to buy it a plane ticket for it to get *near* enough to cross her mind. She simply wondered how Penny could be so nice to the man. She'd never seen them get along well. To be truthful, neither had they, until recently. She was grateful that the dance made her turn around so that the view over Haddock's shoulder was no longer in their direction.

"How is your motorcycle coming along? You said you hit 60 on it the other day. Have you reached 70 yet?" Jill asked.

"No, actually. I, uh, decided to take your and Bobbie's advice."

"And what advice is that?"

"Not getting myself killed."

"Oh, that's always good advice," she said, in disbelief that he reconsidered his recklessness. Between telling Bobbie that he was sorry for being late and this, she wasn't sure what kind of fish she was talking to anymore.

Haddock now decided to return the strange compliment Jill gave earlier with an actually complimentary one. "You look very nice tonight, Jill."

This comment filled Jill with hundreds of different feelings. So, as is the common response to an unhandleable amount of emotions, Jill laughed. "All I did was grab the best-looking things out of the pile of clothes in my suitcase."

"You must have pretty good taste to accidentally look nice."

Jill just laughed again. What else could the poor girl do? She was thankful when he asked her a question next, saving her from having to come up with some sort of coherent reply. "Speaking of suitcases, are you going to be doing any more traveling? Maybe even back home?" Jill opened her mouth to retort, but he cut in quickly, "Not that I'm trying to tell you to get lost—aha! I said it before you could put it in my mouth!" They laughed, then he continued, "I just didn't realize that you were going to be staying for so long."

"Neither did I, to be honest with you. But, Mr. Basset gave me that secretarial job. It gives me enough to chip in to our house's—I mean, *Penny's* house's expenses."

"You must feel at home."

"Well, anywhere I go with Penny feels like home. We grew up together. She's always taken good care of me." Haddock smiled in reply. At last, after a few moments, she thought of what to say next. "My boss actually just wrote and told me that if I want to keep my job, I'm going to have to go back within the week."

"So what are you going to do?"

"I'm determined to stay until at least the end of the month. I'd hate to leave with it only being three-quarters over."

"Why has he let you stay as long as you have?"

Jill was delighted to reply, "At a company party, I saved him from a terrible predicament, and I've held it over him ever since. It involved a hairless cat, a tartan sport jacket, and, ultimately, a toupee. I'll admit that I use it to my advantage when I need to."

"It sounds like he's had *toupee* for it ever since."

And in that very moment, Jill fell completely in love.

# Chapter 24

How did it happen? How did a corny joke make Jill fall in love? It can hardly be known. If the very girl who felt it could not understand it, how could we even begin to? Jill hid the flabbergasting moment with a faint smile. Haddock felt that his joke went unappreciated. But if he only knew what was actually happening! Jill turned her head away to look at the other couples. She found that they were all much more cozily situated than at the beginning of the dance. Jill was endeared by the sight of the older couple but dumbfounded by the other one.

"Ouch!" Haddock suddenly cried.

"Oh, I'm so sorry!" was the regretful reply from his distracted partner.

"For an accident, your foot's got good aim," Haddock replied, hopping on the uninjured foot.

"Here," Jill said, stepping forward to support the one-legged dancer before there was collateral damage. But while doing so, the helpful step forward landed right on his other foot. Haddock, understandably, uttered an exasperated something, then tried to hobble over to a barstool.

"Oh, Haddock! I'm so sorry," Jill cried, again stepping towards him.

"No, no!" he exclaimed, raising his hand. "I've had all the help I can take from you." He then turned and continued towards a seat. Jill cautiously followed behind with carefully guided steps, then gently perched herself on the barstool next to his.

Bobbie walked around the other side of the counter. "I'm goin' out back to get a few drinks—" Cut off by noticing his pained look, she asked in mortification, "What happened to you? Sit on a lobster?"

"Nothin', nothin' happened at all, just get me whatever you're getting," Haddock replied.

"You sure you're alright?" Bobbie again asked.

"Fine, just fine," was the inflicted reply, with his head in his hands and his toes curled. After a few more rounds of motherly insistence, Bobbie finally went out back.

"Oh, Haddock—I'm just so, *so* sorry!" came another trembly apology, one out of a series.

"I've grown to be a little afraid of you. It seems like every time I try to do something nice for you, you retaliate. Somewhere in that ditzy brain of yours, you want to hurt me."

"No, not at all!"

"Here's the deal—once you stop maiming me every time we meet, I'll believe you."

Before Jill could reply, Bobbie came back and slid their drinks over the counter. They thanked her, then began slurping them. Jill began looking between him, then the floor, then him again, then the back door, then back at him, like a nervous pendulum. She finally said, "I think I saw Penny and Adkins go outside on the deck, want to go hang out there?"

"Why not?" came the disgruntled reply. They both were a bit distracted, thus not thinking of the possibility that the two predecessors might not have wanted company. Haddock opened the door for her. With a suspicious side-look, he asked her, "How do I know that you're not going to accidentally push me into the ocean?"

Jill laughed. "I guess you'll just have to trust me, if you can. I wouldn't recommend it." As she walked out, cool air immediately rushed against her. Allow me to compare the air to bricks. The air didn't feel like somebody was throwing bricks *at* her. It was more as if someone had built a wall with them and she ran into it. Many coastal nights can be likened to this, and it may be called an unpleasant sensation. Most don't like the idea of thick air. But this night, it didn't matter to Jill what it felt like. She felt like she had run into a different kind of wall, realizing that Penny and Adkins had left the scene. She turned around and looked through the window, realizing that they'd elusively gotten back into the Coffee House. It was too late to turn back, though. Haddock shut the door behind him. Turning around after closing the door, Haddock seemed a bit confused and surprised, looking like he'd accidentally walked into the ladies' room. "Where'd they go?"

"Inside. Must've snuck back—sneaked? Snuck?"

"Whether they sneaked or snuck, they probably saw you coming and worried you'd step on their feet."

"Who'd blame them?" she replied. Haddock leaned against the railing and looked out over the sea. In front of them was nearly total blackness. The only constant light provided was a nearly full moon covered by stringy clouds, providing nothing but a murky sort of reflection in the black water. There was a slight light behind them, spilling out from the warm innards of the Coffee House. But this light extended only so far. Every other light was outshone by a superior source. A glow struck the rolling ocean, but only periodically. The lighthouse on the mainland's shore held its head high, spewing out a beacon of light at regular intervals, providing illumination only in spurts. Jill joined Haddock's side, leaning over the rail, watching the light skim over the surface of the churning waves. "It's so beautiful, isn't it? This is the stuff poems are made out of."

"Do you write poetry?" Haddock asked, suddenly looking very enthusiastic.

"Oh, a little. I've always been a scribbler," Jill replied calmly, wondering why Haddock was so stirred by the mention of poetry.

"A scribbler, huh? A humble way to say that you've been writing poetry since you were a kid, right?" She only replied with a humble smile. "Well, as far as the evening goes, it *is* pretty, as long as you're not near the light while trying to get some sleep," he said, squinting as the light made another round.

"Tell me about it. It comes right into the house at night. But it's comforting, in a way."

"Like a sporadic nightlight?"

"Essentially."

They were both rather quiet after that. The sounds of the evening were too beautiful to talk over. The water was splashing, and because those few clouds blocked the moon, the darkness wouldn't allow the waves to be seen, only heard. The wind rustled anything that would allow it to. Jill's hair blew to the side and, rather unromantically, in her face.

"I'm no poet—not like *you*, anyways," Haddock said at last, although not looking at her, "but this is one of those nights I'm always going to remember."

He now had unwittingly uncovered a segue for Jill. Words now just rolled off her tongue without first getting permission from her brain. "I'm going to remember tonight, too, for a lot of reasons."

"Oh?" he replied cluelessly.

"I'm going to remember this night because of how nice it was, being with... you."

Haddock's head, which had been aloofly turned in the opposite direction, now suddenly swung towards her. He was utterly discombobulated. She turned her own head away, despite the fact that she had been annoyed with him for not looking at *her*.

"Well, I, I've had a nice time with you, too, Jill. My feet, on the other hand..."

"Ack—I can't tell you enough how sorry I am."

"You didn't apologize as much even when you ran me over with that old car!—"

"Haddock, just how much of a good time have you had with me, exactly?"

"I... oh, Jill! What do you mean?" he cried, getting more discombobbled with each moment.

"Maybe we had different times... that is, different good times."

"That's what I'm starting to think." He then noticed that a tear was starting to streak down her face. "H—hey, don't cry!"

"Why does everyone always *say* that?" she exclaimed through a throaty sob. "It's like they're trying to comfort *themselves* more than *me*. Our whole lives, we're told not to cry, but when things get bad enough that we *do*, they still tell us not to. It's really just idiotic, isn't it?"

"Well, when you put it like *that*, it is—" he said, but then got interrupted. Jill had set her elbows on the old, frail railing without any particular female grace and—well, she leaned on it so forcefully and strongly that it—that is, she *broke* it, and fell over the edge of the deck, and fell into the snapping, crackling arms of the bushes below. Haddock made an effort to grab her hand, but all that he accomplished was grabbing her wrist, thus stealing her watch as it slipped off and the rest of her was embraced by the shrubbery. The deck wasn't very high, so neither of them were in fear of any great injury. "Do you think you're Adkins or something, throwing yourself into the bushes? But Jill, I thought you hated me—didn't you? *Now* you don't..." he said as he pulled her out of the bushes.

"You keep stealing my things," she said with a sniff as he pulled her out of the bushes and snatched her watch back.

"Jill, I have to say this again, even though you've heard it before. I have a girl of my own, and maybe I haven't admitted this much before, but, I do love her. She hasn't been very nice to me lately, but I—I'm pretty stuck on her, and—you've gotta understand me, Jill—I like you a lot, and I have to admit—well, anyways, I hate to see you cry, but—"

"I see now," she sniffed. "I didn't realize you were so serious about her. You're so good that you wouldn't even *think* of loving someone else, would you?"

"Never," was the simple, firm reply. That undying loyalty, even to that twit, made her admire him even more. She looked around listlessly, the lighthouse's beacon illuminating her distraught face every few moments. Suddenly, the back door burst open, Jerry and Bobbie being the interrupters. They were the antithesis of the couple they'd barged in on. Both couples drew back upon discovering the presence of the others. Jerry gave a Downeast cackle, saying, "What are you two doin' out he'ah?"

"I was just about to ask the same of you!" Haddock replied heartily.

"Too nice of a night to not come out and enjoy it," Bobbie said. Both Bobbie and Jerry then began looking curiously at Jill's hair. Instinctually curious, her hand felt around up there, and she discovered a few twigs.

"Oh, yeah, I—I broke the railing and fell into those bushes, Bobbie, I'm so sorry..."

"Oh you did, did'ja? Oh well, you can come ov'ah tommor'ah and fix it up."

"I wouldn't suggest that, Bobbie," Haddock said in that teasing way, "she might tear the rest of it down."

Annoyed and dejected by Haddock's quick recovery from what just happened between them, Jill excused herself and went back into the Coffee House. She walked back into the room with as much dignity as she could muster. The room's inhabitants sat down in any available chair and settled in, half of them chatting, half yawning. Jill sat down next to Penny, who happened to be sitting alone.

"What happened to you?" Penny asked, looking at Jill's distraught face and twig-filled hair with concern.

"I'm tired," was the mild complaint. In turn, Jill looked around the room, leaned over, and asked, "What happened to all the dancing?"

"Well, Jilly!" said Penny, as if the answer was obvious. "Just look at the time." Jill looked at the clock Penny's head was tilting towards and saw that it was 8:30. Jill looked back at Penny in disbelief.

"When I was sixteen, my curfew was two hours later than that."

"Think about it this way: most of them think that a meal at five o'clock is a late dinner. It's about two hours past the fishermen's bedtime."

Jill just smiled absentmindedly in reply. Despite her confused condition, she managed to notice that something was missing from the room. "Hey, where did the old butler go? Did you finally scare him away?"

"He had to go wash some socks or something."

"It was nice of you to invite the poor guy to this thing."

"How couldn't I? He's a good dancer."

Although Jill wanted to know how her cousin knew that the old guy was a good dancer, she got distracted by watching Jerry, Bobbie, and Haddock come back into the room. The two men were supporting each of her arms. Jill and Penny half sat up as they watched them help her over to a chair. Bobbie kept reassuring them that she was fine. "I'm just a little outta breath from all the dancin', that's all," she kept saying. Seeing that Bobbie wasn't in danger, the cousins sat back down. Jill then started thinking about Haddock. It was just like him, having all that care and concern for Bobbie. Her heart warmed, but her head grew hot. Every time he was at his worst, next he'd show his best. She had a feeling that he wasn't always this way. Things had shaken him. She knew how he felt now, and so she could forget about him. Her heart would be stone cold. She didn't believe in the steadfastness of the decision, but with a stung heart, she credulously resolved it. With the resolve came the decision to leave the Isle the next time the mailboat came. It'd be best for everyone.

# Chapter 25

*Wednesday, May 24th*

The next day, there were no lobster boats to be seen. Shrimpy Cove had dragged them away from their usual dwelling on the docks of Petit Homard. The fishing season was about to start, and with this start came an annual competition. This competition took the form of a lobster boat race in Shrimpy Cove's bay. Even if a fisherman didn't get a good catch by the end of the tourist season, he could at least remind his fellow fishermen that he had sped ahead of them during the race. The competition between Petit Homard and Shrimpy Cove, of course, always helped attract entrants. The boat race was one of the few events that could tempt any of the Islanders to pull themselves away from their homeland. Some even thought of it as the most exciting event of the year.

"Aft'ahnoon, Jerry," greeted Bobbie, as he walked into the Coffee House.

"Good aft'ahnoon, de'ah," he replied as he sat at the counter.

"Surprised to see you lally-gagging around he'ah," said Mary, who happened to be in the Coffee House as well. "I woulda thought you'd be on the mainland hours ago by now."

"Well," Jerry said in that drawn-out Downeast way, "I figured I'd just go on ov'ah early tomorrow mah'nin. Why aren't you g'els out the'ah yet?"

"Bobbie isn't feelin' too well," Mary replied.

"Oh, sist'ah," said Bobbie flippantly, being too dogged resilient to admit to it.

"What's wrong with ya, Bobbie? Too much dancin' last night? Heh, heh!" Jerry said.

"Haven't stayed up that late since 1925. Nah, Jerry, just been a little outta breath, nothin' to worry about," Bobbie replied while pouring Jerry and Mary a cup of coffee. Hoping to change the subject, she asked, "Want sug'ah, Mary?"

"I'm too worried 'bout you to drink sweet coffee. I want it nice and bitt'ah."

"Like you two, eh? Nice," said Jerry, nodding towards Bobbie, "and bitt'ah," he finished with a teasing laugh at Mary. He promptly received a thwack from Mary. "Sure is a shame you two aren't comin' to the races, though."

"We'll prob'ly come ov'ah tomorrow mah'nin, if she's feelin' any bett'ah by then."

"But you don't have a boat to come ov'ah on!" Jerry exclaimed.

"I was waitin' for you to offer us a ride."

Jerry laughed. "Well, Pine g'els, I'll meet you on Miss Geraldine at 5 o'clock tommor'ah mah'nin, sharp."

"Good deal, Jerry," was Mary's reply.

"I hope that Miss Geraldine'll make it. Ever since Frog Legs scared me half to death and made me drop a wrench in the engine and jam it up, Miss Geraldine hasn't been the same. But I've been workin' or 'er, and as long as I don't run 'er too hard 'til the race, everythin' should go just fine. Well, g'els," he said as he rose, after gulping what was left in his coffee cup down, "the weather's so wicked nice that I'm goin' out on old Miss Geraldine, and I'm going to take a nice slow turn 'round the Isle. Been ages since I've taken the lap around."

"Don't getcha self lost out the'ah," said Mary in a disinterested farewell. Bobbie said goodbye with only a meaningful glance. With this brief look, Jerry practically said to her, "I'm worried about you, and I care a great deal." It might not sound very poetic on the written page, but one of those involuntarily given looks can fill volumes, whether the author is fluent or not.

So Jerry left the Coffee House, walked onto the dock, and untied the line attached to his old, little boat. He started its sputtering engine, which sounded like it had a case of chronic pneumonia, and steered Miss Geraldine right on around the Isle. He could have taken quite a few laps around if he wanted to, but he decided to take it slow and easy. He made it right on over by the Bassets' mansion, then decided to let Miss Geraldine drift a little. He knew there weren't any terribly strong currents or any shoals near where he was. Even if a current caught him, he'd just have to start up the engine and get himself out of it. He lay down, stretching out on the little deck, his face wrinkling in a smile as he soaked in the sunshine. Such a warm day was too good to not enjoy. He closed his eyes, only for a minute. Minutes have the habit, of course, of turning into hours, if they're left unattended.

~~~

Jerry bounced up from his recumbent position. He had awakened with an unsettled feeling. At first, it was pleasant, the sun shining down on him. But once he opened those creased eyelids and felt the boat rocking in an unusual way, he shot up and looked around. The first thing the groggy fisherman noticed was the increasingly cloudy disposition of the sky. But the next thing that he noticed disturbed him more. Upon realizing where his boat had decided to land itself, his large hands ran up the sides of his head in sheer alarm, making his hat fall off. He stooped over to pick it up while he grimaced—he was practically *on* Mrs. Bloomberg's private beach.
~~~

Recognizing the inevitable danger of being within such proximity of an armed old woman, he quickly looked around to see how he could get himself out of the situation. He was concerned, though, about how chummy Miss Geraldine and a set of jagged rocks had gotten. With a sigh of relief, he realized that he wasn't caught on any of these rocks, saving him from the ruination of any hopes of entering the race. With a few mild expressions of exasperation, he went to start up the engine. But a consternating sound occurred when he started the engine up. Miss Geraldine had made plenty of strange noises in her time, but none of them ever equaled the force of this one. It scared more than half the daylights out of Jerry. First clutching his chest, then his hat, he had a revelation—the boom had come from shore, and happened to coincide with the start of the engine. He impulsively walked to the rear of the boat to get a good look at the shore but was soon greeted with another sample of the noise. He dove for cover, but not before he caught a glimpse of the boom's instigator—a 4' 9" terror with a rifle twice the size of her.

"I surrend'ah, I surrend'ah!" the old fisherman cried, not daring to rise.

"Who's out there? I'm not letting any sea skunks maraud me!"

"It's me, Jerry, ya loon!"

"What?" the old woman called out agitatedly, tilting her head, which supported an off-kilter wig.

Jerry started to repeat himself a few times but was too apprehensive to allow his head to be exposed. Of course, his hat too was a priority, a piece that he had risked his neck and below to recapture. But as much as he didn't want it to be shot full of holes, he was even more wary of its perch getting damaged. "If I lift my head high enough for you to he'ah me, will ya promise not to blow my head off?"

"As long as you're not a sea skunk," she replied in that deep, sophisticated voice of hers. It quavered, both from being too old and from the possibility of having a sea skunk on her hands, whatever *that* was. Although Jerry was unsure of what the qualifications were of being a sea skunk, he felt sure that he wasn't entitled to the position. He meekly peered over the back of his boat, hoping that slow movements would ensure his survival. His eyes couldn't help but catch a glance at the bullet-shattered stern of his boat, which happened to be allowing water into the hull. The quickness of the jerk of his head startled Mrs. Bloomberg's trigger finger, which happened to be the most nervous of her digits. Thus another blow was released, and the bullet took a harrowing journey through Jerry's hat. "You old coot!" Jerry yelled, any shred of patience that was left in him now gone. "Why's your aim so wicked good?" Another blast went off, but in a completely different direction. Jerry was glad to be contradicted in this way. He picked up his cap from the ground, stuck a finger through one of its recently acquired holes, then called out, "Alright, woman, you can shoot at me all you want, but you start shootin' at my cap, and—good gadflies, how many bullets do you *have* in that thing?" He then heard her attempt to reload. Because it seemed that she was fumbling more than reloading, Jerry took the opportunity to emerge and introduce himself. "Mrs. Bloomberg! It's me, Jerry!" Now Jerry and the old riflewoman could look each other in the eyes.

"Jerry? Jerry who?" she asked, as her already transitory wig slipped again.

"Jerry Miller! You know me! I came ov'ah last week, brought you a lobstah."

Mrs. Bloomberg paused her simultaneous wig-readjusting and rifle-reloading to squint at him. "No, you didn't!"

"Oh, that's right, I forgot to—well, I *meant* to." This elderly battle of wits couldn't last much longer. Mrs. Bloomberg's eyes fluctuated from severe squints to wide-eyed ganders, all in some sort of examination. Her head jutted forward as she asked suspiciously, “Do you promise not to maraud me?”

“Woman, I won’t even take a second *look* at you, or your little rifle the'ah, if you'll just stop blastin’ the thing at me every two seconds.”

The old woman, though seeming to be only half-convinced, took the rifle’s barrels in one hand and started back to her house. Unfortunately, the rifle was pointed in the wrong direction when she stumbled over a root in the ground. The gun had pretty good aim all by itself. It shot the set of rocks that Jerry was so concerned about, then ricocheted directly next to the previous gunshot in the stern, creating a larger hole.

Jerry frantically rambled around, finding himself stepping in pooling water. He looked around for something, anything, to plug the hole and save Miss Geraldine. Jerry took off his hat, mournfully bid it farewell, and shoved it into the hole.

~~~

Jerry walked into the Coffee House, huffing and puffing from the excitement of the adventure he’d just been on.

“What are you huffin’ and puffin’ about ov’ah the'ah, mist’ah?” came an unsympathetic inquiry from Mary.

“That old bat Bloomberg woman blew a hole in Miss Geraldine with that cannon of hers.”

“Whad’ja do to her to make her do that?” came another teasing question.

“I fell asleep and Miss Geraldine drifted a bit. I ended up on Bloomberg’s beach.”

“Goodness, Jerry, are you alright? You didn’t get hurt, did’ja?” Bobbie asked, providing the sympathy that the story deserved.

“Oh, I’m just fine,” he replied, sitting next to Mary at the counter.

Bobbie automatically took his order for another coffee. As she did so, she felt something strange inside of her.
~~~

Strange feelings and pains had been building all day, but they increased when Jerry arrived. Despite the evidence her emotions provided, she knew that her symptoms weren't caused by any lovesickness. But like an old, tough Mainer, she did the gritty thing to do and ignored it. Such things, she reasoned, are expected to come with the fiend we know as old age. But as she lifted that same old coffee pot that she'd been utilizing for the past twenty or so years, she wondered why it felt so much heavier than usual. She never remembered it taking so much to lift.

"Now *you're* huffin' and puffin'," Mary remarked rather flippantly.

Jerry, somehow being more perceptive than Bobbie's own sister, leaned forward and asked, "Say, you alright, Bobbie?"

"I've—I've been a bit outta breath, today, but—I'm, I'm fine. Stop worryin' about me, de'ah," she replied, her abnormal breaths describing her symptoms better than her words. As soon as Mary heard her sister say, "Stop worryin' about me," and pat Jerry's arm, Mary knew that they all were in for trouble. The times when Bobbie tried her hardest to convince everyone around her that she was fine were the times when she was the most ill. However half-convincing her words already were, what happened next negated them entirely. Her eyes closed, she moaned in sudden agony, and she slumped forward, trying to support herself against the counter. Mary rushed *around* the counter, while Jerry took the more expedient route and jumped *over* the counter. They then lead her to a booth. They sat her down, and she seemed to make a brief recovery.

"What's goin' on, Bobbie?" Jerry asked anxiously, looking more worried than Mary. But in reality, Mary was the most anxious anyone has ever been for their sister.

"I—I'm not sure," Bobbie replied with an anxious chuckle, leaning forward, her arms crossed on the table. "Ev'ah since last night, I've—I've just been so *tired*, been havin' all these pains in my shoulder—but I figured they must just be from dancin' and stayin' up late. I feel a bit bett'ah, now, though, truly!" The reassurance made Mary even more nervous. Bobbie kept coming up with reassurances as her audience looked at her more and more worriedly. Suddenly, it was all interrupted by an excruciated grunt. Her eyes rolled back, and she slumped forward.

# Chapter 26

That evening, a knock rapped on Penny's door. Both Penny and Jill's heads popped up. Penny set down her mug of tea. "I wonder who that could possibly be."

Jill, unconcerned, returned to her sewing. "Only one way to find out." The knocks on the door then became rapid. Furrowing her brow, Penny got up while sharing a confused look with Jill. Jill watched as Penny jogged towards the door. An unsettled feeling set in when Jill heard Jerry's voice call out Penny's names in distress. She heard the front door creak open, then listened as a rapid exchange of words passed between Jerry and Penny. From the living room, the words were indistinguishable, but Jill could tell that whatever was going on was dreadful. Sensing this fact more and more, Jill rose and decided to head towards the door to see what was going on. However, the door slammed shut and Penny reached the threshold between the living room and the kitchen before Jill did. "What's going on?" Jill asked. Fear set in when she saw the pained, worried expression on Penny's face. It was the first time she had ever seen Penny turn pale.

"That was Jerry," said Penny, so shocked that she still seemed to be reeling.

Jill grew anxiously impatient. "I gathered that—what's wrong? Is he alright?"

Penny's senses returned to her, and with that usual confidence she, at last, said, in her normal, calm cadence, "No, he's fine, just fine. There is something wrong with

Bobbie. She's fainted twice within half an hour, and she's having chest pains. She needs to see a doctor."

"Oh, dear," Jill said, putting her hands over her mouth, staring at Penny.

"He needs me to come with him to the Coffee House, to try and help Bobbie. There aren't any motorboats around the Isle, since everybody's left for the boat races tomorrow, and Jerry's boat got shot." An understandable "*What*?" came out of Jill, but Penny ignored it and continued to relay far more important information: "I need to go and see what I can do for Bobbie, and somebody needs to go and let Haddock know what's going on. Jerry would, but he's getting a head start on patching up his boat. He's also been trying to get its engine to start, but he's having trouble with it. Jerry said that Haddock's the only one he knows that can patch up whatever's going on with his engine fast. And if they can't get the boat going, then Haddock'll be the only one strong enough to help Jerry row Bobbie to the mainland in this weather."

Jill, without a further word, went towards the door and geared up for the rainy weather. Penny dug out a couple of flashlights from the closet, only one of which worked properly. Jill would take the light, get Penny to the Coffee House, then get over to Haddock's. Jill looked at Penny fondly as they put their rainjackets on. "I'm so glad that they came for us. You're the closest thing to a doctor this Isle has."

"I think it says a lot about how much they've grown to trust us," Penny said as she opened the front door. Jill nodded in agreement, and they went into the cold, wet night with heavy hearts and anxious souls. They ran down the hill together, nearly slipping and falling a few times, then separated when they reached the Coffee House.

Jill ran—squelched, really—towards Haddock's cabin. Never had running taken so much effort, with the burden of the rain boots she'd pulled onto her feet. Thunder began to rumble through the thick, foggy air. Although she worried that she might get lost in the darkness, she found her way to and down Haddock's drive. With every moment that passed, she wondered, with pain, if it would be one of Bobbie's last. Out of breath and sopping, she beat on Haddock's door, hoping that he wouldn't take as long to come out as she and Penny did when Jerry came. But Jill began calling out Haddock's name much sooner than Jerry did. She heard rumblings and tumblings from inside. With each one, which seemed to bring him closer and closer to the front door, she tried not to selfishly think about how awkward another meeting would be, after last night. She'd resolved to never seek him out again, yet here she was, pounding at his door, ready to beg for his help. He finally swung the door open, his feet dragging and his shirt halfway buttoned up. He stared at her listlessly. "Jill? What are you doing here? What's wrong?"

She was grateful that the rain streaming down her face hid her own tears. But her voice gave them away. "Haddock, you have to come with me. Bobbie is—she's—"

"What, what's going on?" he cried, leaning out of the door's threshold. "Here, come inside, you look like a melting popsicle."

"No," Jill said firmly, "we have to leave now. I'll explain as you get some rain gear on." Although he was confused, she was glad that he trusted her enough to obey without question. He fumbled around, then found his boots in the dim room. "Jerry came knocking on our door and told us that Bobbie's very ill."

Haddock paused from what he was doing, fear washing over his face. "What kind of ill?"

"Please, keep getting ready," Jill begged, then continued, "He said that she's fainted twice this evening and that she's been having terrible pains in her chest and shoulders." They then paused to look at each other.

Haddock frowned and shook his head, looking deeply saddened. "A heart attack, huh?"

"It must be. Jerry's boat is shot—or *got* shot, or something— anyways, Jerry needs your help getting it working well enough to get her to a doctor on the mainland. If you can't get it going, he said that you two might have to take her in the rowboat."

Haddock shook his head as he finished getting his boots on. "If the heart attack doesn't kill her, going across the bay in this storm with a rowboat will. Bobbie's terrified of the water."

"Really?"

"Well," Haddock said, shutting the door, "it *did* kill her husband and son. C'mon, let's go."

And so the unhappy duo set off. Jill once wanted to walk in the rain with him one day, but not like this. The awkwardness hovered between them, feeling thicker than the fog in front of them. Jill cut her ruminations short, then said, "Oh, look at you, you're slowing down for me. Here, you take the light and run on ahead. I'm too out of breath to go any faster."

Haddock looked between the flashlight and her apprehensively. "I don't want you to get lost out here."

"I'd rather get lost than make you slow down. Go on, just take it, already."

Haddock took it, then took off running, briefly waving at Jill as he fled.

~~~

"I'm goin' with you, wheth'ah you like it or not," Mary said as Jerry and Haddock were preparing to leave. They'd gotten the boat to run. Mary, Jerry, and Haddock were in Bobbie's apartment's kitchen. Penny and Jill were taking care of Bobbie, who was laying down in her bedroom.

"Mary, de'ah," said Jerry soothingly, "Miss Geraldine can barely hold three people. She's built to hold two, and she doesn't like passengers. You've gotta stay he'ah."

Mary, feeling so emotional that the thought of *crying* actually crossed her mind, glared at Haddock, then looked back at Jerry. "But she's my sist'ah. Why does lil' Haddock have to go with you anyways, eh? I learned more about
~~~

boats before he was born than what he knows about 'em now."

"Mary, you know as much about boats as I know about makin' dresses," Jerry countered.

Mary, in a saddened fury, angrily sat down at the table. "So Haddock takes first place ov'ah me again, eh? That's how it is?"

Haddock looked in Bobbie's direction, then shook his head severely at Mary. "Mary, please don't bring this up now." Jill happened to walk back into the room at this moment but cautiously stood in the corner.

"I think this is *just* the right time to bring it up. I'm not lettin' my sist'ah, the only family I have left on this earth, die without me bein' the'ah to—to—" Mary nearly choked up, but with a throaty, irritated moan, she pulled herself back out of it and continued, "to hold her hand. I've lost too many, without bein' the'ah to tell them that I love them more than anything else in this world. And you, Haddock, aren't goin' to stand the'ah, between me and my sist'ah, someone I love more than my own life, not again, not ev'ah again." The room stood still in awed silence. Never had any of them heard anything so warm, yet wrathful, so profound, yet simple, so emotional, yet heartless.

"The last thing I want to do—that I *ever* wanted to do—is separate you from someone you love, Mary Pine. I've lost too many people myself to ever dream of letting you be separated from Bobbie, letting her be without you in what may be her last moments. I've never meant to replace you, Mary. There's no replacement for Bobbie, either, and with each moment that we just, just *stand* here talking about who's going to be with her, we lessen her chances of being with us for years to come."

Mary stared at him, looking a bit dumbfounded. It was the first time in Petit Homard Isle history that Mary Pine ever backed down. She was so unused to the feeling that she barely knew what was happening. Mary slowly got up and walked into Bobbie's bedroom, turning around at its threshold and giving an acquiescing nod to Jerry and

Haddock. Mary knelt next to Mary's bedside, brushed her sister's face with the back of her hand, and smiled tenderly. "Bobbie, I'm goin' to stay he'ah tonight, but only if you promise me one thing."

"What's that?" Bobbie moaned, with a half-smile on her fatigued face.

"That you don't die while I'm not lookin'."

They chuckled together for a few moments, Bobbie's laugh ending as a hearty cough. Mary kissed her forehead in farewell, then Jerry and Haddock stepped forward. As Jerry knelt to help Bobbie get up, he whispered something that Jill thought sounded like, "Hang in the'ah, de'ah—I love you, Bobbie."

~~~

Jerry and Haddock carefully got Bobbie onto Jerry's boat, leaving the ones left behind to go home and somehow try to sleep. Jill had offered to stay with Mary at the Coffee House that night, to keep her company, but Mary stubbornly refused, seeming to prefer to think and worry about the night's events by her lonesome. Before they left, Jerry promised Mary that he'd get someone to come and retrieve her, once he got a chance to find someone to come out and get her.

Jill lay in bed that night, her hands behind her head, looking at the ceiling and replaying each and every moment of the night, but in no particular order. It broke her heart to think about what this heart attack meant for Bobbie's sister and her friends. To have watched that intense conflict between Mary and Haddock— what a sight! What raw emotion comes out during a crisis! Never was Jill more impressed with him until that moment. He spoke so well, so eloquently, so lovingly, firmly. He diffused Mary enough to get Bobbie what she needed. Haddock and Jill shared a poignant look when everyone waved goodbye to each other at the docks. It cut her to the heart, to see him look back at her, going out on a heroic
~~~

mission, but to know that he'd never be her very own hero. But that would have to be forgotten. She didn't want to regret him. She wanted him to be happy. He would go off and live his own life, and she would forget. That's what she wanted. So she tried to put those thoughts aside, and for the rest of the night, she stayed awake, hoping for the best.

The next morning, Jill and Penny got up at the same time. Notice that I did not say that they *woke* up. They merely *got* up, because there was no sleep to be woken up from. In fact, their getting up at the same time was a chance meeting. They met in the kitchen, both in pajamas. Penny came into the kitchen at 5:00 A.M., and there she saw Jill sipping a cup of coffee, looking wistfully out of the little window that overlooked the foggy bay. Jill turned around at the sound of footsteps. "Imagine that—*me* getting up before *you*," Jill said dryly. Penny smiled, then stretched her arms while yawning. Jill caught the yawn and fogged up the window in front of her. She then wiped it off with her sleeve.

"Did you just boil this?" Penny asked, holding up the kettle.

"I sure did," Jill replied, taking another meditative slurp. She listened to the rustlings of tea-making from behind her, then said, "You know, Penny, I think that we're really becoming Mainers. I mean, just look at us—we're breakfasting at five in the morning—excuse me, *mah'nin.*"

"Oh no, de'ah," said Penny with a smile, pouring hot water over a teabag, "you're gonna have to get up wicked early, at least three, to be a real Main'ah."

"So that we can have a late dinner at four, right?"

"Now you're gettin' it, kid."

Now both of them looked out of the window together, both thinking about the same thing. They turned towards each other. "We should go down to the Coffee House, shouldn't we?" Jill asked. Penny nodded. With that, they went upstairs, changed, and reconvened in the kitchen.

The sun gradually rose in the east, and an optimistic day was sure to follow as the sun broke through and dissipated the fog.

With much more calm than the night before, they put on their rain jackets and boots and walked down to the Coffee House. The situation was so uncertain that it left room for the cousins to assume that everything turned out for the best. They walked down the hill, maneuvering around the puddles that seemed more like small lakes. They made it to the Coffee House and peeked into the windows, but no one was inside.

"Someone must have come and gotten Mary," Jill surmised aloud. She then sighed. "I hope everyone's alright."

"Me too, Jilly, me too."

"This is one of those moments that I wish you'd be the kind of person to say, 'Oh, it'll be fine, Jill, they're all alive and well and are eating cake and ice cream.' Is that too much to ask?"

"I'm too honest to tell happy little untruths like that."

"That's the problem with you—you're never dishonest when you need to be."

"That's why honest people die alone."

"Penny! You won't die alone. You're not *that* honest."

"We'll see, I'm right on track—hey, look!" They looked towards the mainland and saw what looked like a bigger version of Jerry's boat. Penny and Jill ran over to greet it. By the time they walked over and waited a few moments, the boat was right in front of them. An old, unfamiliar fisherman threw out a rope towards Penny, who apparently looked like the more capable one out of the two girls. Penny promptly tied a professional-looking knot around the post, while Jill was left to discover that Haddock was on the boat.

"Haddock!" she called, waving to him excitedly. He waved back, then climbed up the ladder on the dock. You see, tides in Maine are so large that ladders are built on the sides of docks, so when the low tide drains most of the water out of the bay, one can get up to the docks despite them being a distance above the boat. "Is everyone alright? What happened, what happened?" came Jill's insistent questioning.

"Let me get off this ladder first—otherwise, I'll fall and you'll have to tote *me* back to the mainland." Reaching the top rung, he put out his hand. "Help me up, would you?" She pulled him up, but unconsciously wouldn't let go of his hand.

"What happened, what happened?"

"We got Bobbie to the doctor, and with some medicine and that gritty will to live, she pulled through just fine."

Jill nearly pulled him into an elated hug, but instead just squeezed his hands to death and sighed with a relieved smile. He grinned as well, then gently pulled away and started talking to Penny. Jill then listened to his account about the perilous journey to the mainland.

"For the last leg I got Miss Geraldine up to eight knots, and we were able to make it to shore in under half an hour. We woke Dr. Jones up, and he and his wife took her right into their house and fixed up a room for her. He said that she's too stubborn to die."

"Good job getting her over there, Haddock," said Penny.

He just shook his head modestly. "I'm just glad it wasn't any worse."

"When can she come back?" Penny asked.

"Dr. Jones wants to send her to the hospital in Westport to run some tests and make sure she won't have another heart attack. She'll probably be back here within a couple of weeks. Mary wanted to bring her back here to take care of her herself, of course, but Dr. Jones convinced her to just go with Bobbie to the hospital. They're going to move Bobbie in an ambulance this afternoon, so I came back to get some things for the both of them so Mary can go with her."

"I bet the doctors will have a hard time telling Mary not to do their job for them," Jill said with a chuckle. Haddock and Penny agreed with laughter and knowing smiles.

Penny now started talking to Jimmy, the fisherman who took Haddock back. This left Jill and Haddock to themselves. Jill pointed back at the fisherman with her thumb. "Do all fishermans' names start with a J and end with a Y? Jerry, Joey, Jimmy—is it a requirement or something?"

"Stick around long enough, and you might meet a Dave or Gary here and there."

"I'd like to meet *all* of the Daves and Garys, but I'm not sticking around."

Haddock snapped out of his aloofness. "What do you mean?"

Jill shrugged, her hands in her pockets. "Now that I know Bobbie's alright, there's really no reason for me to stay. I'm going to leave when the mailboat comes next Monday. I was thinking about staying longer, but—some things came up." If she had said, "But *you* came up," it would have finished the sentence more accurately. But it didn't have to be said. Instead, they walked in the general direction of the Coffee House quietly, thoughtfully. Jill was desperate to know what he was thinking, even though she believed she knew already. But what could he possibly say now? "What a blockhead!" Jill exclaimed mentally. She then came up with a little poem: *"He stays so loyal to that twit, who obviously doesn't care about him a bit."* She refrained from continuing the internal debate about the twit's unworthiness, and eventually, they reached Penny's house. "Thanks for walking me home," Jill said.

"Yeah, sure. I didn't even mean to—that is, I guess I didn't realize where we were going until we got here." Jill chuckled. It was nearly a giggle, but Jill wasn't a giggly person. In fact, she only came close to a giggle when she wanted to cry. "Well, goodbye, Jill—I'm sorry to see you go so suddenly."

"I am too—but, it'll be good to get back to the Southwest. It'll be good to be home."

Haddock looked at her with a soft gleam in his eyes. "You've made this place a lot sweeter, Jill. Safe travels."

He then turned and walked down the hill, and out of her life.

# Chapter 27

*Friday, May 26th*

"...and so, I'm afraid that I have to resign from being your secretary."

If a window wasn't open, Mr. Basset's gasp would have sucked all the air out of the tea room. "Leaving? Leaving us? Did you hear, Dahlia?" he exclaimed, jutting out of his chair a little more with each word. At the end of his sentence, he was positively upright.

"Jill!" Dahlia cried, grabbing her arm, "What are you talking about? I have never had a friend like you! My! If it weren't for the consolation of having dear Remi's friendship, I surely would faint!"

"Well, my dear! That couch you're sitting on has seen plenty of fainting from your female ancestors. Be glad you don't have a corset to entice you further," her father said. Remembering how upset he was, he continued, "But, Miss Jill! I need you for my work! And my daughter longs for your companionship! What can I do to make you stay? I know exactly what I'll do—I'll increase your salary by fifty percent!"

"Oh, Mr. Basset! I couldn't possibly—"

"No, no, of course you couldn't, how stupid of me to make such a minuscule offer! *Seventy-five* percent, of course!"

"Really, Mr. Basset!" Jill returned with a nervous laugh. "It's not at all about the money—"

"Ah! Well, in that case, I could build you a house! A mansion! Whatever you'd like, in whatever style you desire!"

"I am deeply touched that you want me to stay so badly," Jill replied, looking between the father and daughter, their misty eyes increasing her guilt, "but there's nothing you can do to make me stay, truly!" The Bassets despondently sank into their chairs at this reply. "I'm so touched," Jill babbled on, "really, I am!"

"Addie," Mr. Basset said with a sigh, "get me a cup of tea. I cannot cry while I'm drinking a cup of tea. It would be downright un-British, if I may coin the word."

"A truly profound statement, sir," Adkins replied solemnly as he obediently poured.

Jill's heart was now broken, seeing the way they took the news of her departure so hard. "After I knew that Bobbie Pine was alright, I decided that it was best to leave—"

"What happened to Bobbie Pine?" Dahlia asked worriedly.

"Who *is* Bobbie Pine?" Mr. Basset asked confusedly.

"I was rather wondering that myself," Dahlia admitted.

Jill explained the answers to both questions promptly. "Good gracious!" was the long-winded exclamation from Mr. Basset, upon hearing about what happened. "Will she recover alright? What a terrible thing this is! Quite terrible, indeed," he said, shaking his head as he looked down into his tea. He got distracted from his sympathy, though, and his brow furrowed when he saw an alien particle in the murky cup of tea beneath him. He snapped his attention back from inspecting his beverage when Jill replied, "Bobbie wouldn't let anything kill her. And if her stubbornness isn't enough to keep her alive, then her sister's will make up for it."

"Good people, these women are! Why, I remember when we first moved into this house, I sent Addie out to get me a pair of boots, and he returned with a pair lent from Mrs. Pine! Oh, which one of those sisters was that, Adkins?"

"Mrs. *Mary* Pine, sir."

"Right! Out of all the things I had in this house, I hadn't any warm boots. Mrs. Pine lent me a pair that were very practical looking. The poor woman's memory must not have been totally up to shape, however—she forgot that there were holes of substantial diameters in them. It was an awfully kind gesture of hers, though."

Jill and Adkins shared one of those knowing looks that they often had. "It could be said that you ought to be grateful that the vessel she offered wasn't a boat, sir." Jill smiled, and Dahlia laughed, although she wasn't exactly sure what at. Jill coughed, then said, "Everyone on this Isle loves the Pine sisters. I can't help but love them, either. Be sure to say goodbye to Remi for me if I leave before I see him again, Dahlia."

"Oh, that reminds me!" Dahlia cried, flying up and running to the other side of the room. She returned with a canvas in each hand. "Look what Remi brought me the last time he visited!"

"Oh, his art!" Jill said, then remembered that Remi painted one thing and one thing only—a rock.

"Isn't it inspiring in some sort of way?" Dahlia said, looking at the canvases admiringly, though blankly.

Jill's only praise was, "They're—consistent!" She hit on the only praiseworthy thing about them. Jill was amazed by the realism. Remi captured the rock's dullness perfectly.

"Remi's such a good painter, isn't he, dad?" Dahlia asked.

"Quite right," agreed Mr. Basset distractedly, his cravat puffing out huffily as his head drooped, still troubled with his contaminated tea. "Addie!" he called.

"Yes, sir?"

"Look at my tea," Mr. Basset urged, lifting it.

Adkins squinted as he examined it. "Perfectly revolting, sir," was the verdict.

"You know," Jill said, entirely caught up in her own thoughts, so caught up that she didn't even notice that a tea emergency was embroiling, "if everyone on this Isle *really* loves Bobbie, and if they love each other—even if they have funny ways of showing it—why won't they let a doctor come to the Isle? I mean, yes," she continued, getting up from the proper little couch, "I heard that they nearly convinced a doctor to come, but he refused to make the move because there was no accessibility to the mainland except by boat. Everyone is for that bridge being built except them. And when you really think about it," she ranted on, pacing between a fancy vase and an ugly portrait, "it all amounts to selfishness!"

Dahlia had been happily oblivious to both of the concerns raised in the room. She was engrossed in a French-phonetics book. And so, being a faithful student, she decided to begin practicing French vowels.

"Do you think that we ought to fish it out?" Mr. Basset asked his fellow tea connoisseur, while disdainfully staring down at the unwelcome guest in his tea, which was, if you're curious, a little fly.

"That is a decision only the keenest of wits could morally decide upon, sir."

"*Ah*," Dahlia said. Whether she was agreeing or practicing a vowel, they didn't know.

"Indeed," Mr. Basset concurred, "it would save much effort to simply pour it down the sink, but it would be immoral to waste a perfectly good cup of tea."

"*Uh*," Dahlia said.

"But is it still 'perfectly good' if it has been contaminated by a foreign substance?" the butler philosophically countered. Mr. Basset stroked his chin, finding himself wrapped up in a moral dilemma.

"*Ee*," Dahlia said.

Jill's interest in this tea was completely absent. She was too busy being indignant to notice it. "I should go right on down there and give the stubborn old pufferfishes a piece of my mind. Thanks for hearing me out, guys," she said as she marched towards the front door.

"*Oh*," said Dahlia in farewell.

"You oughtn't give them too sizable a portion of your mind, Miss Jopling," Adkins called out, even though she was leaving the room. "You will need every ounce of it if you want to keep some degree of your sanity. Some have given too many pieces of their minds, and now,"—he looked down at his perturbed master—"they have a strange preoccupation with tea." Mr. Basset was too engrossed to pay any attention to Adkins.

Dahlia finished off her self-taught lesson with an "*Oo*," then suddenly snapped her book shut and began walking around the room, daydreaming about being able to speak in perfect French with Remi one day. "Say, Adkins," she said, turning around, "could you get me a cup of tea? Oh, look—never mind, Adkins, I'll save you the trouble, you're done with your tea, aren't you, Dad? Yes, that's what I thought—" and with that, she took the half-empty cup and promptly gulped it. She set it down with a satisfied sigh, then walked out of the room while commenting on what a good brew it was. Her father watched on in horror and was now too shocked to speak. He could only stare at the empty cup.

"You see, sir," said Adkins as he promptly refilled the cup with fresh tea, "things often have a way of working themselves out."

~~~

Jill burst into the Coffee House, disturbing the serenity of all its inhabitants. Prior to this disturbance, Jerry and Joey were sitting beside each other, telling each other stories they'd both heard before. But it didn't matter, because they'd both forgotten them. It was at least the twenty-fifth first time they'd heard them, so they were equally entertained. Mary, in the meantime, was behind the counter, trying not to look out of place while taking care of the Coffee House. It was one of those sleepier evenings, but things were about to get shaken up.
~~~

"Alright, listen up, all you hermit crabs," Jill said as she hung up her coat angrily. "I've had it right up to here," she continued, gesturing towards the chin area, "and I can't take it anymore." Joey was so alarmed by Jill's interruption that he actually looked up from his shoes.

"Take what?" Mary asked incredulously.

"You! And your—your *everything*! Specifically, I just cannot believe how *stubborn* you all are!"

"Isn't anythin' to be ashamed of, de'ah. Why," Jerry said with a chuckle, "your prob'ly more stubborn than all a' us combined!"

"Alright," Jill conceded, lowering her voice. She briskly walked towards the counter and sat down. "Maybe I am. But you—you all take it to another whole level! To be so stubborn that you—you refuse to have a very necessary bridge be built to the mainland—"

"Bah," Mary said, pouring Jill a cup of coffee without being asked to, "buildin' a big ol' bridge is about as necessary as a Nor' Easter on trappin' day."

Although not exactly understanding the terms Mary used, she detected the flippancy of her words. "Mary," Jill said while pushing the coffee away, "because there was no easy way to get back to the mainland, your sister could have *died*."

"Nah," Mary said, pushing the cup back towards her unwilling customer, then wiping up the incidental spillage, "the doct'ah said that Bobbie woulda been alright. Said he didn't do anythin' more than just numb 'er up. Bobbie said she's never felt so numb since that time she fell off Jerry's boat in late Octob'ah, heh, heh!"

"But, Mary!" Jill interrupted, "What if it was worse? What if something happened to her where she needed to go to the hospital in a much shorter time? Listen," she continued, standing up, "I know that all of you think that bandages are luxuries and that just toughing it out can stop bleeding or cure whatever ails you, but that's just not how the real world works."

"You think you know more about the real world than us, missy?" Mary asked.

"I do! Sure, you know a lot more about *your* world than I do, but how are fifty-something years on this tiny island going to make you relate to what goes on beyond Shrimpy Cove? Things happen—you know that! *I* should know, anyways—I've caused more injuries to the people on this island than they've seen in twenty years. What if something serious—I mean, *really* serious—happened? Toughness doesn't cure everything. I think that real life is knowing that you can't always do things on your own. If you didn't put up such a fuss about that bridge, a doctor would come. Families—good people, new life—would come, people to begin a new generation of Petit Homard Isle history. Look at *me*, for example! None of you liked me when I first came here—except Jerry, maybe—"

"But Jerry likes *everybody*," Mary grumbled.

"But you tried me out, and you eventually got used to me, didn't you?" The room reluctantly grumbled affirmatively.

"With each rant you come up with, you're weakenin' your chances of us continuin' to like you," said Mary.

"Well, just listen for another minute—that's all the breath I've got left in me, anyways. Even if you don't admit it, you all care about each other deeply. And if you care, you should sacrifice your independence for the good of others."

"What do you mean, we don't sacrifice? I was the one, mind you, that spent 36 hours and 16 minutes under the same roof as..." Mary began.

"*Oh*," Jill exclaimed, "why do you people always have to drone *on* and *on* about the snowstorm of '38? Why can't you just let it *die*? For people who say they're tough, you like to have all the sympathy you can get! All I'm saying is that opening this island up to newcomers might not be as terrible as you think it'll be. You might even find that the benefits outweigh the costs of having the occasional obnoxious tourist. You all claim that this is the most beautiful spot in New England, and you won't share it? If nothing else, could you imagine all the money from tourists you would rake in?"

"That's why we take the lobstahs to Shrimpy Cove—we don't mind takin' their money, as long as they don't come near *us*!" Jerry said with a laugh.

"Can't you see that it could really be... not awful!"

"You're really sellin' it, Jill," Jerry laughed sarcastically.

"Glad you don't make your livin' bein' a saleswoman," Mary said with a chuckle.

Jill shook her head in awe of their flippancy, then walked back to get her coat. She turned around and looked at them all. "You know, I'm disappointed in each and every one of you—yes, even you, Joey!" She then grabbed her coat, too riled to even put it on, but was stopped before she could leave.

"Hey, Frog Legs, you forgot to pay for the coffee."

Jill turned around and gave her an exhausted sigh. "Put it on my tab," she said, leaving the room. She came back in, and amended, "Actually, put it on *yours—I* didn't order it." And then she left.

# Chapter 28

*Monday, May 29th*

Haddock, as it turns out, hasn't gotten his share in being the focus of the narrative. So now we will give him his due allotment.

It was Monday, and the mailboat had come. Usually, the mailboat signified great excitement and novelty. Letters might come from the exotic land of "From Away," and, although it was a rarity, there might even be a passenger taking a ride. Because Haddock was young and required more excitement than most of his neighbors, little events, like the coming of the mailboat, were nothing little to him. But today, there was no desire to hop on his motorcycle and go flying to see if any communication had come from the outside. Today, the mailboat might leave him something, but it also was going to be taking something away—Jill.

Jill Fargo, as her name was to him… how strange their relationship began and ended. It was brief, informal, odd. But she did leave him something behind—a memory. It could even be called a *fond* memory. There was something so amusing and strange about their time together, that the memory of her wouldn't soon be forgotten, if *ever* forgotten. But even though these sentimental thoughts were well-meaning, he didn't want to have to bid her farewell again, while simply trying to collect any correspondence. It was quite enough to say goodbye once, when he accidentally walked her home. "Goodbyes aren't so bad," he thought while looking out through the morning-lit forest, leaning against his doorway, "it's *repeated* goodbyes that I hate." He looked down at his front step, remembering that just a few days ago, Jill was standing there, looking up at him with desperate eyes. Now he'd never see those eyes again. And it brought him sadness.

Time passed, and the coffee cup resting in his hand became empty as morning grew into afternoon. He then decided that the danger of being forced into saying another goodbye had vanished with the mailboat. Thus, he speeded down to the docks to satisfy his curiosity about what this week's mail had brought. He went into the Coffee House and looked around. Nobody was around, not even Mary. Surprised, he went further in and found an orderly stack of envelopes on the counter. He swiped through them, and his eye caught a thick envelope with a quickly dashed-off address written on it. He squinted at the scrawl, then realized that it was from his roommate, Danny. He tore the envelope open eagerly. Within were three pages, varying in sizes, with two different penmanships. With a rush, he suddenly recognized who the second half of the letter was from! His heart began racing—it was *her*, at last! She'd finally broken her age of silence!

"Haddock!" Mary exclaimed in surprise, walking back in from the kitchen. "Goodness, don't go givin' *me* a heart attack, now. One's enough for the family. I went back the'ah for two seconds, not a soul in the place, and then I come back and he'ah you are, standing the'ah and makin' me jump outta my skin. Say, who'd you get a lett'ah from, anyway?"

Haddock looked up from his enrapture with a glorious smile. "It's *her*! *Her*, Mary!"

"Who? Who's what?" Mary snapped back in confusion. But Haddock couldn't reply. He ran out of the room with the letter clutched firmly in his hands, knocking over any unfastened objects in his path. He needed to get free, get out, so that absolutely nothing could distract him from this letter and this letter only. Finally, after weeks upon weeks of loyal waiting, his love would now be either rewarded or vanquished. He ran around the south side of the Isle for a while, like a startled, gangly colt, desperately searching for the perfect place to read the beloved letter. Eventually, the rush settled down enough for him to sit on a secluded little beach, and there he just read. He was tempted to skip over what appeared to be an introduction written by Danny but then decided that reading it might calm his nerves enough to make him stop shaking all over. Between Danny's rushed handwriting and his own jittery hands, it was difficult to read, but he managed to see that it said:

"Look, before you get too mad at me, I just want to apologize. I know you told me not to open any of your mail, and just send whatever came to you in a larger envelope, but when I saw that it was from HER, I couldn't resist opening it up!"

"*Danny*!" Haddock cried angrily. But temporary forgiveness had to be employed to read the rest of the envelope's contents, so he read on:

"Anyways, let me just say that I'm sorry, and I hope that everything works out between you two. I sent the letter off as soon as I could.

Danny."

"The jerk," Haddock mumbled, crumpling up Danny's page and throwing it into the ocean. Before he could begin wondering what Danny meant by "I hope that everything works out between you two," he delved into the letter, so engrossed that he didn't even notice the seagulls that swarmed in, all of them seeming to be under the impression that the object he threw into the sea was food. The letter—yes, *the* letter—read this way:

"Dear Steve,

Steve, I don't know where to begin. I am full of apologies, and really, that's all that this letter is going to be. First, I am so sorry for not writing sooner."

"Sweet thing," he thought while smiling, even though any other man would've been angry. The letter continued: "Your letter gave me a lot to think about. My cousin, Peyton, invited me to come and stay with her while I thought things over. She is so very kind—she sent me 150 dollars to fly me up to Portland, Maine." Haddock paused to exclaim, "*Maine*?" then read on: "She brought me up to this little island off the eastern coast. It's a darling little island, Steve, you'd love it, I just know. You could write poetry all day long here. I've grown to love it. I'm even thinking about moving here permanently.

"Steve, you've always been so good to me... I feel like I don't deserve you. It breaks my heart just as much as it will break yours, but, I've realized something about myself, and about us. Steve, we are so superficial. We never were friends. We've always been lovers. Love notes—that's all we've ever sent to each other. I think that's why it scared me so much when you asked me, in that poetic little way of yours, to marry you. I've met so many real people here, Steve. You're not going to like what I'm about to write, but as my cousin told me, I must be honest with you. I've met someone here, a man called Haddock. He's called that because—well, it's a long story and doesn't really matter. But now I have to remind myself that I need to be honest—he's a YOUNG man, maybe a year or two younger than you. Steve, he's real. He is so honest, so true. I think that it's very possible that I've completely fallen for him.

"I want you to know that this doesn't mean that I don't care about you. I care for you very much. It's just that we've been hiding behind words this past year... it's so much easier to conceal what we are when we write it on paper. Maybe that's why I like this way of communicating more than any other. But we can't build a life on a foundation made out of paper. I know that sounds corny, but it's true. Meeting Haddock made me realize that, Steve—you and I just aren't real. I'm going to talk to him as soon as I can about how I feel. But I have a feeling that he's going to be as loyal to his girl as you've been to me. But even if nothing becomes of it, I know now that we just aren't ready for each other. I am willing to lose both of you for the sake of knowing what love really means.

"I wouldn't say all of this if I didn't think that it would be best for you. I know that you're going to hurt for a very long time, and it sickens me to think that I'm going to hurt the sweetest man in the world. But it would only hurt you more if I was dishonest and you found out how I really felt after it was too late. After how rotten I've been to you, I don't expect any forgiveness or understanding, but at the same time, I know that you're so sweet, I almost can't expect anything less than perfect forgiveness from you. Please, Steve, love someone much better than me. Please love someone who is vastly more real.

Goodbye, dearest Steve.

Janet-Lily."

It all came crashing down on him—the letter was meant to crush him, but made him fly higher than an albatross on a windy day! He hastily folded the papers up into a neat little rectangle, put it in his jacket pocket, and stood up. He grabbed his head, and a huge, wild smile erupted on his face. His own Janet-Lily was the girl who, before now, he couldn't admit to himself that he loved—Jill!

~~~

Jill Jopling, very conveniently, happened to *not* be on her way to Arizona, like Haddock believed. The day after Steve "Haddock" Carey received what should have been the worst letter of his life, Jill was on a beach. On a beach that was on Petit Homard Isle, to be exact. And this beach happened to be in surprising proximity to Haddock's camp. Whether she decided to go there consciously or was just led by her subconscious, it could hardly be told. But
~~~

there she was, looking out at the sun-brimmed ocean, the expanse being interrupted by the coast of Shrimpy Cove. She stood there, wondering if she'd made good choices over the past year. She never made a choice without fully believing that it was the right one, but that didn't stop her from doubting herself later on. She'd broken her own heart, Steve's heart, and insulted Haddock. Yet somehow, she knew that she did the best that she could.

Aggravation at these thoughts couldn't help but emerge at that moment, and so the natural thing to do was to start chucking objects that happened to be on hand—rocks. Petit Homard Isle had no stereotypical sand beaches to brag about. Rock beaches were all that it had, and so Jill took advantage of their abundance. At first, the rocks she chose to throw into the sea were small and docile. Upon being hurtled, they made nice little whizzing noises as they flew through the air, and finished off their terrestrial existence with a satisfying *sploop* into the water. Eventually, the sizes of these rocks increased as Jill's desire to hear larger splashes escalated. She even got to the point where she picked up a rock that required two hands to carry and proceeded to hurl it away. She clapped the sand off of her hands as she looked at where the giant thing sunk. She frowned, wishing that her anxieties were as easy to throw away. After that satisfying hurtle, she decided that her session was nearly finished. But before she was done, her eye caught sight of a rock that was a perfectly graspable size. She just *had* to bend down and grasp it. It would be immoral not to.

She closed her eyes, sighed, and chucked the rock as hard as she could, not caring what direction it went in. She wondered, "Is this what I've done with my *life*?" Her deep ponderings were halted when she heard a thump, an "*Ow*!" and a clunk in quick succession. Her once irresponsibly closed eyes opened instantly. There in the distance, she saw a stooping figure grabbing its head. She gasped, then began running over, trying not to break her *own* head by letting the rocky beach successfully trip her up. As she got closer, she cringed more and more. She wished that she victimized anyone else except *him*. "Why did it have to be *you*?" Jill cried, stooping alongside him.

Haddock, although overcome with all sorts of feelings, managed to suppress them all at the sight of her, and only revealed his emotions with a tender stare at her. He recovered quickly from his lovesickness, grateful that she didn't notice. It wasn't the time to reveal himself yet. He didn't recover as quickly, though, from the blow to his head. "Sorry for getting in your rock's way. But it's alright, at least I'm getting familiar with your tactics now," he said, half laughing, half moaning.

"I was just throwing rocks, and I wasn't looking at where it was going, and I—oh, here, let's just get you to a chair—or at least a comfortable rock." She took his arm to lead him to one, expecting him to shrug her off, but she was surprised to feel him clasp onto her arm for support, without duress. "I found this one earlier," Jill said, nodding towards a boulder. "It's very comfortable, and it looks like it'll seat two." They sat down, and he smiled at her, then grabbed his head. "Oh, no! I got you good, didn't I? How bad is it?" Jill asked through clenched teeth.

"Not too bad—it only hurts when I blink," he replied, now looking at his hand. Jill looked at it in horror.

"You're bleeding!" she cried.

"No, no, I just spilled red ink on my hands earlier today."

Jill frowned in disbelief. "I see you spilled some on your head, too. Come on, let's get you a bandage or something."

"No!" he cried, rather impulsively. He calmed himself down, then continued, "Really, I can barely feel it, it's just a scratch. You only grazed me. You surprised me, more than anything." Jill gave him an unsure, uneasy look. "Really, Jill, I'm fine. It's even stopped throbbing." Jill smiled unhappily and shook her head. Haddock then started gazing at her again. "I thought you left yesterday."

"Oh—yeah, I was planning to, but Mr. Basset *insisted* that I stay another week to tie up loose ends. I don't think that there are any loose ends to tie up, but he was so depressed about me going, that I just couldn't say no."

"He's a sweet old guy. I'm grateful to him for making you stay, really. I'm glad I got to see you again."

Jill was now completely confused. Just a few days ago, she thought that she was the *last* person he ever wanted to see again, and now he was saying *this*. She only smiled nervously in reply. She wasn't sure if she felt the same way about seeing *him* again. "So—what's new?" Jill asked.

"Besides my latest head trauma caused by you, nothing much—oh, actually, there is *one* thing." Now Haddock's experience of spending a year in drama class in high school would pay off. He was the happiest man in the world at that moment. But for the effect he wanted, he paused with a very heavy-hearted sigh. Jill inclined her head towards him as she sympathetically frowned. "I got a letter from my girlfriend yesterday, and she's... she's broken things off."

Jill was now filled with a hectic assortment of emotions. She reddened, trying to understand what all of this could mean. First, she was angry for him—he'd been so loyal to that awful twit, and now she turned around and cut him off? She fumed at the thought! Next, she was angry for *herself*—all this time he might have thought about her if that awful twit hadn't been leading him on. But next came hope, but not too much hope. It was hope tempered by pessimism. "Oh, Haddock," she said, "I'm so sorry. But really, how could she? How *could* she?" She stood up and started pacing around. "After stringing you along all this time, here the twit up and leaves you! You deserve a lot better than that."

Haddock was grinning at her during the rant, but he quickly put back on a forlorn expression when she turned around to look at him. "I do, don't I?" he admitted. He paused, then looked back up at her. "Would you like to read it?"

Jill sank deeper into confusion; each moment that passed was like another gallon of water gushing into a sinking ship. "I, I suppose I could. That is—do you really *want* me to read it?"

One of the hardest things Haddock had ever done was keep himself from smiling at that moment. His frown was so drawn on that an eraser could've taken it off. But he did his best and nodded slowly. Jill furrowed her brow in bewilderment, sighed with an apprehensive smile, and said, "Alright, then, as you wish!" As she sat down next to him again, his fingers searched around his inside coat pocket, and at last he pulled out the neat little rectangle. Jill laughed in perplexity. "Aren't lovers supposed to carry things like love notes and poetry in their breast pockets?"

Haddock smiled as he passed it to her. "You know that I'm not like most people."

Jill laughed as she nodded with raised brows in hearty agreement. She then went on to open the peculiar little package. Haddock's eyes followed hers intently. If she saw the adoration in his eyes at that moment, the act would have crumbled then and there. But she was too intent on reading the strange letter to notice it. She unfolded it completely at last, tugged some of the wrinkles out of it, then began to read it. But it only took half a moment for her to realize that the letter was oddly familiar. Her stomach flipped as her eyes widened, then flopped as she looked up at him. Both of their hearts started racing. The race ended up as a tie. "How did you get your hands on this?" she asked curtly, mostly confusedly.

He scooched closer to her. "Well, Janet-Lily, you never told me what your full name was, and I never told you mine. I know it's a little late, but, please, allow me to introduce myself: I live in North Carolina, I was born in 1933, and my name is Steve Carey."

Jill was totally, absolutely fried. Her small lips opened, then closed. She stared down at the letter, then got up and began walking away. Now Haddock was confused. He watched her speedily walk away for a while, and then he finally got up and ran after her. "Hey!" he called, "I'd like that back!"

She stopped walking but didn't turn around. Everything stood still—the breeze, Jill, Haddock's heart. But life began again when she finally said, "This isn't a joke? Could—could it be real?"

"I wouldn't joke about this, Jill, you know that."

After he said this, she at last turned around. Her face was expressionless as she looked at Haddock's smiling one. Then all the emotion erupted. With a laugh choked by all the tears, she ran towards him with open arms. She tripped over a rock in the process, but safely landed in his arms. "Ste-e-eve!" she wailed, crying into his chest, "I'm so happy that it's—it's—it's *you*!"

Haddock sniffed as he hugged her more tightly. "And you're *you*, too!" The reunion was too wonderful to be interrupted with words. But after the most intense of emotions passed, he said through his own laughter and tears, "You know, Janet, you're— you're sending mixed signals. I thought that you just dumped me!" They couldn't let go of each other. But they didn't seem concerned about the possibility of it being a permanent adhesion. They only released long enough to look each other in the eyes.

"Oh, Steve—or Haddock—whoever you are—I just don't understand how we ended up here, by chance! Is it real? Is this just a wonderful dream? Oh, how could you bear watching me call myself a twit?" As Haddock laughed, Jill suddenly let go of him and gave him a strong backhand across the shoulder. "Ow!" he cried in confusion.

"You are just awful! You were sitting over there, making me pity you, while you knew all along that it was me! If I didn't see Ol' George take that letter from my very own hands and back to the mainland, I don't think I could believe you. But," she said, coming in for another hug, "I can't help but believe it. You're too real to tell a lie like that."

"I most certainly am, and now we're going to build on a foundation much better than paper, aren't we?"

"Oh, yes, I think so," was the warm reply. She opened her eyes when she felt him gently hold her head. He smiled down on her from that 6' 2" frame and decided to take a systematic approach to what he was about to do next. In an orderly fashion, he first kissed her forehead, then her nose, then, the most common site for such happenings, her lips.

# Chapter 29

After watching the sun start to go down for a while, they decided that they would have to tell everyone about their suddenly decided-upon engagement.

Arm-in-arm, they strolled towards the Coffee House, knowing that most of the people they wanted to tell would be there. As they went, they asked each other every question that came to mind. "Steve, why didn't you *tell* me that your uncle died?"

"It happened so suddenly, darling. I had to come here right after it happened, and I decided that I wanted to hear back from you before I told you."

"That was a little arbitrary of you, wasn't it?"

"Maybe. And I didn't want to depress you. But why didn't the girl I met on Petit Homard tell me that she was from Arizona and that her actual name is 'Janet-Lily Jopling?'"

"Bah, I don't tell anyone my full name. It's a drag."

"But even in your letters, you never told me that people call you 'Jill!'"

"I liked the way you called me by my full name. I didn't want to spoil it."

"Does that mean you want me to call you Janet-Lily in real life?"

"I'm having a hard time deciding. I like this 'darling' stuff, it's very cute. I like you calling me 'Janet'—just don't add the 'Lily'. Hyphens complicate everything."

"Very true, very true. And, speaking of names, why did you always call Penny 'Peyton' in your letters? It was downright formal of you, if I may sound like Mr. Basset."

"Well, she always calls you 'Steven.' I thought it was only fitting. Now tell me this: why didn't you ever send me your picture?"

"Do you really think that a guy would want his girlfriend to know that he had a permanent black eye?"

"That's silly. I have to say that I'm still amazed that Haddock writes sappy poetry."

"It's not sappy!" he protested.

"It's sappier than all the trees on this island combined. C'mon, Steve—'blessings of eternal bonds' and flowers and moonlight..."

"Alright, I admit that I was at my sappiest then, but don't you like any of my poetry?" he asked, the answer seeming to really matter to him.

"I love it all. How often do you get poetry written for you by a fish? The Haddock I knew didn't seem at all like the sappy type."

"I guess that I lost that part of myself coming here. I was in Maine, the rugged country where everyone is supposed to tough things out. Here, I'm Haddock, and in North Carolina I was, was..."

"Sweet Steve," Jill supplied with a smile.

And so the rest of the stroll went on in this matter, happily pointing out all the mistakes made by the other. As the Coffee House came into sight, Haddock smiled down at her while slowing his pace and coming to a stop. "Jerry told me about how you chewed them all out about the bridge."

"Oh," she said with a chuckle, "did he, now?"

"I was very impressed."

"Were you?"

"Absolutely! To have the guts to go in there and tell them to their faces that they're a bunch of stubborn hermit crabs takes oomph! You've got more of it than I do."

"'Oomph?'"

"Yes, 'oomph.' I've known these people practically my whole life, and I'd never do what you did. But maybe knowing them for so long is my disadvantage."

"So you agree with me, then?"

"I agree with everything you say, so yes."

"But about the bridge?"

"Especially that. You're Janet, after all."

"But would you agree if I wasn't Janet?"

"I've wanted that bridge built since I was eight years old! Can you imagine the fun of tearing down a bridge on a souped-up motorcycle?"

As Jill wondered what soup had to do with motorcycles, they came to the front door of the Coffee House and entered, still arm-in-arm.

"Oh, evenin', Frog Legs," Mary said, only looking up long enough from her newspaper to recognize her.

Haddock was shocked. "That's not much of a greeting, is it? Aren't you surprised that she's here?"

"The g'el likes coffee, why shouldn't she be he'ah?"

"But, she was supposed to not be here - I mean, she was supposed to leave yesterday."

"Eh? Oh, yessah, Penny he'ah told me that she's stayin' till next week to keep old Basset happy." Jill and Haddock then noticed that Penny, who was sitting at the counter, was noticing *them*. Mary, Jerry, and Joey were too busy drinking coffee and holding a grudge against Jill to notice. Upon hearing new voices in the place, Bobbie emerged from the back.

"Bobbie!" Jill cried, "What are you doing here?"

"The doct'ahs let me come home with Mary. They said I'd recover bett'ah at home than in that stuffy hospital," she replied with a tired smile. Now there was another in the room who noticed the unusual friendliness between Haddock and Jill.

"I'm glad you're here, Bobbie, because we've got something to say," Jill said with a proud smile.

"We don't want to hear it. We're tired of you comparin' us to ugly sea creech'ahs," Mary replied.

"Oh, just listen. Besides, it's not just about me. Haddock—*Steve* and I have something to tell you all. It's worth interrupting coffee for, trust me." Jill then looked up at Haddock expectantly.

"Oh, so you want me to say it?"

"Don't you *want* to say it?"

"Of course I want to say it, but I thought that—"

"Whatev'ah it is, say it before my coffee cools off as much as my interest has," Mary called out.

"Alright, all you hermit-crabs, Janet and I have something to say."

"Who's Janet?" Mary asked in confused irritation.

Ignoring her for the time being, Haddock drew a breath and began, "Janet and I are—" The announcement came to a screeching halt when, with as much warning as one would have getting socked by a preacher, Mr. Basset burst into the room, closely followed behind by his daughter, his butler, and Remi Roy.

"Well, if it isn't Basset and his fellow inmates," said Mary. The rest of the room was in shock.

"Mr. Basset! What are you doing here?" Jill cried.

"Ah, I'm glad I found you here! Yes, Addie said that I'd probably find you in this nice little shop—allo, allo, everyone. Yes, in fact, it's good that you all happened to be here because I have something very important to tell you. Yes, yes, why don't you all sit down while I say it, hm? Go on, sit—well, as you'd like, as you'd like, stay standing, then, very good—Miss Jill has told me that she wishes to leave this island, but my daughter and I wish that she would stay. We've tried every possible method to get her to stay. I've tried offering money, a prestigious home, an endless supply of trumpets, but nothing has convinced her, nothing, nothing at all! Addie and I were discussing it during one of our intellectual chats, and he mentioned that Miss Jill said something in passing about her wish that a bridge would be built from here to the mainland."

"Incidentally," Dahlia broke in emphatically, "ever since I nearly drowned, Dad has been writing a bunch of letters to the Mayor. If it wasn't for my dearest, sweetest Remi Roy, I'd be washed out to sea somewhere. Dad's been worried sick about me—"

"Because Addie told me during another one of our intellectual discussions—my, we have many of those, don't we?"

"Tis debatable, sir."

"True, true—and he told me that I should be worried about there not being a doctor on the Isle—it's such a pity that there isn't—"

"So he wrote to the Mayor," said Dahlia, "and the Mayor said that there are two reasons why he cannot build the bridge—"

"The first reason, he said, is that he doesn't have the funds—"

"And the second is because my dear Remi has been too shy for all these years to let him build it across Mouton Île—"

"Wait up a minute, the'ah," Mary interrupted, "you mean that the old coot hasn't built it yet because he doesn't have the cash? It's not because *we* don't want it?"

"You can't go around thinkin' you own the place, Mary," Jerry said with a chuckle.

"I could if I wanted to, seein' that the Mayor's got the constitution of a jellyfish with a weak will to live."

"The good news is, I have plenty of money," Mr. Basset continued, not seeming to notice that he had just sprung a revelation upon them, "and I've decided to use some of it to fund the building of a bridge between here and there!" Mr. Basset had a fanciful expectation of uproarious applause in response to his philanthropic decision, but instead, it was greeted by deafening silence.

Remi Roy spontaneously started speaking. "I have something a little shocking to say, myself."

"Isn't it a bit redundant to say that something coming out of your mouth is shocking?" Adkins said smugly.

Remi ignored him masterfully and continued, "Not only will I let the bridge go across Île Mouton, but I too am going to help fund zis scheme of Mr. Basset's, so that his daughter will stop pestering me." Dahlia squealed, then subdued him with a deluge of kisses.

"We have shocking news, ourselves, and we've been waiting a very long time to say it," Haddock called out, pulling Jill closer to him, "Janet and I found out that we're in love, and we're going to get married." The statement caused a veritable uproar.

"Who's Janet?" Mary asked.

"What about your g'el-friend, Haddock?" Bobbie cried.

"She *is* my girl, and she was all along!" Haddock cried back.

"Penny, *he's* Steve!" Jill cried out.

"*What*?" replied Penny.

"Who's Janet?" Mary asked again.

"Jilly, I'm in love, too!" Penny exclaimed.

"With who?" Jill yelled.

"With *him*!" Penny yelled back, pointing at the unassuming Adkins.

"*You are*?" Jill and Adkins cried at the same time.

"Now I feel quite left out!" Dahlia said, then continued with her arms around Remi's neck, "We're in love, too, and Remi asked me to marry him!"

"Who's he?" Mary questioned.

"I am Remi Roy," he said with a sigh, as if he wished he weren't. But despite every indication that he was unhappy, he was as delighted as anything.

"Hold on, now, I've got my two cents to put into this," Jerry said while taking off his hat and looking at the floor bashfully. "I love Bobbie."

"You love *Bobbie*?" Mary exclaimed, continuing her role as the room's confused interviewer.

"And I love you, too, Jeremiah Miller," Bobbie said, going over and standing next to him. With a peachy smile, he put his arm around her, puckered up, and gave her a peck on her cheek.

Mary crossed her arms. "Now all that's left for me is old Basset and Joey."

Then came the passionate confession from Joey, "I kinda like ya, Mary. You make lousy coffee, but I like ya."

"What am I gonna do," Mary moaned, "with all these lov'ahs hangin' around, and with a bunch a' tourists who'll come in and demolish the place?"

"Oh, how bad can it be, Mary?" Jerry said, "We were all pretty steamed when Jill came in he'ah and called us a bunch of old crabs, but aren't we? What can we do about it now, anyway, eh?"

"Alright, look he'ah," Mary said, changing the subject before she had to admit that someone else was right, bending down to get something from underneath the counter, "I made these for you in my spare time. Hope you like 'em." Mary then placed three, handstitched scarves in Jill's hands. "I just used whatever I had lyin' around."

"Oh, Mary! They're just beautiful!" Jill cried, showing them to Haddock, then tying one of them around her neck. "Oh, look! She embroidered my initials... 'F.L.?'" she said in confusion.

"Frog Legs," Mary said, as if the explanation was perfectly natural.

Jill chuckled, then turned to Haddock. "Now don't you steal any of *these*, hm? You'll have both me *and* Mary to answer to, now. And Mary, you didn't just go and dig this fabric out of your sewing box. I've seen this stuff in Peterson's store, and for a pretty penny, too. Oh, Mary, I just can't thank you enough. Really, to receive such a meaningful gift from the toughest cookie I've ever met is, is just beyond touching." Jill then stepped back into Haddock's arms. "But I feel like I don't deserve a going-away gift. I'm not exactly going away anytime soon. Well, I *am* going to the mainland to call my mother and tell her that I'm getting married, but we'll be coming back to the Isle after a little ceremony, and I hope that we won't have to leave for a long, long time."

The Bassets cheered, Penny wiped away a proud tear, and Mary teased Jill about taking her gift while the giver was under false pretenses. But she reasoned that the scarves would just have to be made into wedding presents.

By the end of the evening, everyone had found out surprising things about each other. Jill and Haddock knew each other for a much longer time than they thought. Dahlia and Remi were engaged, and the rest of the couples were soon to follow. And Joey confessed his opinion about Mary's coffee right to her face, while Mary never fully understood who Janet was. It was a thoroughly elucidating evening.

Time passed, and Jill and Steve got married and settled into his camp after she made a phone call to her very confused mother, who was disappointed that she couldn't make it to the wedding and that Jill wouldn't be bringing her back a bumblebee for a while. The bridge was funded soon thereafter, and a few years after the bridge was built, Petit Homard was declared a state park. Steve worked as Mr. Basset's groundskeeper for a while, then after the bridge was built, he took advantage of the tourism and opened his very own auto repair shop, while Jill eventually published a book of poems and got a "tastefully small," as she would say, following of readers. Remi married Dahlia and went on to become a famous painter, and Dahlia came to be his most often used model, being much livelier than the models he usually employed. Adkins and Penny married, Adkins never leaving his post as butler, while Mr. Basset appointed Penny the honorable position as head maid, even though more often than not she was the house's live-in handyman. Jerry and Bobbie married, but their lives didn't change much afterward. Joey got better and better at ignoring people, while Mary made sure that the state declared the area around her cabin a bird sanctuary, which was not to be disturbed. Things often work themselves out, even when we try to make things complicated for ourselves. Haddock learned that very fact with his wife's help. And Jill Carey, née Jopling, found out that Haddock would never stop loving the "awful twit" they once knew. It was but one out of his few major downfalls. But at least now, it was Jill's only trouble with Haddock.

Made in the USA
Las Vegas, NV
11 January 2022

41132248R00164